LAKE MICHIGAN

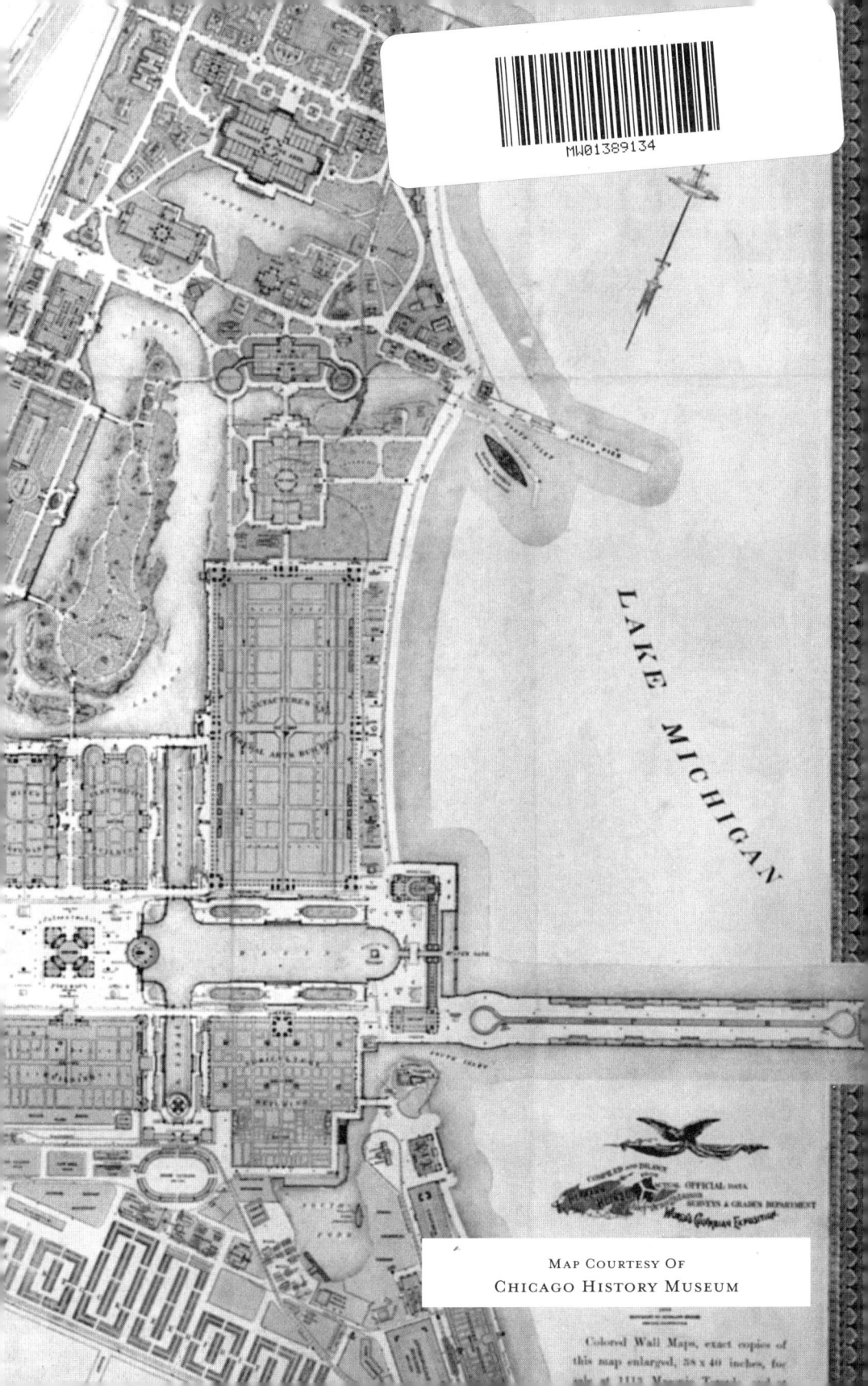

Map Courtesy Of
Chicago History Museum

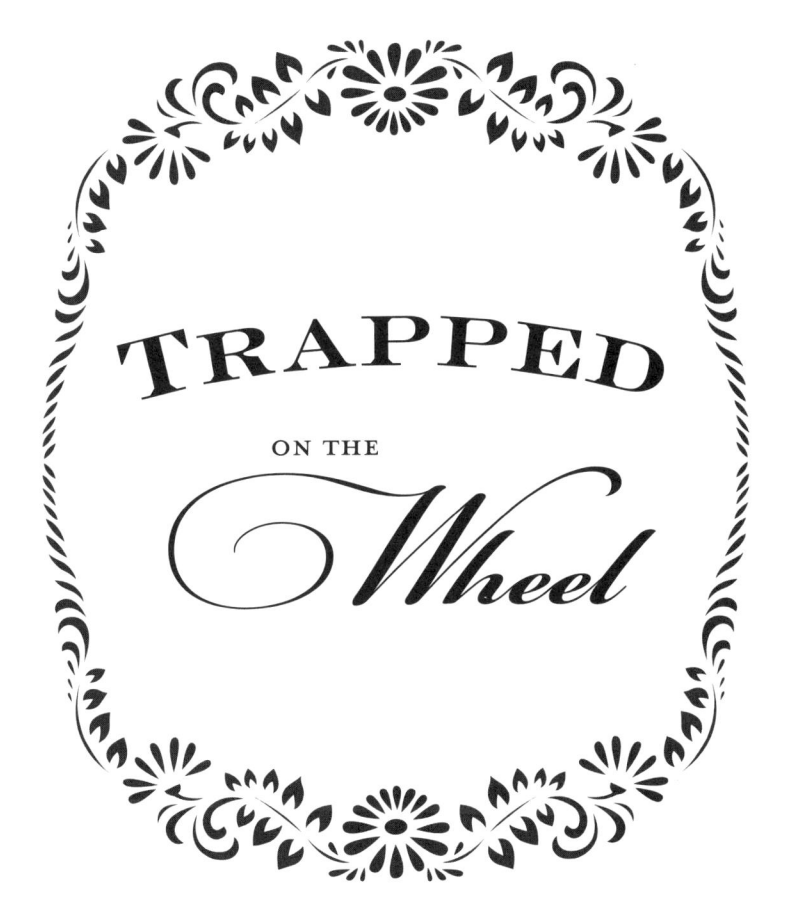

TRAPPED
ON THE
Wheel

Real Estate Investing for the Dumbkuffs
Donald J. Russeau with John Glavin

Building English Skills: Skills Practice Book Blue Level
Including specific materials prepared by John Glavin

TRAPPED ON THE WHEEL
Chicago's Columbian Exposition of 1893
A Novel by John Glavin

Graphics by Lillian Davenport-Partac

Dickinson Publishing House

This is a work of fiction. Names, characters, places, and incidents either are the product of the author's imagination or are used fictitiously.

© 2009 by John Glavin

All rights reserved. Except as permitted under the U.S. Copyright Act of 1976, no part of this publication may be reproduced, distributed, or transmitted in any form or by any means, or stored in a database or retrieval system, without the prior written permission of the publisher.

Printed in the United States of America.

First Trade Edition: 2009
10 9 8 7 6 5 4 3 2 1

Dickinson Publishing House
836 East Seminole Lane
Prospect Heights, IL 60070
www.trappedonthewheel.com

ISBN: 978-0-9822694-4-2 (hard cover)
        978-0-9822694-5-9 (paperback)

Library of Congress Catalog Number: 2009923903

Graphics by Lillian Davenport-Partac
Content editing by Jay Allen
Copyediting by Katherine Glavin
Map courtesy of Chicago History Museum
Manufactured by Adams Press, Chicago

*Dedicated to Saint Jude,
patron of writers who feel hopeless.*

❦ *Preface* ❦

As a boy in a Victorian home, I first learned about the Columbian World's Fair of 1893 on the lap of my grandmother, Jennie Macdonald. She had been thrilled as a young girl visiting the White City. Singing its praises, she hugged me on her rocking chair.

Inspired by Jennie's love of history and stories, I carried her passion in my heart while earning my B.A. and M.A. in English and history at DePaul University. Later as an English teacher, I was a main contributor to a textbook on writing that sold 500,000 copies over fifteen years. Also I co-authored *Real Estate Investing for Dumbkuffs* and *Learning How to Learn*.

After twenty-five years as chair of an English department I retired. While touring the Chicago History Museum that was displaying a huge model of the Columbian World's Fair of 1893, I remembered my beloved grandmother, then deceased. In her memory I resolved to devote myself to researching the fair for the next three years. During that time I collected more than 100 books, several published in the 1890s. Combining the history of Chicago with our family stories I brought Jennie back to life as a young girl who became Lady of the Manor.

Encouraging me on my long odyssey writing this book from 1994 to 2008 have been my wife Retta, my two sons Paul and Michael, and my daughter Katherine. As well, I would like to thank Jay Allen, content editor, and the Off-Campus Writers' Workshop located in Winnetka, Illinois.

Kora

Cyrus

Karla

Nellie Bly

Alessandra

Hermes

Bertha Palmer

Doc Seth

Terese

Rachel

Aunt Ashford

Edith

Trapped on the *Wheel*

Contents

I.	The Gold Coast	1
II.	House of Many Stories	37
III.	Court of Honor	57
IV.	Lady of the Manor	85
V.	Suffer The Little Children	113
VI.	The White City	127
VII.	Under The Big Clock	155
VIII.	Webs of Steel	175
IX.	Seize the Night	193
X.	The Bullet and The Plow	213
XI.	Cold Fire	231
XII.	Journey to Jubilee	253
XIII.	Mirror Image	287
XIV.	All that Glistens	309
XV.	The Truth Shall Set You Free	339

CHAPTER ONE

THE GOLD COAST

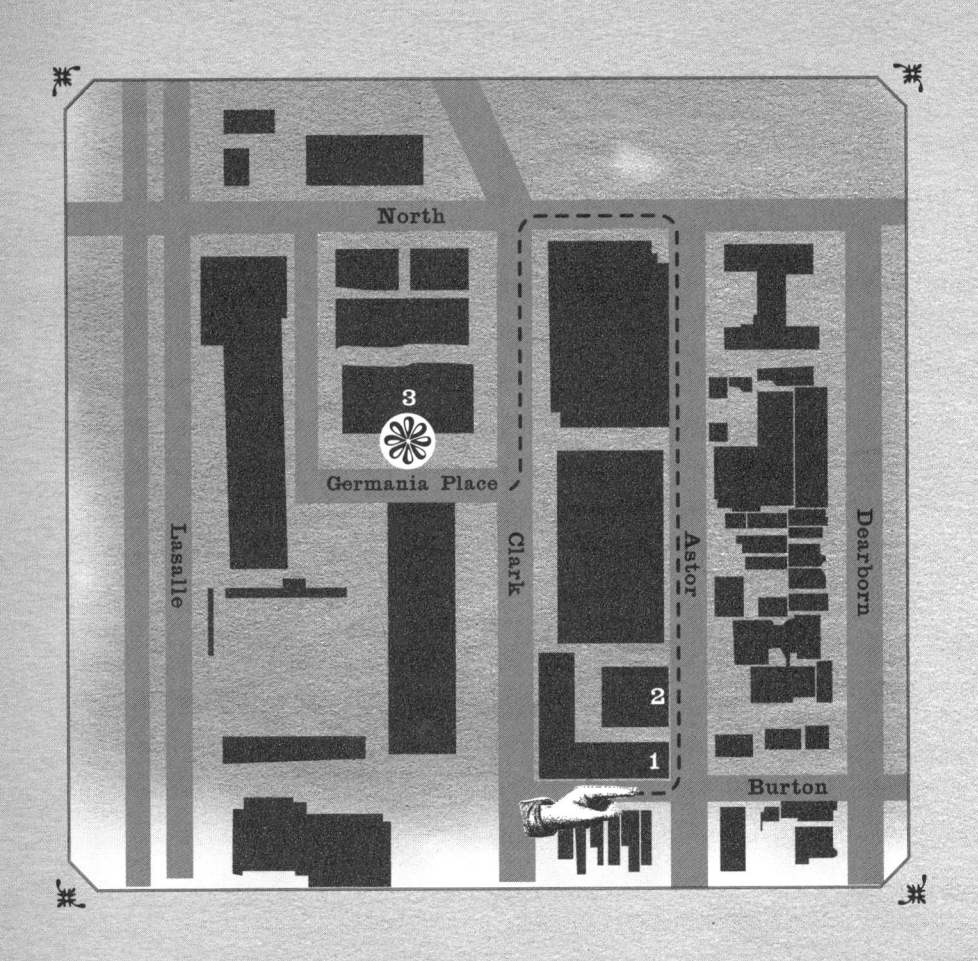

1. Alessandra's Rowhouse
2. Hermes' Mansion
3. Germania Club

Sunday, April 30, 1893

Careening around the corner of Astor Street, the horses pulling our carriage lost their balance on the rain-slicked cobblestones. The rear wheels, skidding over the curb, bumped Karla's knees against mine, her open flask splashing the bodice of my birthday gown. I shouted, "There you go again!" Karla grasped her gold flask as she bounced on the seat opposite me, her white gloves spilling gin into the air. "Alessandra, defend yourself!"

"Karla, why do you always attack me?" With a shudder and a creak, the carriage righted its wheels and rode onward, horses snorting. "Attend to your driving, Curlin!" Then I glared across at Karla's evil eye, peering up at me without raising her head. "Your evil eye of envy doesn't scare me any more. Besides, you're not acting like you're eighteen today!"

Snapping open my fan to cover my eyes burning from Karla's gin, I reached back over my head to slide open the slot behind the driver to address Father. Through the opening, cigar ashes showered down and Father's raspy voice bellowed, "Alessandra, I'm driving now! We're late!"

"But Father," I said, coughing from smoke billowing down, "We're early."

"You tell him, Sister dear," Karla said at me, peering into her flask, "a whole hour."

"Our birthday ball starts at four," I said to Father, the clattering of horses' hooves trampling my words.

"Potter Palmer waits for no man, not even Cyrus Aultman!" With that, Father slid the hatch shut. Raindrops plunked on the canvas roof and zigzagged down the isinglass windows.

Karla laughed at me. "Stir, look at your new gown! What will your beaux Hermes think?" She raised her flask in mock salute. "And your face!"

"Karla, put it away. Your drinking will be the death of you."

"Not drink, dear Sister." Karla leaned forward, her amber hair and green eyes darkened by shadows of the carriage roof. "Passion," she whispered as if to herself. "Passion will be my undoing." Without raising her head she looked up at me, her voice, usually urgent with emotion, settling into a reflective tone. "Alessandra, what is your passion?" She sounded almost sincere.

Above us, Father cursed, cracking the whip as the carriage swayed to avoid an oncoming wagon that loomed at our side as it thundered past.

"You tell me, Karla," I said, rocking sideways. "You always claimed to read my heart." Her beauty once again made me regret being fraternal twins, and not identical, not with my brown eyes and brown hair.

Karla reclined into the corner, green eyes glittering. "Nothing, Sister, your heart is empty, only shreds and patches of trying to please." She steepled her fingers in a mock prayer.

"Ever the actress, Karla," I said, envying her ability to play roles. "Why are you always performing?"

"Well, you're just made of papier mâché of Cyrus," she said, "and shreds and patches of Mother, long departed."

"Well, you're just filled with drink and drugs. Is that what makes you so bitter toward me?"

Karla peered out the window and tilted the alcohol to her purple lips.

"I know I'm Father's favorite only by being the obedient daughter," I said, "If I ever disobeyed him would I lose my way, or find it?"

The carriage hit a rut in the road, jolting us both as it swerved onto Clark Street. The door next to Karla flung open, and her corsage leaped off her lap and flew into the air, followed by her outstretched arms pursuing it. I found myself grabbing her waist with both my hands until the two of us teetered in the open doorway. "Karla, I'm always rescuing you." We passed a gentleman in top hat who gaped at us wide-eyed, his clay pipe descending from his mouth while an urchin playing jacks laughed like a hyena. The carriage swerved, slamming the door shut, and knocking us to the floor.

Karla pulled herself to her feet, bumping her head on a support beam. Adjusting her hairdo, long waves dismantling to bare shoulders, she plopped on the seat and glared at me.

From the floor, I reached up my hand for assistance, but she refused it. I said, "Displaying your usual lack of gratitude?"

"Your fault!" Karla searched for her flask. "I could have saved my corsage but for you—"

Only half listening, I felt a lump beneath my derrière. Shifting my weight on the floor, I probed my hand and retrieved a small oblong object. I waved the flask over my head. "Father forbade us."

Karla snatched it from my hand. "Don't expect a tip." She folded her arms, smirking like my cat. Blowing an errant curl from her forehead, she stared at it until her eyes crossed. She laughed as if a spell were broken, then she relaxed into a smile and offered her hand.

"Karla, you've offered your hand many times," I said, as I rose grasping her wrist. "And you always expect forgiveness." The carriage slid to a stop, jolting me onto her lap. While it shook, we started laughing. "Let's both behave," I said, "for Father's sake. At least for today."

The handle revolved, and the door opened, revealing Father smoking a cigar as he stood beneath a bumbershoot held by

Curlin. I coughed. Immediately, Father flung down his cigar, waving at the smoke with his white glove.

Accepting Father's proffered hand, I stepped down the ladder rungs, raising the hem of my gown ever so slightly. Upon alighting, I looked up at Father's face. The vertical vein that divided his forehead bulged whenever he felt stressed. Today it protruded as thick as a forefinger, as if Father possessed two faces, his left eye as wide and curious as a boy's, his right as narrow and guarded as a judge's. He stepped back, snapping open his bumbershoot, as he offered his arm to escort me to the huge double doors of the Germania Club.

"Curlin," Father said over his shoulder, "attend to Karla."

Father's arm transported me into the belly of the club, with its high-ribbed vaulted ceilings that always made me feel trapped like Jonah in the whale. I yearned for Hermes to take my other arm, like a good blood-brother. Beneath the chandeliers the aroma of roses mingled with the odor of manure from the open windows. A barbershop quartet rehearsing at the far end of the ballroom sang to themselves as tenderly as fathers to daughters. Lyrics of Father's favorite new song drifted on the spring breeze, rippling banners of red and blue. "After the ball is over / After the break of morn."

My reverie was interrupted by a servant balancing a silver tray with four glasses and a decanter of brandy. "Norman," Father said, his voice cracking with nervousness, "has Mr. Palmer arrived yet?"

"Yes, Mr. Aultman, upstairs conference room," the servant replied, gray gloves steadying the stems with his fingertips. "Bringing brandy now, sir."

Patting my hand, Father left without saying a word as he handed his bumbershoot to the servant. I watched his huge back, more round-shouldered than ever, shrink as he ascended the stairway to the meeting. Then my view was blocked by two busboys carrying a banner into the entrance hall.

Trapped on the Wheel

*The Germania Club
Celebrates 18th Birthdays
Alessandra and Karla Aultman
30 April, 1893*

One of the sign carriers spoke to me. "Where do you want it, miss?"

"Why isn't my name first!" Karla said, elbowing me aside.

"Karla, you're acting so childish."

"Put my name first! Use the other side of the banner." Glaring at me, Karla whispered though gritted teeth, "After all, I am one whole hour your superior."

"Karla, calm down. The names are in alphabetical order. Besides, they're stitched on."

Karla marched toward the wall behind the bandstand, bumping into a table displaying hundreds of folded white gloves. The two busboys stared at me for direction. I ordered them not to follow Karla as I shook my head at her little scene. How typical.

"Excuse me, Miss Aultman." Two round tables, each carrying a birthday cake, squeaked past me on the way to the side dining room. I wanted to be everywhere at once: following the two birthday cakes into the side room, watering spots of gin off my gown, racing to the second floor balcony to see everything. Many times I had leaned over that balcony railing, curving out like the bow of Father's schooner straining toward the lake shore, music soothing my face like wind. I needed to be upstairs with Father, to be the watch in his vest pocket. Would Father's business partner Potter Palmer rescue our family from financial straits?

Instead, I found my feet gliding onto the gleaming dance floor, the strains of the barbershop quartet carrying me along. "After the dancers leaving / After the stars are gone." Above my head three crystal chandeliers shivered in the breeze from open windows. As I turned, gleaming oak walls revolved around me like a protective fort while I pirouetted. I spun to a stop, and for a long moment stood silent. My blue gown, festooned with garlands of pearls and crystals, shone like the chandeliers. "Many a heart is aching / If you could read them all."

"Doesn't my being older sister mean anything to you?" Karla said.

I peered into her green eyes with their black specks, expecting to be angry, but instead I remembered being a child again on the roof of our home on Burton Street, staring each other down. Squeezing Karla's hand, I felt eight years old again, sheltering each other from noises of the night. Our rowhouse on Burton Street would talk to wind and rain. In the dark, we would hear beams bending as the spikes ground their teeth. The wooden skeleton of the house shook in the north wind like a dispossessed duchess, resisting its inevitable descent. Was it into an old Indian burial ground that unwillingly had given it birth? During storms, we would share tales of ghosts and little girls lost.

I blinked. Then I found myself curtsying, the hem of my gown whispering on the floor. With a sweep of her arm, Karla bowed like a gentleman. The grandfather clock struck three-thirty, startling us. We hugged each other, then spun to the nearest side table where we collapsed onto chairs.

Karla fingered the ermine trim at my shoulder line. "Is it not exciting? Today—officially—we're the same age as Mother when she met Cyrus. You do recall the family history?" Without waiting for answer, Karla continued. "Tomorrow—officially—the opening of the World's Fair. Right here in old Chicago!"

I retied one of the large blue ribbons at Karla's shoulder that had strayed loose. "But Father forbade us to go."

"He'll collapse like his old opera hat," Karla said.

"No, father's a bear."

"But President Cleveland himself will switch on the new electric lights. Besides, Aunt Ashford and Uncle Chilton are going. They've asked me. Do join us. Bring that scarecrow boyfriend, Hermes. Besides, I hear the Wetherstones have reserved tickets for the speakers' platform."

I untangled pearls on the front of Karla's gown and rearranged the pattern of pink petals. "I don't regret losing your corsage," I said, "not when you make fun of my Hermes."

"Stir," Karla said looking up at the beams in the ceiling, "are you now Cyrus's Lady of the Manor? I mean officially?"

"Father hasn't made that announcement yet."

"Cyrus never will. He takes you for granted." Karla peered into my face with the same level intensity as Mother's portrait overlooking the drawing room. I wished with all my heart I had Mother's face. Taking both my hands, Karla drew me to my feet. "Dance for me. After all, Edith made you the ballerina." Karla twirled me around, the ermine trim of my gown rising and falling like foam.

Spinning across the dance floor, I felt the soles of my feet throb with excitement and pain. Throwing my head back, I squinted like my cat Cerby and watched the chandeliers rotate. Suddenly, I realized those were the new electric lights Father hated. They reminded him that his century was dying like the candles they replaced. I executed a series of quick turns, focusing on the fireplace with Karla chanting, "The fair, the fair, the fair."

Round and round I revolved, like the tiny mechanical dancer on my music box Father gave me as a child. Dizzy, I spun off balance into Karla's arms, laughing.

"Father's favorite all right!" Karla growled. "Sister even laughs like Cyrus."

"Karla, do you have to be jealous even today?"

When the ballroom stopped circling, I focused on Karla's face, and felt a welling of love for her. Why did we have to fight over things neither of us caused? Why couldn't I express my love for her? In Karla's eyes, I thought I saw the same feelings, but I wasn't sure.

Grasping her waist, I dragged her to the nearest window, now darkened by afternoon rain clouds. I pointed to both our faces in the reflecting glass. "Karla, look how beautiful you are!" I said. Her amber curls framed high cheek bones, and her skin glowed beneath powder and rouge. Daily doses of vinegar and arsenic had whitened it. For myself, I preferred the sun in our garden, even though it made my face unfashionably tan. Karla's eyes glittered with the energy of a fever.

"Sister, you do have Father's face with your brown hair and brown eyes," Karla said. "Because you're his obedient daughter, I won't tell you I've already accepted Aunt Ashford's invitation to the fair."

"It's so like you, Karla, always deceiving me."

"Then why do you trust me?"

"That's how I am. I trust people."

"Since I'm his disobedient daughter," Karla said, "I can't expect the honor of Cyrus' first dance. Even though I'm the elder by a full hour."

"No, Karla, Father won't show you the disrespect you show him." Taking off my glove, I offered her my hand on it. Karla removed her glove and shook my hand, her skin ice cold. She bit her lower lip, sharp teeth drawing a drop that bubbled. Suddenly my right hand twitched as if pierced by thorns. I stared at three long scratches throbbing like pink threads, pain shooting through the back of my hand.

Karla snapped out of her trance. "Look at you!" Dabbing at the back of my hand with her lace handkerchief, Karla leaned over and kissed it.

I pulled away. Just like Karla, anything for a scene.

"What gets into me? One minute I'm quiet as a doll. The next minute—" Karla tapped me with her closed fan. "Impulsive, that's me," she said with a strained laugh. "Even Aunt Ashford agrees passion will be the death—" She looked to see who might be overhearing her. No one was near. "Sister, dear, you know I love you and isn't that what love is—a crime of passion?"

"Wasn't that a quote from a play with Aunt Ashford?"

On the bandstand the musicians were arriving early. The clicking open of their cases echoed off the wooden beams. A half dozen young men tested their trumpets, puckering their lips and hesitating, as if for a first kiss. Trombonists extended their arms and pulled them back, directing traffic. A gray-haired man, with a watch fob like Father's, held time in the palm of his hand. He swiveled his head as if wondering where to hide an Easter egg.

Karla advanced toward them. "Gentlemen, play me a number."

"But Mr. Sousa—" the tallest trombonist said.

"Yes?"

"Mr. Sousa's not here yet, Miss."

"Perfect!" Karla clapped her glove with her bare hand. "Before he arrives to say no, play me a tune."

The tall youth, who resembled Hermes with his shoulders hunched, looked at his comrades for assistance. A drummer with cherub cheeks addressed us, "But ladies, we are not tuned." The musicians exchanged glances with the gray-haired man holding the watch, who responded with a bass voice. "Mr. Sousa does not allow—"

"But I desire to dance. Today is my birthday. Oh, and hers too!" Karla waved her empty glove at a wall banner behind them.

"Karla, don't," I said, "you're causing a public embarrassment."

The band members did not bother to look.

"Furthermore, I was just bragging about John Philip Sousa to my sister here." Karla replaced her glove and folded her arms. She glared at them, tapping her foot.

They did not move.

"Need I remind you of the only reason you people are here?"

"Karla, you're not on stage now."

From a table along the wall near the winding staircase, four middle-aged men with mustaches arose. One of them sounded four notes with a pitch pipe, signaling them to hum. He coughed, stepping toward us with a slight bow. "We, however, are pleased to serve young ladies."

Hand on hip, Karla stared at the band, as I called out to the quartet, "After the Ball." Karla's back stiffened at the mere mention of Father's favorite song.

After a brief flurry of throat-clearing and head-bobbing, the singers settled themselves by tilting their heads toward each other.

Snapping open her fan, Karla turned her back on the bandstand and strode toward the comfort room without a backward glance. As she left the dance floor, a single trumpet cleared its throat, notes cracking like sticks in a forest. A drum rumbled a threatening storm around Karla as she maneuvered amongst tables and chairs. Reaching the far wall she passed beneath the portrait of President Cleveland, who beamed like Falstaff dressed as a banker.

"Thank you, Miss," said the old man with the watchfob.

"Please excuse my sister," I said, "We're twins in name only."

When two trombones joined the trumpet in a crescendo of noise, the barbershop quartet ceased singing, and huddled like footballers. I felt sorry for them. One head bobbed up like a tom turkey's to glare at the band with the arrival of a youthful conductor. The man with the watch whispered in the conductor's ear, pointed to the quartet, and then to me. Glancing at our birthday banner, unchanged, the young conductor tapped his baton and stroked his mustache.

A pitch pipe screeched the barbershop quartet to attention, but the tap-tap of the baton drew my eyes to the upraised arms of the conductor, who looked over his shoulder at me and winked. The downbeat of the band, and the opening notes of the quartet produced a noise I had never heard before—a barbershop quartet accompanied by a band.

Laughing, I applauded and walked toward the entrance. A string ensemble entered the club, some covering their ears against the sounds. They shuffled toward the smaller room that contained our two birthday cakes behind sliding doors. The last member to enter shut the large doors, catching his fingers. A muffled curse rumbled.

The memory of the last line of the song filled my mind. "Many the hopes that have vanished after the ball." Near the main entrance of the club was a tall thin figure, waving at me. Raindrops dripped from his closed umbrella as he coughed nervously. "Alessandra, I was supposed to pick you up. Hustings told us you left an hour early!"

My aching hand forgotten, I felt drawn once again to Hermes with his accepting eyes that had warmed my heart since I was a child. He smiled, and held out his long arms, dropping the umbrella with a sharp rattle. Overlooking his clumsiness because it was part of his boyish charm, I lost myself in his deep set eyes once again.

We grasped each other's hands.

"You feel so warm," he said.

I could see in his eyes he wanted to embrace, but the Germania Club was too public. Instead, Hermes grinned, his head bent to one side as if peering around a corner. "Where's Karla? Sent to the corner for misbehaving?" After a servant retrieved the bumbershoot, Hermes and I sauntered arm in arm toward the cloakroom where his parents were standing, adjusting their formal evening wear. Dr. Wetherstone fingered the last moisture from his walrus mustache as his wife Edith pirouetted playfully, every movement worthy of my old ballet instructor. We hugged and kissed cheeks, careful not to disturb hairdos nor crush corsages. Her back stiffened. Did she detect the slight aroma of gin? Appearing puzzled she whispered, "Karla's doing? Enlighten me later." When she squeezed my right hand, however, I winced. It wasn't the pain of my hand that caused my discomfort as much as facing another looming lecture from Mrs. Edith Wetherstone pretending to be my mother.

"Alessandra," Edith said, "What's wrong? Let's examine that hand."

"Oh, it's nothing," I said, regretting not having covered it with my glove.

"Nothing does not hurt." Edith stared at the back of my hand as I looked away, ashamed to be calling attention to myself. "My dear, such scratches." Edith clucked her tongue. "Don't tell me. I can guess." She tapped Dr. Wetherstone's shoulder. "Inspect, dear Seth," she said, offering my hand.

Dr. Wetherstone stared at it as he would at tea leaves. "Superficial abrasion. No concern. Skin scratched red, but clean." He smiled, teeth gleaming beneath his moustache. "My patient will be billed for services rendered—one kiss."

"No bill will I more willingly pay," I said. His cheek felt warm and accepting. Why did I feel closer to Doc Seth than to my own father?

"Isn't it my turn?" Hermes said.

"Decorum, son, decorum." His father chuckled and took out his snuffbox. "Let's retire to the bar." Suddenly, Dr. Wetherstone looked about himself. "By the by, where's old Cyrus?"

"Father's upstairs in the Astor Room with Mr. Palmer." With Father's German pride how could he bring himself to request another loan from his financial partner?

"Oh, high crimes and misdemeanors, eh?" Doctor Wetherstone said, "More risky real estate?" I wished I knew what the properties were. Their high risk for high reward had not paid off so far.

"Don't converse like that, Seth. You're supposed to be Cyrus's best friend."

"Speculating in real estate has proven the downfall of many a good man on Astor Street." Dr. Weatherstone said, "But you Aultmans still live in the only rowhouse left on Burton, don't you?" His voice turned serious. "Cyrus complains to me about the downturn threatening his real estate holdings. Even though he needs money, he won't sell his house to me. He knows I dream of building a mansion for you and Hermes." I loved Doc Seth for feeling this way, but I refused to marry his wife's old money.

Before I could reply, he hugged me with one arm. "Can't you talk the old bear into it?"

"You're embarrassing my darling," Edith said, securing her arm about my waist. "You men find the bar while you have time. Alessandra and I want to share."

Hermes linked arms with his own father, and blew kisses to me as they headed for the bar beyond the cloakroom. I wished with all my heart that my Hermes took after his father instead of his mother.

"Now that we're alone," Edith said, "there is something I need to address. The business of the first dance. Seth is afraid that Cyrus will shun Karla by refusing first dance to the elder sister."

I could not meet her eyes. Instead, I fidgeted with my white gloves. My father could not be that cruel in public. It might embarrass him. Although his feelings were hurt by Karla, I believed he was strong like a bear and would shrug it off.

Edith guided me to a corner. "Just what did Cyrus say?"

"You know Father—"

"Indeed I do. Pardon me for speaking plainly, but Cyrus is more stubborn than Seth. Worse than Chilton. But thank the Lord, Cyrus is more responsible than his older brother. My lands, the way Chilton and that actress aunt of yours flaunt themselves in public—"

Feeling my eyes moisten, I wished Edith to cease. I loved Uncle Chilton for being a lifelong comfort when Father misunderstood me, but I also wished he would not be a lapdog to Aunt Ashford.

"Oh, forgive me, child. Seth is always telling me I gossip enough for both of us." She hugged me. "I can see why Karla so envies your self control."

"Then why can't Karla practice some herself? Why can't she be more like a real sister?"

A draft swept toward us as more guests entered the club. I turned with great anticipation hoping with all my heart it was my ideal Lady of the Manor.

"There's Bertha!" Edith exclaimed, releasing me with an "excuse me dear" as she hurried toward Mrs. Palmer who was almost surrounded by her entourage. Bertha's gold-belted gown, her head topped by a diamond tiara, framed her at the entrance doors like her portrait-in-progress I saw in her mansion. Her Kentucky drawl poured invisible honey into the air. "When Ah think of the short time left, Ah get so nervous Ah cannot sleep. Tomorrow is Opening Day for the fair."

A stocky woman with a black choker said, "We can't open!" Her gray curls shook. "Roads muddy! Fairgrounds impassable! Buildings damp! I should know, you appointed me Chief of Installation."

I shook my head in disbelief. The drawings of the fair in the *Tribune* had been so romantic. My favorite was the elevated train encircling the entire fair like a wedding ring. I moved closer to hear Bertha Palmer. I imagined Hermes sliding the ring on my finger making him more precious to me than just a blood-brother. Then we would mirror the ideal marriage of Bertha and Potter Palmer.

"Amey Stark, not today." Bertha waved her fan. "Today is one special occasion. We've been anticipatin' the Aultman twins' comin'-out ball for years!"

I moved even closer. To me, Bertha was the sun to warm my dreams. "But Bertha, what instructions for my ladies?"

"Tell the workers the Exposition means just one thing—government has finally discovered women. Isn't it about time, Alessandra?"

I snickered behind my hand, while the ladies tried to stifle Amey Stark. My throat was so choked with delight that

Mrs. Palmer would address a question to me that I could not respond.

However, Mrs. Stark's complaints persisted. "Five weeks I barely existed. Living in rubber boots, furs, mackintosh. Morning 'til night—cold and wet!"

I was irritated by her spoiling our coming-out ball but Mrs. Palmer smiled at her with warm charm. "Amey Stark! Do join me on my dry pedestal. Did you all know the Gold Coast was constructed atop an Indian burial ground?" She waved her lorgnette. "My lands! I do see Mrs. Wetherstone. Edith, we have arrived. Missed anything?" She embraced Edith and touched her cheek. "Where's our distinguished doctor? With Potter upstairs?"

I stared in awe at my ideal Lady of the Manor being so close to me. The stem of her lorgnette tapping her bare shoulder resembled the wand of a fairy godmother.

Amey snorted. "And Jack Ellis is smack-dab in the middle. Cutting our budget again! Bertha, why in blazes don't you just have Potter write a check?"

"Ah do declare, Amey, you really don't trust men. Now, do you?" Mrs. Palmer reached out for my wrist. "Now look you here, one of the guests of honor herself. Bless you, Alessandra darlin'." She pressed her cheek to mine and, peering over my shoulder, said, "and here appears the other half. Greetings, Karla honey, happy birthdays, both."

"Kindness for an outcast?" Karla's voice, deeper than usual, told me she had been crying. Her face, even paler than when she had arrived, her eyes wide and staring, spoke of extra doses of vinegar and arsenic. Karla stubbed her toe on a rug; she kicked at it.

Blood rushed to my cheeks. Without taking my eyes off Mrs. Palmer, I could imagine Karla's evil eye of envy trying to intimidate the queen of Chicago culture into contributing funds to Aunt Ashford's touring company. How could I rescue Karla from embarrassing herself? While I remained paralyzed, Edith acted. She spread her arms, eagle-like, and swooped up Karla, turning her around. "Time to form the receiving line, my dears. But first, let's tidy up."

"But I just came from the ladies—"

"Alessandra, you're part of this, too, you know." This was what I hated most about Mrs. Wetherstone: her assuming command of us as if we were her daughters.

Mrs. Palmer's voice tried to restrain me. "Miss Aultman, darlin', Mrs. Stark needs to talk with you. Oh, dear. Oh, well. Do hurry back you-all!" I wanted to ask Mrs. Palmer about the fair and my intense desire to attend. Perhaps she could prevail upon Father to change his mind.

Passing the stairs, I saw a shadow cross my path. Long and wide, it rippled like a wave, followed by the raspy voice of Father. I smiled, willing the shadow closer. Had Father's meeting gone well? Had it relieved our finances? Suddenly Father laughed, and my heart resumed beating. Then his voice assumed its business tone, a loud staccato, like an ax convincing a tree to become a log. "So, Potter, my old partner," he said, his voice chopping away, "Is it a deal? You know my love for any real estate speculation. But really, isn't the property too far south? Thought you'd abandoned Prairie Avenue for good." Was that the location of Father's property? I wish I knew.

"You mean Millionaires' Row?"

"Where's the new location of my investment property?"

"Hyde Park."

I stopped as Edith and Karla paused. "Strange name," Father said at the bottom of the stairs, sniffing the rose in his lapel. "Can't we change it?"

"What to? Something more German?" What about Irish, Father, to honor Mother?

Arm in arm with white-haired Potter Palmer, Father looked more vigorous than usual, with no trace of headache. His brown eyes, deep set in shadows, flared in the light reflected from a sconce in the hallway. He puffed on a slim cigarillo held by the gold holder I gave him last Christmas. Although he had seen me, he was pretending he had not. Father loved a captive audience.

Mr. Palmer smiled at me, nodding his head. "Cyrus, old stock, what would you suggest?"

Father peered directly into my eyes and beamed. He swept his holder with a flourish. "Alessandra Park—of course!" he said, ashes falling to the Persian rug. Father strolled toward me, his arms as wide as a fishing net. I nestled into his embrace. Hugging me tightly, he planted a kiss of brandy and tobacco smoke on my forehead. He held out his left hand to Karla who was now returning; her gloved hand hesitated as if approaching a rabbit snare.

"So what have my birthday girls been up to? Over your pouting? Talking fashions? Hairstyles?"

"You know us, Cyrus," Karla said, "that's what we live for." That's just what I meant, Karla. You're always knocking off Father's top hat with your sarcasm.

"Karla, remember our agreement," I said. How many times have I begged Karla to be more civil at least in public?

"The agreement was only with yourself."

"Why do we even need an agreement to be pleasant?"

Father frowned and ceased hugging me. He stage-whispered, "I prefer your sister when she is rude only in private."

Listening nearby, Mr. Palmer narrowed his eyes but laughed. "Well, happy birthdays, to both young ladies!" With his gray hair and silver mutton chops, I found it hard to believe he was the husband of beautiful Bertha and not her father.

Smoke flowed from Father's nostrils. Then he shrugged and embraced us girls, keeping his eyes on Mr. Palmer's face. The furrows on Father's forehead deepened like knife wounds. With the back of his huge hand he rubbed his chin, and I knew he was in pain. With a nod to Mr. Palmer, Father strolled with him to the bar, leaving us bobbing like boats imprisoned in their wakes.

I watched with pleasure as Hermes raised his glass in a toast to me before I turned and faced Karla, her evil eye a burning coal. I felt embarrassed for her, but then she put her hand on mine and whispered, "Some day you will understand Cyrus." What is to understand? I trusted Father, and he trusted me.

"Oh, but I do understand Father. Haven't I always?"

"Stir, you're so childish."

"Childlike," I said, smiling at her attempt to embarrass me. "Doctor Wetherstone calls me childlike."

Another breeze carried drops of rain that fell near our feet as more guests arrived. "Did I miss the receiving line, boys and girls?" Aunt Ashford's high-pitched voice soared. Turning, I saw my actress aunt untie the purple ribbon at her throat and swirl the cape into the waiting hands of Uncle Chilton, who always seemed to be at her side. Blond and petite, Aunt Ashford posed with one hand on hip, the very picture of Karla twenty years from now. She held everyone's attention. I noticed her green eyes followed a trail of rose petals that littered the floor where Father had walked. She displayed the same expression as Mother's portrait.

"Well, this won't do!" my aunt exclaimed. "You people act like it's the end of something—not the beginning!"

I had always admired Aunt Ashford's boldness. In Edith's absence I marched toward my aunt. "Time to form the receiving line," I said, "Shall you and I begin?" I felt joyous to be taking charge of her instead of vice versa.

We ladies lined up, facing the entrance—Aunt Ashford first, a space for Edith, Karla, and then me. I wondered why my aunt had previously advised me not to shake hands, to only squeeze flesh, but after several couples passed through, I grudgingly realized the wisdom of her experience. My admiration for her good judgment sat uneasily on my deeper feeling of anxiety, with her trying to take the place of my mother. Aunt Ashford beamed at Karla like the hostess of the ball. Just who did she think she was? Thank goodness, Edith rejoined us in the greeting line, but now Edith also seemed to be standing in for Mother. Why can't Mother be here herself?

Usually guests would pause to say a few words as I pressed their flesh. Mrs. Marshall Field whispered, "Your mother, God rest her soul, should be first in line. Not that actress!" My cheeks tightened in what must have seemed a frozen smile. Mrs. Field caressed my face with both her hands as she moved on. "I know, dearie, you can't speak." As he followed his wife, Mr. Marshall Field asked me, "Where's the old bear? How's he balancing his books these days?" I glanced at the base of the stairway where Father, Dr. Weatherstone, and Hermes stood in the shadows, holding champagne glasses. I'd never agreed with the old custom requiring gentlemen to stand off to one side. How could they seem so jovial? They must not be discussing finances.

Mr. Field grunted and edged toward them, replaced by Mrs. George Pullman, who said, "Alessandra dear, announcing your engagement soon?" I replied, "It's not official yet, but you'll be the first to know." "Hermes is such a catch!" Mrs. Pullman said. "We need a young doctor down on Prairie. Do hurry, dear." Mr. Pullman shook my hand. "Fraternal twins are so much more interesting than identicals, don't you agree? Needless to say, we'll see you at the fair tomorrow Miss Aultman?" His wife poked him with her elbow. "Oh pardon him, he forgot," Mrs. Pullman said. "Your father hates the fair. Ever since his best friend the architect died. Didn't Mr. Burnham change the original plans when he brought in those New Yorkers?" They moved on. Mrs. Glessner stroked my cheek. "But don't resent him dear. I hate the fair too." It's not too late for Father to honor my birthday wish to attend the fair.

The back of my neck tightened, like a marionette with invisible strings, when I heard Father's nervous chuckle. What was he laughing about? And why didn't he explain to me why he hated the fair? And why did he forbid me?

When the stream of guests ended, the band in the ballroom struck up "After the Ball." Father's voice cut into my ear. "Time for first dance." Turning around, I saw him nodding at Edith while strolling past me to pause at Karla's side. Had he changed his mind? Father's shadowy silhouette darkened Karla's profile. The crowd, milling and murmuring, waited for the first couple to dance. He reached out his hand, but then Karla smirked at me as she slapped Father's hand away, publicly embarrassing him. My breath left my body. By rejecting Father's hand for the first dance, she had betrayed my trust once again. Brushing past me, Karla muttered, "Thank you Stir, for being so trusting." I said, "Karla, you just derailed yourself again." Father stood stock-still, a muscle in his jaw rippling his cheek. As the guests nearby gasped, Aunt Ashford stepped forward, taking his outstretched hand and leading him to the dance floor. The crowd parted, creating a pathway. Being an identical twin Aunt Ashford gave the illusion to me of Mother and Father dancing.

The nearby pocket doors slid open and the odor of strawberries from our birthday cakes flooded my nostrils, making me sneeze. I hated strawberries as much as I hated the sight of blood. But I realized that strawberries were Father's favorite.

Dr. Weatherstone and Edith joined Father on the dance floor, soon followed by the Potter Palmers. I was rescued from my shock at Karla's rudeness by Hermes putting his arm around me and guiding me to the dance floor. Short of breath, I barely got out a thank you.

"Don't talk," Hermes said, spinning us into the rhythm of the waltz. "Remember, words always get in our way." His gloved hand rested on my shoulder as he maneuvered past other couples, who smiled at us. The look in Hermes' sunny blue eyes lifted my spirit like my Chinese box kite in a gust of wind. "Remember, Alessandra, my mother is old money." That's the problem. I wouldn't take advantage even of Edith just to solve our financial difficulty.

I twisted my head away from Karla and her new boyfriend waltzing nearby. Once again, trying to protect her, I had been deceived. Karla and her little acts of vengeance—why did she hate Father? Why did she only call him Cyrus? Had Aunt Ashford told lies to Karla about Father?

A kiss on my forehead penetrated my reverie. "When you frown, Sander, you are more beautiful than when Karla smiles." Once again Hermes rescued me from self pity with his casual charm.

I squeezed Hermes' hand. We pivoted faster and faster. Toward the climax of the dance someone tapped Hermes on the shoulder. It was Father. Stepping in front of Hermes, without looking at him, Father seized my right hand and kissed the back of it. "You are loved, Alessandra," he said as he glanced across at Aunt Ashford, who was now dancing with Uncle Chilton. Taking me into his arms, Father waltzed me away, whispering, "Do the scratches still hurt? When Karla hurts you, it's like she's hurting Cora." Tenderness from Father always came as a sweet surprise that felt like aloe soothing any hurt I tried to hide.

I shook my head. "Not now," I said, dancers crowding the floor, but bringing us closer. "Karla's always sorry when she's cruel to you, Father. She truly loves you, but she can't seem to—"

"Alessandra is beautiful tonight," he said, "my Lady of the Manor." His strong arms continued holding me into the second song, "Daisy, Daisy, Give Me Your Answer Do." Sinking into Father's shoulder, I felt my eyes water until they focused on the little rose clinging to his buttonhole, its petals having worked loose. The deflowered stem seemed absurd in the crevice of the wall of Father's formal jacket. I heard myself laughing. Father cocked his head at me. "Happy?" he asked. I nodded. "Das is gut," he said. As we passed an open window a breeze carried the stink of horse manure. Smiling, I looked up at him. "Yes Father, I'm happy, as long as your arms protect me."

The dance over, Father escorted me to the dining room where twin birthday cakes awaited. Hermes linked my other arm as the three of us wended our way beneath floating balloons, streamers, and confetti. The crush of people forced all of us closer. I loved crowds of friends; they could not be close enough.

The people gasped at the sight of the two tables displaying identical birthday cakes—four-layered white frosted devil's food with strawberry fillings. Supporting the top two layers were tiny pillars with eighteen gold candles adorning each cake, freshly lit by our family chef. Doffing his baker's cap, Alsace bowed his long frame toward us, cocked his head and winked at Karla. For once I felt envious of Karla and how she attracted male companionship, even extending to our chef.

Within moments, the band in the grand ballroom struck up "Happy Birthday to You." As more people entered singing and dancing, the crush of people moved me deeper into Father's arms. I saw Karla watching us intently, her eyes glittering like a cobra's. Father's body tensed as he released me. Moving away, he whispered something to Dr. Wetherstone entering the room. I could not hear because of the happy bedlam that surrounded us. The good doctor frowned, but nodded. Waving his walking stick, he accidentally struck Hermes on the shin, making my own leg ache. Instinctively, Hermes raised his arm against his father. *Someday you must rebel against your father, Hermes, but not now, not this way.*

"Oh, Hermes, don't!" I shouted.

"Edith, dear wife, take your offspring in hand." Then he spoke German to Father who laughed and said, "Fair enough, Seth." The two men shook hands.

Why doesn't Father do the honors himself? Maybe Karla was right: when the occasion called for him to rise to the challenge, Father would collapse like his opera hat.

A penguin climbing an ice floe, Dr. Wetherstone, assisted by the chef, waddled atop a chair, waving his cane for order.

The buzz of the crowd quieted to a murmur. "Gentlemen—and ladies of course—I have been asked the honors to do. Who am I to say no? Most of you good folks know me, and you others don't care. Family doctor to the Aultmans, among many others here. For instance, you over there, Mr. and Mrs. Armour, and the Marshall Fields, and the Frank Lowdens, and of course my old favorites, the George Pullmans—so this speech will be short." He swayed on the chair. "I'll take another glass of champagne. Briefer I'll be with glass in hand." Quickly, he was offered four full glasses.

"Later, Seth, later!" Edith said. So like Mrs. Wetherstone to squelch her husband's happiness.

Clearing his throat and rocking on his heels, Dr. Wetherstone held onto Alsace's shoulder to steady himself. "Brought those two Aultman girls into this world, I did. Ireland it was." Then he looked down. "God help them—I lost their mother—" He tapped his cane against a passing balloon. "Today, both complete eighteen years and—yes, eighteen years without their mother." Why did Mother have to die giving birth to Karla and me? My best birthday present would be Mother's hand squeezing mine. I yearned to read her only letter once again. I preserved it in my remembrance book awaiting my future wedding pictures.

"Cut the cake, Dad!" Hermes yelled. "Cut the cake," chanted people in the crowd, shoving toward the cake tables. Someone jostled the doctor off his chair, and he fell forward toward the cakes, a cheer erupting from the crowd. Father sprang with the grace of a bear to catch the doctor in his arms. They both crashed to the wooden floor, their impact rattling the pyramid of newly filled champagne glasses that leaned like the Tower of Pisa, paused, and then splashed on top of them.

I looked around for Hermes who rushed to my side. Struggling to his feet, Dr. Wetherstone shouted, "Let me go! Arrumph! I'm not finished with my speech!" He thrashed about, buckling a limb on one of the tables holding one of the cakes. Frozen in horror, I watched as the four-layered cake, tiny pillars swaying, inched to the edge of the table directly over Father's head. When I tried to scream, my throat choked. Hermes peered at me, reading my face. He gulped, then leaped toward the cake and caught it midair. Bent in half, stiff-legged as a deer on ice, Hermes stared at me, smiling in triumph. I applauded. Mistake. Karla slapped Hermes on the back. "Good going, skinny!"

A slim atlas losing his grasp on the globe, Hermes tilted forward on his toes. In slow motion the tall cake slid, layer by layer, out of his hands through the air, onto the two forms struggling on the floor, burying Father and the doctor in whipped cream, strawberries, and devil's food.

Karla laughed at first, then began screaming, "Good God, my cake is ruined!"

People lounging at the bar straightened and stared our way. My Gawd, Bertha and Potter Palmer are staring at the floor.

I wanted to die.

Aunt Ashford said coolly, "You mean Alessandra's cake is ruined." Her sharp-edged voice brought Father from under the table, like Poseidon arising from the sea, dripping whipped cream. "Enough indignities!" Sputtering devil's food, he grasped my wrist, his fingers a manacle. Then he took Karla's wrist and with both of us in tow, strode toward the other table. Trying not to look down, we stepped over broken glasses and splattered cake. "Finish this charade, dear sisters! One cake for both, with one bloody knife!"

My cheeks burned in embarrassment for Father. Was he afraid this public display would endanger his financial backing from Mr. Palmer? Why must we be so vulnerable financially because of Father's risky real estate? Should I thank Potter Palmer or curse him?

He picked up the large silver carving knife, his eyes searching for the ensemble which perched, open-mouthed, on a little stage at the end of the dining room. With a curt nod, Father signaled for them to begin playing. The strains of "Happy Birthday" filled the air as Father slapped the gleaming handle into my palm and reached for Karla's left hand. Aunt Ashford stepped between them. Father glared for a long moment.

Dropping her glance from Father's eyes, Aunt Ashford led Karla over to him. He motioned for her to remove her left glove, so I removed both of mine. Father placed Karla's bare left hand on top. The crowd, breathing hot on my neck, sent cold shivers down my back. I turned and realized it was Uncle Chilton who winked at me. Always I felt comfortable with Father's older brother because he taught me to play the harp piano and encouraged me to be myself.

With renewed energy, Karla seized the knife handle from my hand. "I'm the first born!" She grabbed my forearm and positioned my right hand on her left, raising the point of the blade. Then she smirked at Father for the first time, dark and knowing; it chilled my very soul.

The crowd grew silent. The grandfather clock in the corner struck four-thirty, clunking its metal tongue.

Karla inserted the long knife blade into the bottom layer of the cake and, as she withdrew it, strawberries stained the blade. She plunged the blade into the cake again, creating a wedge, sliding the flat of the blade under the triangle and lifting it, with the dark devil's food dripping bloody crumbs. The blade shook and the wedge of cake wobbled, threatening to fall to pieces.

"Catch it!" Karla ordered.

Instinctively I reached out my hand, open palm stretched toward the tilting slice of cake. The long silver blade sliced a thin line across the palm of my left hand.

Strangely, I felt nothing; my hand was numb. Blinking in disbelief, I looked around to see who had noticed the cut. No one. Father dusted frosting off Dr. Wetherstone; Hermes sipped champagne while scraping cake from his shoes; Aunt Ashford stamped her foot as Chilton lit her cigarillo.

Karla placed the knife down on the table cloth with the precision of a surgeon. "You finish cutting the cake, Sister dear. This is all your fault anyway. I feel faint." She left the table and headed toward the comfort room, leaving me to stare at the thin pink cut oozing across the lifeline of my left hand.

The crowd shouted, "Cake! Cake!"

Aunt Ashford removed the knife from the table, handing it to Alsace who dispatched the other wedges. If Mother were here, none of this would have occurred.

Shoved aside, I searched for Father. He was lighting his pipe at the bandstand after having patted the doctor on the back. Edging to the outskirts of the crowd, I recognized shock in the eyes of people who stepped back from me. Looking down, I saw blood dotting my sky blue damask, the pink chrysanthemums turning auburn.

A woman pointed at my dress. "The poor thing cut herself!" Another said. "No, her crazy sister did it." A third, "I don't see anything." A fourth reached for my hand. I pulled it away. "Nothing! Nothing happened!"

"Let us help you."

"No. Nothing's wrong." I broke free from clutching hands, leaving smears of blood on someone's white glove as I grabbed a napkin from a table and wrapped it around my left hand. My legs felt leaden, and my corset squeezed my ribs. Stumbling through the crowd, I searched for refuge within a curtained opera box to one side of the ensemble. Reaching the door, I opened it and groped up the narrow steps to the little balcony while sounds of Mozart's "A Little Night Music" from the other side seeped through the curtain. Taking a deep breath, I peered into the little loge separated from the ensemble. In the dim light I saw boxes, boxes, boxes, wrapped and tied with ribbons, white, yellow, red. Long boxes piled on every foot of floor. Short boxes stacked on chairs, a miniature city of boxes. As I sidled among them I noticed the tags—all for me and Karla. Finding a Morris chair I collapsed upon the smallest box of all. Tightening the napkin, now pink, around my hand I cursed Karla and reached under myself to retrieve a little present with my name on it. Holding it balanced in my good right hand, I eased my neck onto the headrest. Was this the day I had waited for eighteen long years? Shaking my head, I undid the gold ribbon, unwrapped the textured paper, and lifted the cover. A note inside read:

Alessandra,
This pendant belonged to your mother Cora. I saved it for your 18th Birthday, my little Lady of the Manor.
Remember you are loved,
Father
P.S. Do not share it

I recognized the same acorn pendant that adorned Mother's neck in the photograph in my room. How I yearned to wear it, but Father told me to wait until I became a woman of eighteen.

After removing the note I held up the box. In the faint light, the silver acorn shimmered on the silver chain. I closed my eyes. I kissed the acorn. Lifting the chain, I swung it like a pendulum before bowing my head. I imagined Mother adorning it around my neck. It would help me trust people, just as Mother trusted her love for Father. At that moment, I vowed to wear Mother's pendant each day for the rest of my life.

Relaxing, I felt my mother's chain touch the gold locket from Hermes that he had given me for my birthday last year. I retrieved it to snap open its heart shape, and to gaze once more with love at Hermes' picture displaying his cowlick that I had once snipped and secured in the opposite side of the locket.

Mother, if you were here, would you love Hermes as much as I do? You could help me transform him from my blood-brother to my husband. And you could handle Edith. We used to get along fine in ballet, yes, so much so that she took me into her home for one whole summer five years ago. Something mysterious had happened between Father and Karla. Afterward, Karla took to the stage with Aunt Ashford providing her wigs, makeup, false eyebrows and eyelashes. However, at school all the boys and girls in our class tormented Karla by constantly chanting, "White crow! White crow! Fly away to Kokomo! White crow! White crow! Burn your wigs before you go!"

Well, that was the beginning of our being tutored at home. For me, I missed my friends at school, but Karla sought out new acquaintances by sneaking out at night to roam the streets of gray Chicago, meeting older men. Aunt Ashford was often on tour, Uncle Chilton was usually inebriated, and Father could seldom stop her. Karla told me she lost her last shred of respect for him and would henceforth call him Cyrus. However, I tried to make it up by being extra obedient, but this made Karla hate me even more.

My reverie in the loge must have lulled me because a tap on the door, followed by the calling of my name, awakened me. How much time had passed I did not know. The music had ceased, and I heard only a few murmurs from the dining room. Then the door opened, revealing a pair of hands, the finger of one drawing a line across the palm of the other. Hermes stepped inside. "I hoped you would be in our old hiding place." Stumbling over boxes, he caused a cascade of noise. "Take that, Karla," he said, kicking a box. Muttering to himself, Hermes moved closer to me. "Karla's always causing trouble," Hermes said, "at least that's what Mother tells me. She wants to know why you still trust her." Untangling his ankles from ribbons, he reached my chair. Taking my hand, he inspected it as if it were a present. Kneeling, he removed the layer of cloth and replaced the bloody napkin with his own handkerchief and tied it. As he peered into my eyes, I could almost see his mind fumbling to form the proper words. Would he rescue me tonight? Would Hermes finally ask me?

"Aless—Alessandra," Hermes said, "Now that we're alone, I can—"

I felt the throbbing of Hermes' locket. Why did society forbid me from asking him? We've wasted so much time. But our family finances have stood in the way. Why couldn't the Aultmans be old money?

"Sander, you could always read my heart. You know how I feel, that's why I don't have to use words."

"What are you trying to ask me?" I said, his hand shaking in mine. I have waited for Hermes to profess his love for how long?

Sitting on the floor at my feet, Hermes looked up at me. He kissed my ring finger. "Sander, why do you let Karla hurt you? Mother says a real Lady of the Manor would not allow it. You need to be your father's Lady of the Manor before we can—you know, just for a few years. Until I graduate Harper College." Who cared what his mother said? Edith always intruded herself between Hermes and me. Is she still bitter at my refusing to join her ballet studio? Why can't she realize I want Hermes and me to have our own dream.

Suddenly all the birthday presents around me that a moment ago held promises seemed to collapse, burying me alive. I could not breathe. I heard myself muttering, "I need some air." Rising from the chair, I stumbled away from Hermes toward the door. To clear a pathway I kicked at Karla's boxes. Then I paused, my fingers trembling on the knob. Letting myself out, I slammed the door, leaving Hermes alone. When would Hermes stand up to his mother and be his own man? A few more years of waiting, indeed! Was Hermes to remain only my blood-brother?

Halfway down the small stairway, I leaned against the wall to steady my limbs for a brief moment. It was my fault expecting too much. Pushing away, I limped down the steps and eased open the door to the ballroom. Where had all the adults gone? One of the few people left was Amey Stark, who immediately approached me. Were my emotions exposed on my face?

"My dear, so sorry for your accident," she said. I wondered what she was talking about. "How's our little hand?" Why do you care? You're not my mother.

Trying to clear my mind, I shook my head. "Where is everybody?"

"Oh, most people already left. I stayed behind to see the doctor's son. You know, that handsome fellow."

"Pardon me?"

"My best worker, he is!"

"What?"

"Whenever Hermes manages to skip class, that is. That boy's not afraid of work—carting crates, dusting paintings, fixing plumbing. Not to mention taking photographs of my exhibits!" She moved closer and hugged my waist too tightly. "Don't tell anybody but the whole fair is a bumblebee that cannot fly. A half-built bumblebee at that!"

"What do you mean?"

"State secret, my dear—under-funded, under-appreciated, under-staffed." She studied the mural on the opposite wall, and yawned. "If Bertha don't give me more willing hands to help, the fair won't—"

"I'm sorry for you," I said, pulling away. Why did other people tell me their problems? I felt if I told mine I would be imposing on them.

"But dear, don't misunderstand. As Chief of Installation I wouldn't dream of asking." She flounced her hair and frowned. "Contrary to my expressed wishes, Bertha Palmer appointed me. That's what comes from complaining." She patted my arm. "Will you be attending the fair tomorrow?" What can I say? I felt like a little girl whenever I asked permission from Father.

"I hope to attend the fair, but Father—I'm looking for him now."

Mrs. Stark examined my face. After a moment, she shrugged and reached out to the lone couple seated nearby. Was she going to ask them for help? I almost regretted my little lie about looking for Father.

Pretending to search for him, I walked across the dance floor to the mural with a banner proclaiming *GOLD COAST*. To avoid conversation with stragglers, I pretended to examine the painted waves of Lake Michigan with ships bobbing upon white caps. In the center of the mural, red scars slashed the face of Chicago with its main streets—State, Lake, Clark, Astor. Bordering the bottom of the mural were oval portraits of Father's life-long friends—Potter Palmer, Joseph Medill, Robert Todd Lincoln, George Pullman, Mayor Carter Harrison. Topping the wall was a mountain of clouds revealing the gigantic face of John Jacob Astor, glowering like a demon. This was the picture of Father's world, but was there any room for Mother or for me? Mother, how did you mature into an eighteen year old woman? Help me do the same.

As I stared at Father's portrait, his disembodied voice boomed all around me, as if emerging from the wall mural. "Alessandra! I'm ordering you home with Dr. Wetherstone."

I blinked my eyes as I turned around, but found myself facing Hermes instead. "I'll escort her home, sir, granting your permission, of course."

Stepping back, I bumped against the mural as I stared at them. Before I could respond, I saw Karla at the far end of the ballroom near the sliding doors. She waved theater tickets in the air. Was she leaving with Aunt Ashford and Uncle Chilton? Why did I need Father's permission anyway?

"My dear," said Doc Seth, "I need to treat that hand."

A choking sensation flooded my throat, forcing me to cough into my bandaged hand. I felt like a volcano about to erupt. Was it becoming eighteen that made me feel rebellious? How much longer could I contain my true feelings about hating being the obedient daughter?

After Father put my cape about my shoulders, he presented his arm to escort me to the exit. He and Doc Seth marched me across the empty dance floor. Nearing the sliding doors, I heard Karla's high cackle. It had taunted me all my life. Aunt Ashford and Uncle Chilton stood at Karla's side, laughing at me. "Thank you, Alessandra dear," Karla said, "I owe you." Why can't I be my own woman and curse Karla publicly for hurting Father once again?

Father's face reddened with embarrassment. "Ignore them," Doc Seth whispered. Hermes sneezed in the draft from the open door to the street.

The little volcano inside me rumbled and, deep inside, my control snapped. My fingers tore at the clasp of my cape. I rushed toward the moist air at the open door. At the threshold, I motioned for the doorman to step aside. Feeling dizzy, as if looking down from a great height, I tottered on my toes. Stepping outside, I felt the spring rain pelt my cheeks. I was suddenly aware my face had grown numb. The doorman reached out to steady me, but he froze upon seeing my expression. I marched past him, not even waiting for Curlin to bring up our carriage, and launched my body into the crosswind. Puddles soaked my new dancing shoes. Lifting the hem of my gown, I watched my feet strike against the bricks, the staccato sounds stamping out voices from the club shouting for me to return. I advanced to the same corner where only hours ago Karla and I had careened in our carriage. Avoiding a gap in the sidewalk I scurried toward our house a few blocks away. To me, everything seemed broken—a smashed gas light, a cracked window, two lovers back to back beneath a bumbershoot on a bench. The volcano inside me burst through the conventions of society that cemented on top of my heart. I felt like the dead arising from the grave. Home. I must go home.

With rain joining tears on my face, I realized the truth: that beneath these bricks lay spirits of Indians arising from burial grounds the Potawatomi had blessed, but the white men had cursed—calling it Astor Street.

Chapter Two

house

of

many

stories

Later that Night

*F*lames from the fireplace in my bathroom flickered orange, like iodine. The Chinese screen protected me from the draft. Was it only an hour ago I had collapsed into Odette's arms at my front door, unable to explain why I had fled my own birthday ball?

Pouring aloe on my wounded palm, I shook it trying to banish the cut. Why had Karla hurt me? Didn't I try to help her? Hadn't I always trusted Karla? Why can't I trust her now?

Odette, my personal maid since childhood, spilled water from the kettle she was carrying into the bathroom. Cursing in Creole, she pushed a mat with her foot to blot the puddle. Then she placed one kettle on the floor, and poured the other into the bathtub.

I sponge-bathed my nude body so the warm water dissolved cold rain on my shivering skin. I squeezed the velvet-covered sponge onto the base of my neck, letting water trickle down my white bosom, unfashionably full and cursing Karla whose chest was fashionably flat. Restless on the pullout seat attached to the marble tub that Karla and I had fought over as children, my feet made ripples in the shallow water.

After Odette emptied the second kettle, she hobbled toward the door to fetch more hot water from the kitchen stove downstairs. Wanting to embrace her, I refrained, knowing such a gesture would embarrass. Instead, I wondered if the water pipes in the house had been repaired. If they were working, they could spare Odette another backache.

Crossing my fingers, I turned on the golden faucet, shaped like a swan's neck. I listened to the rusty pipes deep in the bowels of our old house rumble complaints as water began to force itself up to my fourth floor. I heard my own stomach rumble. What did Karla mean by saying I helped her with the first dance? Did she just use me to hurt Father? Why?

I soaked the sponge in the newly warmed water and squeezed hard, wishing it were Karla's heart. Beneath me, the pipes rattled in the basement boiler. Water pipes creaked like the bones of my old dog Banks that Hermes had given me before Father had her put to sleep. The sound then climbed to the first floor pantry where our chef Alsace in a starched apron would meet with Mrs. Dibbs, the housekeeper, each morning to plan the next day's menu. I vowed to replace Mrs. Dibbs when I become Lady of the Manor.

The rattle ascended to the second floor drawing room, containing Mother's portraits above the harp-piano Father did not play anymore. On the third floor the pipes banged through the room reserved for Aunt Ashford whenever her touring company performed Gilbert and Sullivan in Chicago. A small door led to the bedroom for Mrs. Dibbs. The other side of the third floor contained the master bedroom where Father paced nightly. The pipes whined as they strained to reach Karla's bathroom on the fourth floor, signaling my turn at last.

I loved the old house since ours was the last rowhouse left standing on Burton Street. I remembered an old daguerreotype showing six rowhouses shoulder to shoulder for support. House by house, year by year, they were sold to Doc Seth and ripped apart until our home was the last standing. When I asked Karla why Father called our rowhouse a manor, she shrugged and told me it was Father's conceit. My consolation was that the reporter Nellie Bly, my hero, was born in a rowhouse. I yearned to become an independent woman like

Nellie Bly. I devoured her book *Around the World in 72 Days, 6 Hours, 11 Minutes*. My imagination ignited at the thought that Nellie Bly traveled unchaperoned, and at the worst time of year, November. On short notice and on a dare, Nellie had clutched a one-way ticket to London accompanied only by a constant migraine. As if shot through a pneumatic tube, Nellie circled the world as she made up her itinerary on the fly. That was in '88 when I was all of thirteen years; Nellie was twenty-one. Every heartbeat of Nellie's conquering the globe, I followed. After her journey, Jules Verne, the famous French author exclaimed, "Brava! Nellie Bly has outdone my fictional hero Phineas Fogg who went around the world in eighty days." I preserved the newspaper clipping in my remembrance book.

Now I watched the faucet shake, cough, and shake again before disgorging spurts of rusty water. Instinctively, my feet lifted to the side of the tub as the faucet expelled fish bones, belched centipedes and vomited blowflies that wriggled on their hairy backs as they spun in whirlpools. Beetles twitched, trying to regain their balance. From the yellow water arose the smell of decay. Shutting off the faucet, I yanked the chain attached to the drain plug and watched them fight against the whirlpool. And with a smile I christened each insect after Karla as they were sucked slowly down the drain.

Odette reappeared with two more kettles. "A tout hazard!" she screamed at the insects, splashing the contents of one of the kettles into the bathtub, flushing the remaining little visitors. After placing the other kettle on the floor, Odette embraced me, and we rocked as we did when I was a child. I always imagined she was Mother. Finally feeling reassured, I stood up. As Odette eased me into my terrycloth robe, she toweled me down by patting me all over, while muttering words of endearment in her native Creole, and humming lullabies I had heard all my life. Unlike me, however, Karla could not stand being touched. Usually when I remembered

Karla's steady stream of boyfriends I would chuckle, but nothing could console me tonight.

Closing my eyes, I remembered Hermes trying to tease me as he did when as children we played on our roof after a spring rain. Wind had exposed Hermes' auburn hair when it blew off Father's opera hat. When the hat rolled to the edge of the roof, it tilted like a seesaw on the gutter. Hermes slid down the shingles, stretching his arm to rescue it. Another breeze twirled Father's hat off the roof as Hermes slipped down the slope to the edge. The toes of his shoes hooked into the gutter halting his slide but his weight bent the gutter to the breaking point. Hearing myself yell, I reached out to him, fingers grabbing his sham collar, the stays popping off. After throwing the loose collar over my shoulder, I hunched farther down the roof, while clinging to a corner of the dormer. Snatching a handful of his yellow suspenders, I watched them stretch as he hovered over the edge of the roof, his back buttons snapping one by one. Staring over his shoulder at the treetops four stories up, Hermes prayed aloud for me to rescue him. Wrapping the loose end of his suspenders around my waist, I dug in my heels. While I tugged at him, his fingernails scraped into the shingles. The gutter snapped. Hermes scurried up to my side, squeezing me against the dormer. For a long time, the only sounds were our labored breathing and the wind whipping branches. With Hermes' head in my lap, I stroked his chin and raised his head ever so slightly. His eyes were closed, but a smile twitched his face. Without thinking, I kissed Hermes full on his lips. Was this the action of a child? Shocked at my boldness, I held my breath, but I did not regret the kiss.

What would Hermes think of me? For an unknown reason I wondered where Father's opera hat had landed, thankful for once he was not home but at his office. Meanwhile Hermes sat up, reached into his hip pocket, and pulled out his Swiss knife. He unfolded the blade and dipped the point into the blood already covering his thumb. Then he cradled my thumb as he inserted the tip of the blade into my flesh, releasing droplets of blood. Pressing his bleeding thumb upon mine, Hermes whispered, "Blood Brother, Blood Sister—Forever!"

Now concluding my toilette, I leaned onto Odette's small frame as I shuffled along the hall to my bedroom, my flat slippers whispering across the threshold. I instructed her to apologize to Father for me, feeling unable to join him in our dining room for the celebration with the Potter Palmers after the ball. Strangely I did not feel guilty disobeying Father.

After Odette left, I tried to sleep, but even though I pulled Mother's comforter over my head, my heart beat too fast. Tossing upon my down mattress, I couldn't close my eyelids being too excited about teetering, at last, on the threshold of adulthood. Questions jabbed at my temples: Should I reject Father's security to pursue freedom like Nellie Bly? Or should I marry Hermes' old money to rescue Father from our financial ruin? Frustrated, I threw off the covers. After staring at the ceiling I rang for my favorite libation, opium cordial laced with morphine. That always soothed me. While waiting for Odette, I listened to rain drops drumming on the roof. In my mind's eye, I envisioned rain trying in vain to assault my secret hideaway on the flat portion of the roof between dormer and chimney. I had safely protected my book from the elements, wedged beneath loose shingles and eve. Dry as myself nestled my Nellie Bly book about a girl's journey to freedom. Would it ever be mine?

Nellie Bly. How could I resist imitating her when we had so much in common: We were both Irish, we both mourned a dead parent; we both loved midnight snacks of peaches and pears; we both craved coffee when sorting things out. Naturally, I also parted my hair down the middle like Nellie's. Whenever she advertised anything I purchased it: A double-peaked English cap; elastic stockings of rubber threads; Doctor Morse's headache pills extracted from Indian roots; Faultless biscuits, cakes, and crackers from the Wilson Company; a checkered long-coat with traveling satchel. The only item I failed to secure was Nellie's recommended LaCigale Cigars. Father refused to switch, insisting on smoking his expensive Havanas. In addition, weren't Nellie and I both five foot five inches? Besides wasn't I trying to lose weight off my one hundred and twenty-five pounds down to Nellie's one hundred and twelve?

Of course leave it to Karla to quickly taunt me by pointing out the faults also shared: staying up too late and then sleeping in; hiding migraine headaches; bumping into furniture whenever we tried too hard to appear dignified. Just to annoy Karla I would sing lyrics from one of the many ditties about Nellie Bly: The way / She walks she lifts her foot / And then she brings it down / And when it lights, there's music there / In that part of town.

Now I bit my lip. Although I could not tour the world, at least I could tour the fair. Didn't it bring the world right to Chicago? Why can't Father give his permission? But why did I need permission? I'm eighteen. Besides Karla was going with Aunt Ashford and Uncle Chilton to Opening Day. And why didn't they want to take me?

My reverie was interrupted when Odette laid the bed tray on my lap, the aromas of coffee and opium mingled with freshly baked shortbread. She relayed Father's displeasure with me by causing him public embarrassment. Fighting back a tear I nodded to Odette who left me alone. Was I no longer Father's favorite daughter? What had I done? Why did it bother me?

I punched my pillow to calm myself. Sipping the cordial, I felt its warm comfort. I settled down to gaze on the objects in my room as I always did when I could not sleep. As usual, I began with my favorite—Mother's daguerreotype standing in the place of honor on the mantel above the fireplace. Within its silver frame, Mother's hair was parted in the middle like mine, but pinned in a bun. Her face was turned slightly toward the camera to reveal her pug nose, deep set eyes, dimpled chin. As a child, I thought the cleft in her chin was really a button I would push, just like the pearl buttons on her blouse. She wore a pendant upon her heart.

Mother provided my life with a center of gravity. When faced with an important decision, I would ask myself what would please Mother. I thought when I reached eighteen I would outgrow listening to her voice in my head. But I needed her more than ever.

In Mother's picture her identical twin—my Aunt Ashford—wore a peasant blouse exposing a scoop neck as she flaunted naked shoulders. Hair bobbed, Mother's sister glared into the camera lens with the same evil eye of envy I saw in Karla's face last night at the ball. My mother and my aunt were eighteen years old at the time of the photgraph, but Mother would never see nineteen. The photograph had ended at the waist. Many hours I stared at Mother's waist, trying to detect the hint of a bulge.

Leaning against Mother's picture frame was Father's collapsed opera hat, the same hat I begged him to give me after our first opera. I loved the hat trick Father taught me. At the touch of a secret button the hat flattened, but he shared with me that by touching another button it popped up, tall and proud as Father himself. Oh how I had brushed his hat so many times it glistened, even in the semi-dark. My glance moved above the mantel, to the posy holder that Karla had fabricated for me six years ago on our twelfth birthdays. With a grunt of disapproval, I recalled how she had insisted on lecturing me on the language of flowers that she insisted described me: chamomile for initiative; larkspur for swiftness; poppy for enthusiasm. I disagreed, knowing she was describing herself instead of me. Karla christened the lacquered flowers *Carpe Nostrum*. I remembered there was a spring storm thundering outside and when Karla attached the tessie to the wall a lightening flash ricocheted light against the mirror above the mantel. We both screamed in fright, and jumped into each other's arms, embracing like real sisters.

Next to the tessie, hung my frayed ballet slippers. How many hours of practice had I endured under Edith's tutelage? My favorite time was with Edith after the other dance students departed. How often we talked together. We even shared the dream of my own ballet studio. Yes, being with Edith after ballet class was almost like being with Mother.

Then my glance to the corner of the room fell on Father's favorite gift to me—my doll house where I pretended to be Lady of the Manor. Placing my half-empty cup on the tray and setting it on the sidetable, I scooted out of bed, squatting close to the doll house, Indian style, and pulled Mother's comforter about me. As always I stared in awe at my doll house, a scale model of Father's rowhouse, constructed by John Wellborn Root, his good friend, the original architect of the fair. It had removable walls and roof permitting me, almost God-like, to see clearly into all the rooms. I pitied Karla for what she had done to her own dollhouse.

Little wooden replicas of our family members filled the dollhouse with life. I chose to imagine only happy times in each of the rooms—I loved the cellar kitchen where I learned baking bread from Alsace; I loved the drawing room where Father would play duets with me on the harp-piano for the Wetherstones; I loved the parlor, where I imagined Mother at her desk alone, sunlight through the stain glass window rainbowing her hair.

As I grew older, it became harder to sleep, so I would snuggle next to my dollhouse listening through the open grid of my heating vent moving little figures into the rooms where I heard conversation taking place. At times, Father would defend himself in the parlor from his older brother Chilton demanding money to finance Aunt Ashford's next Gilbert and Sullivan. I would listen to Karla entering late at night through the kitchen door left unlocked by Alsace, and tip-toeing up the squeaky back stairway. Then, one time something happened I never quite understood. After the family had attended a local performance of Aunt Ashford's musical, Father stalked to his master bedroom and slammed the door. I heard through my open vent Aunt Ashford sobbing and scratching to get into Father's room. When I mentioned this to Karla, she just cackled and walked away, calling me childish.

These meanderings would lull me into a recurring dream. Mother's photograph would spring to life, with Karla as a child in a corner of the frame. Mother Cora would ignore her and beckon me to abandon Father's side as I hugged his leg while he took the photograph. The artificial flash, followed by a muffled explosion, made Karla scream, but it did not frighten me. Breaking away from Father, I would skip toward Mother while she pirouetted like Edith, full skirt billowing, inviting me to enter. Once enfolded within it, I would feel warm and loved as in my comforter. Clinging to Mother's leg, I sobbed for joy. Then, Mother would kneel to kiss away my tears, whispering my name over and over, while Karla lowered her head and peered up, cursing us both with her evil eye of envy.

※   ※   ※

The next morning, Opening Day at the fair, I was still brooding on Karla as I headed down the front stairs to join Father for breakfast. Odette scurried to throw my house robe over my shoulders covering my chemise nightgown. Descending the steps, I felt my temples throb as the floor clock in the dining room ticked louder with each step. Entering the room, I observed Father seated as always at the head of the oval table, tapping the edge of the prayer card in his left hand. Time for grace.

Still in a daze from a restless sleep, I had not realized I was not properly attired. When I assumed my assigned place mid-table with the big clock at my back, Father clicked open his pocket watch to gaze at Mother's photo. His meditation, at this moment every day, smoothed his forehead as well as my aching heart.

Father's throat rumbled as he snapped shut the watch and replaced it in his vest pocket. "Alessandra, you are loved, so I grant you leeway to breakfast in your houserobe. You are, after all, eighteen years old. But as you know such attire is acceptable on Burton Street, but not acceptable on Astor."

The wall clock that grandfather Oscar bequeathed us ground its gears, gathering strength to strike quarter hour after nine. Close to the big clock, I felt less fear, like being close to Father.

"Where is Karla? Did she come home with you?" He touched the bandage on my left hand that Odette had applied. I winced. "Pardon me, my dear, I would never hurt you to save my soul." I believed him; we trusted each other.

Staring at the azure breakfast plate before me I wondered again about the painted figures. Those tiny Chinese travelers poised in the middle of the bridge—would they ever reach the opposite bank? My eyes moistened. "Father, could we pray now?"

He extracted the prayer card from its cellophane protector, grown amber over the years, and placed it against the base of the silver saltcellar. Moistening his lips, and smoothing his mottled beard, Father tapped his fingers. "Now let us close eyes, bow heads, and join the spirit of dear departed Cora. Let us pray the words Cora herself wrote on the back of my calling card."

Folding my hands in the middle of the table, I closed my eyes as I had done countless times. Taking a breath, I prayed that Karla would not barge in to ruin this moment shared by Father, Mother, and me. Always at such times, I felt warm and accepted in the security of being Father's favorite daughter. But over the years, Karla had always seemed to be the pin poking at my balloon.

"Be present at our table Lord." Father's voice sounded softer when he prayed. "Be here and everywhere adored." But how many times had I giggled as a child picturing the Lord as a door. Would he swing like our pantry door? "And these bounties bless."

Opening my left eye, the one away from Father, and turning my head ever so slightly, I saw him sneaking a peek at Mother's words. Poor Father, was his memory so altered by mercury poison from his hats that even Mother's sacred words he recited each morning were forgotten? "And grant that we—" Did I hear a sudden rustle of a skirt behind the pantry door? "Grant that we be in paradise with thee. Help us live the words of the Bible—John Eight, Verse Thirty-Two. 'If you abide in my word you shall be my disciple indeed, and you shall know the truth and the truth shall set you free.'"

In unison, Father and I chanted, "Amen." But did I hear a little echo in the pantry?

Father picked up the prayer card, kissed it, and slipped it back into its cover. He stored it in an inner shirt pocket covering his heart, his face bathed by an inner light. Once when I was a child, I had asked why he looked happy only then. He lifted me onto his lap, and whispered that he was remembering Mother's voice. At those times my little fingertips would trace the vertical crevices in his cheeks. Each time I would ask what they were called. He would repeat with a smile and a hug, "St. Peter's tears." I would ask if I would grow such ditches in my cheeks? He would laugh, and blow in my ear to make me giggle. But I would not want Father to do that now.

Father stared into his cup of black coffee, "Daughter, why did you embarrass me by leaving Germania Club without me? I was afraid for your safety." He picked a piece of lint from the sleeve of his new morning coat of olive and brown that he had received as a business gift from his friend Marshall Field. My feeling of peace was evaporating. I did not want to lie, but I did not want to play Judas by accusing Karla. While Father awaited my answer, he tugged out his gold watch again, but without opening it. Instead, he rubbed it between his palms like Aladdin's lamp. As a child, I believed that Father was conjuring Mother's spirit to join us at her empty chair at the foot of the table opposite Father. Ever since I could remember, a complete table setting with food was reserved for Mother. Each meal I sensed Mother's presence. Father told me she was warm and understanding, like me. At such times I implored her to give me strength as an adult to take her place in Father's heart as Lady of the Manor.

"Mrs. Dibbs," Father said, "clock is two minutes tardy. Have Hustings correct it."

"Yes sir, wish to be served now?" After a flick of Father's wrist, Mrs. Dibbs hastened to the pantry. Father leaned my way. Was I being forced into a corner? My throat went dry. "My future Lady of the Manor," Father said, sighing, "what is today's menu?"

"Your favorites, Father: broiled sheep kidneys, kedgeree fish, and milquetoast." Everything Karla hated. However I wondered how Father could afford to pay the bills. Yes he needed me to rescue him.

The pantry door swung again. Mrs. Dibbs and two servants flowed around the table, rattling dishes and silverware, setting breakfast before us. I removed a sprig of parsley from the medallion-shaped kidneys with my silver fork. As I pressed into the kidney, a screech made me jump.

"Get your bloody cat out of my way!" Karla burst from the pantry, attired in my own Gibson girl red outfit. She swung her leg to one side, sweeping away Cerby without spilling a drop from the teacup she held above her head like a trophy. Cerby jumped onto my lap. "No applause expected, Cyrus, although I know red was Mother's favorite color." I said, "Karla why are you wearing my dress?" While maids whisked past her as they returned to the pantry, Karla paused at the head of the table to peer down on Father. The vein in his forehead pulsated with each heartbeat as he stared straight ahead. "I'll wager you odds, Cyrus, you bet I'd be late again." She patted the tonsure on his crown. "But I forgive you—again. Isn't that what your old bible says? Seventy times seven? But with you, I've used them all up." Karla took her usual seat directly across from mine as Mrs. Dibbs pulled out a chair for her. Why did Mrs. Dibbs respect Karla and not me? Sitting, she glanced at the full plate at the foot of the table. "Oh Mother, you're not eating?"

Gulping ice water, I gagged at Karla's words, spilling the precious cubes that rolled like dice across the table. Gambling. We were all gambling on the future: Father with his risky investments, Karla with her risky way of life, and me with a risky blood-brother for a future husband.

"Uncle Chil should be breakfasting at the club instead of always eating breakfast in his room," Karla said. "But then he gets only a measly allowance from—"

"Karla don't," I said reaching for her hand. She withdrew it, raising the teacup to her lips, and leveling her gaze at Father's bowed head. His bald spot turned crimson whenever he was embarrassed. Now it was beat red. I yearned to kiss it. Instead I said to Karla, "You missed Mother's grace again."

"Stir, that's Cyrus' line," Karla said, waving a triangle of toast. "You should know that, our dear future Lady of the Manor."

"Jealous?" I asked. Was it possible that was Karla's secret desire?

One maid removed the ice cubes, blotting the water on the table, while another placed a full glass before me. Karla's tone of voice chilled the air. It never sounded so totally self-righteous before. What transpired between Karla and Aunt Ashford after the ball?

"Remind me, Cyrus, isn't blind faith enough? Who needs prayers? Didn't your precious mother Cathleen teach you that?" Karla nibbled the toast as if it were covered with caviar. "Aunt Ashford told me last night you used to be a decent

Lutheran like your father, Oscar. Didn't you? That is, until you met Cora, our pious Presbyterian."

"Karla this is a new low even for you," I said.

Father picked up a gleaming silver knife, and gripped the handle so hard I thought he would snap it. On the crack of the table, my plate tilted like a seesaw whenever I tried to eat. I moved it off the crack toward Father's direction. Palming the fork, he stared at his dish before stabbing at a kidney. He sliced it in half, in fourths, in eighths, then cleared his throat and laid the silverware on his plate in the pattern of a cross. "Mrs. Dibbs," he said pushing the dish away, "the kidneys are cold. Remove them."

Although mine were warm, I did not wish to embarrass Father, so I motioned for Mrs. Dibbs also to remove my plate. As I did so, I felt Karla staring at me. What secret seemed to lurk in those black specks within Karla's eyes? She claimed to read my heart; why couldn't I ever read hers?

Karla speared a piece of kidney into her mouth, "Mine's warm," she said, staring at the ceiling. "And I don't even like it."

Father scraped his chair back, and ordered at the top of his voice, "Brandy!" Then from an inner pocket, he produced a Havana cigar. At such moments of confusion I felt total trust in Father. He snipped one end with a tiny guillotine that dangled on a gold chain from his vest pocket. Snapping his thumb nail on the head of a wooden match, he ignited a sturdy blue flame to heat the underside of the cigar. Drawing on the Havana, he crossed his legs, and then after inhaling deeply, he tapped one cheek, admitting a perfect halo of gray smoke that rose slowly to hover above his head. Father looked at me, and winked. We shared the secret of survival: trust in each other.

With that, the sliding doors rumbled partially open as Husting's head appeared. "Begging your pardon, Mr. Aultman," he said twitching his owl whiskers, "the Wetherstones, sir." For the first time today, Father smiled. Nodding, Hustings stepped aside, revealing Edith and Hermes waiting in the vestibule. I gasped in surprise and pleasure. Dr. Wetherstone waddled into our dining room with his medicine bag, while Hustings shut the door behind him. "Greetings to my second family! Breaking fast are we?" I loved him but felt totally embarrassed.

At the sound of his high pitched voice I arose, apologizing for being in my house robe, as Karla left for the pantry, in a blur of red taffeta and feathers. Then, I heard Karla's muffled curse from the pantry. "Bloody Oaf! Spilling coffee all over Sister's favorite dress. Now I'll have to change."

"Alessandra my love!" Doc Seth said, waving one hand while placing his bag on Karla's deserted chair. "Oy, never mind your attire, my girl. I brought you into this world not properly attired. In fact, naked you were." He came around the table to hug me. "Ah, my future daughter-in-law." I loved his embrace but I refused to marry his wife's old money. Peering over my shoulder at Father, he said, "Cyrus, old man, when will you sell me this last rowhouse? You know why I bought up your neighbors." He peered into my eyes. "I want the whole slice of Burton Street so I can build a mansion worthy of my Hermes and my Alessandra." Father blew a smoke ring in the direction of Doc Seth. As I resumed my place at table, the good doctor sat in Mother's chair. He glanced at me, "Don't worry Alessandra, your mother wouldn't mind. She, like you, had a trusting heart." To Mrs. Dibbs he said, "I see the brandy's uncorked. A dram I'll have." While the maids finished clearing dishes, he added, "I've advised you Cyrus," he said, glancing at the remnants on the plates, "become a vegetarian like Chilton." When his snifter was filled he raised it first to me, then Father. "Since no longer you come to my office I thought I'd bring my office to you." He whispered to me, "Catch the old bear in his lair."

My cat Cerby licked my fingertips. Hugging him to my breast, I stroked his ears until his whiskers stood straight out.

"Cyrus, too much worry you carry," said Doc Seth tugging at his earlobe. "Remember us as young boys? Old Oscar told us to dig that cistern? When he discovered we dug in the wrong location, what he did he tell us to do? If you dig wrong hole—just stop."

He glanced at me for support, but what could I say? My heart was brooding on attending the fair. I prayed Doc Seth would find a way for me to attend. I trusted him.

"So stop digging already. Take holiday. Opening day, go."

I scratched Cerby's white throat to calm myself. Since Karla was going to the fair with Aunt Ashford and Chilton, why couldn't I go? Wriggling free, Cerby sprung off my lap.

"Cyrus, about you I care, not the fair," Doc Seth said, "But don't tell me again how your bosom buddy Johnny Root died building it. And I know all about Danny Burnham selling out to those New York Architects. Just remember fresh air is fresh air."

Father sat quietly, fingering his empty brandy glass.

"Help me talk him into going," Doc Seth said to me.

"What?" I said, distracted by remembering those romantic sketches in the *Tribune* of Wooded Island with its million roses surrounding me and Hermes on our wedding day. If I couldn't even persuade Hermes to propose, how could I get Father to relent?

"Cyrus," Doc said, "your spells are getting worse. Stop wearing those mercury hats of yours. Burn them. I've warned you: mercury poisons and kills. God forbid you ever become a mad hatter. Listen to your doctor for once, and prevent a stroke." He gestured to Mrs. Dibbs to remove Cyrus' glass. "To your study shall we go?" The doctor stood and picked up his medicine bag.

Father ground out his cigar and shook his head.

"It's here, then. Remove your waistcoat." He nodded to me with a tight smile. "Cyrus, if you won't come to the fair at least let Alessandra join us."

Instantly accepting his invitation, I nodded feeling blood returning to my limbs. Hastening from our dining room, I slid open the panel doors. My final glance backwards showed Father slumping in his chair like his old opera hat. As I stepped from the dining room I closed the pocket doors behind my back, I leaned my shoulder blades against the closed doors, feeling a cold chill grip my neck from a slit where the panels failed to seal. With a shudder I realized I had unfinished business with Father and Karla both.

"My beloved daughter-in-law to be," Edith said, flinging her arms wide to embrace me. Then she froze, her eyes widening at the sight of my houserobe. Edith turned to Hermes lounging at the front door. "Hermes my dear, please wait outside in our carriage." When he had gone with a smirk, she spun me around and marched me up the stairways to my bedroom. Upstairs, Edith hustled my body to my wardrobe, snatching apparel willy-nilly and handing them to Odette with instructions to clothe me forthwith. While Odette dressed me, Edith muttered, "That old bear Cyrus shan't deny my future daughter-in-law the experience of a lifetime!" As we stumbled out my bedroom, I paused at the standing mirror, trying to see my image, but before I could, Edith whisked me past it.

"Stop treating me like a child!" I shouted. Another reason to resent Mrs. Wetherstone. Is this how she would control me as her daughter-in-law?

"Opening day won't wait," Edith announced. "The speakers! The platform! The World's Fair! That is, if we ever get there on time!"

CHAPTER THREE

COURT OF HONOR

The Next Day

𝓑reathless at being rescued by the Wetherstones so I could share the thrill of experiencing the whole world brought to the fair, I felt my heart throbbing. I scurried down the staircases too impatient to await Hustings to open the front door for me. This time, I pleased myself by leading Edith, but isn't that what adults do: take turns?

Emerging from Father's Manor, I was greeted by sunlight peeking between rain clouds as thunder rolled over my head. Bounding off the outside steps, I splashed through puddles as I ran toward the Wetherstones' carriage, enclosed, with Hermes' head poking from beneath a bumbershoot held aloft by Chas, their driver. "Sander, it worked! You're coming with us!" Hermes bellowed, "We hoodwinked the old bear."

I shook my head in denial as I ran toward him, the feather on my robinhood hat loosening, the fumes from Father's cigar smoke lingering. As I started to reply I wet my lips, but instead tasted kidney from breakfast. When I stretched my arm toward Hermes it prompted him to hop out and flip down the riser steps. Suddenly he stopped to stare at my clothes and snicker. What was wrong with him?

Upon reaching the carriage I paused and followed Hermes' gaze. Then I realized what was wrong—my clothing. Indeed what garments had Edith chosen, willy nilly, when she ordered

Odette to clothe me? Halting in the middle of a mud puddle, I stared down at red Turkish trousers, blue stockings, and white common-sense shoes. To my further embarrassment, I was also wearing a man's yellow shirt from my costume rack. But at least the shirt was partially covered, if only by a Scottish plaid vest. Why hadn't I noticed all this before? Why had Edith hurried me so? Why did she dress me like a clown? Thank Gawd I wore a cloak.

"A lady is not only what she wears, my dear," Edith said catching up, her arm claiming my shoulder. "Take it from your mother's best friend. Bless her soul."

"Mrs. Wetherstone I can't leave the house wearing children's clothes."

"My dear, if you return to the house, Cyrus the old bear will never let you go with us." She squeezed my shoulder. "Make your choice my dear, what will it be: obedience or the fair?"

As I stared at my common-sense shoes, I heard Hermes yell, "Hurry up Nellie Bly!" Yes, indeed, what would my Nellie do? I rocked on my toes like a teeter totter.

Then Edith sniffled, while she revolved her gray gloves for my inspection. "And my heart was so set on ivory gloves for Opening Day."

The self-pity in Edith's voice freed me to laugh at myself at being so indecisive. Her driver descended from the coach to escort us into the cabin. Hermes secured the door and kissed my hand.

While I untangled the straps holding binoculars and camera around Hermes' neck, Edith exclaimed, "Here comes his royal highness. And about time."

Indeed, Doc Seth was hopping around puddles as he clutched his medicine bag like a footballer at Harper. Puffing, he managed to say, "Don't look, my dumplings, but the old bear is sneaking a peek between the front curtains. At Alessandra, our new grownup."

"Then stop talking, fool, and climb in!" Edith shouted, "Before we even get there the fair will probably burn down!" Hermes opened the door and pulled Doc Seth into the cabin.

※ ※ ※

After the carriage stopped at Randolph Street station, the four of us transferred to the Illinois Central Railroad to continue our trek to the fair's 64th Street entrance.

Through a dirty train window I searched for the Wetherstone carriage and perceived Chas waving his horsewhip as he shrank into the distance. After being seated opposite Edith she hid her eyes behind her purse. When Doc Seth noticed my mouth agape, he chuckled. "Detected you have, that Edie dear detests train rides. But today she made exception. Just for you." He waved the tickets. "Reserved ducats from Bertha Palmer for speakers' platform." I smiled, feeling relief at the assurance of special treatment and the fact that Karla was not here to ridicule my outfit. She would arrive later with Aunt Ashford and Uncle Chilton. But we would be first and comfortably ensconced so I could afford to pity Mrs. Wetherstone's fear of trains.

"I love train rides," Hermes said, chewing gum. "Specially steam engines." His eyes avoided my outfit.

"But why?" I asked Doc Seth as my teeth rattled from the vibrations of the car. I hoped Hermes did not notice.

"Trains remind Edith, trains do."

"Of what?" I tried not to peek behind Edith's beaded purse.

"Just because my eyes be closed," Edith said, "does not mean I'm deaf, too."

"Missing the passing beauties of the day you are, my dear." Doc Seth said. "Just passed Van Buren Street."

"Oh that's where they dock the Columbian steamship," I added, craning my neck. "Hermes, could we—could we sometime?" I reached for his hand. "So romantic."

Hermes, however, adjusted the lens of his binoculars to ogle fellow passengers in the railway car. "Well, if we had started earlier we could have taken it."

"Not without our future daughter-in-law," Edith said around the corner of her purse, eyes shut. "Heaven forfend!"

The train conductor's voice boomed through the loud speaker. "Passengers, we are approaching exposition grounds. Portside windows."

Some people scrambled to the right while we squeezed left. From our vantage point, I smudged my nose against the glass to stare at the fair's stone walls. The very first sight of the fairgrounds caused my jaw to drop—I saw bears that walked like men. Or were they men who stalked like bears? The dust on the pane made me stifle a sneeze. The bear-men lurched with every upright step as if they were riding our train; I gaped as they pawed at each other's furs. They inspired my imagination to hear their animal roars, to smell the musty odor of their hairs, to see the beads of sweat bubbling on their foreheads, red with heat and white from fatigue. My skin shivered and sweated as if I were one of them.

"Esquimaux Village," Hermes said, waving his Rand McNally guidebook. "Required to wear fur coats and hats all day long no matter the temperature."

"Children too?" I shouted, "How quaint!" My further view was then blocked by an elevated train circling the fair. "Hermes! Let's share a ride on that."

Hermes stood, binoculars jammed to his face, as he pointed at dozens of tall white buildings covering the entire north end of the exposition. He looked at his father.

"State Buildings," Doc Seth said, "Twenty in a cluster."

I wiped the window with my handkerchief. The sun shone on dozens of domes, cleansed by night rains, flashing in clear morning light. "I see a ship's tall mast atop one of the buildings," I yelled amazed. "I see a giant Spanish adobe with dome and oh such a delightful rooftop garden." I turned to

Hermes, "How I'd love to luncheon with you on a rooftop garden."

Hermes dropped his binoculars to his chest. "My Gawd," he whispered, "White palaces, a city of white palaces."

"And look at the giant art gallery. Packed with oil paintings from around the world. Read about it in the *Tribune*." Suddenly I felt Edith's presence between us. She stood as stiffly self-righteous as in church.

"Well," Edith said staring me down, "Did you cause my son to curse? Don't I have duty as a mother?" Interrupting, Doc Seth said, "Behold Edith, every state and territory with a building. And all tucked into just the north end of the fair."

"Two huge towers of marble," Hermes said. "My Gawd, in the sun they resemble ivory."

I laughed. "But look right next to it. What is a French gothic cathedral doing there?"

"If you ask my favorite," Doc Seth said, "It's Independence Hall from Philly." Placing his arm around his wife he added, "Edie my dear, what's your favorite?"

Rising to her tiptoes, Edith exclaimed, "My little Rhody, I can't see my home state Rhode Island."

In the meantime, other passengers yelled names of their favorite buildings. "That one's Illinois—the largest—ain't you bloody proud?" Another said, "There's the little model school of the future. Imagine all these buildings in one little corner of the fair."

"The Chicago fair is enormous!" Hermes proclaimed, "And wait till you see the rest of it."

"With all them canals?" a sailor said, "Couldn't count them all. Bloody Venice in Chicago."

"Please," Edith said, "Everybody cease cursing."

To distract her, I asked, "What is that imposing building sliding past us? See it? With a glass conservatory on the roof?" Edith aimed her gray gloves. "Woman's Building, of course! Imagine one whole building filled with enlightened women. And designed by a woman, if you please."

I studied its three-storied white silhouette embedded in a forest of stately oak trees. Dozens of open archways and creamy balustrades were fronted by luxuriant shrubberies, and brilliant flowers. Its corner pavilions overflowed with hanging gardens decorating a rooftop restaurant, but I could not see what I had read about. I yearned to be closer to see the Woman's Building, to see it reflected in a nearby lagoon, sparkling in the sun. The very thought made me squint harder.

"You do look confused Alessandra dear," Edith said, "You should know the building style is Italian Renaissance. Just ask."

I shrugged. "And that little building next to it?" I pointed at a smaller building with children dancing on the lawn. When they did not move I realized they were statues. However the grassy yard was also filled with real children flying box kites crisscrossing in the winds. A dozen other real children were leapfrogging and playing tag. "At last," I whispered aloud, "The first public park in Chicago created just for children."

"I love the Children's Building," said a lady in a straw hat next to us. "I'm a wet nurse there."

Curious about the mere existence of a Children's Building, I asked how she had secured a position when I was interrupted by Edith tugging at my sleeve. "Alessandra, what are you thinking? That's no place for Lady of the—"

"But I must visit it," I said, "I know Nellie Bly would." As I reveled in the banquet of buildings sliding by us, a large island of trees came into view. "What is that?"

"Japanese Wooded Island," a sailor said, "That's where I'm headed, you know. Pagodas, roses, and geishas. My ideal trifecta." He twirled his white cap and whistled through his missing teeth.

The conductor's voice bellowed, "Passengers please be seated. Our train will now veer away from the fair to pass over the eastern portion of Midway."

We staggered back to our seats and collapsed in happy giggles, our minds filled with sights we never could have imagined, seduced by a vision of how the world ought to be. Doc Seth muttered contentedly, "Goliath, himself, he could stride across all those rooftops of all those buildings all the way to Lake Michigan!"

As the train ground to a halt, rattling the windows, Doc Seth stood up, "Hagenbeck's Zoo I see, that's where they skin a lion every week. Cyrus, the old bear, would love that lion show."

"Where's my Libby Exhibit?" Edith asked. "I've read so much about it, but now I'm here looking down on Midway I can't find it."

Hermes whooped, "See that building outside the fair? Buffalo Bill's Wild West Show!" He pointed to a huge wooden stadium open to the elements with countless pennants flapping atop its tall walls.

I only half-heard, my mind lingering on the little image of the Children's Building. I longed to see the inside. I wondered if it contained a gymnasium for children especially for girls only, so boys would not hog it assuming it was their right, it being a boy's world and all. I hoped the children needed me. Blocking my view was smoke from the engine as the train resumed rumbling.

After we halted at the 64th Street entrance we descended from the train, with Edith leading us through the gates straight to the kiosk selling chocolate while Doc Seth paid admission fees. It began drizzling. Looming over us was a strange windowless building. I felt it would collapse on top of me. Despite myself I enjoyed the happy faces of people entering the building with ice skates tied over their shoulders.

"That's the Cold Storage Building," Hermes said. "We'll visit it later."

Weaving through a crowd of countless tourists we munched on chocolate, until we finally secured the base of the speakers' platform only to be rebuffed.

"What do you mean, we can't be seated!" I heard myself shrieking at the base of the speakers' stand. We had elbowed our way from the train station entrance to the Court of Honor for Opening Day ceremonies so how could the Columbian Exposition start without us in our reserved seats on the speakers' platform?

Glowering above us with arms outspread, a Columbian guard barred our way up the ladder. He might have thought he resembled an American eagle, but to me just a busboy, the flat top of his cap collecting rain, tassel drooping. In the crosswind, he bit the strap attached to his cap. He peered past me as if overseeing lawn croquet instead of hundreds of people jostling against the head-high speakers' stand. Being ignored by the likes of him was worse than not being seated.

"Read the tickets," Doc Seth yelled, "Four reserved seats on Speakers' Stand—signed Bertha Palmer." Rain swirled off the waterproof tarp covering the table holding the gold key that controlled all the electricity in the fair waiting for the President's touch. Hermes tried to distract me from the delay by pointing toward the cloudscraper buildings surrounding the court, but I found such excess a waste. Raindrops rolled down the neck of my birthday cloak, so I flipped up the hood and fastened it. As I wriggled my toes, I looked down at my water-soaked shoes, caked yellow with mud and manure. After scraping them against the rung of the ladder, I stared up at the Columbian guard. "Sir, are you blind?"

"You're no better than those working folks. Platform's at capacity. So back you go!"

"If Father were here, you wouldn't—" Then I saw the guard possessed one normal brown eye and one blue eye made of glass. In his glassy orb, I perceived the reflection of tiny palm trees on delivery wagons. Fascinated, as if studying Karla's crystal, I saw men as small as ants crawling up sides of buildings.

Doc Seth waved the tickets. "See here young fellow! Four reserved seats from Bertha Palmer!"

The guard slapped his baton against his trouser leg. "Capacity! Nothing personal."

Turning, Dr. Wetherstone appealed to the crowd, murmuring behind us. "Fair is fair," he pleaded. The crowd booed him.

"Who the hell's Bertha Palmer?" a man yelled, making the crowd laugh at us. The man waved his arm like a policeman. "We want to see President Cleveland too—even if we didn't vote the bum." The crowd cheered. "And we don't flash no phony tickets!"

At that moment, the ladder rung cracked beneath my feet, throwing me off balance. A stream of people, avoiding carriages, pushed against me pushing me into a maelstrom of buttons scraping my cheek, umbrellas poking my eyes, fingers pulling my hood. Hermes lost his straw hat, his square eye glasses dangling from one ear. Together, Hermes and I were swept from the base of the platform by a troop of horse soldiers clearing a path. Borne away from the stand, I saw Doc Seth's cane waving above the crowd, and Edith's ostrich feather bobbing like a distress signal.

Pushed and pulled by the crowd, Hermes and I found ourselves near an enormous fountain, amongst children splashing each other as women screamed at them to stop, and men protested being jostled against their will. Gusts of wind sent bonnets soaring like balloons, while white gulls swooped from the tops of ivory buildings. Guards lugged rolled Turkish rugs as they ramrodded past people eating sandwiches and drinking wine. From the terminal station on the other end of the huge square, shouts arose. "Here they come. The Indian chiefs!" But I could not see a thing.

Then the drizzle ceased, bringing forth a rainbow as thousands cheered. Halfway across the face of one of the buildings, a little man climbed, spreading his arms as if he might jump; he hollered, teasing the spectators below him. Suddenly, he lost balance, spinning downward, the crowd gasping. He disappeared into them. Other people, unaware of his fall, swarmed along the edges of the white buildings lining three sides of the court like happy ants at a holiday picnic. Windows bulged with heads and arms, some shooting rifles that emitted belches of smoke, although I couldn't hear the reports over the nearby bandstand blaring "America the Beautiful."

A horse's nostril snorted rudely in my ear. Startled, I saw its red eye flair and its mouth foam as the riderless horse reared on its hind legs, flailing against the crowd, sunlight glinting off its wet harness. At that moment, hundreds of flags and pennants unfurled downward from the roofs of all the palaces as the horse galloped and leaped the railing into the water fountain.

"It's President Cleveland!" I heard Hermes yell a few feet away as I sat down on a stone bench. "He must have pressed the gold key!" Joining me near the bench, Hermes looked down, his head blocking the sun, creating a silhouette outlining his oversized ears. "Alessandra, history is being forged today and here you are resting!" He reached for my hand. "Besides you're making me late for my job!"

Standing on my own feet a little too quickly made me dizzy. Steadying myself, I stared through fountain mist, golden in noon light, and perceived what looked like a mirage. A massive oblong basin stretched a hundred yards before me, with dozens of giant plunging sea horses, leaping dolphins showering droplets, mermaids posing on chariots as Triton threatened the skies. A tall statue at the stern steered a gigantic barge. Father time? Columbus? Were those obedient maidens at the oars propelling themselves into deep waters?

"Alessandra," Hermes said, "Great idea of yours to dodge my folks like you dodged your father!" His chuckle sounded strained. "But, you're looking in the wrong direction. My job's over there. Past the fountain and that stupid army horse."

"But the speakers' stand is the other way!"

"We'll grab a water taxi." Hermes' long arm surrounded my waist.

"Wait a minute," I said, changing the subject. "Did you ever see such a beautiful sight?" At the other end of the Grand Basin stood a huge statue of a lady. "Who is that? I want a closer look." Searching his eyes, I wondered if Hermes was really listening to me.

"That's just another woman." I felt his arm release my waist. Around us, soldiers tried to restore order. Hermes grabbed my hand. "I'll protect you." He jerked my body toward him, snapping my head back.

I heard myself protesting, "Hermes you're hurting me! Besides, I don't need your protection, you know that."

Hermes' smile faded. "Your spectacles are wet," I said, "Here, take my handkerchief." I straightened the straps of the camera and binoculars tangled about his neck.

A Columbian guard, looking like a member of McVicker's cast of Gilbert and Sullivan, apprehended the army horse which was using the fountain for a comfort station.

"Sorry I irritate you, Miss Aultman," Hermes said, his voice deeper than usual.

I sidled away from him as a voice boomed from the public address system. President Cleveland, sounding like Father, bellowed; "On this exalted mission the world cooperates in an enterprise devoted to human enlightenments—" A little boy spat on my shoes, then peered up at me, blinked, and kicked my shin. "And in this undertaking we exemplify the noblest sense of the brotherhood of nations." Passing us were men in derby hats cursing Indian chiefs arrayed in feathered royalty, smoking pipes of peace. "Hold fast to the meaning of this ceremony. Don't lose the impressiveness of this moment." Hermes stood atop a railing, encircling the fountain, taking photographs of the speakers' platform. "I torch this machinery giving life to our vast Exposition. At this instant, let us awaken forces which influence the dignity and freedom of all mankind."

Thunderous applause followed, mostly from people who had not been listening.

Hermes, back at my side, squeezed my elbow as he hailed the driver of a large electric launch in the nearby canal. Before we could reach it, a portly lady carrying three small poodles clambered aboard. At the launch's side bobbed a tiny battery boat, its huge motorman already half filling it as he chewed an unlit cigar butt. Blocking our path, two elegant older ladies fumbled at their drawstring purses for proper fare. Hermes dodged around them, then whispered into the ear of the motorman. Glancing at my midriff, Hermes wrinkled his brow, then held out his hand, winking at me. What did he mean? Dismissing the two ladies, the motorman planted one boot ashore, while extending a beefy hand in my direction. Hermes guided me into the little boat with unaccustomed deliberation. Before I could object, we were both ensconced in the tight quarters of the battery boat, rocking outward from the dock. While the engine sputtered, I leaned toward Hermes. "What in the world did you say to the man to get us seated?"

Blushing, Hermes stretched one arm about my shoulder and with his other hand patted my midriff, smiling at the motorman, who grinned at me.

As we drifted from shore, my astonishment at Hermes' resourcefulness mingled with my secret pleasure wishing his baby fantasy was true. But why was Hermes so inconsistent? Was he toying with my affection? I also felt uneasy that the farther we went into the fair the more I would be hurting Father's feelings. His loyalty to his dead friend Root seemed to me to be inappropriate and inconsistent with my feelings. Already I felt slipping in Father's affections. Would Karla succeed me as his favorite daughter? Would she become Lady of the Manor? My brooding was interrupted by a commotion at the elevated speakers' platform. Were Doc Seth and Edith scanning the crowd for us? I grabbed the binoculars dangling around Hermes' neck and stared into the blurred lenses. Adjusting focus, I crouched for a better balance.

"Don't, Mother!" screamed the motorman. "Don't deliver in my boat!"

Forgetting that the binoculars were attached to Hermes' neck, I stood, jerking his head. His eyeglasses popped loose, splashing into brown water at the bottom of our boat. Sputtering louder than the engine, Hermes ducked from under the strap. Lassoing it around my neck, he said, "Here! Wear it in good health, Mother."

As Hermes bent to retrieve his eyeglasses, the waves from a nearby electric launch rocked him headfirst, bumping him onto the bench.

"Stay down, mate," shouted the motorman. "A bloody armada's headed down our throats!"

Indeed, the prow of a Venetian gondola rose and fell like a sea serpent as their gondolier threatened us with a long pole. Musicians on board ceased playing, hiding their faces behind guitars and mandolins, preparing for a head-on collision. Our motorman rose regally, and bit his thumb at them.

The gondolier in the other boat stabbed the water with his pole, and at the last second managed to change his boat's direction. The hulls thudded against each other, the eyes of the musicians bulging as they swept past us.

After Hermes wretched over the side, he looked at me with a sickly grin. "Well, I did pay him to hurry." A dozen other boats sailed in the wrong direction straight at us—launches, sailboats, gondolas.

Our motorman cursed, swinging our boat so sharply we almost capsized. "Pay me bonus, mate, for taking shortcut wrong way."

"Hermes, are we headed in the wrong direction?" I lowered my head in my hands, and noticed my red Turkish trousers were soaked. The plume from my Robin Hood hat was floating at my feet.

Commenting on my outfit for the first time today, Hermes said, "Bicycling are we?"

Straightening my spine, I faced him, "Hermes, answer me. Where are we headed?"

"Shortcut to work."

"Your work? But how? You're in college. Did you get expelled?"

"Spare-time only."

My tapping foot splashed water.

Passengers waved and whistled at us from a launch that narrowly missed our boat. "A month ago, our professor invited Mrs. Stark to lecture on the fair. She needed volunteers, or the fair couldn't open."

"But you never volunteer for anything," I said, as a sailboat spun in circles, creating a whirlpool as we passed it. I noticed a lady wearing a familiar raven's wing hat like Karla's. "And you kept this from me." Then I said to Hermes, "Opening Day's part of your assignment?"

"No, my idea was to take a few photos. But now you made me late for work."

Before I could ask more, our boat pulled to shore where a small guard with a loose collar screeched in a high-pitched voice, "See here, pilot, you're not supposed to dock here. Besides, I should ticket you for sailing against traffic!"

"Bug off, baby britches!" the motorman yelled back, bumping our boat against the cement wall. "You ain't authority. Go get a copper!" When the guard saw the size of our driver as he rose to his full height, his eyes bugged out. People on the shore laughed, applauding our boatman who tossed the rock anchor onto the dock, startling a sleeping dog. Our boat secured, he held out a ham-sized hand to Hermes. "Forgive me, mate, must charge for three."

Hermes bit his lip before reaching into his vest pocket for change which he handed over to the motorman, who chomped on each coin. Climbing the metal ladder, I remembered the Columbian guard at the speaker's stand. His glass eye haunted me. Waiting passengers were queued for an electric launch, while workmen replaced broken wood on the sidewalk with cement.

"Good luck to youse two—I mean three!" the motorman yelled, removing his soiled captain's cap. "Name the little one after me—Bertrand—if youse will allow."

Almost stepping into fresh cement, I was rescued by Hermes. "My new avocation it seems." For once, I felt glad to be protected by him.

Zigzagging through the crowd and down a narrow street, I saw the corner of a white façade peeking out at me. As I approached the archway I saw large medallions depicting children of different races in national costumes. Stopping, I read the inscription: "The hope of the world is in the children." I said, "Oh, Hermes, this is my kind of building! I saw it from the train." But he had lagged behind when a hansom cab passed him with a young couple. I envied them as they hugged each other. Hermes jumped back as a mounted police man galloped after a speeding bicycle, whistling it down. I resumed studying the replicas of children's faces. This simple building in the midst of the fair's artificial extravagance moved me in ways I did not understand. I clapped my hands and exclaimed aloud, "This is the first building I must visit!"

"You can't!" Hermes shouted in my ear. Without waiting for my response, he rushed beyond me, heading to the building next to it. "I'm late as it is."

I felt the same public embarrassment as when the Columbian guard refused our seats earlier in the day.

As Hermes walked backwards like a guide, he mocked my expression. "You should see yourself. Sometimes you have the same evil eye as Karla."

"But I don't have to work at it!" I must have shouted too loudly because a woman clucked her tongue at me, while the man with her smiled.

"The sign on the door," Hermes said, "Did you not read it?"

I returned to the entrance as a cluster of children swirled around two adult females at the closed front door. They were staring at a posted announcement.

The Children's Building will be received by Mrs. Bertha Palmer Public Ceremonies 10 A.M. June 1st

"Follow me," Hermes yelled from a distance. "My building's open. Yours isn't until next month."

I followed him, dragging my feet.

In contrast to the simplicity of the Children's Building, the Woman's seemed pretentious with its four pillars of Greek goddesses dwarfing Hermes. However, as I studied the figures of such classic women, I was soon filled with awe. Motioning me to hurry, Hermes entered the east loggia where we passed visitors opening lunches next to a sign, *No Picnic Area.*

Inside, we tiptoed down a passageway to the main hall. On each side were wall murals, one showing a dozen women in an idyllic forest scene crushing grapes, carrying water, nurturing babies. It was labeled *Primitive Woman*. I loved it. The other mural displayed women picking fruits of harvest, playing lyres, dancing. It was labeled *Modern Woman*. I loved that one too. The archway connecting the two murals stated, *President Bertha Palmer, 1893*. I doubted that Karla would like either one.

Succeeding rooms revealed display cases of pottery, textiles, sculptures. I yawned. Portraits on the walls were of women only. I asked Hermes for an explanation, but he shrugged and said, "What do you expect? It's the Woman's Building."

"But you're working here?"

"Shush! They'll never guess." Hermes bumped past me, not lingering for a glance at the displays. Racing through the crowd, he stamped his foot at the elevator being out of order; then he lurched toward the stairway. I pursued his shadow to the second floor, where we encountered long corridors choked with milling people. When we reached the arches of the rotunda, Hermes stood rubbing his chin with the back of his hand, "She must be in here."

"Who are we looking for?" I asked him, but he didn't answer. My attention was distracted by the vast dimensions of the assembly hall, three stories high, arched by stained-glass windows pouring rainbows of sunlight across hundreds of display cases. Wall signs pointed to the modern electric kitchen in Connecticut room. I wanted to visit it. Hermes snapped his fingers. "The roof garden!"

"What?"

"That's where she holds court."

"Who you talking about?" But Hermes, gone again, elbowed through people in the assembly hall to God-knows-where. I followed him, of course, until we reached a winding stairway with walls only half-finished. The waiting crowd jammed me against the unfinished wall, my lace gloves sliding along loose boards and nails. As we ascended the stairs, I heard a piercing voice exclaim, "Get these garbage barrels out of here! We open soon. Got two hundred reservations coming to the opening, and where's Mrs. Riley?" Hermes reached the summit of the stairway first and paused. The voice continued. "Boston Cooking School didn't teach Mrs. Riley to furnish enough chairs, cushions and tables!" When I reached the doorway at the head of the stairs, Hermes told the Columbian guard, "I work here and so does she." We wedged onto the roof garden where I found an open-air restaurant readying itself for business. In the center of a whirl of waiters, waitresses, and porters stood a recent acquaintance of mine. Her gray hair stacked atop a bold forehead, a blue choker at her throat gave the look of a tired teacher. When she spoke, I tried to recall her name. "You!" She pointed at Hermes. "About time!"

"I'm sorry. I'm simply abject. I'm—"

"Take charge of porters. The fair director hired muscles, not brains. Have my porters haul garbage barrels down the stairs." She turned to me, her voice softening. "Would you believe it, miss? The idiot boss turns the elevators off at night to save money. Then they don't start next morning."

I turned to Hermes for an explanation, but he was already rounding up porters who had been smoking and sitting on railings.

"For five whole weeks, young lady," she said, amidst clanging plates and moving tables, "I lived in boots, furs, macintosh. Cold, wet, hungry morn' til night."

I reached for her hand. "My sympathies," I said, to stop her talking.

Squeezing my hand, she burst into a huge laugh. "I'm not complaining, mind. I'm describing. Lord knows, I volunteered for all this." Her eyes darkened as she dabbed a corner with the edge of her apron. A movement caught her eye. "Hey you, Ellis!" she shouted at a bearded porter. "Careful rolling that barrel. You'll soil this young lady's unique outfit." Extending her hand to me, she paused, wiped it on her apron, and offered it again. "Chief of Installation." She bowed in self-mockery. "You don't remember me, do you?"

"Of course I do. I'm Alessandra Aultman of Astor Street."

"Friend of young Hermes, are you?"

I looked around for him.

"More than friends? Oh, never mind. At least you're not starry-eyed, thank God. Not like do-gooders they send me." Her eyes never rested, taking in the faces of porters packing garbage into barrels, and waitresses setting tables. While she observed others, she seemed focused on me. "Volunteer?" she asked again.

Behind her, I saw a skinny white-haired woman with birdlike movements wipe her brow from perspiration that did not seem to be there. She waited her turn.

"Of course, you're not a volunteer. Too bad. Always did like the ones too smart to join up." She patted my hand like a nurse taking her leave from a hospital bed. "When I think of the needs of all my people," she sighed, heaving her bosom.

"Cannot rest." Then she tilted her head. "Do I hear a nervous foot tapping behind me? Could it be Mrs. Riley, here at last?" With that, she swung her attention to Mrs. Riley, who coughed behind a handkerchief.

Hermes shouted, "Over here, Alessandra. By the railing." He motioned to a wicker armchair where porters had lounged.

I joined him and reclined gratefully, my ankle starting to ache. Unbuckling my shoe, I noticed my gloves had become frayed at the knuckles from scraping along the walls of the rough stairways. Removing the gloves as if an outer layer of skin, I flexed my fingers, knuckles cracking like twigs.

"I thought only I was king of knuckle crackers," Hermes said, removing his own gloves, stained green and brown. From his short topcoat dangled strands of lettuce, carrot tops, and parsley while his woolen suit, wrinkled and wet, hung loose on his thin frame. His v-neck sweater, twisted sideways, was half-hidden by the weight of a box camera about his neck. The straps tangled his binoculars like vines around a young sapling. I wanted to sit Hermes down and untangle him again.

"Oh, this?" Hermes said, glancing down at the camera as at an albatross. "My spare-time assignment. Photograph displays." Untwisting a spaghetti of straps, he laid them aside. Then he knelt, and cupped the heel of my shoe. With the gentle hands of a son who had observed his father's doctoring, Hermes freed my aching foot from the shoe's control. At such moments, I realized that Hermes was trying to express his affection by massaging my foot in the warm sun.

Over his stooped shoulders, I observed Mrs. Riley approaching with a basin of water that spilled over one hand and then the other. Pausing, she closed her eyes as her lips moved. Was she counting numbers? Springing to take the burden, Hermes said, "Thank you, madam. I'll tend to her."

Mrs. Riley squeezed her moist hands on her leather apron, and blinked as if the sun were too bright. "Have to get back. You don't know Mrs. Stark."

After she left, Hermes placed a warm cloth around my ankle, then patted it with a dry towel before I studied my foot. How disappointing. The foot appeared disgustingly normal. I couldn't ask Hermes to care for it much longer. Glancing about, I watched busboys rubbing down table tops and waitresses placing fresh roses into porcelain vases. I sensed Hermes staring at me, so I confronted his eyes, sparkling in sunlight. "Yes?" I asked, inviting him to find the right words. To myself I thought, Hermes you are loved.

He gulped, cheeks reddening. But instead of speaking, he propped my foot, inspected it again, and then he muttered, almost to himself, "No broken bones. Just a strain." After a long moment, he looked up and grinned. "Bad luck—for me."

I retrieved my foot and kicked at him, feeling childish.

"And I could have been a hero."

Mrs. Riley returned with a waiter, who carried a tray holding a coffee pot with a short stem rose next to it. I nodded. She clapped her hands, and another waiter brought cup and saucer. "We're not really open. Not 'til lunchtime. But the so-called help already consumed half the food. However, we can offer English muffin and jam."

"Thank you, Mrs. Riley. Could you make that coffee an opium cordial?"

"Rest assured, dearie," she said, flapping her handkerchief as if giving permission. She ordered the coffeepot taken away. Later, she returned with the cordial and poured it herself. After I took the first sip, I smiled my approval so she bowed and departed.

My hands, warmed by the cup, still trembled in thin sunlight. Although the cordial burned my lips, it soothed my throat. Relaxing into the wicker chair, my body told me how tense it had been. I should not be here. I should have rejected the Wetherstone's invitation. Karla will tease me endlessly about disobeying Father.

"Stop brooding, Alessandra. You look like Karla. Enjoy the view." Hermes handed me his binoculars.

I focused the lens, using the vertical bars of the iron railing as a reference point, as he had taught me. In the distance, two massive girders braced themselves like limbs waiting for a giant torso to be attached. Pointing at them, I almost spilled my cordial. "What is that going to become? A bridge?"

"Do you mean that viaduct?"

"No, funny, far beyond it."

Shielding his eyes, Hermes stood on his tiptoes. "Oh that. Those are two support towers." He rocked on his feet, as he always did when he knew something I did not. I hated Hermes when he was smug.

Wasn't there something I could say to put him in his place? "Come to think of it, little man, shouldn't you be working? Besides, where's your boss?"

Hermes sat down, and waved to a waiter for a regular coffee for himself. "Oh, all right, nosey!" He put an arm around my shoulder. "It's the base for the wheel. A bloody fairy wheel."

Readjusting focus, I asked, "But where's the wheel? I just see two limbs."

"Look closer, Columbus. There's an axle connecting them."

I giggled to myself, because Hermes and I had been invisibly connected all our lives. He sensed that I was feeling something unsaid because he cocked his head, peering at me. Then he leaned closer and whispered, "Do you want to ride it together?"

I let go the binoculars to dangle against my breasts.

"Sander," he continued to whisper, "the Ferris Wheel will be ready next month. Will you be?"

I took a deep breath. Then another.

A voice echoed from the enclosed café. "Ellis! I've told you to accept all exhibits. Don't run people away. I'll find room even if I have to build cases myself!"

"I like her after all," I said, "maybe because she knows the porters' names, like Ellis."

"Oh, you're such an innocent. She calls everybody Ellis."

"I don't understand."

"If you would read the *Tribune* half as much as that chef of yours, you would know Mr. James Ellis, Chicago millionaire and collector of antiques, and—by the by—your father's friend, he's chairman of the budget committee." He raised an eyebrow, the sophisticated one, and waited for me to applaud.

All this rushing about made my head swirl. I could not understand Hermes anymore either. I sought solace by enjoying the opium cordial's gifts of drowsiness and exhilaration. I did love them so! That was one thing at least I could thank Karla for.

Hermes was called away to the enclosed café. That was fine with me, because although I was alone, I did not feel lonely. I needed to sort things out. Why would Hermes not commit to me? But then if he did, I would not marry for his mother's old money, despite Father's financial troubles. Squinting at the sun, now brighter, I held up my left hand to protect my eyes. In my half-drowsy state, I rotated my hand, fascinated with the orange outline around my finger nails buffened to a new length. In my imagination, I labeled my palm as Father; my index finger as Mother. Then what would my itchy middle finger represent? Perhaps school? Even Harper? Oh, I know. Our house, waiting for its Lady of the Manor. My ring finger, of course, belonged to Hermes; however what could my little finger mean? Well, why not the fair? Still staring at my upraised hand, I realized that I belonged to Father, I belonged to Mother, I belonged to Hermes, I belonged to the house. If I'm not careful, I might also belong to the fair.

Shaking my head and dropping my hand onto my lap, I reached for a muffin, no longer warm, and spread the raspberry jam to taste its sweetness. In my distracted state, the red jam had fallen onto the palm of my left hand. Dabbing it clean with a moistened napkin, I was surprised to note that Karla's cut from the birthday knife was not as deep as it felt at times. Squeezing my eyes tighter, I rubbed them with my right hand imagining myself on my rooftop, my back against the chimney. I would be reading my favorite book by Nellie Bly, *Around the World in 72 Days*. With my knees raised to support the book, I'd be turning the pages with my thumb—my wet thumb, and I would—wait a minute—maybe that's who I am—I'm my own thumb. Putting the muffin down, I inspected my left hand again, this time crossing my thumb to touch each finger nail—my index, middle, ring, and little. Then I touched the palm with my thumb. What would my hand be without my thumb? Could I even have a hand without a thumb? Where is my life without my thumb? Without me?

As I sank deeper, I thought I heard voices nearby. "Mr. Ellis, I don't agree." Then a man's voice, "Well, the walkup did my constitution good." Then the woman, "But you must fix the elevator. Workers will strike if you don't—" "Let them strike! So you, dear Amey, you can catch up on your delinquent inventory."

Folding my arms, I chose to snuggle sideways deeper into the chair, my back to the sun, my thumb curled snugly into the center of my palm.

The man's voice was fading. "Which reminds me of the purpose of my visit. Health inspectors complained about garbage spilling down your stairway." The woman's voice, "Can't take barrels down the elevator. It doesn't work." The man stamped the floor with what sounded like a walking stick.

It brought me half-awake. Through the slits of my eyelids, I saw a stout man in a serge suit sporting the latest turned-down collar. He twirled his bowler hat atop his walking stick like a roulette wheel. "That's your problem, Stark!" The man pounded his walking stick, nearly bouncing off his hat. "I—don't—care!"

Mrs. Stark snapped her fingers at a porter. "You, Ellis!" A young man, smoking behind a barrel, leaped to his feet. "Roll that barrel. Make sure it's full. Roll it to this railing." Mrs. Stark strode from the real Mr. Ellis, knocking his bowler off his cane. As he reached to recover it, another porter, beckoned by Mrs. Stark, kicked it away, waking me fully.

Bending over the railing, she shouted to the street below. "Heads up down there!" To the porters, now snickering, she pointed to six barrels belching garbage. "Lads, drop those delicious contents. Don't drop the barrels!"

Mr. Ellis rushed forward, swinging his stick like a whip, barely missing the shoulder of a porter, "Put them down you blackguards!" Everywhere, barrels were lifted, garbage spilling over the railing.

Hermes hurried to my side, bumped by a porter who pushed him against a barrel. He grabbed the open top to regain balance, but slipped on lettuce leaves and fell. The barrel teetered on its edge, then rolled straight toward me.

Aroused by the chaos, I hopped on my shoed foot to a corner behind a potted palm tree. The barrel smashed against my empty chair, spitting garbage between the railings. Hermes crawled toward me on his hands and knees as porters scooped up armfuls of garbage and deposited them over the side. A hail of orange peelings, celery stalks and coffee grounds showered into the air as a light rain began to drizzle through the sunlight.

"You're finished!" Ellis shouted.

"Tell that to Bertha Palmer!"

Ellis threw his walking stick to the floor. "My Gawd! Do you hear it? It's working!" The elevator was rumbling up to the roof garden. "There's your first customers, Amey. Clean up this damned place!"

Rasping like a mechanical snake, the elevator door slid open. A folded pink parasol protruded from the elevator, as if sniffing the air. With raindrops spotting it, the parasol popped open and spun, shaking off the drops. Everyone in the roof restaurant froze, as if playing statues.

From the open elevator strode a sky blue taffeta walking costume with a short coat of Louis XV design, a skirt with twirled rolls of satin, and a hat rimmed with ravens' wings, jauntily tipped to one side, partially hiding the face beneath it. A porter shouted "Momma Mia!" His praise drew the attention of the lady as she sashayed with an actresses' gait on the arm of a sturdy man in a fireman's uniform.

Hermes had ceased crawling. Behind a palm tree I stared at my upturned hands as they filled with raindrops. I closed my eyes. Everything would just go away if I just ignored it. However, Mrs. Riley's bird voice chirped as if on a branch above me.

"Do you know this young lady in the corner? She seemed to have twisted her ankle, so I served her an opium cordial. Would you like one, miss?"

When I opened my eyes, the sun shone brighter than ever. Hermes stepped around my palm tree where I crouched and, putting his arm about me, assisted me to my feet. Rejecting his arm, I stood shakily. Peeking between my fingers, I saw a woman. The evil eye that had stared at me yesterday afternoon in the carriage now pierced my heart.

After a long silence, my sister spun the closed parasol that I had given her for her birthday.

"Do you two know each other?" Mrs. Riley asked.

"Oh, no! How could a lady like *moi* possibly be an acquaintance of a clownish waif soaked in garbage?" Spinning on her heel, my sister ordered, "To the café! I'm still dizzy from their bloody battery boat driving the wrong way on the canal. It almost sank our sail!" She poked her escort with the tip of her parasol. "And you, dear Kelso, bet me I couldn't find my sister after she almost sank us. Can't wait to tell on her!"

With Karla's back toward me, the center of my very being melted. I sank into the half-broken chair that had cradled me only minutes before. Burying my face in my hands, rocking like an orphan, I willed myself borne home to my own bed, longing to feel Father's soothing hand as it smoothed my brow, forgiving me for having such a disobedient heart.

Chapter Four

Lady of the Manor

The Next Day

The palm of a hand, cool and firm, pressed against my forehead dissolving my nightmare into images—palm branches lashing my face, waiters' towels igniting white flames, garbage barrels bursting like bombs. Spirits floated by—Father shaking his head in disapproval, his vein cleaving his head in two; Karla toasting me in mockery with her flask; Hermes chewing his lip off, unable to speak his love for me; Amey Stark, beckoning me to drown in the swamp buried beneath the fair.

The hand cooled my fever and soothed my heart, half-broken by its disobedience to Father. I heard myself speaking to a skull I held in my hands. "Father, forgive me. I should have listened to you," his skull crumbled in my palms as my nightmare ended.

Sitting up in bed, eyes still closed, I flung my arms around Father and hugged him. "Forgive me for going to the fair," I sobbed. Father's neck felt thinner. "I'm sorry for embarrassing you at the ball in front of your Astor Street friends." His shoulders seemed narrower. "As a child you always forgave me with your comforting kiss." His chin felt rougher.

A gentle laugh, familiar to me from childhood, opened my eyes to full wakefulness. Light from the kerosene lamp next to my bed glinted off spectacles. Startled by the frightening appearance of a pince-nez balanced on the bridge of a nose, I saw my reflection glaring back at me.

"My dear, calm down. The end of the world it's not. Your old uncle is here to get you on your feet again."

"You are not my uncle!" I whispered, "You're just our family doctor."

Sighing, he removed his eyeglasses with thumb and forefinger, to dangle on a red cord against his plaid vest. "Your image must bother you, my dear."

"Where's Father?" I demanded, feeling foolish mistaking him for Father. But, then, how could I mistake him? Doc Seth's eyes were always the kindest in the world. I threw my arms around his neck, yes thinner than Father's, but this time with my eyes wide open. "Forgive me, Uncle Seth. You mean more to me than I realize. I love you, you know you're like a second Father. It's just that—"

"My dear, I understand. Eighteen years old you are."

"Is there a cure for it?"

"Yes, Alessandra, become nineteen. The sooner the better."

From downstairs, a loud rasping cough signaled that Father was pacing. My back stiffened. "I must apologize to Father."

Doc Seth clicked open his pocketwatch. "Your foot and your hand I've attended, but to your heart you must attend. Love surmounts every obstacle, even old money. I know." He smiled, revealing the gap in his front teeth. "Rest you need. Cyrus, the old bear, needs time to lick his wounds, self-inflicted as they may be. Best to himself you leave him."

"But I can't sleep without his forgiveness."

"Then with insomnia learn to live."

Would my apology to Father be misunderstood, angering him further? Would a rift give Karla an opening? A small voice within me knew a confrontation with Father must come to pass.

Doc Seth sighed, turning off the lamp. "Alessandra, your Father believes you think too much." He winked at me. "I believe, not enough. My prescription for you is—my son Hermes." He placed his hand on my forehead again. "But in doses small." Clicking shut his medicine bag, he arose, and glanced toward the door of my bedroom. "Truth be told, with me Hermes came. A class he's missing. Permission to send the young scamp in? Then my customary cognac with your Father?"

"No!" I shouted, pulling Mother's comforter tightly under my chin. "I need time to think." Doc Seth was already out the door. Peering around the jam, came a familiar face, ears sticking out.

"Is, is this the roof garden?" Hermes' tall frame brushed the top of the open doorway. His short topcoat was unbuttoned revealing a maroon college sweater. Tiptoeing in, he pretended to photograph me with his box camera, its strap around his neck. "Karla sends her best wishes."

I pulled Mother's comforter over my head, and to make him disappear. The scraping of the wooden limbs of the chair across the floor, however, told me he was settling in. When I peeked out, he had seated himself, straightening his red bowtie with both hands while the camera swayed like a loose branch.

"Aren't you supposed to be someplace else—like in class?"

Hermes ignored me by peering out the window next to my bed. "You don't send signals to me at night anymore." With both hands, he steadied the camera.

"Is that what you came to tell me?"

"My father says I have to get to class soon. He says he'll drive me there himself."

"Hermes," I said, "yesterday was a fiasco." I felt anger, but I also felt attracted to his sensitive eyes, reacting to every shifting light and shadow. "Hermes, why didn't you protect me?"

He leaned toward me, fiddling with his camera. "I've been thinking about you, and me. I need to tell you how I feel."

Is he finally going to ask me? I smoothed Mother's comforter with my palms.

Hermes chomped on his lower lip, and gazed at his high-buckle shoes. "I—I don't know what I would do—if anything happened to you." He tapped the shoes together. "You know I'm only a freshman in college, and Mother tells me to wait." He sank back in the chair. "But Father says if I'm a man I'll tell you how I feel." His eyes searched the room as if looking for a hidden door, then alighted upon Father's opera hat, collapsed on the mantle. "I'll bet his hat size is the same as mine."

I couldn't stand the moment any longer. "Hermes, your father is ready to drive you to class. Have you come to say something?" Why was it against the rules for me to ask him?

Hermes glanced at the dollhouse in the corner. "I wish—I wish we could be small enough to live together in your dollhouse."

"Are you the one with the fever? Do you have something to say to me, or not?"

Removing the strap from around his neck, he put the camera down. He shifted forward. Studying my eyes, he stammered, "Sander—would—would you be my, my Lady, Lady of the Manor?" He turned my hands over, and gently kissed my palms. I closed my eyes, and eased back against the headboard.

In my imagination, I pictured the two of us living happily in the dollhouse.

Hermes let go of my hands. "Mother's right. I should wait, but I must have a commitment from you or else I can't go on. Mother's solution is for you to gain some experience. Being Lady of the Manor for your Father would be ideal—but just for a few years."

Behind my closed lids, tears welled up. My throat choked with disappointment. I half-opened my eyes and waved Hermes away. As he stood, he kicked his camera. The chair toppled backward to the floor.

"Alessandra, I can't believe this! Are you rejecting me? Karla warned me downstairs you would spurn me! And after all we've—"

"What does Karla have to do with us? Were you flirting with her again?"

Hermes lifted his head, eyes widening like a crazed pony. Picking up the fallen chair, he slammed it straight down on the floor. He stared at me without blinking, then he bolted toward the door. I pointed at the camera lying on the floor, and he returned in a crouch, stretching out his arm and hooking one finger around the strap, avoiding my eyes as if I were a box of dynamite. He dragged the camera across the floor. At the doorway, he stood, the camera cradled at his stomach, and heaved a sigh of relief. Then he took out a blue handkerchief and dusted it off.

After Hermes left, Odette entered the room. Her face flushed, she applauded. "*Oui, Ma'mselle!* Lady ze manor. Mrs. Hermes Witherspoon, *n'est ce pas?*"

Shaking my head, I said "Not yet!" As Odette replaced Mother's comforter around my shoulders, I added, "As Karla would say—time is out of joint."

Odette fluffed my pillow as she giggled, "You are secret engage?" She kissed my forehead. "You happy, me proud!"

Gazing at Odette's cherub face, I realized I could no longer go to her like I used to as a child when Karla would taunt me. Needing to be alone, I asked for a tray of cocoa and pastries.

After Odette left me, I cried. Reaching for my kerchief on the night stand, my glance wandered idly about the room. As I put the cloth to my nose, my eyes rested on Mother's daguerreotype. Her protective arm around Aunt Ashford made me pine for it around me. I yearned to be enfolded in her long skirts. Staring at her, my eyes ached. I imagined her face gradually moving within its frame the second after the click of the shutter. Mother would slowly turn her head toward me instead of her sister. For the first time in my life, I imagined I saw Mother's full face. Her eyes burrowed into mine and for a moment we were one person.

Needing to sort things out, I sought my remembrance book with the double A for my name. In it, Mother's only letter was worn from many readings. I leaned my back against the headboard, and unfolded the faded green paper.

Prayer for my helpless unborn. You are loved. I don't know if your name will be Alexander or Alessandra, but you are loved. May G-d shine his grace upon you. May you find love in marriage as I did with your father, Cyrus.

Closing my eyes for a moment, I imagined Hermes as my loving husband. Sighing, I had to admit I needed to do a lot of work.

We will cherish you as our precious gift. I can't wait to cradle you.

Through tears, I gazed at Mother's picture on the mantle before continuing.

Oh Lord, dispel my fears and selfishness. Grant to me, a frightened eighteen year old girl, a woman's heart.

Yes, that's what I need, Mother, a woman's heart. But what is a woman's heart? Must she desire to please everyone?

Protect our baby from the world's evil eye that always threatens to twist our good intentions into evil.

I saw Karla's tessie on the wall needed dusting. When Karla had described me, I knew it was herself. Is it her fault she inherited the evil eye from Aunt Ashford? Mother's letter was meant for both of us but Karla didn't treasure it.

My thoughts and prayers are transcribed by my maid of honor, Edith. Bless her and Seth for coming back to Ireland to be with me, in my hour of need.

Trapped on the Wheel

Why was Edith the maid of honor and not Mother's sister?

Seth, the good doctor, pronounced me too weak to handwrite a letter but I must, must reach out to you from my own helplessness. So, I'm really obeying him because I'm not writing a letter, I'm talking it to Edith. (You'll need to be clever, too, my darling Celt.)

Yes, Mother's Irish blood made me long to rebel, but Father's German commitment to duty held my heart.

My fever burns brighter and all my bones ache. So I must hasten.

My ailment, dear Mother, called conventions, restrained women with rules made by and for men. It's a disease even Doc Seth could not cure.

I fear most of all, that you would ever share my fate as an orphan. Little one, you need to know my dear Da, Alexander Sully, loved us, but hard times came after our Ma (Moira) died. Da was forced to beg the holy nuns to take his children in. Later, it was G-d's will that Da be lost at sea.

I have fears, too, Mother. Do I leave Father by marrying Hermes or find my own way like Nellie Bly?

The Larken family wanted to adopt me, but only me alone. Naturally, I refused unless they also adopted my sister, Ashford. Reluctantly, they did. But I've never understood why—from that day forward—Ashford hated me for it.

Ashford is so like Karla, using the evil eye to turn around good intentions.

Being such a burden to other people humbles my heart. But I must confess my heart has acted with enthusiastic disobedience.

I held Mother's letter to my heart and felt it throb.

Someday, my beloved helpless unborn, you will know the whole truth. I trust you will accept and understand. Perhaps when you give birth yourself to a baby of your own.

Enthusiastic disobedience? What could she possibly mean?

I pray for Cyrus. He needs your love because his intentions, at least, were pure.

I put the letter on my lap and stared at it. No matter how many times I reread it, her meaning always escaped me. Did Mother mean I must spend my life with Father as Lady of the Manor? Or must I uncover truths hidden from my eyes? What would such secrets unleash upon our family?

There are more deep feelings in my heart, but they must remain locked away until you and I can hear the lilt of each other's voices. Edith's hand must be tired. She is shaking the blood back into it. So I bid adieu, little one, but never goodbye. I pray that you too will feel the overwhelming joy of a baby of your own.

Remember you are loved,
Cora
P.S. Erin Go Bragh!

A tap on the door and Odette reentered bringing my cocoa and pastries. She placed the tray across my lap, and touched my forehead. "Mon dieu! Fever? She is worse!" I took a sip of cocoa, and peered at the picture again.

When I finished, I set the tray on the floor and rose to choose the proper adult garb for Lady of the Manor. Should it be a lightweight cotton blouse with ruffle cap, skirt of wool? No, too frilly, lacking in dignity. Karla would wear it. As Odette picked up the tray, she shook her head at me and returned to her chores. I let her go. I had to do this on my own, even with a fever. Should I wear my Gibson Girl outfit with its long-sleeved blouse, bow tie, black belt, ankle-length dress? No, too informal. What then? Glancing over my shoulder, I stared at Mother's profile. This time no matter how hard I stared—she remained a profile. It was up to me.

Then I saw my yellow-check gingham housedress, its high collar layered with bands of lace and trimmed with ruffles at shoulders and wrists. Its front closure of brown had a matching sash around the waist. I held the housedress against my body, and studied it in the full-length oval mirror. Nellie Bly would never wear it. Mother's acorn pendant dangled from the adjustment knob. I raised the chain over my head.

A tiny purr at my feet told me Cerby approved of my choice as he brushed my ankles.

What to do next? Consult Father about my list of duties as Lady of the Manor? Even while thinking this, I heard the front door slam, signaling Father's exit for work at his real estate office on LaSalle Street. He would not have to be concerned about what to wear. Why did I? I envied Nellie Bly, who often dressed as a man. Hers was the kind of liberty I yearned for. But at the same time I needed to fill Father's heart by becoming his Lady of the Manor.

With my gingham house dress secured and fitting comfortably, I realized what to do next. Leaving my bedroom, I conducted an inspection of each and every room in Father's house, making a list of restorations on the backside of my tutor's slate.

※ ※ ※

An hour later, ignoring the puzzled frowns from the staff, I took a fresh cup of cocoa outside toward my favorite spot for sorting things out—the gazebo in the middle of the garden.

The midmorning sun welcomed me, its warm rays soaking into my cheeks. Walking the winding pathways, I found myself judging the growth of spring flowers. If the dried tessie on the wall of my bedroom told me mostly about Karla, what would a similar tessie tell about me?

In the gazebo, I sat on the glider, meditating, newly appreciative of Father's house with its Persian rugs, Turkish sofas, and ottomans from India. On the walls hung two-dimensional patterns of Japanese cranes, bamboo, and plum blossoms. The stain glass window, cracked by Karla, bulged with grapevines. The parlor table shimmered with blue willow china. In the corner, bloomed open Japanese parasols. Divans from Arabia rested beneath a ceiling of stars, resembling the Sainte Chapelle in Paris. All these were models for my dollhouse.

Oh, but how I loved Father's real ceilings! As children, Hermes and I would take hand mirrors and pretend to be high-stepping over the door beams in the ceiling, a gangway for passengers aboard ship. Staring into the silver frame I would pose my profile trying to look like Nellie Bly, but no matter how hard I tried I always resembled Father. As we marched through Father's rooms, our mirrors filled with chandeliers appearing as icy Christmas trees in one room, followed by painted murals of lakes and mountains in another. The journey always filled my heart with the feel of freedom. Humming, we would bend foreheads and listen to our knees thudding against our mirrors like tiny toy drums.

Sometimes on these stalking Safaris I wore Father's opera hat, but it being so large would slip off and collapse upon the floor. Hermes would retrieve, snapping it back to its full height with the magic button and donning it on his head at a rakish angle.

Now my thoughts were interrupted by a bumblebee buzzing past my nose, perhaps attracted by my wearing Mother's perfume from Ireland. I swatted at it with the slate. The bee did not irritate me half as much as my guilt at not noticing over the years the changes to Father's house. Who had encroached Mother's role as Lady of the Manor? Father wouldn't have changed anything—must be Mrs. Dibbs—only she could have chosen that ugly strawberry wallpaper in the vestibule. What happened to the Moroccan bound classics in the glass bookcases? Who introduced those dead dry flowers cluttering the house? All those awful smells of glue and dust, dye and chicken feathers, glass beads and toilet paper! And who put those stick crosses into shadow boxes? It seemed to me, no surface of Father's house was free. No room for human beings to breathe, not with everything horizontal painted; everything vertical, draped.

Although the gazebo lay open to the breeze, I lurched back on the bench gasping for air, feeling entombed. My secure nest had been transformed by Mrs. Dibbs into a mausoleum.

I burned with the need to talk to Father about restoring his house to grandfather's original furnishings. However, the very thought of confronting him made me tremble. Would he support Mrs. Dibbs instead of me? So I decided to hide my plans locked in my desk for the following week. As usual, Father dined at Germania Club as often as necessary with Mr. Palmer and his business partners. However, when he was able to be at home, Father and I loved to talk for hours after dinner about my studies with the tutors. It was the favorite time of day for both of us. Father always praised my excellent marks, calling them the hallmark of a first class mind. We never discussed Karla.

Later, Odette came to the gazebo to remind me of a planned dinner Saturday night with Potter Palmer and Bertha as guests. Would Father announce publicly his choice of Lady of the Manor? Karla would be certain to cause a scene.

When Saturday evening arrived, I set aside my thoughts of Nellie Bly and chose a Swiss muslin dress, off-white with pink piping, and pink bows. Odette told me Karla had instructed Mrs. Dibbs to change the procedure for dinner service. Karla proclaimed the new style was called service *á la Russe*, restaurant style. Astor Street considered it so smart. The *nouveax riche* riche of Astor Street competed against Prairie Avenue's old money with the number of settings, sometimes high as ten, each with new place settings and with dozens of pieces of tableware per person. Fear of germs was the social excuse; but I was certain Karla's purpose was to bankrupt Father. Myself, I preferred the traditional manner of selecting food and then passing the serving dishes without waiting for the servants. Would the Palmers prefer Karla's changes? When dinnertime came, I could not judge their reactions because the table's new centerpiece (three feet wide, three feet high of dried flowers) almost buried the bust of Bacchus and blocked my view.

When wine was served, I controlled my nervousness with Negus, a concoction of port wine, hot water, sugar, lemons and nutmeg. Seated at opposite end of the oval table, Aunt Ashford and Karla dismissed the wine and Negus, demanding instead, champagne. To Father's left, Uncle Chilton gulped ice water, whining about enduring another of his dry spells.

While sipping my second Negus, I studied the menu card and, despite the golden light of table candles, my mood became even more restless. The silver place holder, resting on a blue china dish, presented choices of crimpcod and oyster sauce, fried perch and pigs feet a la Bechamel, boiled fowls and vegetables, with meringue a' la crème completed the menu: Dessert jelly molds, puddings, and blanc manges. All my favorites. I was surprised and pleased.

After a nod from Father to announce dinner, Mrs. Dibbs directed servants to remove the centerpiece. It took two of them. The new view allowed me to observe that Father, with Mr. Palmer sitting at his right hand, had been slipping notes while drinking champagne. For a half hour I listened to table talk about real estate, the fair, the opening of the new Gilbert and Sullivan with Aunt Ashford. Karla said not a word. When Bertha Palmer engaged in small talk with me about my possibly working at the fair, she smiled warmly while ignoring Karla.

During the five courses, Mrs. Dibbs stood expectantly against the wall. She relayed orders from Father to the servants with just a flicker of her eyes. To me, she seemed far too composed. Had she tried to convince Father I should not become Lady of the Manor? I felt everyone was staring at me.

Before dessert, the clinking of a glass drew everyone's attention to Father. His forehead, smoother than in weeks, shone in candlelight. He glanced at Mr. Palmer as if asking for permission. Mr. Palmer nodded. Then Father hoisted his great weight to his feet and raised his glass. "Propose a toast, friends and family, to my new official—Lady of the Manor." He gestured towards me. "My very own Alessandra!" Everyone stood except me, of course, and Karla. After the other people emptied their glasses and planted them upside down on the tablecloth, Father ordered Karla to stand.

"I'll stand, Cyrus," she said, jumping to her feet. "I'll stand for anything—except Sister as Lady of the Manor." Aunt Ashford grasped at Karla's hand, perhaps to stifle her, but Karla shrugged her off.

"Lady of the Manor?" Karla shouted, aiming her evil eye at me. "You're bizzare! You don't even know the names of servants. Besides," she said looking at Aunt Ashford, "I'm the elder sister. In all fairness, Karla should become Lady of the Manor!" The truth of her words knifed into my heart. Everyone's eyes seemed to burn my face. Could I crawl under the table? Everyone sat down, except one.

Father whispered in a hoarse voice, "Karla, I order you to sit!"

"Name one servant, Sister, besides Odette, Alsace, Curlin."

Three tumblers of Negus made my throat dry.

Karla swayed on her feet, spilling champagne. "Name laundress, kitchen maids, groom, footman! What are duties of the steward? The housemaids? Can you keep accounts? Being Lady of the Manor is not just house visits!" Karla waved her champagne glass at Mrs. Dibbs, who stood with edges of her mouth upturned. "Do you want to take her position? Would you exile that woman onto the street?" With that, Karla threw her napkin down, pushing from the table. Striding to the door, she growled, "For me, I'm having my dessert with Kelso at the club." When she stopped, she spread her hands on the indentations of the closed pocket doors. "Sister," she said to her hands, "You're at last taking your mother's place—but it took you eighteen bloody years!"

Karla thrust aside the pocket doors with such force the table candles blew out. A movement from Mrs. Dibbs' eyes ordered a servant to relight them. The air seemed to be sucked from the room. Father's vein throbbed in his forehead as his body collapsed, like his opera hat, onto his chair. I glanced at Father's full-length portrait on the wall displaying his once proud stance, thumb hooking his leather vest and hand squeezing a lion-headed walking stick, borrowed for the occasion from Mr. Palmer.

As Father buried his face in his hands, Mr. Palmer embraced him. I also rose to comfort Father, but Mrs. Palmer clapped her hands twice and motioned Aunt Ashford and me toward the withdrawing room. The tears welling in my eyes made it difficult, but then my ideal Lady of the Manor took my hand, and I felt almost her equal following her lead.

❊ ❊ ❊

Later that night, as I sought refuge in bed under Mother's comforter, I seemed to hear her voice as I drifted to sleep.

"Who was first born? Who knew the names and duties of the servants?" But, Mother, I argued, I could still improve their lives. "Alessandra, do you want to take my place or not? You believe Nellie Bly is more important than your own mother!" But Mother, I'm confused; I don't know what I want to be. Hermes' wife? Father's Lady of the Manor? Or Nellie Bly?

Next day in church, I could not attend to the sermon. Instead, I stared at the list of servants and their duties scribbled on a card Odette had written for me, and tucked into Mother's prayer book. Was this the map of my future?

I felt determined to please Father. I chose a natural beginning: Monday, collection day for laundry. Having confided in Odette about my plans, I ordered her to awaken me at dawn.

She dressed me in a brown basque jacket with skirt of checked wool and high-topped shoes. My long brown hair she tied back with a lace handkerchief. Odette advised me that visiting the laundress' room would cause embarrassment, so I agreed to meet in the laundry room off the basement kitchen. When Odette finished dressing me, I thanked her and strolled down the back stairs. When I arrived, the laundress was already there. As she introduced herself as Dolly, I hid my shock at her utter plainness. I had never noticed Dolly's horse face of protruding teeth. As she tried to hide her hands in apron pockets, I observed scars on the palms. What had scarred them?

In the laundry room, smells of soda crystals, yellow soap, and lime burned my nostrils. Dolly soaked and poked the clothes in hot soapy lye. She loosened the dirt by rubbing hard on a corrugated washboard. Then Dolly hummed as she pounded the clothes with a strange contraption—a short five-legged stool holding a three-foot post with a two-foot cross stick. In response to my question, Dolly called it a Posser. "I thought Father bought the house a new washing machine?" I said. Would I have to be burdened with such details?

"Lordy, miss, that there new washing machine's just a tub with paddles to tear clothes," she said. "Just have to mend them later." Then Dolly heaped table linens from Saturday's dinner, stained yellow and brown. I noticed tell-tale markings of the Negus I had spilled. My face felt warm. Never had I realized how my carelessness caused unnecessary work for other people.

"Dolly," I said, interrupting her humming. "Why do you appear so happy doing such difficult chores?" I knew I wouldn't.

"Ah, Miss Aultman, pardon me boldness, but you are a sweet pea to ask." She blew wisps of hair from her eyes. "But it's the only work a laundress do." She smiled, her tongue licking her teeth. "No cooking for old Dolly! No dressing people hand and foot! No kneeling to scrub no floors!" She straightened her back, and wiped her forehead with her apron. "Just wash, dry, iron. Wash, dry, iron. Six days a week. And on Sunday? Sunday, Dolly owns herself. Sunday is Dolly's time to spoon."

All this activity made me hungry. But when breakfast was served by Alsace at the little table adjacent to the kitchen, Dolly whooped for joy. "Great leftovers from Sunday," she said to the food Alsace served in silence. "Brown bread, boiled potatoes, good strong tea!" We sat among fly papers suspended from crossbeams. Embarrassed at Dolly having to eat our leftovers, I poked at the scraps while a horsefly hovered above my hands. *Am I rehearsing to become Hermes' Lady of the Manor?*

Afterwards, Dolly heated flatirons on the low stove to use on starched and dried clothes. When she removed a flatiron, Dolly tested its heat by spitting on it. If the spit bubbled the iron was ready. If the spit did not jump, she returned the iron to the stove. When she retrieved the second hot iron, I asked if I could hold it. Dolly frowned, shaking her head, but instead handed me a cold iron. Surprised at its weight, about ten pounds, I dropped it, barely missing my foot. Picking it up, Dolly placed the cold iron upon the trivet. Sighing, I asked why she did not use the electric iron Father had purchased for the house. Dolly laughed. "Does Dolly want sparks and weird noises? Sparks scorch the bed sheets." Then, Dolly wrapped her hand within a cloth to pick up the hot irons. As she did so, I noticed again purple scars upon her palm.

As Dolly finished storing the ironed linen, she began to sigh and whistle off key. Pausing, she stretched her neck, rotating her shoulders. Dolly's fatigue seemed to be my own, so I laid my hands upon her back to rub her to a bit of relief. At my touch, Dolly jumped as if assaulted. "Miss Karla would never touch me like that," she said. Shaking her head at me in disapproval, Dolly bid me a quick adieu, and exited the laundry room. Alsace averted his eyes and attended to cleaning his stove.

※ ※ ※

Wednesday, needful to restore my energies, I chose the fresh air of the garden. I wore a white poplin dress with a green carter's frock. My high collar, open at the throat, displayed Mother's acorn pendant. However, my straw skimmer kept blowing off. I shivered in the gazebo as the sky sprinkled rain. When the wind changed direction, it blew the rain through the gazebo, ruining my temporary shelter. I had to retreat to the security of Father's house.

※ ※ ※

Next day, I resumed my observations of the housemaids' duties. What were their names again? Odette informed me they were Maggie and Em who wore uniform gingham dresses, white caps, white aprons. Each maid carried a box containing brushes, cloths, cleaning powder. I learned the maids did not possess rubber gloves either. At six in the morning, I greeted them with a smile to witness their daily tasks. They surprised me by wearing leather aprons instead of white ones. Maggie's first job was lighting the fire in the kitchen stove to allow Alsace to cook breakfast for the house. Then, she swept the front steps before dusting the parlor and igniting fire places on all four floors. I admired her skill in not burning her fingers. Maggie carried up a kettle of hot water to Father's bedroom for his morning shave, while I waited in the doorway.

During Maggie's tasks, I wondered what Em did. She later told me she opened all the shutters on the lower floors, and stoked the fireplaces Maggie had just lit. Then, Em sprinkled carpets with damp tea leaves to lay dust before brushing. She set table in dining room for breakfast before she carried the tea tray to Mrs. Dibbs' room. Behind a closed door, Em dressed her. Later, Em and Maggie changed to fresh cloth aprons to dust furniture in their assigned areas in the house.

After lunch, Maggie and Em changed clothes again, this time black uniforms with white starched collars and cuffs. Observing them at their work made me realize that I'd never noticed that layers of soot coated every object in the house. The light of coal fires, candles, and gas lamps had seemed so romantic to me when Karla would chase me, as barefooted children, playing tag. Now, I had a different aspect. Each day every single inch of picture frames had to be dusted; as well as furniture polished, carpets brushed, china cabinets dusted, painted walls washed. Worst of all, for me, was watching their endless kneeling to scrub wooden floors. At night, I dreamt my own hands were tied to brushes that plunged relentlessly into buckets of scalding soda water, swirling with foot-long bars of yellow soap, stinking like rotten eggs.

When I awoke I needed a holiday from the manor, so Friday I bicycled to nearby Lincoln Park. But even in clean air I still smelled rotten eggs. I rode my safety bike in figure eights so many times I lost count. When my feet ached, I sought a shady tree to prop my bicycle. From its wicker basket, I uncovered my Nellie Bly book, thumbing to the section I had bookmarked after reading in my nook on the roof. I puzzled over the question, "What are unmarried girls good for?" I searched for Nellie Bly's answer. She told me, instead, to ask questions of the man's world, and also choose the largest small action leading to the goal, and then act. Her watchword was "Forward!" But how did the men in Nellie's life react to all this?

※ ※ ※

On Saturday, taking advantage of the false dawn, I tiptoed, shoes in hand, down the front stairs because they did not squeak. I felt like Karla. Once outside, I slipped on my common sense shoes and circled Father's house to cross the manicured area outside the kitchen. The aroma of freshly baking bread finally erased vestiges of rotten eggs.

A wrought-iron railing led down a flight of steps to the back entrance. The doorknob felt cold and unyielding. Should I have worn gloves? Was I guilty that our servants could not afford gloves? The bottom of the stairwell lay in total darkness.

As my eyes grew accustomed, I tried the knob again. Locked. Drawing a deep breath, I felt dawn air chill my lungs. When I struck my knuckles on the door, cold shivered along my forearm into my elbow. Shaking it off, I placed my ear against the door, and listened to the shuffle of slippers across the flagstone floor. Another moment of silence. Then I heard a cat meow. Had Cerby sneaked down to the kitchen again to chase mice? Suddenly, the locks on the door snapped open, echoing. I jumped.

In the open doorway, a ghost appeared with a kerosene lamp held aloft: Alsace. He blinked into my face. Shaking his head, he retreated from the door and bumped into a chair. Entering,

I closed the door behind me. When the lock clicked shut, it unexpectedly opened a door of memory within me. As a child, I had spent many hours in the kitchen with Alsace teaching me to cook. The kitchen was Alsace's private domain. Mrs. Dibbs refused to set foot below stairs, claiming the kitchen was beneath her. The kitchen, then, meant a refuge to Alsace, and a womb to me.

Standing with my back to the door, I studied the kitchen because, when last here, I was absorbed with Dolly. The cooking range still sat in the wall, the stone sink still had its familiar leaky water tap, gray slabs were still firm beneath my shoes. The food slicers, egg-whisks, and cream-whippers were nestled in a corner. The aromas of the kitchen caressed my memory.

Alsace, recovering his composure, drew himself to his full height—taller even than Hermes—clicked his heels, bowed, and swept his mushroom hat in a half circle. "Franlein, zee honor bestowed, she is underserved." Puffing out his cheeks, he winked.

"You were expecting my sister?"

He put a finger to his lips. "For you, Fraulein, today you are my favorite sister."

"I came to bake bread."

Shaking his head, Alsace cleared the largest table. "Nein, nein. Alessandra, for you I member your favorite recipe. Bread, she can wait. For you, your favorite, plum cake." Turning up the gaslights, he brought out several wooden basins and a sack of flour.

"How much?" I asked, taking out my little notebook from my pocket.

Without looking at me, he held up one finger. Then he poured flour freely.

I wrote down one pound flour. "Why don't you measure it, Alsace?" I asked, wetting the point of the stub pencil with the tip of my tongue, like Nellie Bly.

"Sugar, half pound."

I wrote it down as Alsace broke a bar of butter with one hand, beat the butter, and then poured the cream into the basin along with flour and sugar. Slicing a lemon he dropped it in, then spilled one-half pint of milk into the basin and mixed the ingredients. Taking a heaping teaspoon of bicarbonate of soda, he stirred two tablespoons of milk, adding them to the batter. Then he beat the combination in the basin.

"How long do you do this?" Alsace glanced at me and shrugged. He added, what appeared to be, half a pound of currant and perhaps two ounces of candied peel, both unmeasured. He continued mixing. Buttering a tin, he put the dough into it and offered the cake to the oven.

"For how long?" I asked, pencil poised as Cerby sniffed at a mouse hole in a corner.

"'Til she tells me."

Shaking my head, I sat down and stared at my scribblings, "Alsace, how can I write a precise recipe when you don't measure precisely?"

Alsace chuckled, scratching powder from his large nose. After spying into the oven at the plum cake, he wiped his hands on his checkered apron. Sauntering toward me, he took my hands and turned them over, causing my pencil to clatter onto the flagstone. "*Liebchen,* the recipe for life, you search for—Pardon poor Alsace for speaking so plain: cook not with your head, cook with your heart."

Scratching paws across flagstone, Cerby pounced onto my lap. I hugged him to my breasts and promised him a piece of plum cake. Cerby licked my palms. Was he approving of my new status?

✼ ✼ ✼

The next Sunday after church, I kissed Mother's acorn pendant and begged her for strength. Her small voice told me to restore Father's house. Therefore, pretending I was Karla, I began by ordering the servants around, changing their routines, authorizing daily menus over Mrs. Dibbs' objections, selecting food purchases without consulting anyone in order to save time, and designing detailed plans to restore Father's house to its total original condition. The most important step would be to audit Father's account books. After several rebuffs for an appointment he finally allowed an audience with him.

"What's the meaning of this?" Father demanded. I took a deep breath and then explained that it was the duty of Lady of the Manor to review household finances. "But Mrs. Dibbs didn't even know—"

"Mrs. Dibbs is not permitted to know where account books are located." Father smacked his lips. "Only I know that."

"But Father, that was before. You were alone then. Now, I'm helping—"

With a wave of his arm, Father dismissed my words. "Helping? By changing my life? By upsetting Mrs. Dibbs? The maids? The laundress?" He sat down, "Alessandra, about them I don't really care." He motioned for me to sit. "About you I care." He peered into my face. "Is this too much for you? Are you ready?"

Placing my hands on the table, I eased myself onto a chair, doubling my right leg beneath me for support. "But Father, now I'm an adult. I've taken Mother's place. One friend of mine has had a baby already. Just like Mother. Besides, my friend Katherine is already a Lady of the Manor."

"They are not you, Alessandra. You are loved. During these eighteen years you belonged to me. I, that is, your mother Cora gave you these eighteen years with her very life."

I felt so selfish, but I needed to speak. "But Father, I've got other things on my heart. Remember our harp-piano? We don't duet anymore. We don't worship together anymore. Not since the birthday ball. No, please don't start to leave. Tell me why you hate the fair. Father you don't explain yourself to me anymore."

"My old Alessandra did not ask questions. She always aimed to please her father, like a dutiful daughter."

"But I wasn't eighteen yet. Now I'm Lady of the—"

"For your mother's sake, I will explain only once," he said, leaning forward. "As you well remember, the man who made your dollhouse, my best friend John Root, died only one year before the fair was scheduled to open. Died also our vision of the fair: a peaceful gathering of the world's countries with their own native architecture." He sat back and sighed. "Then that bastard Burnham sold out to those New Yorkers." He slapped his open palm against the table top. "White City! My ass! White tombs."

Father stood, banging his crown on the low chandelier. "Dammit! I'm Lord of the Manor." The sound of grandfather's floor clock chimed throughout the house. Father yanked out his vest pocket watch, popped it open, and glared at Mother's picture. This time his forehead vein did not become smoother, but more protruding. "Thank God, Cora's not present to hear you sassing your dear old father."

"Father, we used to be so close, but ever since my growing years, you've drifted—"

"Mrs. Dibbs informs me you have plans for the house."

"Yes, Father, let me share them."

"Burn them, instead."

I felt breathless, as if I had fallen off my cycle.

Father's shoulders slumped. He seemed to stare at nothing. I prayed he was not suffering the stroke Doc Seth warned him against. White foam surfaced at the corners of his mouth, turning black hairs gray. He sank into the chair with a grunt and muttered at his hands, sulpher-scarred from the great fire. "Cora, Cora, why do my good intentions always go wrong?"

He stared at Cora's tintype in his open watch. Then he raised it to his lips and kissed it. He took out an oyster-colored handkerchief and dabbed at the foam stains. He snapped shut the watch, pocketed it in his vest and thrust his chin like a trapped horse struggling to free itself from a muddy ditch.

Standing, Father puffed out his chest and announced to the chandelier, "Audience is terminated."

"But what do you want me to do as Lady—"

Father lurched toward the door as I rose to aid him, fearful of his falling.

At the doorway, Father paused and spun on his heel to face me, his eyes unblinking and darker than ever I saw them. From beneath his shirt he lifted a brass chain on which dangled a small brass key. Father growled, "This key. This key is to the household accounts. It's the one key Cyrus Karl Aultman shares with no bloody servant!"

After Father slammed the door in my face, I stood transfixed and stared without seeing. Was I no longer Lady of the Manor? I did not understand Father anymore, nor Mrs. Dibbs who refused to leave her room since I took over, nor the servants when I attempted to reform their lives. For my pains, they politely ignored my simple requests. Such rejections made me feel like Nellie Bly lost at sea with a rebellious crew. I needed a north star to steer by. Since I prayed to Mother for direction and she had answered me, surely my intentions must be correct. So then it must be my fault. Perhaps a house call to Bertha Palmer at her mansion would clear the clouds from my mind. So tomorrow, Decoration Day, I determined to visit her early in the morning.

❂ ❂ ❂

Alighting from our carriage, I instructed Curlin to wait. Approaching the huge front doors, I saw flags flapping from every window, buntings rippling from every turret, and red and blue streamers twisting in the wind of the multi-million Palmer mansion on Lake Shore Drive.

For all the countless times our family had visited the Palmers, I never noticed one fact. The doors had no doorknobs! Instead, a thick golden cord hung suspended near the round stainglass windows. After I tugged at it, a single drop of perspiration rolled all the way down my spine. When a second drop started, the massive doors clanged open, and the brow of their new butler appeared in the opening. He frowned but permitted my entrance. He informed me that the Lady of the Manor was engaged in her office at the fair. When I displayed my visitor's card, the butler pointed me to the front parlor to deposit it on a silver tray before departing. Thereupon, the new butler returned to his duties. I felt the stranger, instead of him.

In the parlor, the sound of my shoes echoed off high ceilings. No sun shone through the stain glass windows. I burned with curiosity to search for the unfinished portrait, but instead I deposited my card, and turned to leave. Then I noticed in a dark corner an easel covered by oriental tapestry. Glancing about for the butler, and not seeing him, I tiptoed toward temptation. With both hands, I loosened the top corners of the covering that fell, revealing a golden tiara crowning silver hair, penetrating eyes, aristocratic nose, uplifted chin. A gavel rested upon a bare shoulder, the wand of a fairy godmother. Staring longer at her than ever I would in real life, I immersed myself for one golden moment in the image of the perfect Lady of the Manor. I soaked up her essence of regal humanity. But I also realized that as much as I adored Bertha Palmer, she was a north star to steer by, but too distant for me to reach.

Returning home, I spoke not a word of my usual chatter to Curlin nor to Hustings. Instead, I raced up the stairways two steps at a time to my bedroom. Slamming the door behind me, I collapsed onto the mat next to my dollhouse. It had always comforted me in the past. But somehow the dollhouse seemed smaller; its interior decorations suddenly old-fashioned.

My eyelids grew heavy, then heavier. Before I knew it, I surprised myself by awakening from a catnap. The floor must have been drafty from open registers because my spine began to tingle, producing goose bumps all over my body. I rolled off the mat, my stomach quivering as something ugly started to rebel inside me. I sat up trying to control my body. My throat filled to bursting. Then my mouth exploded with vomit splattering all over the dollhouse roof, dousing dormer, chimney, and oozing down the side windows. Again and again, my frame shook. Half-fainting, I fell backwards, slamming my head on the wooden floor. I tasted a bitter truth that I was no longer Father's favorite daughter. I had become his favorite servant.

Chapter Five

SUFFER THE LITTLE CHILDREN

Thursday, June 1

*L*ost in limbo, I drifted though my daily duties as Lady of the Manor. Whenever the corner of my eye detected the distant shadow of Father shaking his head in disapproval, I felt a failure. Father's cigar smoke clouded my days, while Mother's pendant burned each night. Odette informed me that whenever I was not present the servants, prompted by Karla, ignored my orders. My elaborate restoration plans for Father's house remained in my desk drawer, locked.

One morning, to console myself, I went to the basement kitchen to knead dough alongside Alsace. I only half-listened as he struggled to improve his English by reading aloud headlines in the *Tribune*, "Re-cess-ion Deep-ens." "Fair at-ten-dance Fair." "Ded-i-cate Child-ren Build-ing To-day."

"What?" I grabbed the newspaper from his hands so roughly that Alsace, with his feet propped on a chair, almost lost his balance. Skimming down the newspaper column, my glance halted at the sentence, "Teachers needed for deaf children."

"I'm needed," I whispered to myself. Muttering my thanks to Alsace and waving the front page over my head, I hurried up the back stairs to my bedroom. After I sponged the dough off my hands, I changed into my Gibson outfit. Although I enlisted Odette to accompany me on the carriage ride, I changed my mind when we reached the cable car. I realized I needed to chaperone myself. Since I was unable to fulfill

Father's vision without becoming servile, and unable to imitate my ideal Bertha Palmer, perhaps I could still become an enlightened Lady of the Manor like Edith, but in my own way.

Riding unaccompanied in the cable car, I avoided the prying eyes of fellow passengers who must have been shocked at the sight of a young lady traveling without a male escort.

To contain my feelings of excitement and embarrassment, I wrung the newspaper in my hands until the black print stained my palms. Finally the cable car screeched to a halt at 63rd Street. At the exit door, I stepped down only to be swallowed by the crowd of pedestrians pushing towards the entrance to the White City. Jostled as I paid the fee, I yearned for Hermes' protective arm, but today he was ensconced in class at Harper. Which way should I go without him?

Fortunately, the blaring of the band informed me with its "God Bless the Child." While most of the people turned right to the huge Horticulture Building, with its obscene overbearing size, I resisted the crowd by turning to the left.

At the Children's Building, a woman's voice boomed through a megaphone. Bertha Palmer. "Ah humbly receive this dedication in the name of the little folks! It belongs to them. Suffer the little children to come unto me—from babies in their cradles to girls in their gymnasium." Although she was my ideal Lady of the Manor, why couldn't I at least become an enlightened one?

The front entrance was blocked by the speaker, the band, and the milling crowd, so I drifted over to the side of the building by the fire exit where people elbowed each other at the arched doorway. An ugly mood seemed to be growing. "Twenty-five cents to get in?" a woman shouted, "Ain't got a nickel!" Another yelled, "I'm dropping off my baby!" Then a change purse landed at my feet. When I put my foot atop it, so no one would steal it, a buxom woman kicked my shoe. At the same moment, the side door before us swung open, and a woman stepped out, her gray hair shining in the morning sun, taut as strings of lead. Each of her hands cuffed a little girl's arm; one child, about three years old, chewed on a ragamuffin doll; the other, about five, hopped to the rhythm of drums banging behind her in the semi-dark.

The woman in the doorway squinted at us. "Volunteers? Volunteers can step out of the hot sun."

"I hear my baby!" screamed a lady in front, holding yellow balloons. "I came early to collect her from yesterday. I demand her back."

"You volunteers raise your hands."

My arm seemed to raise itself, so I brushed aside the balloons to reach the doorway where the woman at the entrance asked me, "Do you have your work application?" Looking at my face, she smiled. "That's all right, dumpling, fill one out later."

Heaving a sigh of relief I edged inside, pausing with my back against the wall until my eyes grew accustomed to the dim light. Images emerged at the back of the room: nurses in striped uniforms with white caps and long aprons bending over row upon row of baby cradles. The odors of powder and urine filled my nostrils as I moved toward them. In the center of an enclosed playpen dozens of toddlers were standing, falling, crawling.

At my side stood the woman from the doorway. "We call that the pond."

"Do you have it—The form to teach deaf children?"

"Oh, no, you're confused. I'm Jenny Garret. My twin sister Mary is on the door today." She grinned and offered her hand. It felt hot and sweaty. "We like to confuse people."

Pointing at the children I asked, "Their ages?"

"A few weeks to six years. We sit them. Parents start dropping off morning at seven." As children swirled around us, she peered into my face. "Don't be concerned. Mothers must sign papers promising to return that night. But we're always desperate for wet nurses."

I felt tricked. "Wait a minute. Who's in charge here?" I shook the rolled up newspaper like a stick. "The deaf children. The *Tribune*—"

"No, no, dear heart. Paper's all wrong. To feed the babies we need wet nurses with their—"

"Not me! I'm not even—"

"Then can you change diapers?"

"But that's not being a wet nurse."

"Young lady, a wet nurse is what I say a wet nurse is!"

"But I simply can't—I thought I'd be needed to teach deaf children."

"Yes, it is simple—I teach. You learn."

As we were speaking, other volunteers had poured through front and side doors, heading straight for babies, picking them up and hugging them.

The very thought of being forced to be a wet nurse tied a knot in my stomach. Nellie Bly wouldn't be a wet nurse. Why hadn't I paid closer attention to Odette when she cared for Karla and me? My hope of having children in the future should not begin like this.

I barely noticed a tug at my skirt. A clinging toddler stared up at me, her eyes crossed, her lips bubbling. Jenny Garret went about her business. Dropping the newspaper, I placed my hands under the little girl's arm, raising her up to bring her cheek next to mine. Her tiny hands fingered the edges of my skimmer straw hat. Laughing, I crowned her tiny head to her shoulders, her giggle muffled as I cradled her in my arms.

After a few moments, I returned the hat to my own head. Then, with a sickening feeling, I realized her diaper had become damp. I looked around for a real wet nurse. However, every volunteer seemed occupied. I realized who the wet nurse would have to be.

"No, no, dear heart," Jenny Garret said, taking away my wet bundle as she motioned to a uniformed nurse with thick glasses. "Back into the pond for little—" Garret studied the tag fastened to the toddler's shirt. "Little Jeanette," she said, handing her over to the nurse.

I walked away, passing another nurse, this one seated, caring for seven babies at a time—one across her knees, one at her breast, four in double cradles, and one baby bouncing in a jumper swing attached to a ceiling beam. The nurse's red cheeks glowed and her eyes contained such contentment. She sang softly, "Oh dear, what can the matter be? Oh, dear, what can the matter be? Cook has forgotten the salt."

Jenny Garret gripped my elbow, stopping my progress toward the exit. "Professor Harting needs help. He sent a message from the gym for more volunteers," she said. "We need you."

With relief at being needed, but regret in leaving little Jeanette, I volunteered.

"Good, follow those ladies through that door." She patted my hand. "We need more of your social class down here."

I hurried as they headed toward the rear of the building. Behind me Jenny bellowed, "Mary, send me more volunteers!"

At the door I asked a Columbian guard, "Deaf children. Where are they? I really came to teach them." He shifted from foot to foot as if needing a comfort station. Waving me into the hall, he closed the door. On the walls of the hallway, colorful murals from folk tales flowed past me, including two of my favorites: *Hansel and Grettel* and *The Handless Maiden*. I hastened toward the muffled cheering. Reaching the door to the gym, I paused to let my breath catch up. Turning the knob, I pushed, but bodies on the other side prevented my entry. I leaned my hip against the door and shoved. The bodies must have moved, because I swung with the door and almost fell on my face. Somebody caught me. "Welcome to the girls' gymnasium!"

My eyes saw controlled chaos. A huge gym two stories high exhibited a hundred little girls, and only girls, in exercise uniforms of blue flannel bloomers trimmed in white. They were climbing poles, somersaulting on rings, swaying on trapeze bars. It seemed a delightful playground. Upper ramps with iron railings encircled three sides lined with adults, four deep, shouting encouragement at each and every movement of the girls. Large flags from many countries were suspended from the vaulted ceiling, but the only one I recognized was our own stars and stripes.

The whistle of the ringmaster reduced the chattering of the crowd. He stood calm as a statue in white starched shirt, ivory coveralls and black bowtie. The gymnasts froze in their movements in a grand tableau as the ringmaster addressed people in a brisk Prussian accent. When he blew the whistle again the children sprung back to life. I stared transfixed as their little bodies spun upside down and around pole ropes. Girls cartwheeled until they became rotating spokes. Bodies swung stiff-legged around wooden horses while shouting whoops of delight. I squinted until gym suits and flesh became abstract patterns, rearranging themselves like my old kaleidoscope.

The nurse with thick eyeglasses came to my side and whispered, "Look up. Girl on high wire is yours. After exercise, escort her to lunch." As directed, I craned my neck to observe the little girl on a tightrope high above the trapeze artists.

She placed one toe before the other without aid of balancing pole nor security of safety net. Never peering down, she always stared ahead at Old Glory suspended from the ceiling as she launched her voyage. From my position far beneath her, I could not see her face but her ramrod spine, straight shoulders, and quiet head bespoke maturity. I imagined she was Nellie Bly putting on a performance just for me.

As my high wire walker shuffled closer to the American flag, the gymnasts gazed upward, holding their breaths. The tumult in the gym subsided to a murmur. The ringmaster paused, whistle dangling on his chest, as my walker reached the flag and hovered within one step of her goal. Her small feet squeezed the rope. What was wrong? Why was she hesitating? Had she lost courage?

With my own fear of heights, my ribs ached from holding my breath. Had she seen her own reflection for the first time in the high windows? She stood in total silence as the crowd stared up. The only sound was the heavy breathing of gymnasts. Would silence unnerve her when noise could not? The ringmaster wet his lips as he fingered the whistle, without taking his eyes off her.

Suddenly the crowd roared. While I had been watching the ringmaster, the girl must have pivoted, after taking her last step. Raising her slim arms, she smiled at the applause, revealing high cheekbones, deep-set eyes, and the almond skin of a beautiful Oriental.

The crowd gasped, and their applause stopped as she descended the ladder to the floor of the gym. Stepping off the bottom rung, she shrank to the size of an eight-year-old.

The contrast between my image of the high-wire artist and this little child standing before me made me laugh. Seeing my expression, the little girl bit her lip, and turned away.

"Miss," I called to offer apologies, but she kept strolling.

Not to be ignored, I stamped my foot and hurried after my little charge to give her a piece of my mind about manners.

As I reached her side, she was gesturing to the ringmaster, who shook his head and shrugged. Seeing me approach, he said, "Ach, young lady, you sent to take mein star—little slant eyes—to lunch, nein?"

Words to reproach her gagged in my throat at his crudeness. However, the ringmaster misread my face. "Ach, mein manners. You be shocked." He bowed, beads of sweat falling to the floor. "Permit inductions. Meet Professor Harting. Director ze Exercise." He extended his hand, and we shook, his handshake surprisingly weak.

"Alessandra Aultman of Astor Street," I said. I also held out my hand to the little Oriental, whose expression had not changed, her brown eyes warm as a fawn's. She bowed to me, and instinctively I embraced her. The ringmaster shook his head in disapproval as he blew his whistle and shouted. "Dismiss!"

Putting my arm around my little charge, I guided her through the crowd toward the exit. Making signs with her fingers that I did not understand, the little gymnast sighed and mouthed the word, "Follow." She led me to an inner door. Wedging ourselves between gymnasts and parents, we squeezed through an exit that plunged us from a bright gym into a darkened room. The odor of fresh varnish burned my nostrils. In the dark, objects emerged as if from black water—long tables, straight-back chairs, high bookcases. A woman's voice said, "Oh, helpers at last! And us just turning off those newfangled electric lights. Hope you brought a load of books with you."

I stopped in my tracks, but my little companion kept walking in the semi-dark as if she had not heard. So rude.

"Well, if it isn't our little friend from Siam," the woman said, making hand movements. When I tugged at my starched collar, it squeaked like a mouse. I reached out in the dark for a chair, feeling weak.

"Hi, we're Clara Bates. We'd turn the lights on again but only half of them work."

I sat on the nearest chair, but the seat was so small I almost fell off. A loud click told me the little girl had found the wall switch. Half the ceiling glowed on, revealing a forest of bookcases—all empty—filling the room.

"Welcome to the number one unique library in all Chicago!"

I shook my head. All tables were too short, all chairs too small. No adult could ever be comfortable here.

Mrs. Bates must have read my eyes. "Exactly," she said. "This is a library only for children."

"But—but no books, all empty shelves."

"Did we introduce ourselves?"

"Forgive my manners," I said, "I'm Miss Alessandra Aultman of Astor Street." I glanced at my little gymnast for her to say her name.

Mrs. Bates hugged her. "Your diminutive escort is also our assistant." She kissed her cheek. "I've christened her Terese." A flurry of finger movements were exchanged between them. Then Mrs. Bates said, "Terese just informed me her stomach is telling her lunchtime."

"Mrs. Bates, I'm lost," I said, tapping my forehead. "I came to the Children's Building to teach deaf children. But they started me as a wet nurse, then as an escort to a gymnast, and now I'm in a library denuded of books!"

Mrs. Bates wiped one of the low tables with her apron. "The hallway should be passable now." Her lower jaw jutted out. "We follow Terese. She knows all the secret passages." The three of us joined hands and weaved through the walls of bookcases to a small door at the other side of the library. I felt like a servant who had entered the wrong house.

"We're not really a librarian, you know." Mrs. Bates said, as we moved. "A writer of stories for children. Mrs. Dunlap hired us to select books using children standards, only." She stopped and stared me in the face. "So we contacted public and private schools for them to send us lists of their students' favorite books. Hundreds and hundreds of letters." She tapped my chest. "Know which book was the children's favorite?"

I sat down, knowing she wasn't finished.

"*The Mill and the Floss*," she announced. "Don't ask why. So we wrote all the publishers requesting book donations to give to children visiting the fair." She sat down next to me. "Know how many books we received?" She swept her arms toward all the empty shelves. "See for yourself!"

I leaned over and held her hands. "What are you going to do now?" I refrained from correcting her on the title of the children's favorite book.

While we talked, Terese skipped ahead and flipped off the lights. Following her to the hallway, we almost bumped into a troupe of uniformed girls marching two by two, in muslin caps, with badges of knives and forks crossed and tied with red ribbons. They carried straw brooms like rifles. Marching in unison, they sang "Oh, dear, what can the matter be," over and over while led by a high-stepping major domo of a woman, long legged in black bloomers.

"Good show, Miss Huntington!" Mrs. Bates shouted. "We love your kitchen gardeners!"

Without missing a step, hunching her wide shoulders like Hermes as if to protect her neck, Miss Huntington clasped her hands behind her back and stepped even higher.

To me, Mrs. Bates said, "They're returning from lunch on the roof. So now's a good time to go up." She smiled at Terese and held out her hand, but Terese took mine instead.

I enjoyed the rickety ride in the elevator because Terese had chosen my hand. She squeezed it all the way to the roof.

Upon reaching it, I half expected to see Amey Stark and Mrs. Riley, but then recalled they presided next door at the Woman's Building. On the roof, I saw wire netting ten feet high surrounding the veranda to protect children from falling.

When Mrs. Bates grabbed Terese's other hand, I squeezed tighter. I pointed to a little girl clambering half-way up wire mesh. She reminded me of Karla scaling the lattices of our gazebo to perch on the roof to throw stones at me when we were children. Now a waiter stood expressionless, his arms shielded by a soiled towel. When little Terese freed herself from both our grasps, she raced across a sandbox to join other little girls and boys elbowing up a ladder to a circular slide.

"She loves it," Mrs. Bates confided to me. "Every time after exercise she flies straight for it."

I could scarcely hear Mrs. Bates, what with the laughing children, clanging dishes and rumbling elevator. So I watched the woman finally grabbing the ankle of the little girl, dragging her down the netting while she kicked and cried. If I were the mother, what would I do?

Since Terese was occupied at the slide, Mrs. Bates and I selected an open table with straight-backed chairs. I noticed that nearby girls in gymsuits gossiped over lunches while their chaperones gulped sandwiches. Mrs. Bates sidled her chair until it bumped against mine and whispered, "What think ye of little Terese?"

"Beautiful face," I said, "a China doll."

"A doll, yes," she replied, "a China doll, no. Siamese, really." She motioned to an approaching waitress, who smiled at her and walked past. "Miss Aultman," she continued, "did you volunteer or were you conscripted?"

"It was my fault. I took things for granted."

"If we may be so bold—have you even graduated school? Or are you one of those rich tutored students?"

I tried to smile. "It shows that much?"

Appearing at our side, Terese giggled. Mrs. Bates patted the cushion next to her, but Terese sat on my lap, avoiding Mrs. Bates' eyes.

With Terese so peaceful on my lap, I touched Mother's pendant at my throat. "Where are Terese's parents?" I asked Mrs. Bates.

Mrs. Bates smirked. "If you had your eyes open in the nursery you would have seen them. Did you not notice a Siamese couple taking notes and photographs? They're on government business for King of Siam."

"Why did they travel halfway around the world?"

"They brought latest nursery equipment—each Siamese crib holding four children. Somehow King of Siam believes Americans are progressives. What do you think?"

I shifted Terese's weight on my lap. "I don't know. Not qualified to judge."

Mrs. Bates sniffed, flaring her nostrils. "You're the humble one, you are."

I tried changing the subject again. "Mrs. Bates, all those bare bookshelves—whatever to do?"

"Call me Clara." Mrs. Bates looked away, waving at a waiter. "What will you order?"

Picking up the menu, and skimming the list of offerings, I shrugged. Terese wrenched the menu from my hand.

"She orders the same items everyday."

"Mrs. Bates—I mean Clara—I must know something. Why don't her parents lunch with her?"

Mrs. Bates patted my hand. "Tell you later, dearie." Then her voice assumed an edge. "Terese must be heavy."

A bundle of feathers filled my lap.

"Here comes our waiter," Mrs. Bates said, frowning. "Terese, you should sit in your own chair like a big girl." She tapped Terese on the shoulder with her menu, mouthing the words again, and pointed to the empty chair between us. "And don't pretend, Terese, you can't read lips!"

Terese put her arms around my neck and peered deeply into my eyes, her almond pupils floating in milky amber. I felt myself melting inside, as if I were being pulled into unblinking bottomless vessels.

Mrs. Bates slapped the table with the palm of her hand, rattling forks and knives. "Now, Terese! Now!" The table vibrated, and Terese leaped to her feet. Mrs. Bates pushed back against the chair and shouted, "Sit in your own bloody chair!"

With exaggerated reluctance Terese pirouetted, keeping her eyes fixed on me. Oh, how I envied her spirit of freedom. Can a little deaf girl teach me to risk a voyage across a high wire — like reckless Karla — when I'm so afraid of heights? Then Terese draped herself across my lap like a dying swan, and hugged my knees.

Chapter Six

The White City

Wednesday, June 14

*V*eering toward the shore of Lake Michigan, the steamer transporting us to the fair pivoted into the path of its own black smoke, belching from its stacks. I held my breath, but smiled.

As clouds of oily smoke rose up to the second deck to engulf us, I tried to protect little Terese, who was clinging to my side. I lost my grasp on the railing, knees buckling as if on a tightrope. Any fall to the deck was halted by Terese's small hands hugging my waist. Regaining balance, I mouthed "thank you," grateful to have persuaded the Garret sisters to allow Terese to accompany me, along with Hermes, Karla, and Kelso to the fair this afternoon. For clothing, I had imitated Karla's white taffeta with pink piping by wearing my own identical outfit. Shopping at Marshall Field's with Terese, I purchased similar attire for her.

During the past two weeks I had served at the Children's Building, so Terese was provided an intimate look at my weaknesses as a wet nurse. However, her almond eyes were always accepting of my faults. I requested permission from the Garret sisters after a monetary donation. When I mentioned Mrs. Bates, the sisters shrugged, and said she wasn't even a librarian. She was only a writer, like Nellie Bly. I bit my tongue.

Despite Mrs. Bates, or because of her, Terese and I had grown closer than a loving niece and her doting aunt. I felt this an important small step in becoming an enlightened Lady of the Manor.

As the boat cleared the breakwater nearing the pier, the setting sun fingered the mass of shadows bordering the lake into silhouettes, the buildings emerging before us as a veritable dollhouse for a giant. Thanks to thumbing through Hermes' guidebook, I was able to identify the buildings. To our left, I pointed at the Krupp Gun Exhibit that Father should certainly visit. When I had informed Father I was working at the fair, he was furious, claiming it was beneath our family name. When I added that my duty was a sort of wet nurse in the Children's Building, he pretended to wash his hands. Was it of me? Next to the Krupp Gun Building, I could barely see the small Indian school. Terese begged to visit it.

Overshadowing everything loomed the Agriculture Building. My own favorite site stood directly before us at the end of the long pier. Sweeping my arm at the two giant bookends of buildings connected by a hundred Roman columns, I located the Casino and the Music Hall. Behind them, lay the Columbian basin that I remembered when Hermes and I were at the Court of Honor six weeks ago.

Behind the Casino and Music Hall towered the Manufacture and Liberal Arts Building with its observation roof top, the largest building in the whole world. To my disappointment, Terese had stopped following my directions after she saw the Indian school. But I didn't have the heart to scold her because Terese's thin arms outstretched to embrace the entire fair.

From the other end of the railing, Karla peered at us over her fan. "Alessandra! Your little organ grinder so reminds me of the old you." Kelso and Hermes stood far too close to her.

I barely heard Karla, so exhilarated was I in seeing the White City. It brought back the feeling when I first saw my very own dollhouse. I recalled being awakened on my eighth birthday. Odette had brought Mother's comforter to cover me moments before a little procession marched into my bedroom.

Carrying a slab with something I could not see on top, were my Father and his good friend John Wellborn Root, the architect. Despite the strain of the load, Father's forehead was perfectly smooth. Mr. Root was whistling "Happy Birthday" as Uncle Chilton followed in their wake, balancing a wooden box on his head.

Springing out of bed, I hopped into the parade as it passed by, heading to the far corner of my room. Dashing in, Hustings and Curlin raced to the front of the line, muttering apologies for their tardiness as they slid my desk away, allowing a space for the slab Father and Mr. Root carried, oh so delicately. Knees creaking, they laid their burden upon the floor. I heard small wheels roll across the grooves in the wood as I sniffed fresh oil and paint. Odette encased my head with the black hood Karla used in a history play when a beheading was required. Then Odette led me, my arms outstretched, as if sleepwalking. At the count of three, she whisked off the hood, dazzling my eyes at the sight of the wooded replica of Father's four-story rowhouse, complete with roof, chimney and dormer.

Uncle Chilton unlatched the roof separating the façade as he placed figurines of our family members and servants, carved in wood and brightly painted. He identified each with one hand, while trying to hide paint-stained fingers behind his back. With my heart pounding, I stared down at the dollhouse as if from a cloud. I swear my fear of heights began at that moment. Feeling overwhelmed, my eyes closed as I prayed for the first time to become Lady of the Manor. I must have swooned. When I opened them again everyone had gone.

A horn blast from the boat shocked me into looking far below. Karla's face was pink from shouting. "Stir! Are you deaf?" She opened and closed her parasol to attract my attention. "I'm first in line to disembark. But what good is it if you don't see me?" Karla stamped her foot. "You dressed like me. So follow me!"

I signaled with my lace handkerchief for her to wait for us, but Karla twirled her parasol and linked arms with her firefighter to disembark. After Hermes handed me his camera case, he offered his arms to Terese and me, escorting us to the lower deck with the other passengers shuffling to the dock.

After disembarking, Hermes paid the entrance fee for us three, while I wondered how to travel to the other end of the pier. Would we select the movable sidewalk that stretched two thousand feet? Or the railroad with its hollowed-out cable cars, its inner seats pulled along? With gestures, Terese told me she wanted to just stroll the edge of the dock and watch dozens of sailboats, windjammers, and launches churning white caps on the lake.

While contemplating choices, I was interrupted by Hermes handing me Italian shaved ices that half-spilled as he pointed his arm toward Karla and Kelso. "Slow down! You two!" he shouted. When he grabbed my arm, one Italian ice fell. "How can I win my bet," Hermes growled, "If you two are slow and those other two cheat by running ahead?"

Karla and Kelso elbowed strollers aside, dodging screaming children and zig-zagging between sofas and armchairs. Passengers leaning out of railcar windows cheered them on, waving beer bottles.

Willingly, I followed in Karla's wake, but Hermes would not. "I'll lose my bet!" He yanked at my wrist, dropping the other ice on the pier, and hustled Terese and me onto the stationary walkway too close to the water's edge. "They call this a movable sidewalk?" shrieked Hermes, as strollers, rescuing a poodle out of the drink, refused to move out of his way.

"Hermes." I tugged at his sleeve. "The movable sidewalk's over there. Tell me what bet did you make?" His camera case banged against my knee. Was it the bet he was after, or really Karla? "Why didn't you tell me before?"

Hermes shouldered us toward the sidewalk, crowded with couples cuddling on benches and mothers chasing children.

Poor Terese almost crashed into a kiosk selling the new-fangled hamburgers. I grabbed her just in time, and stopped to blow into her ear to make her giggle.

At the moving sidewalk, Hermes, out of breath, doubled over clutching his knees. I slammed down his camera case between his feet. After asking him to repeat what he was mumbling, he looked up and whispered, "Three miles an hour on this so-called movable sidewalk. I'll never catch up." He glanced at the train nearby, then back down at his camera case. His eyes widened. "The cable car!" he shouted.

"Oh, no," I yelled, looking at Terese, but we were blocked by people hurtling their bodies past us on all sides.

"Over there!" Hermes shouted pointing to the stop located halfway along the pier for tired walkers to board. We joined the queue. When it became our turn, I stepped inside, fully expecting to see cables above our heads, but the oval ceiling contained advertisements for Havana cigars, Smith Brothers cough drops, Pabst beer. Where were the cables? The throbbing of machinery vibrated through the soles of my common-sense oxfords. Why were things never what I expected? Guiding us to vacant seats, Hermes plunked his case atop my foot.

He peered out the window and screamed, "Cycle!" Then he bolted up the aisle, bumping standees as he exited. I stared after him until our seats were jolted into movement by cables underneath. Through the glassless window frames, I squinted as he stopped a bicycle ridden by a ten year old boy who shook his head until Hermes took out a fistful of something. After he handed it over, the boy clambered onto the handlebars. Hermes leaped on the saddle of the cycle, like a pony express rider. He wheeled away, pursuing Karla and Kelso, just to win his bet. Didn't Karla know that if Hermes wasn't at my side, he could not propose again?

Abandoned to our own devices, I let Terese sit next to the window. We watched a little girl skipping alongside the cable cars, and a boy with a wooden stick rolling a five foot metal hoop. Then, across the aisle, I detected frowns of disapproval from suffragettes. I wondered why they were glaring at Terese and me. One stopped reading her Rand McNally guidebook to stare over her rims. Another, with a boy's hair bob, cooled her face with a fan picturing the Ferris Wheel, while a third pulled a hat brim over her eyes. I peered out the window, wondering if Hermes had caught Karla.

As we gathered speed, the passenger seats moved along the high platform within the stationary shell of railroad cars. Provided with a view above the heads of hundreds of strollers on the pier, I searched in vain for any sight of Hermes. The curved ostrich feather on the hat I had purchased for Terese tickled my nose, making me sneeze. I removed a black pin from Terese's hair before setting the hat onto her lap.

She smiled, without showing her teeth, and touched her throat as she shook her head. Putting the long pin into my hair bun, I felt more secure. But would Terese ever find security in years to come if people stared at motions of her hands in sign language? Could I protect her better as Lady of the Manor?

I loved having her at my side although I wondered how she appeared to those suffragettes with their sashes declaring *Equal Rights*. Terese however, seemed oblivious of them, as calm as when she walked the tightrope.

When we pulled into the terminal, the train slowed to a halt, making my teeth chatter as I re-pinned her hat more securely. The suffragettes rose to join the herd of passengers elbowing their way to the front. The bubbling rhythm of ragtime, Karla's newest craze, clashed "The Maple Leaf Rag" with the hissing of the cable cars. Karla loved young Joplin's music, although I could not see why. I preferred classical.

We jolted to a halt. Still seated, I felt my skimmer shoved over my eyes by the elbow of a rotund gentleman in a red and blue striped jacket. He pushed past the suffragettes who poked at him with their closed bumbershoots, but in vain. As passengers exited, I eased back in my seat, and put my arm around Terese. Was this how Edith felt when I would linger as a child after ballet practice to soak in the safety of an adult female? Most of the shoes had trampled past Terese and me.

In the aisle, a ray of sunlight glittered on something crushed beneath boots and high heels. It resembled a huge butterfly with sky blue wings, now soiled and twisted. With the aisle cleared, I stood as Terese crossed in front of me, and knelt in the aisle. Over her shoulder, I inspected the object on the floor with its thick ribs splintered, and a design of a fan map of the fair. Placing the camera case next to it, I motioned to Terese. She scooped up the damaged map, a bird with broken wings, and handed it to me. I nested it in my purse.

Picking up the case, I led our way down the aisle, stepping over empty whiskey bottles, cigar butts, children's broken toys. One image on the fan-map was of a little French café. Today was dedicated to honoring France. My imagination pictured red-and-white checkered table cloths on small round tables with glasses of white wine. Hermes would toast our future together. Karla, of course, would be our waitress.

The toot of the horn, and a uniformed conductor clearing the cars, told us to hasten. Reaching the exit, I paused at the top step of the platform to shield my eyes from the setting sun as I searched for Hermes. Ignoring the ragtime from a band shell, I turned and hugged my quiet companion who surprised me with the firmness of her embrace.

"Over here!" Hermes voice sounded strident. "I'm waving! Beyond the gate!" Releasing my embrace, I turned around but, despite the vantage point of the top step, I could not locate him. The tip of a finger poked me between my shoulder blades. Terese smiled, and aimed her finger like a pistol at an oak tree where Hermes bounced, up and down, waving his arms as if exercising.

Flattening my skimmer and grabbing the handle of Hermes' camera case, I made my way down the steps with Terese, and through the milling throng toward the gate, without taking my eyes off Hermes. As we struggled through the turnstile, Hermes spun on his heel, and motioned toward the twin buildings ahead of us. "The Casino!" he shouted, beginning to run up the incline. As we hurried, the strains of Handel's Messiah drowned the Ragtime. "But the Music Hall!" I yelled after him. With the camera case banging against my shin, we passed a caramel stand, the sweet smell enticing my senses. I yearned for that cool glass of white wine in the French café.

Finally, at Hermes' urgings, we passed the stand and clambered to the top of the knoll where the Casino stood. The three stories of Roman marble shaded two bearded young men crouched next to a skinny lad, about twelve years old, rolling dice and cursing his bad luck. A Columbian guard lolled against a pillar, munching an apple. "See, Hermes, see!" I shouted at him as he knelt, tying a shoelace. "I told you the name casino sounded like a den of gambling." Terese smiled whenever we seemed to be arguing. She frowned at Hermes.

We paused at the huge double doors of the casino, several times the size of Germania Club's. I thudded the camera case onto the pavement. Terese pointed at the closed doors. "Hosannah!" I yelled, hoping the gambling casino was locked.

Opening the case to examine it, Hermes shook his head in disapproval, "If you damaged anything—"

"The Music Hall," I said, "you promised me—"

With that, the huge doors creaked open and a guide, gold braid glinting, poked his head out, "Anybody gone away?" Then the doors swung fully open. "Just joshing, folks. Need to keep out the heat."

The crowd around us rushed the steps toward the entrance. "Don't hasten folks. We have room for two dozen more."

Clicking his camera case closed, Hermes led Terese and me up the steps with the stream of visitors and past the portals. Once inside, I saw a second guide, standing upon a desk, making announcements. "Public comforts to the right. Baggage rooms to the left. Check room straight ahead." He resembled a mechanical man. "Second floor—dining room that seats over a thousand. Only an hour wait."

Hermes frowned at Terese, while squeezing my hand, as we moved closer to the guide.

"On third floor, a café for men only, of course." Hermes moved ahead and tugged the trouser leg of the guide, interrupting his pronouncements. "Oh, mister guide, don't want my girlfriend to overhear this, but—" Hermes said, looking up at him, "Where's the gambling? You know, the den? This is a gambling casino, is it not? I told her it was."

For the first time, the guide showed emotion. Bending down he stared into Hermes' face, and burst into a huge horse laugh. "Gambling! Gambling you say!" He straightened, and spread his arms as if to surround the crowd. "Folks, do you hear this boy?" Then, he poked his thumb against Hermes' nose. "You college kids. Don't they teach you no law? Gambling's against law, boy." He grabbed Hermes' ear. I sidled through the crowd as close as possible to hear the guide whisper "Boy, you can get laided, but you can't get faded."

Shaking my head at my own naïveté, I hurried as ladylike as possible, with Terese in hand, toward the public comfort station. But when the guide had said to the right, was it his right or our right? After wandering for a minute, Terese found the door with the image of the Lady of the Republic. She was almost knocked down by a young woman in a walking costume of white taffeta with blue piping, beneath a hat trimmed in silk flowers and crow's wings. The outfit was all too familiar.

"Stir!" she shouted, after colliding with Terese. "My land! Just because you didn't like my little joke on you. Don't use her to kill me." She straightened her rows of bias-cut satin.

"Or are you still searching for roulette wheels? Come for the gambling have you?"

Suddenly no longer responding to nature's call, I turned on my heel and stalked away from Karla. How could Karla ever qualify as Lady of the Manor? Notes of chamber music from a large parlor transformed my mood. I wandered into the parlor's relative darkness, ambling past large islands of round couches, and back-to-back armchairs, the palm trees beckoning me to enter. My contempt for Karla made me forget Terese for the moment. I walked alone to the open archways facing Lake Michigan, and allowed a delicious breeze to caress my skin. Resting against the nearest pillar for support, I inhaled deeply, trying to take in the lake air. I stared at the long pier with its sidewalk transporting people standing like statues, alongside the cable car train. Farther off, I heard the horn of the Columbus steamboat silhouetted on the water, and for the first time realized it was shaped like a whale. Gazing lakeward, I absently opened my draw purse, and lifted out the fragile fan. Easing apart its wounded framework, I studied the soiled map with the curiosity of a treasure hunter. Was this map my passport to the world that had come to Chicago? With my thumb, I located the Casino at the west end of the movable sidewalk. As I did so, the chords of *"O Solo Mio"* enveloped the parlor behind me. That was the song Aunt Ashford had tried to teach Karla and me, but only Karla could carry the tune.

Brooding about Karla brought a memory I had tried to forget—why she hated me for wanting to share my dollhouse with her on my eighth birthday. The sunken memory slowly surfaced of when Father, John Root, and Uncle Chilton left me after presenting my wooden dollhouse. I scurried to Karla's room to share my joy. Knocking at her door, I remembered waiting for her voice but just hearing heavy breathing. My second knock moved the door slightly ajar. My fingertips pushed it open to show Karla's bed, usually in disarray, unslept in. Wall posters of the Mikado, Pinafore, and Antony and

Cleopatra were half ripped off the wall. Karla's night gown was torn and heaped upon the floor. My eyes almost popped when I saw Kara's naked back with her head down, looking headless. Approaching, I perceived her sitting, Indian style, facing the window. Her alabaster skin was layered with soot as the odor of thin smoke hovered over something piled in front of her.

Standing behind Karla, I detected shards of cardboard stacks slightly smoldering. Paper cutouts, resembling people, were balled up like baseballs atop a twisted cardboard roof on a tiny pyre that flickered, and smelled of urine.

"Kar—Karla, come see my—my birthday gift?"

With her head slumped, Karla said, "You're welcome to my birthday gift."

"What happened?" I knelt beside her. "A fire? Father warned you against smoking."

I remembered Karla's shoulders convulsing. Was she sobbing? I placed my arm around her naked shoulders, and at that moment I felt closer to Karla than any other time before or since. "Karla, tell me how to please you."

She was motionless as a sphinx.

"I know," I said, "let me share, share my birthday gift with you."

"Share! Did Sister say share?" Karla's green eyes enlarged to fill her face. "Everything is mine! By birthright!" Karla threw her head back, and cackled like the witch she played in *Hansel and Gretel*. She leaned her body backwards, her arms straight back, glaring up at me. Lowering her voice, she growled, "Because you had to be born too! You killed Mother." She spit the words into my face.

I stood, unsteady, and took one step backwards. With a grunt, Karla turned her face away, bending over, hugging herself as she rocked and groaned. As she peered at her blistered fingertips, she sniffed at the smoke fumes still lingering above the burnt remains of her dollhouse. "Be warned: what you have, Alessandra, really belongs to Karla. Karla vows to claim them!"

Outside her window, crows pecked at the glass, demanding their delinquent feeding from Karla, who flapped her elbows, her long blond hair rippling on her shoulders like feathers. At such moments, I believed that my sister embodied the living reincarnation of an evil spirit. The pecking of crows grew louder as I shuffled away, half bent, my eyes riveted on them. I tripped over Karla's newest poster, my foot unraveling the figure of Cleopatra, as if from a carpet. It scrolled back against the stop.

Closing the door, like a doctor bandaging a wound, I heard a sudden scream beneath my feet. Cerby. Scooping my cat into my arms, I hugged his warm fur, retreating to the protection of my own bed with Mother's comforter. Why did Karla hate me? Was it my fault I was born an hour after her? Did I cause the hemorrhaging that took Mother's life?

"Alessandra, why are you sobbing?" Before turning, I closed the fan, and slipped it into the safety of my purse. "What's that you're hiding?"

"Only candy for Terese."

Hermes frowned at me.

"Do you want one?" I asked, before realizing I'd left them at home.

Hermes reached out his hand, then restrained himself. "Don't be childish." He grabbed my wrist, "Karla and Kelso have already left the casino with Terese. They want to show her the fair from the elevated train."

"Oh no!" I said, "I wanted to do that. I told Karla."

"Why do you still trust her?"

"I trust people. I must." I stepped backwards. "Besides, aren't we going to gamble here?" I said, wondering if he knew I had overheard the guard tell him the truth. I wondered if he would pretend he knew it already.

"What?" He slapped his forehead. "Gambling! It's against the law. Anybody who's anybody knows that."

I shook my head. "When I feel lost I get so hungry."

"Eat here? Meat and potatoes? That's all they serve at Casino. Old American food. Fit only for tourists." Hermes strode toward the exit.

After a final gaze at the lake, where two sailboats circled each other like swans, I followed him to the rotunda. I noticed the elevator had a wrought iron cage enclosing it. "Hermes," I said, "how precious, classical music from a cage."

"You're in a cage yourself," he said, snorting. "Only with you the cage door is wide open, but you stay inside."

"What?"

"Well, that's what—"

As the elevator ascended, the seated string quartet played, "Oh Promise Me." The lyrics rolled through my heart as I squeezed Hermes' palm. "Take my hand / The most unworthy / in this lonely land / And let me sit beside you / In your eyes I am seeing / The vision of our paradise." In a dream-like trance I almost bumped into the desk supporting the guide who was repeating his misdirections to the next incoming crowd.

Outside, the doorman saluted as we paused on the top step. I had the warm feeling that Terese was throwing rice as Hermes and I were leaving church after our wedding. Then suddenly, I realized that Hermes had forgotten something. "Your camera case," I said, thinking he would be furious with me for not reminding him.

Instead, Hermes shrugged as we descended the steps, and walked among the crowd. "Karla told me to pretend it was Sunday, not Wednesday. Told me to take a day off." Hermes puffed his chest. "So, of course, I checked my case in the cloakroom."

The sweet smell of cotton candy from a nearby concession stand distracted me. The aroma of sponge sugar sweetened the stench of manure from horses hitched to fire wagons.

"My Gawd!" Hermes shrieked. "I've just been ravished!" He emptied all his pockets, elbows flailing at passersby. "My guidebook!" he said, shaking his head, searching for a bench. "Without my guidebook, I don't know where I am." He sat, a pigeon pecking at his boot.

Needing a moment to think, I bought cotton candy. When I sat next to him, I offered the cotton candy to Hermes. He shook his head. Laying the candy aside, I took Hermes' hands and held them, trembling within mine. I massaged his palms and fingers until they stopped shaking. "It's not important where we are," I said, "as long as we're side by side." I peered into his blue eyes, foggy and lined with red veins. "Hermes, you probably left your guidebook in your camera case. Why do you suddenly panic?"

He kicked at the pigeon.

"Hermes, here's another thought. Today is French Day."

"What made you think a dumb thing like that?"

Part of myself wanted to tease Hermes about his tri-colored eyes. Instead, I said, "Inhale that aroma. The French bakery. Those long warm loaves."

Shouts of sailors on the Santa Maria, exchanging curses with the Nina crew, echoed across the narrow inland of water surrounding the peninsula. Their voices gave me a headache.

Sensing that Hermes' body had calmed, I stood and tugged at one of his arms. "How can I follow you, Hermes dear, if you don't lead?"

Standing unsteadily, he moaned. It reminded me of when he first learned to ride a cycle with a six foot front wheel. Oh, how he loved to peer down upon the world from his lofty perch. How he kept getting traffic tickets for speeding over ten miles an hour. I recalled the day Hermes was showing off outside my window with figure eights on uneven grass. Inevitably, it tossed him onto his left collarbone, breaking it. Because he felt ashamed to let his own Father treat him, Hermes kept it secret. It mended poorly by itself. As a consequence, his left shoulder was hunched up, and when he looked at me, even straight on, he always appeared peeking around a corner. Why doesn't Father feel sympathy for Hermes like I do?

Now, as we trudged along the shoreline of south pond, I pointed to two swans entwining their long necks, releasing them, only to enwrap them again. I ardently wished Hermes and me were swans.

"Alessandra, why are you pretending to know where you're going?" Hermes said, "when I don't?"

Saffron ruins of the Yucatan surrounded us, the stench of decay so real I held my nose. The façade of a temple resembling a gigantic serpent, coiled beneath thick vegetation. "Those stones, how did they get them here?" I said, "How old? Two thousand years?" The hot wind blasted sand against the huge paws of a sphinx. I fingered my collar, perspiration seeping from my pores. Dare I free the top button? In my bones, I could appreciate Karla's obsession with the posters of Cleopatra, and her hope that the voices in her head meant she was her reincarnation. Karla never heard Mother's voice. I freed the top button.

At my side, Hermes chuckled, "Two thousand years!" He ran and leaped onto an ancient rock, kicking at it, a young Napoleon. "How long lasts plaster? Cement? Hemp?"

"What? I wasn't listening."

"These buildings, all built of staff. But, when it hardens, my dear, it's so tough a man needs to saw through it."

I stared at him. "What are you talking about?"

"See beyond the Dairy Building? That long one as long as the football field at Harper?"

"What's the building named?"

"That one I remember. The Forestry." Hermes came back and put his arm around me. "See that extra high roof? Inside that building, they created all these ruins you see before you."

He studied my face, and his expression changed. Then he ran, and jumped on the other paw of the sphinx, and spun around in his dusty boots. Sweeping his arms in a circle to include the entire fair, he shouted, "All these ruins! All these buildings! All the White City! Even the Casino we were just in! All made of staff!"

"Stop it!"

"You wanted to know the truth."

"Not this way." I said, striding toward the French colonies, and suddenly wondering if Odette had visited them. Maybe she mentioned it once, but I was half-listening. Children playing among simulated ruins flung handfuls of crackerjack at each other. Hermes rushed past me, scuffing sand. I shouted at his back, "Tell me how long these beautiful buildings will live!"

As he bumped into a crowd of sightseers applauding troubadours, Hermes shouted over his shoulder, "First tell me where's that French café." Dark-skinned natives screamed at us, ululating their tongues.

Following Hermes, I hurried toward the countless windmills that dominated our west bank. Sunset, glinting off the large steel blades, made me lose sight of him. My head spun at the churning, churning of huge steel fans. I caught up with Hermes, pausing for breath in the shadow of an old Dutch Mill that clanked above his head.

"I'm dying here," he gasped, "Dying for a beer." Hermes cupped his ear, expecting me to respond. I looked around and saw the elevated train, partially visible, near the Indian school leaving the station. Hermes thrust out his hand without looking at me. "Peace treaty?"

Entwining two fingers behind my back, I said, "Yes, but only if you tell me."

"How's that?"

"Don't taunt. How long will they live?"

Hermes rocked on his toes, like Cerby spying a crow in the gazebo. "In hell," I heard Hermes say.

"Don't curse like that."

"No really, inhale, smell that oven bread." He placed one arm around my waist, and lifted me almost out of the sand.

"I'd rather drink some cold cocoa from the Holland Mill instead," I said, breathless from the strength of his arm. "See these pretty Dutch maidens clicking their wooden shoes?" He put me down to look at them.

Then Hermes hustled me along the intramural road to an ugly ten story building with awkward wings. "It looks like a factory trying to fly," I said.

"As usual, Sander, you don't understand." We paused, so he could hold both my shoulders and peer into my face. "I have to educate you on everything. It's not a factory; it's a plant. Shipped all the way from Paris."

"Just because you're at Harper."

"Well, they don't enroll Ladies of the Manor, if that's what you mean. It's no place for you. Don't even think about it."

I jogged ahead. "Wish you'd never read that guidebook."

"Five giant ovens! One thousand loaves of bread each day."

"Should have brought Alsace, not me."

"He's too tall."

Branches of a willow tree sheltered little round tables on a brick patio outside the bakery. "There!" I shouted. "How romantic." Each table was draped with red and white checkered cloths flapping in the wind at the corners. One table alone remained unoccupied. I ran ahead to a chair and collapsed onto it just ahead of four male students wearing West Point beanies. As I slumped, they surrounded me with frustrated eyes and muttering mouths. Fortunately, they were all short, so when Hermes appeared, he stretched his six-foot-whatever frame and grabbed the two smallest lads by the napes of their necks. My heart leaped with pride.

"See here, rascals!" Hermes shouted. "You see before you a Columbian guard on holiday with his pregnant wife!" I tried to blush, while patting my stomach and nodding.

The other two cadets stumbled downhill toward launches recharging. One of the two remaining lads cursed his fleeing comrades but when he, himself, struggled free he hastily joined them in deserting the field. The final shavetale in Hermes' possession took a roundhouse swing while held at arm's length.

I waved at a waiter nearby to aid Hermes, but he just flapped his towel, and held up empty glasses as his excuse for retreating to the bakery. Meanwhile, Hermes spun the lad around, and kicked him in his shiny pants. "Get out, you army mule."

Returning up the slope, carrying large rocks in each hand, were the two cadets who had first fled. Seeing them, Hermes unbuckled his belt, whipping it free, and wrapping it around a fist. The West Pointers halted, stared beyond Hermes, and dropped the rocks as they bumped into each other, stumbling down the bank to the pond. Thereupon, they climbed aboard a launch, followed by their two classmates.

A man at a nearby table shouted, "Army brats!" while ladies applauded. Putting his belt back on, Hermes winked at them, and sat at our table. I rewarded my hero with a kiss to the cheek. Then, I noticed a husky Columbian guard, partly hidden by the branches of a willow tree, who nodded approval before returning to his post.

Our waiter cleared his throat, and asked for an order. Hermes fingered the cheek I had just kissed. "I've worked up a sweat," he said, "I need a beer—make it Pabst."

"Oh Hermes," I said, "not beer in a French café." He needed a lot of work.

He tipped his chair as the waiter tapped a pencil against his front teeth. Then Hermes leveled his chair onto the bricks, and peered into the waiter's eyes. "What's your pleasure?"

"Ach," said the waiter, "Beer."

I gulped, and glanced away at the pond. A swan seemed to guide the launch as it left shore, the four cadets waving obscene gestures as they crouched among the passengers. "Merlot," I said. Why aren't good intentions enough? Hermes is so inconsistent.

"Make it two glasses," added Hermes, "And a loaf of warm French bread with a ton of honey butter."

As the waiter left, I listened to the tri-color snapping on the wooden wings of the bakery. The breeze, however, also brought the stench of cattle from nearby stockyards. I sniffed in disgust. Why wasn't the White City perfect?

Hermes smiled. "You are smelling the biggest dog in the world, three hands tall, three hundred pounds."

I found myself staring at the tablecloth of red and white squares. Something tugged at my memory. As my eyes blurred it resembled the chessboard Father had purchased to instruct me and Karla in the appropriate moves when we were thirteen. Father always insisted our most important move would be castling. In one game, Karla disobeyed his order to castle. Father pounded the chessboard so violently the pieces leaped into the air, and onto Karla's lap. Staring down at them, she cackled like a harlot, making Father more furious. Overturning the table, he stalked from the room. I felt abandoned, so I pursued Father while Karla stuffed the knights down the front of her blouse as she peered at Father's back with her evil eye.

"Sander," Hermes said, interrupting my thoughts. "Please don't look at me until I say something." A wasp hovered above my fingers. "I'm no good at this," he said. The waiter's hand placed two glasses of red wine on the tablecloth, next to a basket covered with red cloth. "I've kept busy at Harper and at the fair, but it hasn't worked." Hermes squeezed my hand. "I dream of Alessandra. When she's not here, I wonder about Alessandra. When she is here, I can't speak." He emptied his glass in one gulp. "Just can't wait anymore."

The wasp glided over the table toward the honey butter, as Hermes squeezed my hands until my bones almost cracked. I could not wait anymore either. I looked into his face. His eyes brimmed with tears. "Hermes, what are you saying? Are you asking me?"

Releasing my hands, Hermes leaned back, and cracked his knuckles. "Can't you help me with this?"

I closed my eyelids. At last, has Hermes found a way? So many times I imagined our wedding at our Presbyterian church, my bridal train straightened by Karla, my frowning maid of honor. My flower girl Terese would scatter rose petals. Father's strong arm would guide me down the white runner to Hermes standing tall, awaiting me at the altar. With such a vision of orchids in my heart I chanted yes, yes, yes loudly inside myself. But had I said yes aloud?

Opening my eyes to receive Hermes' kiss of love, I was shocked to see him peering past me at God-knows-what. I searched his face for recognition of my acceptance of his proposal.

"Holy Hades!" Hermes shouted. "Karla! She's giving me the evil eye." He waved as he stood up.

The elevated train rattled to a stop behind the tree tops. I fought back tears as I fingered my full glass of merlot. Had Hermes really seen Karla? Standing, I studied the elevated above the French Bakery, but the glass windows were so glazed I could not detect any faces at all, much less Karla, Kelso or Terese. I could not see what Hermes saw.

Hermes waved, rising on his toes, "Karla," he shouted, "I forgot to tell Alessandra." Then he sighed, as the elevated train resumed its ride circling the fair. As we sat, Hermes stared at his folded hands, "Karla planned for us to dine later today at the Electricity Building. But I forgot to tell you. Sander, why do I always let everybody down?" He reached into the bread basket, and uncovered the napkin releasing a warm aroma. Grabbing a long loaf, he gave it a twist, then another, until crumbs and broken fragments littered the checkered squares like broken chess pieces. Placing chunks of bread onto a dish, he handed it to me.

Accepting the plate, I wondered if I had missed something. As I pondered, I dug the nails of my two thumbs side by side into the bread's underbelly, and cleaved it open like a dead lobster. To my surprise, I observed a tear moisten the crumbs fallen into the palms of my hands. Frustrated, I wondered if Hermes had even noticed.

Crumbs, like clumps of puffed rice, littered the table cloth. I reached for my napkin, but it was not there, and Hermes' chair was vacant. Catching the attention of our waiter, busy taking orders at the next table, I pointed to the empty chair.

He nodded toward my feet, and rolled his eyes. I pushed away my chair, and peeked under the table cloth. A crown of auburn hair with a cowlick bobbed as Hermes retrieved my napkin. Bumping the table with the back of his head, Hermes knocked my wine glass over, staining white squares red.

Plopping onto his chair, Hermes handed me my napkin, crumpled and soiled. Before I could react, a busboy took it out of my hand and replaced it with a freshly ironed one. I clutched at it, cursing the rules of etiquette, forbidding me to ask Hermes to marry me. I took a deep breath, and held it for a long time.

"Alessandra, your expression sometimes is just like Karla's. What's wrong?"

"Did you really see Karla on the elevated?"

"What?"

"What time is Karla's reservation for us?"

"Oh, not to worry, as Dad always says. She's scheduled dinner after dark. Electricity, don't you see? Bet you don't even know where it's located."

"Yes, I do. Planned to take Terese there."

"Well, where is it?"

"In your guide book," I said, refusing to display the slightest disappointment. Is that castling, Father?

"*Garcón,*" shouted Hermes, "Another round."

"Not for me," I said. "Feel dizzy." Why are Ladies of the Manor forbidden to show anger?

"Stockyards?"

"No," I waved my hand, "all those windmill blades, revolving and revolving."

Snapping his fingers, Hermes signaled for our waiter to bring the tabulation. After he paid, he stood, assisting me to my feet. "Let big brother cure your vertigo." He took my arm as we strolled down the sloping bank. "I'm the spirit of light and love," he whispered, "To my unseen hand 'tis given to pencil the ambient clouds above." He squeezed my arm as it nestled in his, "and polish the stars of heaven." Hermes peered at the sky.

I looked at the pond: one swan had slid over to be fed. I regretted not bringing French bread from the table.

"Betcha can't believe I made up that poem myself?"

One of my tutors had taught me "The Song of the Lightning," a poem celebrating the invention of the telegraph. "Of course you wrote it, Hermes." Beaming, he thrust out his chest. "So let's hear another stanza," I said.

Hermes tripped over a root protruding from a nearby stump. He pretended he hadn't. "My dear Sander, inspiration cannot be automatic, like those new-fangled Kodaks."

I scooped crumbs in my pathway and tossed them to the swan, now joined by her mate. "Oh, Hermes," I said, "Let's not talk. For us, silence speaks so much sweeter." As we moseyed along the bank with other strollers, I listened to the sound of cranking windmills, shouting whalers, hammers of pioneers building cabins. I envisioned Hermes and me bicycling upon his union cycle. We would circle the base of the tallest windmill with its hundred foot frame. We would offer free rides to children playing hide-go-seek near those launches being recharged at the shore. Someday we would have children. Perhaps if I were Lady of the—

I pointed to a launch, but Hermes had his own idea. He waved his arm at an Italian gondola depositing a young couple at the cement stairway that descended into water. Each end of the gondola rose like pointed slippers from a folk tale Karla and I played as children. In the center of the boat perched a hut. Was it to hide lovers from prying eyes? A single gondolier leaned on a long steering pole. Despite yearning for the launch, I felt romantic when the gondola scutted against the dock with the gondolier singing in a full-throated baritone, *"La commedia e commenciare."* He jutted his chin while his long black hair hid the rest of his face. As he finished singing, he burst out laughing so loudly the two swans flapped their wings.

Without a word, Hermes led me past the launch to the gondola. Nodding to the couple who had disembarked, Hermes high-stepped into the boat, and turned to offer his hand. When we were seated in the hutch, gently rocking, the gondolier grinned at us so broadly I thought his white teeth would pop out. Motioning, the gondolier pointed with stiff fingers to his chest, *"Me Ruggiero."*

"Me Orfeo!" Hermes shouted, and then glared at me for my identity.

I swallowed my tongue. What could I say? I puffed out my cheeks, and whispered, *"Me Euridice?"* The gondolier whistled. I stood to take a bow, bumped my head, and sat down with a thump. I resolved to forget my discomfort and open myself to the evening.

"La gente paga e rider vuole qua," sang Ruggiero, as Hermes rubbed my head. When finished singing, Ruggiero held out an open palm and recited the same line in English, "The passengers pay for laughter." Hermes reached into his pocket, and produced several silver coins that appeared to be too much. Ruggiero leaped forward, seized all the coins, and kissed Hermes on both cheeks while singing, *"A stanotte e per sempre tua saro."*

Hermes' face flushed as he peeked outside the hutch. "Stop the foreign yodeling. Sing American, or don't sing at all!" Rattling the coins in his red pantaloons, Ruggiero grinned. He sang as he leaned on the long pole, and pushed against the steps, casting the boat deep into the center of the pond. "Tonight and forever I'll be yours." The gondola surged with each thrust, until it settled into its own rhythm. "Oh, Columbina, your harlequin awaits." The shoulders of the boatman, framed against orange clouds, hunched as he hummed to himself, polling.

Wordlessly, Hermes and I tilted our heads together as if being glided into a daydream. I imagined huddling on the lovers' seat in my gazebo with Hermes, pretending to be newly married while we both made up names. I closed my eyes. Did I dream or had Hermes' lips touched my neck? His breathing, deep and slow, made me realize mine was quick and shallow.

Opening my eyes, I was surprised to see that Hermes had fallen asleep, even though a battery boat sputtered past us, heading for a recharge. On board, little children giggled into their hands at Hermes' open mouth and thrown-back head. I shook my handkerchief at them not to awaken him. The Italian lights outlined their craft as did the small bulbs around our hutch. I saw the canal tunnel fast approaching. Around the entrance green lanterns swayed in the breeze in semidarkness. A battery boat passed us, kicking waves that rocked our gondola and flopped Hermes' head side to side. Golden sconces, lining the walls of the tunnel, flickered splotches of brightness onto Ruggerio as his pole thrust, pushed, and pulled us through the waves. With Hermes' head resting on my shoulder, I felt the present moment ease the pain of Hermes being distracted during his proposal, and my accepting him only in my mind.

After rowboats passed us, the black water suddenly burst into a brilliant white. As I faced the stern, I realized we had exited the tunnel into the Grand Basin.

Leaving the hutch, and staring toward the bow, I beheld a miracle. Thousands of electric bulbs on every building on every bridge on every face lining the basin blossomed like sunflowers.

Ruggiero blinked his eyes at the brilliance. "See little fish! See little fish!" He motioned toward the water. At the starboard side of the gondola, I peered over the railing. Countless tiny silver fish darted close to the surface, chasing each other.

Then, I heard our gondolier chuckling at me. "Fish, no fish. Fish, no fish." He pointed the dry end of his pole toward the east end of the Grand Basin. Craning my neck, I saw the massive statue of the Lady of the Republic. The electric spotlight, highlighting the laurel crowning her head, caused hundreds of reflections to dance upon the waters.

Laughing at myself, I studied the tourists ten deep, encircling us. They were watching swimmers racing each other across the width of the basin. A sailor tossed his cap into the water and belly-flopped.

"Ridi, Pagliaccio, sul tuo amore in franto," Ruggiero sang softly. He grinned at me. "You sing American now?"

I sang as I translated, "Laugh, clown, 'cause your love is over!" Our voices echoed as musicians on a nearby launch took up the melody with violins and balalaikas. As our gondola toured, spectators applauded, and yelled encouragement. I waved at people on rooftops of cloudscrapers surrounding Court of Honor. Searchlights from Liberal Arts criss-crossed the water, playing tag. Odors of cigar smoke, whiskey, and steaks beckoned to me on the breeze. I rested my head against the railing, closing my eyes, and listened to the pulse of water throbbing at my temples. Although Hermes and I had missed signals tonight, I must believe that while we blunder, we also persevere.

The jarring of the bow, scuffing the cement steps, awakened me. The gondola had returned to its beginning. Hermes, refreshed from his catnap, already had sprung ashore to anchor the gondola. Ruggiero was assisting another young couple aboard. I stepped ashore, and fell into Hermes' arms. As held me, he whispered, "Couldn't bear to awaken you, Sander." He pulled me closer. "You seemed so childlike." Hermes held me tighter, peering deeply into my eyes. "Sander, what were you dreaming about?"

"Me?" I peered into Hermes' blue eyes for a long moment and said, "A box of chocolates."

Chapter Seven

Under the
Big Clock

The Next Day

Dreaming of the White City composed entirely of white chocolate, I lost my self-control. Gobbling down the biggest building in the world I gorged myself until my body swelled to the size of the fair's Captive Balloon. I tugged at it to free myself until finally I snapped its chocolate cable. As I sailed past the Ferris Wheel, I bumped my head against it, awakening me to find that it was the edge of a small box.

As I pried open one eyelid, I beheld a blurred array of crinkled chocolate holders. Sliding the empty box, I knocked it off my bed onto the floor, producing a hollow noise that echoed within my aching head. Once again, chocolate taught me the truth that I could never get enough of what I really didn't need.

Roiling about, I crunched more unseen wrappers, sounding like Hermes cracking his knuckles. That thought of Hermes prompted me to remember dinner and too many drinks last night with Karla and Kelso at Electricity Building. After an argument with Karla about her taking charge of the schedule, Hermes and I left early to return Terese to the Children's. Later, we strolled to the rail terminal. Hand in hand, we agreed to meet today at noon for lunch at Liberal Arts under the Big Clock.

Now sitting up in bed, I swung my legs over the side. My bare feet recoiled from stepping onto the upturned corner of the box. Deciding to kick it aside I rubbed one sole against the other, as I heard Odette's shrill voice, "Mon dieu! She not dead from the wine and the chocolate? Such naughty conduct for Mamselle ze Manor."

I didn't need to see Odette's face to know it was flushed with shame. I cradled my head in my hands, sinuses throbbing. As Odette rustled the debris around the bed, she kept scolding me. "Mamselle, white wrappers should be our wedding. Odette she saves you, but how? Tell poor Odette." How could I tell her that Hermes had finally asked me, but possibly didn't hear my acceptance? I knew I blundered.

"Fresh bread," I groaned into the palms of my hands. "Bring it. Fresh bread alone can save me." Through fingers interlaced, I peeked at Odette's back. "And don't mention wedding. Not yet."

"*Oui*. And marmalade?"

"But only mandarin."

Scooping the remnants of my last night's indulgence into her apron, Odette headed for the door to fetch my usual wake-up food.

"Wait Odette! On my desk you'll find tomorrow's menu for Alsace. Give it to him, and cancel today's appointment with me. I'll be lunching with Hermes at the fair."

Near the doorjam, Odette turned on her flat heels, and clutched her billowed apron containing candy wrappers, her elbows crunching the box against her side. "Detritus, menu, breakfast." She pursed her lips. "Which come first?"

My heart went out to Odette. With an effort, I sprang to my feet, feeling dizzy, and gave her a bear hug. Her buxom body felt warm as when I hugged her as a child while the box and its lid clattered to the floor. The cutting voice of Karla preceded her into my room.

"Stir, you're tardy. Get bustling." She stepped around the clutter in her passion pink outfit. "Such disarray. What would your mother think of you?" Her glance surveyed the floor. "And Hermes tells me you have no bad habits!"

"Don't talk to me," I said. "Why did you kidnap Terese from me?"

"Such ingratitude. Don't you know? Little old Karla cleared the field for your lover lad. So tell me. What finally happened?"

Releasing Odette, I helped retrieve the box. "Forget food, Odette. But do take the menu." Odette withdrew, averting her eyes from Karla.

"Stir, are you servant today or Lady of the Manor? Which mask are you wearing? Mr. Aultman probably would like to know."

Ignoring her the best I could I selected my blue Gibson outfit and threw it on me. But the mention of Cyrus' name reawakened a worry gnawing at my brain. Grasping Karla's hands and peering into her face, I guided her to my bed, and sat beside her. "Karla, forget about us. I'm desperate. No, don't start yawning. This is serious. About Father. He paces the floor every night. And he imbibes."

"So?"

"I mean he imbibes afternoons now. Is Father worried we're going bankrupt?"

Karla laughed. "Stir, I get your point. It must be you. He certainly doesn't worry about me."

"My Gawd, then is it Hermes?"

"You know Cyrus. He can't suffer Hermes."

"Why?"

"Don't you understand anything? When Cyrus looks at Hermes, he sees himself thirty years ago."

"What do you mean?"

"Full of hope. Aiming to change the world."

Downstairs, the gong rumbled for family breakfast. "Karla, there's no time. Hermes begged me to lunch with him today."

"So?"

"He might try to ask again."

"Why tell me?"

"If you accompany me to the fair, Father will have to let me go."

"Hasn't poor Alessandra ever caught on?"

"What do you mean?"

"Cyrus is his own opera hat. Press the right button, he springs up. Press another right button, he collapses."

"You're wrong. Father's a bear."

Karla yawned. "So, where's this illicit rendezvous of yours?"

"Under the Big Clock."

"Hold on. I'm going to Midway, not White City."

"Just get me inside the gates of Midway."

Karla rocked on the bed until she brushed the headboard. Her glance swept the room. "Notice my tessie's still on your wall." She examined her fingernails, tracing one across the palm of her hand. "Thought you'd have thrown it away after—" Lowering her head and peering into my face she started her evil eye. "Don't think I owe you one." Then she crossed them, and cackled. "You're on your own."

Disappointed, I left the room, followed by Karla. As we descended the stairs, halfway down, we froze midstep. Peering up at us from the base of the stairs was Father. "Ach, you forgot to remind me." Father stepped to one side, revealing his lederhosen suspenders, short pants, knee socks, and a peaked cap atop his head.

Karla and I stared at each other, open-mouthed.

"Cherman day!" Father shouted. "Krupp Gun."

I gulped. He can't be coming with us. Not today. Not when Hermes might ask me again. "But Father you hate the fair."

"My Dumkupf daughters." Father snapped his suspenders. "How could you ever forget Cherman Day?"

"But—but I'm famished," I said. "Breakfast." I must delay and talk him out of going to the fair, ruining my rendezvous with Hermes.

"Vienna Café eat." Father swept his arm toward the front door. "The Aultman family carriage awaits!"

While Curlin drove us to Midway entrance at 49th Street, I concentrated my thoughts all on Hermes. To the rhythm of the horses' hooves, my mind drifted back to my birthday last year, when I thought I spied from my window an intruder by our pond. I hurried down the back stairs, pretending to be Lady of the Manor rousting a burglar. The noise grew louder. One car of the model railroad blocked my view, brake parts scattered on the grass. With my common sense shoes munching the ground covered with thyme and ferns, I stalked the intruders' footsteps past the evergreen tree to reach the rusted side of other railcars on the track. Peeking between engine and tender, I saw in the middle of the pond our old life-sized twin statues, carved when Karla and I were twelve. I almost laughed aloud at the bird droppings bleaching Karla's cheek, but then, I saw that my own statue had been tipped off balance by a recent storm.

"And you call yourself Nellie Bly?" said a familiar voice.

"Lady of the Manor, if you please!" I said pretending not to be startled. I peered through the little cow-catcher, and recognized a back with bony shoulders beneath a French flannel shirt, striped black and brown. "Impersonating an interloper," I said, "and on my seventeenth birthday!"

Sprawled on the bank, Hermes stopped splashing in our pond, and stood up in water, dungarees rolled to his knees. He turned to face my justice, while tugging at his waist of gray doeskins.

"Or did you come to ogle me?" I said. "On my birthday? Indeed!"

"That's just what I was gonna say." A silver chain dangled around his neck. He tapped it, "Just for that, you won't get this!"

"Oh, Hermes, are you really sweet after all?" I said, strolling around the traincar, and striding toward him. When I noticed his unbuttoned dungarees, I burst into laughter.

He peered down at himself, hauled his body about, and started to restore his privacy. I covered my mouth, expecting him to be furious. But instead, he shouted over his shoulder while raising one arm in surrender. "Peace! I brought you a peace offering—this dang button—peace offering to my Lady of the Manor."

When he resumed facing me, dignity restored, he waded toward me to plant one barefoot on the bank of the pond, black mud squishing between his toes. As he began to place his other foot on the muddy slope he lost balance, teetering on the brink.

I stepped forward and grabbed him.

"That's a dumb thing to do, Sander," Hermes gasped, my arms around him. "Now, we're both for it."

I dug in my heels, tugging at him like he was a stubborn mule. I pulled too hard. When I tumbled backwards on the grass, we collapsed upon each other. We lay there, breathing heavily, while I heard mandarin ducklings padding down the embankment to bellyflop into the pond.

Hermes whispered in my ear. "I'm truly sorry, Sander. But then I always seem to be saying that."

"Thank you for the gift, anyway, even though it's an odd way to deliver it."

"You don't understand. I'm banned from your house."

"Father's furious with you again?"

"Oh, I can solve that. All I have to do is just propose sometime."

I sat up. The ducklings were splashing circles around momma. "What did you say?"

"Called on your new telephone," he said, rolling onto his side.

"What?" A frog croaked on the opposite bank. How could Hermes be so flippant about proposing? That's what Father thought was Hermes disrespecting me.

"I hoped you'd be up early for a change, but instead Mr. Aultman answered. At first, he thought I was Potter Palmer calling about a property but when I laughed he got angry."

One mandarin duckling strayed from momma and swam toward the frog. "But why did you call at all?"

"Mother instructed me to apologize."

"Your mother, it's always your mother."

"She says I'm always doing something wrong." The frog hopped onto a lily pad. Hermes sat up. "Hey, you've ruined my new leisure clothes. Mother will kill me."

"You didn't!" I shouted as the stray duckling paddled toward the lily pad. "You made Father furious?" I imagined Father's vein throbbing in his forehead. "Hermes you never take anything seriously."

"Well, look at them," he said, pointing to mud stains on his dungarees. "Besides I've lost some of my buttons."

I jumped to my feet, fists on hips. "I should crown you for making Father frustrated. He's got enough worries. You're so smug because of your mother's old money."

Yawning, Hermes skipped a stone across the water to overturn the frog on the pad. "But I can straighten it all out."

I stepped away from him, and leaned on the engine for support. "No wonder," I said thinking aloud, "Father has standing orders 'not to let that silly boy enter our house.'" I should have warned Hermes, but I didn't want to displease him or Father.

Hermes sprang to his feet, fury in his eyes. "Boy! He called me boy? How dare he."

"You're missing the point again. Why can you boys express hurt feelings but not girls?"

He waved me away. "My dad will take care of old Cyrus. Eighteen is not a boy."

I sat down on moist grass. "Hermes, we have a problem. We shan't have Father feeling about you this way." I drew up my knees, and leaned my cheek against them. "We just can't. It's not fair to you. And it's not fair to me."

Hermes sat down beside me, and took my hand. "You're right. As always. Life is not fair. Someday, your Father will respect me as a man."

I glanced at Hermes' profile, edged with flickering sunlight from the pond; its beauty always surprised me, especially when I was irritated. Then, a question I always wanted to ask him fluttered into my mind like a monarch butterfly. After a long moment of silence I said it. "Why have you chosen me and not Karla?" The question hung in the air between us. I'd surprised myself with my boldness.

Hermes' profile did not change expression. He skipped another stone at ducklings leaving the pond on the opposite bank. "Karla scares Mother." He tugged at his big ears. "Besides, Karla's got the evil eye." He turned his head to face me. "Sometimes, so do you." Is that all that I meant to him?

Examining his face, I sensed that something was missing. "Where's your eyeglasses?"

Hermes straightened out his long limbs, and slipped the chain with a locket from around his neck. "Do you want this stupid thing, or not?" He held it up.

"Thank you," I said, reaching. Was he making up? He was so changeable like mercury.

"Your father won't object." he said, holding it higher, beyond my reach. "It's made in Germany."

"You shouldn't have."

"I know." He said laughing and kissing my temple. He opened the locket to reveal a tiny tintype of himself. He snapped it shut, and placed the chain around my neck. "This will have to do until—"

I hugged my knees, the locket against my bosom, to keep close the feeling of being special to Hermes. This moment with him quieted my uneasy innards as they had not been pacified, since I don't know when. "Hermes, I promise to wear your locket until it's a part of me. I'll wear it so much I'll even forget I have it on." A blackbird dove at a raccoon climbing an oak tree. "Maybe tomorrow we'll be given a way out of this."

"A way out of what?"

"Father's banning you from our house."

"Oh, I forgot." Hermes voice deepened. "Yes, I do have a problem." He rubbed his eyes. "Never gonna find my eyeglasses."

He squeezed my hand, and I closed my eyes as we held each other close.

Now, the surge of the carriage stopping at Midway entrance halted the rhythm of the horses' hooves. Jolted out of my memory, I followed Father and Karla through the gate. Father marched stiff-legged, as I hurried to catch up.

Inside, he lectured us on Midway's spectacular display of the evolution of the human race, starting with the aborigines within the gate, and extending to the far end glorifying British Civilization. While Father talked at us, Karla muttered to me under her breath how different people and exhibits appeared in daylight.

I hastened my pace to pass the smelly stables of the military outpost. As we approached a farm of ostriches, I was amazed at their pencil-thin limbs rocking their oval bodies. They stretched their feathered wings in vain, trying to fly. A young ostrich scraped gravel with the side of its head. I had been taught by tutors that ostriches hid their heads in a hole in the ground, but this one only pressed its cheek. Maybe it was too young to know as much as my tutors. Rifle shots, from nearby Indians pretending to attack the army fort, spooked the ostrich. Leaping to its feet, it ran flatfooted around in circles, as if on hot coals. The gamekeeper started chasing it, losing his cap. Finally, his assistant threw him a canvas sack. What for? Hooking his arm around its neck, the gamekeeper pinned the ostrich to his chest, slipping the hood over its head. Then, lifted off his feet, he was carried along. Moments later, the ostrich slowed, stopped, and stood stark still, trembling, trembling, until the hood was finally removed.

Father yanked my wrist rather rudely, to get me back onto his schedule. Karla, however, kept making her own suggestions about what to see next, much to Father's annoyance. When Karla asked about visiting Sitting Bull to see him in his own cabin, Father muttered that he had been assassinated years ago. When she exclaimed about the beauty of the Eiffel Tower, Father complained that the replica was only twenty-five foot tall. When Karla pitied the wild man of Borneo imprisoned in his iron cage, Father snorted that it was only a man in a gorilla suit.

The exhibit I was drawn to was the biggest bicycle wheel in the world, twenty-five stories high. It filled the sky, blocking the sun. Father, however, strode past it with nary a glance. "Damn fool, Ferris!" he muttered, "He used his own money. Now what kind of example for young people is that?"

Despite Father's opinion, I paused to study it, anyway. Its huge spokes of steel, interlaced, resembled dozens of gigantic steel spider webs. Its height flooded me with fear, even though the carriages were large as Pullman cars and seemed secure. As I stared at it, the Ferris Wheel became a mountain for me to climb. Karla poked my ribs and pointed at a placard: *Opening in 6 Days*. I breathed an audible sigh of relief.

"Old Vienna straight ahead!" shouted Father, as a German band on a stand oom-pah-pahed for a large, boisterous crowd. I turned to share the sight with Karla, but she had already wandered toward the tethered Captive Balloon straining at its cable. As it swayed in the wind, it reminded me of a character in a classic book my tutors made me read, but I couldn't remember the title.

As I arrived at the outdoor beer garden, Father led me to a wobbly chair. While I waited watching the band members who were dressed like Father, I fidgeted, worrying about Hermes. Father stood in line for an Old Style and bratwurst for him, hamburger and ice coffee for me. To distract myself I closed my eyelids, and absorbed the sounds surrounding me: African chants, Chinese flutes, and the tolling of the bell from the replica of St. Peter's. When a beer mug thudded on the table, I opened my eyes, and saw Father towering over me, gulping a second beer without taking a breath.

"Father, I'm confused. Do you hate the fair or not?" I said, even though I knew he didn't explain his actions anymore to anyone except Potter Palmer.

The June breeze mingled smells of camels, tobacco, and gun powder. After two bites of the burger, my stomach felt queasy so I returned it to my plate with sauerkraut. When Father finished his second stein, he grinned and started to go for a third. I touched his hand and said, "Krupp Gun?"

With a shrug, he gulped down his bratwurst and sauerkraut, wiping his mouth with his bare arm. "Nein," he said with a big grin, "First, zoo. Hagenbeck's Zoo."

The two of us passed Cairo Street with snake charmers tempting fate, the Palace of Moors with its hall of illusions, and a Fire Drill team rescuing a baby from a building with orange and red ribbons fluttering from all the windows.

Finally, we stopped in front of what resembled a Roman Coliseum, but much smaller: as if it had shrunk in the rain. Father, however, was too impressed, bouncing from foot to foot like a boy. At that moment I decided not to judge him but to join him in his joy, but when he glanced about, his face frowned. He watched Karla entering the Natatorium, probably to swim off the morning perspiration. Shrugging, Father waved at me to join him at the Coliseum that boasted the sign *Hagenbeck's Zoo.*

We hurried inside to be greeted by aromas of popcorn and peanuts, making me smile. I grasped Father's hand, feeling like a child as we wended our way to the queue at the ticket booth. The first ring exhibited a baby bear balancing high on a tight rope. My heart leaped; I thought of little Terese. Father pointed beyond the baby bear to the second ring with a tiger riding in a chariot drawn by six Alaskan huskies. I preferred the third ring at the other end where ten dwarf elephants stood, their front hooves on each other's rumps, while they all marched in a circle. I laughed with the crowd at a midget in red vest and boots waving a pistol, cracking a whip.

Father and I sat down on the last seats, located away from each other in the crowded bleachers. To console myself I observed a sight in the large center ring that I still do not understand. An old lion sprawled on sawdust before a huge round mirror. He appeared to be fascinated by his own royal image as a young lady, resembling Karla dressed in lion's skin, curried his mane. Behind them, careful not to be reflected in the mirror, three hunters crept forward. One lugged a huge elephant gun, another dragged a large webbed netting laden with weights and knives. The third man motioned for the girl to continue brushing the lion. As he pushed a cart loaded with twenty flat lion skins and seven lion heads, he wielded a huge glittering cleaver. The spectators, especially children, were deathly still. So as not to alert the hunters? The lion? The girl?

Nervous not to be sitting next to Father, I craned my neck to see him. He stared open-mouthed, mesmerized by the center ring. Each time Father started to applaud, he caught himself, forcing his open hands to keep apart. I sensed an electric charge pulsating between his palms, generating invisible rays of electricity. Meanwhile, the lion kept posing, the girl kept brushing, and the three hunters kept advancing. The man with the net swung it high in the air in ever-widening circles, as the man with the elephant gun raised it to his cheek. I stood up, wanting to scream a warning to the old lion.

But instead I fled toward the exit, the scream choking in my throat, as a gunshot echoed behind me. Children and adults cheered, stamping their feet. Won't they ever stop? Did they kill the old lion? Didn't Doc Seth tell us on the train Father would love this show?

Finally outside, I rested against a white-washed boulder, catching my breath. After a minute I sat upon it, my knees pulled to my face. Father's behavior lately had become so erratic. Was it the mercury in his hat? Was he losing his bearings? I tried to fight back tears. In a few minutes, people started exiting, so I knew Father would soon be searching for me. Drying my cheeks with my wrists I awaited him. As the crowd thinned, he sauntered out with a half-full stein of beer, and a self-satisfied smirk.

Upon seeing me, Father started cursing in German for my leaving early, and embarrassing him in public. What if someone from Astor Street saw us? Sliding off the boulder, I only half-heard Father's tirade. Instead, the whoosh of the water-propelled bullet sled was whisking from one end of the mile-long Midway to the other in mere seconds. As we marched away from the Coliseum, I saw the speeding sleigh streak toward Father's head, unknown to him, and like an Indian arrow gave the illusion of burrowing into one of his ears, through his skull, and drilling out his other ear.

I heard someone laughing hysterically. How embarrassing. I crossed my hands over my mouth. It was me. Would Father feel disrespected? When he saw me laughing he blinked his eyes, threw his head back, and flung his empty beer stein into the air over his shoulder, howling like a bear. Never had I seen him act so crazy. It occurred to me public embarrassment was permitted so long as Father did it. He pulled me into his arms, his bear hug lifting me out of myself. When my feet left the ground I realized that playing a servant for Father might come at too high a cost.

As we left Midway to enter White City, Father and I found ourselves pausing at a crossroad. I wanted to visit the Children's Building to see little Terese. If I couldn't meet Hermes under the Big Clock today, couldn't I at least present Terese to Father as a surprise? But how could I deflect Father to the Children's Building? Pretending I had to visit its comfort station, I begged Father to escort me over there.

Without waiting for his response, I hurried toward the friendly façade of the Children's Building. Fearing she would be disappointed, I hoped to explain to Terese that the planned outing to the Ferris Wheel with Hermes had to be postponed.

Reaching the entrance, I rang the bell chimes and stepped back to watch the window pane reflect Father's image pausing behind me at a distance. I could ease my own regret in missing Hermes with the pleasure of sharing Terese with Father. I trusted him to accept her as I did.

While I contemplated another ring of the bell, I heard my name called from an open window above. Shading my eyes, I perceived the Garret twins chuckling and poking each other. As I started to wave, a little brown face bobbed up between them. With her chin resting on the window sill, Terese whistled at me. The three of them were a picture to behold, healing my hurts of the day. "Terese!" I heard myself blurting out, "I need you to live with me at Father's manor."

Father's voice growled. "Jesus Judas Christ! Look at the three of them. Talk about a stink willy between two roses!"

Shocked, I peered up to see Terese's face but she was gone, the window closed. I turned on Father. "How could you embarrass me like this? Why would you hurt Terese's feelings?"

"Daughter," Father said, now standing between me and the Children's Building. "You are beyond the pale!" He peered into my face, his vein purple and throbbing, "First, you embarrassed me by stomping out of Germania Club. Then you used Doc Seth to sneak out to the fair, and disgraced our family name by being a wet nurse. Worst of all, you failed me as Lady of the Manor. And now, you lied to me in order to follow you here. And all for what purpose? In my presence, you have degraded yourself with that pipsqueak oriental. To top it off, you dare invite her to live in my Manor!"

Before I could gather my thoughts to reply, the entrance door flung open. Out dashed Terese, wearing the blue sailor suit I had purchased for her at Marshall Field's. With sailor cap leaping from her head, and pigtails flying, Terese swooped into my arms, spinning me like a maypole, her feet fleeing the ground as we twirled, giggling and hugging each other off balance.

Breathless, I braced for introductions, but saw Father striding back to the sedan chairs, whereupon he pivoted and pointed his arm at me. "Daughter, as your father, I hereby forbid you to disobey me by seeing that brown slant eyes ever again. And if you do dare to bring that little monkey into my manor I—shall—disown—you!" After a deep cough, he muttered hoarsely, "So help me Gawd."

When I looked to comfort Terese, I realized she had fled back to the Garret sisters in the open doorway, whereupon she buried herself midst their billowing skirts.

I felt frozen for an eternal moment. I felt myself straddling the center of a teeter-totter, rocking uncertainly in the air, comforting Therese or obeying Father.

"I won't wait!" shouted Father. He rode away in a sedan chair toward the Krupp Gun Exhibit.

Biting my tongue until I almost tasted blood, I pivoted on my heels away from the Children's Building. Head high, I marched straight to the shadows of a willow tree, scuffing my common-sense shoes at every stone in my way. Reaching the sedan bike, I half turned and saw a fleeting glimpse of Terese's face framed in the upstairs window. Seeing her, my throat tightened at Terese being a lonely orphan. Was it my own fears of being abandoned? I stared at her doll-like features, her eyes large and empty, her chin collapsed upon the sill. I wondered why didn't Terese at least cry? Her silence condemned me for betraying her. Was my soul the price of being loyal to Father?

I knew the route because I had pestered Hermes to share his guidebook. I pumped toward the Illinois Building, past the Haytian Pavilion where a tall Negro was speaking to a crowd of whites and coloreds, as a young woman distributed pamphlets. The fair was fast becoming a blur.

Finally, I halted my sedan bike at the outdoor banquet garden next to the Krupp Pavillion. Already Father was seated at a table by himself, stuffing his mouth with boiled potato, cabbage, and one of his favorites—weisswurst, a delicacy consisting of pork and veal stuffed into a casing of links. Biting my lip, I joined him at his table, in the shadow of the belltower at the Deutschland. Without a word of greeting to me Father finished his draught beer. Beyond his shoulder, I scanned the innocent faces of children playing leapfrog outside the gun exhibit. I wondered if Hermes would be searching faces of passersby under the Big Clock, and gulping his second opium cordial? Was Hermes missing me? I certainly hoped so.

After Father burped, he steered me to the entrance for the next tour. As we paused before entering he pointed upward at the stone eagle sculptured in an alcove above the doorway. "See that eagle? Makes me remember father Oscar." I craned my neck and studied the eagle, wings outspread, neck stretching, eyes searching the sky, as it struggled in vain to free its talons forever imprisoned in cement.

Entering with the polite crowd, I heard a foreign voice proclaim, "Behold! Behold ze Gun Krupp, greatest peacemaker in ze world!" In the semi-dark, I detected a German sergeant waving his arm at a monstrous cannon on the east wall, fronting Lake Michigan. It aimed its massive barrel in the direction of the incoming steamer Columbus, docking at the long pier. Lining the wall were sixteen smaller cannons. I must have been counting aloud because Father poked me in the ribs.

A stocky officer clicked his heels, and saluted as he addressed the sightseers. "Permit introduction. General Schofield, United States Army, at your service. Observe these sixteen cannons from Herr Krupp surrounding the largest cannon in the world, with a barrel sixty feet long. This cannon can salvo a truck all the way to the Michigan side of the lake."

The crowd murmured approval as Father clapped his hands. I edged away to a stone bench against a sweaty wall. The General raised his arms for quiet. "The horror of war is over! War is trumped by a worse horror! The Krupp Gun becomes the ultimate peacemaker for Germany!"

Beneath the skylight, applause echoed off the high iron crossbeams. The sun, filtered through the grid, created shadows crisscrossing every person, and every cannon in the exhibit hall, like a massive web of steel.

Shrinking into a dark corner by myself, I felt sick to my stomach. To avoid the spider shadows, I tucked my feet beneath me. I could not detect Father's face, but his laughter told me he had located himself next to the General in the heart of the crowd. Father seemed lost to me in the tangle of bodies and shadows. Then a thought came to my heart, unbidden; a question I had buried in a cave inside of me. In my endeavor to rescue Father from collapsing, I had failed to ask myself: Did Father want to be rescued? And in rescuing him was I in danger of losing myself? The bell tower of the Krupp Pavilion struck twelve.

Chapter Eight

WEBS of STEEL

Thursday, June 21

That same night, returning in the dark from the fair, I felt orphaned. In my bedroom for companionship I lit a candelabrum to signal Hermes at his house. I must have displeased him by failing to meet under the Big Clock. Had I also displeased Father by not believing the Krupp Gun would be the great peacemaker for the world? But how can violence prevent violence? Lighting the fifth candle in the center, I clung to the wooden match too long, searing myself. Raising my fingertip to my mouth, I tasted sulphur, making my lip rusty. In trying to please Hermes was I hurting myself?

To forget the sting, I thought of stealing another cigarillo from the hidden inner compartment in Karla's desk, since she had not returned home. As I rose from Mother's rocker to go to Karla's room, a candle finally flickered in Hermes window.

Rushing to the round table, I snatched up Mother's comforter to shield and unshield the candles, sending greetings in our secret code. Did Hermes still remember it? My heart rumbled with surges of guilt about missing our date, with resentment over obeying Father, with my own desires, with bitterness at failing Mother as Lady of the Manor.

Perhaps hearing me stir, Odette brought in an opium cordial. After a sip, I saw the candle in Hermes' window blink out a reply, "No anger." My heart skipped. Had Hermes forgiven me? Then Hermes added, "Beg forgive." Puzzled, I signaled for him to telephone me. But he replied, "No." Instead, he signaled, "Photos."

So, that was it. Hermes had chosen Mr. Arnold's photography assignment over me. Shaking my head, I collapsed onto Mother's rocker as I drained the cup. Further flickerings from Hermes were dimmer, like fireflies perishing.

I blew out my candles, and rocked in darkness, while branches of my oak tree scratched the side of the house, mocking me. The cup slipped from my hand. Mother's rocker squeaked, as I squeezed its wooden arms, thin as an old lady's, but strong enough to support me. Tell me, Mother, did Father take you for granted as Lady of the Manor? Were you enlightened or only a servant?

The rhythm of the rocking chair and the faint aroma of candlewax dragged me into a nightmare. I found myself cocooned in the barrel of the Krupp Gun. Wriggling to be free, I inched upward toward the open mouth. I grasped the iron lip, and pulled my head up to peek out. A cackling at the base of the cannon made me stretch my neck. I peered down at Karla, naked, wearing Father's opera hat. Cackling again, she ignited a huge wooden match with her hand like a claw. She leered at me from the darkness with her purple eyes as she lit the fuse. She put one finger to her lips, "Shush!"

Staring at the burning fuse in my nightmare, I struggled to escape, extracting half my body, like a caterpillar hanging upside down from a branch. At that instant, an explosion catapulted me upward out of the barrel, crashing me against the ceiling of my bedroom, and splattering me into a thousand pieces.

Flying shards of something real cut my cheek as I shed the caterpillar skin of Mother's comforter, and fell from the ceiling. Awakening me from my nightmare I saw that a broken branch from my oak tree had shattered glass over me.

It had actually crashed through my bedroom window. Odette screamed, and Uncle Chilton dashed in, scooping me into his arms, and staggering toward the door. "Drawing room!" shouted Odette. "Drawing room's safer!"

Each step down the back stairs jarred me as the smell of gin stung my eyes, reminding me I was finally awake. When I squinted, I saw the widow's peak of Chilton's toupee nudge left, nudge right. Then, thunder roared around the house like an angry bear as I snuggled deeper into Uncle Chilton's soft arms.

As we burst into the drawing room, I saw something that fully opened my eyes—my harp-piano. Uncle Chilton slid me onto the bench like a caring mother. He dabbed the blood from my cheek with his handkerchief that retained a scent of lavender.

Taking a deep breath, I focused my eyes on the vertical harp of iron and gold rising at the back of the keyboard embellished in gold design, so light, so elegant. How many times had Father and I played duets, blending our hearts? Gaslights flickered on the two portraits suspended on adjacent walls, Grandfather and Grandmother, staring away from each other. Oscar's baby face frowned within his muttonchops. Did he scowl because he hated music? In the portrait on the wall to my right, Grandmother Cathleen's vertical vein divided her forehead like my father's. It seemed to throb. Were the rumors true that it pulsated from hiding the secret of Chilton's adoption at Oscar's insistence? Did Chilton's swarthy complexion resemble that of the Spanish maid who had suddenly disappeared? I felt guilty believing these forbidden rumors while in Uncle Chilton's arms. I kissed him on his smooth cheek.

"Alessandra, remember how you christened these 'torture gloves'?" he said retrieving them from behind the music stand. He held the two black gloves, weighted at the tip of each of the ten fingers. Father had ordered this aid to strengthen my fingers while I learned to play. He called them his magic digitorium. Whenever I complained, he silenced me by shouting they belonged to Mother. The swollen black fingertips resembled claws of a skeleton from the ashes of a fire.

Shaking my head at the prospect of donning those gloves again in my lifetime, I closed my eyes, and instead touched the cold keys with my bare flesh. A shiver of pleasure surged through my hands. I teased out a few notes by striking the hammers above the keyboard again and again, until the three boxes blended sounds of violin, cello, viola.

Sitting next to me, Uncle Chilton laid his hands side by side to mine as he had done so often during my growing years. He always provided comfort whenever I cried from those torture gloves.

Tilting his temple against mine, Uncle Chilton played and sang softly in his sweet tenor voice. "A little maiden climbed an old man's knee / Begged for a story—" He winked at me, and paused until I added my part.

"Do uncle please," I sang, "Why are you single? / Why live alone? / Have you no babies? / Have you no home?"

Uncle Chilton straightened his back, pounding the piano as he howled in his falsetto: "I had a sweet heart / Years, years ago / Where is she now pet? / You will soon know." Then, he held down the chords as he sang, "List to the story / I'll tell it all / I believe her faithless / After the ball."

Placing his arm around my shoulder he played the melody as I the chords. Our duet was drowned by thunder rumbling outside our drawing room. Branches lashed against windows, making gaslights blink. We just sang louder: "After the ball is over / After the break of dawn / After the dancers leaving / After the stars are gone / Many the heart is aching—"

My voice cracked. The lyric stuck in my throat. I felt my head bow onto Uncle Chilton's shoulder like Terese's onto mine. It was a relief to become a child again for a little while as I nestled into his embrace of acceptance.

❧ ❧ ❧

With a start, I awakened from a dreamless sleep to my old nursery with Mother's comforter over my head, wondering if I had really become a child again. As I peeked out at dusty sunbeams slanting into the nursery, I recalled last night's nightmare. The branch from my oak tree had actually crashed through my window. I remembered being rescued by Uncle Chilton. Now my vision was interrupted when I heard voices drifting from a room below the nursery. The open potbelly stove in the corner carried Father's voice arguing with Doctor Wetherstone. "I'm not afraid to bet!" Father shouted, "But you're just tricking me into going to the fair."

Doc Seth said, "Cyrus, it's your chance to win back some cognac you've given me. Your prize would be a vintage bottle of cognac Normandin, 1840!"

"Hell, that's from Edith's old family stock. Besides, what would you win?"

"That Civil War revolver you hide under your pillow." I crept out of bed, ignoring the cold floor, and crouched next to the open stove door, as Karla and I did as children.

"Cyrus, you used to brag about your great eyesight. But not the last few years. Know why? Those mercury hats of yours. Dimming your lights."

"Prove it."

"Exactly. I bet you can't see your precious Krupp Pavilion from atop the Ferris Wheel."

"Move your fairy wheel out of the fair and I would go."

"But you went to German Day."

"I did?" said Father.

"You used to like big bets."

"Did you say Cognac Normandin 1840?"

"Cyrus, all you have to do is get a sighting of Krupp at the apex of the cycle."

Father laughed. "And you would bloody believe me?"

"I would Cyrus—with the carriage attendant as your sworn witness."

"What about you, Seth?"
"I'll be in another carriage car with another attendant."
"Doctor, I swear you will never touch my revolver."
"It's done!"

❀   ❀   ❀

Thus it was that the clans of Aultmans and Wetherstones found ourselves back at the fair, sweltering in June heat. The relentless sun slowly hatched a foreboding within my heart. Would today threaten a different direction for my life?

All Astor Street, it seemed was assembled in their finery at the base of the Ferris Wheel for its delayed opening. The odors of fresh paint and varnish assailed my nostrils while the blaring of the band from Iowa State assaulted my ears. As our party waited in line at the foot of the wheel, the strains of "My Country 'tis of Thee" belched forth from one of the Pullman-sized cars above our heads. The curved slides of trombones poked between crossbars, and retreated as the tune trudged the carriage sway. Music echoed off enclosed walls at the base surrounding us, and the hundreds of passengers on the six railed platforms on the north side of the wheel.

Father stood on my right side, and Hermes on my left, neither one looking at each other, but both holding my hands. Dr. Wetherstone and Edith stood in front of us. I for one did not care that Karla and Kelso had wandered away. The crowd squirmed in mid-afternoon sun: ladies fidgeting with parasols, men fingering their collars, children fanning their faces with programs.

In response to my earlier question, Hermes pointed out Mr. Ferris seated among dignitaries with Mayor Harrison and his young fiancée. To me, the only one relaxed was Mr. Ferris himself, inventor of the biggest bicycle wheel in the world, as Hermes called it.

Squeezing my hand too tightly, Hermes prevented me from repeating my chatter about the tree crashing through my window that interrupted my nightmare last night. I told him I had slept overnight in my old nursery, while the stable boys repaired damage to my bedroom. "Didn't Mr. Arnold have an assignment for you today?" I said, to stop him asking questions. It sounded petty, but I could not resist.

Then I noticed Mr. Ferris did not possess the image of an inventor. Instead, he dressed as a groom with formal black tails, a boutonniere, and white cravat. Did it nestle a diamond stickpin? Next to him, I assumed, was his wife, in a blue bonnet with roses, tied to secure it from crosswinds. They held hands and looked into each others eyes. How I envied them.

I pointed out Mr. Ferris to Father, but he snorted and said, "Oh, you mean that man with wheels in his head?" I felt sorry for Father's closed mind.

The crowd quieted when Judge Vincent introduced himself as secretary of the Ferris Wheel Company, and expressed his gratitude at being named Master of Ceremonies. He implored speakers to be brief. In turn Mr. Hunt, president of the company, was pleased to point to representatives of the fair Mr. Handy and Mr. Fearn, who were also pleased to defer to the man in uniform, General Nelson A. Miles. He reminded me of the officer at the Krupp Gun.

Father muttered aloud. "Wonder if Miles knows the General from the—from the—what was his name again?"

Father's poor memory worried me. Drinking? Mercury? Money? I distracted myself by noticing that all of the speakers seemed to agree on two things: Mr. Ferris should be praised and short speeches were too long. When Mr. Ferris stood to speak, he appeared young and slim in contrast to the others.

He stated that his wheel was higher than any cloudscraper in Chicago, as well as an engineering marvel surpassing the new Eiffel Tower in Paris. Applause. "I express the hope this giant wheel be worthy as representative of skill and daring of American engineers. In that spirit, I dedicate the Ferris Wheel." I wanted to cheer, wishing I had also accomplished something important.

Judge Vincent leaped to his feet and proposed three cheers, although Mr. Ferris seemed to have more to say. The judge prompted Mr. Ferris' wife to stand and present her husband with the official whistle, glistening in sunlight. Mr. Ferris puffed his chest, and let go with a blast that made me jump. It startled birds within fifty feet into sudden flight. I was amazed how they avoided collisions as they darted among St. Peter's, Parisian stores, and the fire station. I noticed a long black shadow on the pavement stretching eastward, enveloping both sides of the Ferris Wheel. "We're in for it," I whispered to Hermes, as I shivered at the birds' near misses.

"What?"

I pointed to the growing shadow. "Rain's coming."

Hermes laughed at me. "Dummy," he shouted in my ear, "That's just the shadow of the Ferris Wheel."

After a second blast from the whistle, the door of the carriage for dignitaries opened. "Can they all fit into that one car?" I asked Hermes. "When is our turn?" My fear of heights grew within me.

"Not to worry, as Dad tells me, simple math," Hermes said, "Thirty-six carriages, each holds forty people. Six carriages load at one time on three different levels, each a house story apart." People nearby stared knives and forks at us. "The wheel stops a total of six times to load to capacity, and with standees, totals two thousand passengers for each trip!"

"Marvelous, Hermes, how do you know all that?" I asked him as if I didn't know.

He held a Rand McNally guidebook, and grinned.

"One thing more," I said, "As you know, I hate heights. Hope it doesn't drop too fast." My stomach started to churn. "Sander, it's called an observation wheel, not an amusement wheel."

I appreciated his thoughtfulness. But then he smirked. I hated Hermes when he smirked.

As we waited to load, the band in the carriage above began a barbershop rendition of "The Ferris Wheel Waltz." "Gently moving up higher yet / Nearer to heaven may we get / Then yearning to returning / Back to home and earthly debt."

I thought about Father's finances.

While I enjoyed the music, Hermes held his ears, and swept ahead by his parents to enter the third carriage. Inside, Hermes turned back, peering through the plate-glass window. He mouthed the words, "Alessandra, you're supposed to be here at my side." Why did he leave me? As the door began to shut, he squeezed out and rushed toward me as his parents' carriage clanked upward to follow the band and dignitaries in their two carriages. A fourth car swung into place, itself almost full with reserved passengers, but it stopped to permit Father, Hermes and me, plus a dozen others to enter.

The inside of the carriage smelled of face powder and sweat. It seemed larger than any Pullman railroad car. The seats were wire-backed stools bolted to the floor, and facing the windows on both sides. The stools revolved. With the crush of bodies, I clung to both Father and Hermes, despairing of ever seeing out a window.

"A cattle car," Father complained. "Told Wetherstone to get us reservations. I must see the Krupp Pavilion to win my bet."

At that moment, a young man doffed his derby, and offered me his stool next to a window. I accepted with a nod of gratitude, and sat side-saddle, my skirt being so voluminous.

Behind me, Hermes placed his hand on my shoulder to reassure me of his presence, calming my fear of heights. It felt warm being so close to him. I patted his hand, but worried at its coldness.

The entrance door slid shut. The abrupt start produced a horrible noise, like rust scraping rust on steel plates. Conversation ceased. On the ground below, performers from Cairo Street pointed up at our noise, laughed, and ran over to see the source of the racket. When the carriage brakes released, the wheel ratcheted in the opposite direction downward until it caught. The gnashing of steel gears and the vibration of small cogs meshing swayed our carriage. As we ascended, the dancers and tumblers from Cairo Street cheered and waved good luck with Karla and Kelso in the middle of them. Everything outside the windows sank by slow degrees, as we swung cradled in a giant hammock. Conversation resumed at once.

Our carriage advanced to the next pause, allowing passengers below us to board. We were as high as the Captive Balloon. In the basket, a woman with ostrich feathers waved at us. Our carriage rose to another level. Remembering I had secured Father's opera glasses in my purse before we left, I took them out, and adjusted the focus. Straight ahead in all its June greenery spread Washington Park. Didn't some planners want Midway there? To my left, Oakwood Cemetery seemed as large as Midway. In between, I focused on gray hovels that seemed too small for people to breathe in. I pitied their occupants living so close to main gates, but without possessing entrance fee.

Suddenly a gasp on the other side drew my attention. "Look at the lake," a woman shouted, "I can see Lake Michigan." Passengers who had bumped against us to see Chicago, now pushed the opposite way to see the lake. The carriage tilted.

Where is Father? I needed to hold his hand to hear him accept me as an enlightened Lady of the Manor. I asked Hermes where Father was standing. He pointed to a far corner where Father was lighting his pipe beneath the sign *No Smoking*.

Now I had to see the lake, too. I asked Hermes to steady me as I climbed onto the seat and took hold of a leather strap dangling from the ceiling, available for standees. Swaying, I peered over the heads of people previously blocking my view of the lake.

Trapped on the Wheel

Focusing Father's glasses, I saw brilliant whitecaps of the lake rushing toward the dock. As the carriage swayed, I picked out the German Pavilion which seemed smaller, until I realized it was the Spanish. In the center of the lagoon, the Wooded Island reminded me I was mad at Hermes because he had taken photos of the Japanese consul, instead of meeting me under the Big Clock. However, he later reminded me of the huge rose garden he promised to show me.

My new shoes started slipping so Hermes guided me down, supporting my waist with both hands. I loved Hermes protecting me—but only sometimes. As I sat, I peered out my own window again. To my right, beyond the north wall of Midway lay an odd assortment of buildings, some several stories high, some facades, some only foundations. Odd that Dr. Wetherstone would allow his son to attend school at a place only half built. Did they allow females to enroll?

Next to me, I heard an animal whining and grunting. Swiveling on my stool, I searched faces around me, thinking someone had smuggled in a dog or cat. Perhaps a baby. Then I saw Hermes' face, beet red; his eyes bulged, resembling a cornered ferret. I'd never before seen Hermes as a wild man. Lurching, Hermes banged his head against crossbars on the window. The attendant blew his whistle. Hermes moaned, and chewed something in his mouth. Was it his tongue? I almost fell off my stool. Was this my future husband? The father-to-be of my children?

The attendant placed a protective arm around Hermes, and whispered in his ear, but Hermes threw off the attendant's arm, like a wet cape after a storm. Hermes pushed the attendant's chest with both hands, sending him sprawling backwards, toppling people like ten pins. Hermes needed me. I reached out for him, but he rushed past me, a horse escaping a burning stable. The crowd blocked his exit. A frustrated moan emitted from his throat, veins purple, and fit to burst. Hermes struck at me, but Father pulled me to safety. Then Hermes, like the wild man form Borneo, tried to bend the crossbar on the window. I could not move; I was so paralyzed with fear. Letting forth a primitive yelp Hermes bent the bar, his whole body shaking.

The attendant and policeman flung themselves upon poor Hermes' back, smashing his cheek against the window and twisting his arms behind him.

I screamed as if for my own life.

At that moment, the carriage jolted to a pause for the loading of more passengers on the ground. Loose bolts on the floor flew up, clanking against a metal fire extinguisher, ceiling, windows. One bolt binged against the opera glasses in my hand. My only fear was that Hermes might harm himself.

With calm restored, people on the opposite side resumed enjoying their view of Midway. However, my side now had our view encumbered by rims and spokes of the giant wheel, like a huge spider web.

Concerned about Hermes dripping sweat, I took out my handkerchief and started to wipe his forehead. At first touch, he jerked away, slapping my hand. To my relief, Father stepped between me and Hermes. With his back to him, Father clasped my arms as tears started to cloud my eyes. I couldn't look at Father because of the public embarrassment Hermes was causing him. Father lifted my face by cupping my chin with his thumb and bent index finger. At such moments I felt a child again, sitting upon his lap after he read me *The Handless Maiden*. Peering into my heart he would whisper, "Alessandra, you are loved." At such moments, I did not need to listen to Mother's voice.

When our carriage paused on ground level to load to full capacity, people cheered, probably thinking the ride was terminated. I heard Hermes sobbing and laughing as he blurted out apologies. He expressed relief his parents had not been there to witness his conduct.

Some boy yelled, "Ride's too short!"

Father escorted Hermes to the exit, until the attendant announced, "Door's locked. Automatic. Phone line's not attached. Can't interrupt the two cycle trip to let no man off." People groaned and cursed. "Must follow this here schedule. Second cycle lasts ten minutes with no more stops."

As he spoke, the carriage engines roared, shook, and resumed ascent. The movement sprung Hermes from Father. He spun in a circle, flailing like a farmer's scythe cutting a path through a field of people. Children screamed in terror. Father pulled the fire alarm that clanged louder than the engines. Hermes pulled his Swiss pocket knife, and snapped open a blade that flashed in a beam of sunlight. Total silence. Outside the windows, Midway sank from sight. So did my stomach. In the corner of my eye, I saw Father hide against the far wall. The attendant who had stepped toward Hermes jumped back at the sweep of a knife blade. Hermes whimpered, his neck stretching, and his head flopping upon his shoulder. Poor Hermes reminded me of the ostrich laying his head on the sand. The policeman pulled out his pistol and several big men surrounded Hermes who stabbed the point of the knife against his own wrist. This was a living nightmare.

Remembering the gamekeeper's trick of throwing the canvas sack over the ostrich, I unbuttoned my overskirt, letting it fall to the floor. I stepped out of it. Picking it up, I crept behind Hermes. At that instant, he must have sensed people were peering at me, not him. I flung my skirt over his head. As if by signal, attendant and policeman grabbed Hermes by the neck, my skirt covering his head, and wrestled him to the floor. As the attendant rolled Hermes, the policeman stomped on Hermes' hand, freeing the knife so another man could kick it away. The attendant perched on Hermes' back as the policeman handcuffed his wrists.

The passengers gave a holler of relief as we attained the summit of the Ferris Wheel. I saw Father on his tiptoes, straining to see the Krupp Gun Pavilion. Men patted attendant and policeman with congratulations. I felt relieved that Hermes could no longer hurt himself or anyone else. But had he just altered my future?

To calm my panic, feeling trapped on the wheel, I looked out the window. In that moment, I realized I could never be free on the ground, never free from Father, from Hermes, from the fair. Anchored on the ground I met only obstacles. Even as enlightened Lady of the Manor I was not free. Up here in the ether, on the other hand, I saw a vision for the first time. Harper. Harper could lift me above my obstacles on the ground. But would I be walking on a tightrope without a net? Would I have to become as brave as Terese? What if I fell?

A woman took my hand, "You poor lass. A flying bolt must have hit you. Are those tears in your eyes?" A man laughed. "Heroes don't cry."

With increasing speed, the carriage descended to the ground. When it shuddered to a stop, the door rattled open as the attendant rose from Hermes' back, and assisted him to his feet. The policeman returned my outer skirt with a tip of his cap. Thanking him, I put it over my inner skirt, as ladies circled me so I could readjust my garments. A young woman said, "I'm a reporter. I must interview you for your daring-do.' Her blurred face seemed strangely familiar.

"No, no thank you," I said, moving away. "Hermes, are you all right?" I left the covey of ladies. "Father, where are you?"

As passengers were exiting, Father was talking to attendant in a far corner. He reached into an inner coat pocket, and produced his wallet. Licking his thumb, he dealt out several money bills onto a waiting palm. Then Father hesitated before dealing several more bills. After a moment, the two men nodded, and walking over to Hermes as the policeman unshackled his hands.

When I finally reached Father's side his face was pale, the vertical vein cleaving his forehead, as if splitting his head into two faces.

Expecting an embrace for my action, I opened my arms. Instead, Father twisted away from me, shaking his head and muttering. "Daughter, disgrace I shan't endure! Your misconduct made me lose my bet with Doc Seth!"

"But Father, my outer skirt is restored now."

"That's but half! Just look at yourself!" Father folded his arms and whispered hoarsely at the wall. "Your skirt is on backwards!"

Before I could inspect my outer skirt, Father strode toward the open exit where he clapped Hermes on the back, whispering in his ear. When Hermes glanced at me, Father turned Hermes' head away with his thumb and index finger. Then they both strode out the door. Men. Would I ever understand them? What had brought Father and Hermes closer together? I felt invisible.

Smells of stuffed cabbage and sauerkraut from nearby Vienna Café slithered through the open door of the carriage. Pushing my back away from the window, hot from sun, I pinched my nostrils refusing to inhale the noxious odors. Holding my breath longer than ever before in my life, I felt I was swimming underwater.

If being alone was the price of freedom, so be it.

Chapter Nine

seize THE *night*

Friday, June 30

*C*lutching the postcard of the Ferris Wheel I was filled with new energy and resolve. I smoothed the wrinkled and torn image I had gripped throughout the night determined to preserve it later in my remembrance book.

The morning light flooded the parlor with the paleness of new beginnings. Mother's desktop, too high for comfort, forced me to sit straight as Bertha Palmer even though my sinuses felt stuffed. Laying the crinkled postcard on the oak surface allowed me to study it, as I would study a cathedral.

In my memory, I relived the event of the Ferris Wheel. Poor Hermes. I never imagined he could break down. Why didn't he tell me of his secret seizures? How could he ever protect me? How could I ever trust him? And Father seemed a total stranger when he consoled Hermes instead of me. Why didn't they both realize something happened deep inside me? It was Harper College. Harper with its new buildings, some partially completed, like me. I experienced a vision I could not explain to anyone else. When Mother's chair squeaked beneath me, I wondered what she would feel about all this. Mother was the only person who understood me. Not Hermes, not Father.

From the center drawer, I brought out the fan map of the fair and laid it flat. I stared at it, as if riding in that Captive Balloon floating high above the fair, but tethered to the earth below. But even as I did, my imagination drifted away from the clean beauty of the White City. Turning the fan over, I peered at Midway, resting my chin on my hands, and wondered how the nighttime transformed the fair. When Karla, Father and I had toured Midway in the daylight last week, it did not seem romantic. But somehow, the night always lured Karla back to Midway time after time, like an addict. Why?

My eyes located the Captive Balloon between Chinese theater and Indian Village. As I scanned the map, however, an annoying thought buzzed like a gnat within my head. Being taught at home, would I even qualify to enroll at Harper? I must add more knowledge! Could a trip to the fair be educational? Near the Ferris Wheel was the diorama of the destruction of Pompeii. Why hadn't I noticed it when I rode the wheel?

Then, I realized I still had duties as Lady of the Manor. At least I had to go through the motions to avoid embarrassing Father even further. The servants, according to Mrs. Dibbs, needed my supervision; daily menus by Alsace required my approval. Shopping at Marshall Field's for my own proper attire as well as Terese's demanded my presence; not to mention my volunteering several days as wet nurse at the Children's Building. Before I realized it, a frustrating week had passed.

Then one afternoon, playing croquet with Karla on our back lawn, I suggested visiting Pompeii at night. Wouldn't it be romantic? She readily agreed. At her prompting, Hermes borrowed his dad's new carriage without horses, but when he parked at our curb I lost the race with Karla to the vehicle. As loser, I scrunched down in the backseat, and had to watch Karla in the front snuggle too close to Hermes. I overheard her say, "Hurry Mr. Ferry Wheel, Midway at night awaits you and me." Then she cackled and peered back at me with her evil eye, while slinging her arm around his neck.

After Hermes received a ticket for speeding, we parked at Midway. I resolved this time to win the race to the Pompeii Exhibit. Out of breath I awaited their arrival, but then I wondered why they sauntered so slowly. Were they holding hands? Maybe I made a mistake by not giving Hermes enough sympathy for his seizure. I took out my fan map to locate the exact site. The electric lights trimming and illuminating the Ferris Wheel did not aid my reading, so I sidled closer to the fire barrel. I shouted at Hermes, "The destruction of Pompeii. The diorama—where is it?"

Hermes stopped within the shadows of the Persian concession. Was he holding Karla's hand?

"It's supposed to be here. It's drawn on the map!" I waved it at him. "But it isn't here!" A skinny Arab boy with his hand out, begging, perched his bare feet on the exact spot mapped for Pompeii.

A mocking laugh from Karla crackled like sparks springing from the flaming barrel. "Stir, the first rule of the Midway at night is—say, don't you know it?"

She waited for reply, but I refused to play guessing games. Instead, I stared at the fan map rattling in my hands like a snake. Hermes advanced out of the shadows toward me and the fire. "Abandon—all—reason—ye—who—enter—the—Midway." He waited for my response. None came. He shrugged at my denseness. "No cash, don't you see? The boodlers ran out of cash. They never even built it. Anyway, that's what Mr. Arnold told me. So your precious snap-map is all wrong!" Verdict rendered, Hermes folded his arms like a judge pronouncing my death sentence. Crowds flowed around me, allured by bright lights of Algerian Village with snake charmers, harem girls, jugglers. Others hurried to Chinese theatre with its tales of unrequited love.

Taking a deep breath, I spread out the fan map I had previously mended, and ripped it in down the center. Then I snapped each wooden spine, naming one Lady of the Manor, one Father's servant, one wet nurse, and one Nellie Bly. I strolled to the fire barrel. Furious at myself for being so trusting, I balled the map in my fists, and scattered the remnants, some small as seeds, into the hungry flames. "Destruction!" I shouted. "I demand destruction!"

Karla stepped to my side, shadows dancing on her face. "Now you sound like a new Alessandra. Last week you were just a showoff on the Ferris Wheel."

"But tonight you are a crazed woman," Hermes said, "I never saw you like this. You're terrific, but you frighten me!"

I dusted my hands of remaining flakes, but a few stuck to my palms. A mule stopped to stare at me. I wet my lips. "Karla, don't you have to meet your newest beaux?"

Hermes put an arm around my waist, in what I was sure he considered a protective gesture. I did not. Pointing with his other arm he said, "Over there, Sander, do you see the tallest building on Midway? The Hawaiian Volcano. Won't that do instead?"

"Perfect!" I shouted, striding away from him, and toward it. "I could play the volcano myself." As I approached, I saw above the entrance the Hawaiian goddess of fire, Pele, luxuriating in carved flames while holding aloft a torch. The spotlight glowing beneath made her eyes glitter, as if with a fever. I thought of Karla as I hurried toward the replica of the greatest volcano on earth.

Striding into a building shaped like a silo, I paid my fifty-cent fee, fully expecting an immediate volcanic explosion. Instead, greeting my eyes was a curving panorama one hundred feet long, depicting the nine stages of a living volcano. Even in the semi-dark, I made out a huge sign on a back wall, *Science can show you how—but never why.*

Displayed before me, the nine panels of a volcano's life seemed to echo my own life. Above each panel, a key word in yellow emblazoned each stage of development. I marched past Extinct, Dead, Dormant, Reposing and Sleeping. Then, I paused at Restless. A recorded voice, activated by foot pressure announced: "The oil glows deep inside the earth. Decaying elements produce friction and heat so intense it melts all boundaries." I moved to the panel Awakening: "Rising slowly along its faults and growing crystals the volcano nears the surface." I thought of my wanting to be equal to men and others equal to me, but inequality ruled society.

The next panel Active said: "Dissolved gases boil out of fissures erupting lava from vents in small explosions of fire and smoke." I thought of my disappointment at Hermes for his break down on the Ferris Wheel; of my disobedience to Father; of my hatred toward Karla. How can our weaknesses bring us closer when our strengths keep us apart?

I strode to the next panel, Destruction. "Hot blocks of lava spew forth, plowing down the slopes of volcanic cone, ripping trees in a lethal mud avalanche." I stared at destruction, as if at my own face in a dark mirror.

The final panel was labeled Alive: "Lava cools into rough clinkers in a cycle of rumblings, destructions, and recreations of the earth's body." The moving crowd had flowed along with me slow as lava, oohing and aahing at the panels with their eyes popping, their mouths gaping like miniature volcanoes. Nearing the exit, I scarcely glanced at the plaque listing positive results of the volcano's destruction.

Leaving the cyclorama, I mingled with passengers exiting the Ferris Wheel. I envied the joy in their faces.

From the Persian concession, Hermes' voice caught my attention. "Alessandra, what took you so long? Karla couldn't find her beaux!"

I don't trust you. "Where did she go?"

Hermes grinned like a thief and stepped aside, revealing Karla crouched behind him. She leaped to her feet, a Turkish cigarette dangling from the corner of her purple lips, smoke squinting shut one eye. Her face, white with clown make-up, glowed like a full moon while her head, topped by a fez, bobbed inspecting me. "Stir, you do need work." Karla removed her Moorish vest, gemstones on the tapestry flickering like fire flies in the torchlight, and motioned me to turn around. When I did, she slipped the vest on my back like a pair of wings. Turning to face her again, I saw Karla step back, rubbing her chin. Was she laughing at me? Taking off her fez, Karla placed it upon my head as a crown. "Stir, welcome to my world!"

I was not amused. The very possibility of Karla mocking me was worse than Pompeii not being there.

"Stir, you're angry at something."

As usual, Karla read my heart. "I need a complaint department like Marshall Field's."

"You'll soon be in the right hands." She hugged me. "The complaint department here is the unofficial mayor of Midway, Sol Bloom."

"I heard about him in class." Hermes said. "He's just a kid. Twenty-one. Mr. Arnold tells me Mr. Putnam of Harvard is the real director of the Ethno—"

"Mr. Bloom?" I said to Karla, ignoring Hermes. "Where's this Mr. Bloom? I need to register my complaint about Pompeii."

Karla's attention was distracted by the flute of a snake charmer, crouched in the sand at the edge of the bazaar.

"Karla are you hypnotized?"

She pulled a riding crop with a yellow tassel from her sash and, with her elbow against her breast, pointed it toward the Algerian Village. "See that little gent at the café table, almost buried by dancing girls? He's your complaint department."

I hurried, with Hermes at my heels, through the crowd that was inspecting rugs, sampling perfumes, bickering over prices. From the corner of my eye, I noticed Karla with her newest boyfriend, trailing me at a distance. I passed a boy riding a donkey with a sign *Yankee Doodle* around its neck, and a bearded conjurer balancing an egg on his nose. I passed dozens of open booths lining both sides of a narrow street containing Arabs carving ostrich eggs, pulling taffies, sewing tents, until I approached a booth defined by tapestries for three walls enclosing a Turkish rug for a floor. The area contained six small round tables, each holding a coffee urn on a brass tray, with a half-dozen demitasse cups filigreed with gold.

"Hi, you young thief!" shouted Karla, suddenly at my side.

On Sol Bloom's table the coffee urn had been removed to occupy a nearby stand. In its place, bubbled a hookah, its long stem resting its tip in the mouth of a dark-haired young man with deepset black eyes. He lounged with one booted limb bent over an arm of a chair. An Algerian girl's arms encircled his neck as she leaned behind him. Girls on each side begged for the mouthpiece of the pipe. Mr. Bloom's eyes focused on me.

"Here's another complaint for you." Karla shook her crop at him. "Another complaint about another exhibit not built."

After drawing on the mouthpiece of the waterpipe, Mr. Bloom placed the tip into his vest pocket, irritating the two girls at his side, who stalked away as they pulled the hands of the third girl who still clung to his neck.

"Karlotta, my beauty, do you mean the Tower of Babel sixty stories tall? No? Do you mean the mountain range suspended in air containing a Swiss restaurant with orchestra? No? Then how about—"

Reaching his table, I shouted over the din of the bazaar. "Destruction of Pompeii!" I yanked Karla's fez from my head and slammed it on the table. "How can I get educated if Pompeii is not there to be destroyed?"

Mr. Bloom studied my face with intensity of an artist. "My beauty, I have not had the honor." He took the arms of the girl from around his neck, shooed her away and stood up, shorter than me and bowed. "Mr. and Mrs. Bloom's favorite son Solomon, at your service."

He oozed romance.

"We're wasting time," Karla yelled. "You promised me Palace of Moors." Mr. Bloom raised his black-eyebrows, as he kept his eyes on me. "Would a palace of illusions make up for Pompeii, my nameless beauty?"

Karla circled the table to Mr. Bloom's side, planting a kiss atop his head while extracting the mouthpiece from his vest pocket, and sucking on it. I wondered what it tasted like.

Mr. Bloom roared with laughter. "Karlotta, your passion will be the death of you."

My cheeks flushed. "My answer to you about Palace of Moors is yes, but only if you guide us." Why was I being so forward? The old Alessandra wouldn't even be here.

Taking back the mouthpiece from Karla, he blew on it while pulling her onto his lap.

"See here," said Hermes, "I don't fancy your attitude, Mr. Salmon. It's too—too New York."

"San Francisco, old chap," Mr. Bloom said, without taking his glare off me. "My answer, young debutante is—thank you—no." He sucked on the mouthpiece. "Have to finish whatever I start."

Hermes pulled on my hand, dragging me away from Mr. Bloom's table. After a few steps, I broke away and returned, retrieving the fez. As I left, I bumped into Karla's newest boyfriend who stood with arms folded, his face looking as if he had been munching a tasty peach, but had just swallowed the pit. "I'm told to wait here."

"I'll be your guide," Hermes said, straightening the fez on my head. "Palace of Moors directly across. Alessandra, what's gotten into you?"

Taking Hermes' arm, we dodged a riderless camel, its tail like a spear, grasped by a screaming Arab boy scuffing up sandy surf with his bare heels. When we reached the Palace, Hermes searched for entrance fee as Mr. Bloom's voice bellowed in my ear. "Guests of mine, Achmet." Mr. Bloom tapped the ticket taker with the riding crop I had first seen in Karla's hand. "Allow my guests to pass." I stared at him in awe.

As we paused at the roped gate, Karla joined us and Mr. Bloom said, "Permit your humble servant to impersonate a guide. Palace is calculated to confound the naïve Occidental."

The three of us followed Mr. Bloom into the Hall of Optical Illusions, amid aromas of burning wax and smoky incense filling the semi-darkness. Poppies and lotus blossoms seducing my nostrils, I nearly lost my balance on the lumpy carpets covering the sand. My throat felt dry and scratchy as sandpaper. Feeling dizzy, I reached out my hand to steady myself and gripped an aisle rope. Tugging on it, hand over hand, I stumbled along, but I started to hum.

"Behold, the Hall of Magic Mirrors!" Mr. Bloom announced. I stopped, breathless, expecting to see mirrors, but instead saw an Arabian oasis moistened in the moonlight by fountains cooling a desert that stretched for miles. Enchanted, I recalled my own garden at home with its gazebo. Mr. Bloom snapped the riding crop against his leather boot. Immediately, garden, fountains and desert disappeared. I envied his power.

In its stead arose the interior of a Moorish Palace with arched doorways, concave ceiling studded with jewels, and in the center of the marble floor, a heap of gold coins spilling from an open treasure chest. "A million dollars should impress even my Astor Street friends," Mr. Bloom said. Ordinarily, the sight of financial independence for Father would have delighted me, but instead I recoiled at the image of so many gaudy coins vomiting from the mouth of the chest. Seeing my expression, Mr. Bloom snapped his crop again, the crack echoing off mosaic walls. The lights went off. When they come on again, the million dollars had vanished. Hermes groaned. I laughed, thrilled to be in this world of illusion.

I heard music of the Marseillaise as ceiling lights revealed a guillotine that dominated the center of a French courtyard. A woman in a low-cut Empire gown faced us as she knelt at the base of the guillotine. She studied the huge blade as it rose inch by inch high above her head. It paused at the apex with a loud click, shining like a giant cleaver.

I rubbed the back of my neck while Karla's eyes narrowed to slits. Hermes picked his nose with his little finger. Mr. Bloom lit a cigar. What riveted my attention was the woman waiting beneath the guillotine. She possessed a calmness I understood, as she contemplated the end of life as she knew it. A sign to one side of the platform read: *The Execution of Marie Antoinette.* The pensive lady offered the nape of her neck, long crimson hair cascading over her head like a rivulet of lava. Drums rolled, and French music swelled for so long it seemed forever before the blade moved at all. Then it shivered down a few inches, and stopped. A woman in the audience screamed, begging the blade not to fall. I grabbed my throat with both hands, and willed the blade to descend, knowing its fall would be fatal but necessary. The drums and music ceased. A man in the audience cursed. Then the silver blade trembled, and descended in a hungry rush. At the very second it struck the bowed neck of Marie Antoinette, Mr. Bloom snapped his whip, and lights went out.

Instead of witnessing the lady being decapitated, we now stood within a Greek Temple. Surrounded by seven marble columns, a statue of a young girl was being chiseled by an old Greek sculptor. Music from a lyre caressed my ear. I stared so intently at the statue of the young girl that her bare limbs seemed to tremble, her bosom seemed to heave in controlled passion. She reminded me of myself when I was a ballet dancer. I would pause for a brief moment of well earned rest denied by Edith's inhuman standards of perfection. After a final click of mallet against chisel, the sculptor stepped back and discarded his tools, casting them to one side. The clang of their crashing onto the marble floor startled the young statue into fluttering one eyelid. The spellbound audience gasped as the sculptor shook his head in bewilderment. Then he approached her face, and breathed on it. Her other eyelid fluttered and, as the sculptor took one step backward, the statue opened her small mouth and—yawned. A wide lingering self-satisfied yawn.

Hermes whooped out loud, totally embarrassing me, and breaking the spell.

I found myself applauding Galatea's small gesture of independence. Her slight blush revealed her yawn as an involuntary act of nature. Nodding my head vigorously in her support, I shook my fist at Pygmalion, shouting he should have taken the place of Marie Antoinette. Mr. Bloom's riding crop cracked. In a blink, the scene disappeared.

While the rest of our group lingered, Mr. Bloom embraced me. I yielded to him as he led me out of the Hall of Optical Illusions into a narrow winding corridor. Energized, I felt fully alive for the first time, until he released me at the sound of Karla's heels clicking in the hallway of full-length mirrors. Different shapes reflected images of our bodies. Stunned as if spied upon by voyeurs, I froze.

In the torch-lit maze of mirrors, I found myself accused by reflections of Alessandra, in a concave mirror that swallowed her body, a convex mirror that ballooned her body, a cracked mirror that splintered her body, a rippling mirror that snaked her body.

Feeling faint, I looked about me. Karla kissed a convex mirror that enlarged her face, while Hermes punched a cracked mirror, bragging he had broken it. Mr. Bloom fenced his own reflection with the riding crop. I shut my eyes and stumbled farther down the corridor of mirrors, desperate to escape counterfeits of myself.

Opening my eyes, I found an emergency exit and shoved my hip against it three times before I tumbled outside, falling on my face in the sand. For a long moment, I lay motionless as the statue. When I opened my mouth I spat out sand, but so thankful was I to have escaped the Palace of Moors with its illusions I felt like kissing it.

"Oy! Don't leave," shouted Mr. Bloom from the opened emergency door. "Next is our flight to the moon, the assassination of Lincoln, then Suez Canal—"

As if awakening from a trance, I rose and clutched my knees to regain balance. I stood shaking like a spent mountain climber. In front of me, Bedouins on their small Arabian steeds fought with curved swords against French Foreign Legionaires on a mock battlefield. Rifles cracked, and camels squealed around me, as I ran over a broken sign, half buried in the sand, *Wild East Show.*

Somewhere behind me, I heard Hermes shout, "Alessandra, wait! How can I protect you, if you don't need me?"

At the sound of Hermes' voice I ran faster dodging burros, sedan chairs, and crowds of tourists, until I made my way to the center walk. On the street of Cairo, I passed two muscular wrestlers, attired only in vests and loin cloths, who upended a table overthrowing a fortune teller along with a bride and groom in wedding garb. A rope charmer dropped his flute, collapsing a vertical rope, causing a naked boy to drop upon the wrestlers' shoulders.

"Forget them!" shouted Mr. Bloom, grasping my waist, as he pointed toward the Egyptian Temple. "Inside there is something interesting." At the entrance we paused to collect our breaths. "This exhibit. A knock-out draw for me in Paris four years ago," Bloom said. I followed him into the Temple hand in hand where smells of olive oil soaked into my pores, my ears detecting lispings of unseen snakes echoing from high ceilings with ornate draperies. Catching up to me, Hermes poked my shoulder as he pointed at the semi-circular stage lined with richly colored divans displaying Egyptian dancing girls. Hermes whistled through his fingers. Karla sneezed as she rejoined our group. On each side of the stage, beaded curtains scarcely veiled dressing rooms of female dancers smoking cigarettes and sucking on mouthpieces of water pipes. I wanted to join them.

A sweating usher in red pantaloons guided us to straight-backed chairs at the front of the theatre. We sat amongst a crowd writhing in their seats like snakes. Behind the performers on each side of the stage hung huge mirrors, ten foot long and five foot high that reflected the audience. The mirrors allowed our images to become participants on stage. As we sat, Mr. Bloom waved at his reflection in the mirror. Next to him, I was disappointed that only half my face and half my fez were reflected by the edge of the mirror. I straightened half my fez.

Hermes sidled close to me like Cerby and nuzzled my cheek. I shivered, and turned my head away. As an amber spotlight glinted on the beaded curtain of the women's dressing room, the audience quieted, and leaned forward as a bass drum throbbed in the dark. Slithering between the beaded strands, fingernails of exotic hues appeared ringed with jewels and gemstones. Two slim hands parted the curtain to release a long naked limb to the audible delight of the audience. Around one ankle, gold bells tinkled. On the other ankle, silver bells jingled. Applause erupted from the audience led by me.

"Hoochie, koochie!" Hermes shouted.

Mr. Bloom snapped his riding crop against the back of the empty chair in front of him. "*Danse du Ventre*," he snarled, opening a black leather flask as he glanced at Hermes. "Sir, have you no class?"

"Belly dancer?"

During their exchange, I lost track of the lady's entrance. Now she possessed the center of the stage with the authority of the Queen of Sheba. The spotlight illuminated limbs only to hide them, an elbow appearing only to recede as a shoulder teased. The undulation of her hips began to rotate so slowly and so luxuriously it mesmerized me. Some in the audience stood, until cautioned to sit by roving ushers, while dozens of long beaded necklaces clinked against the dancer's bosom. Her nude navel glittered with an embedded ruby. The pace of the stringed music increased as the dancer spread her knees, and simulated to me riding an invisible pony. My mind ridiculed the image, but my heart responded to the erotic motion. She embodied passion.

I whispered to Mr. Bloom. "Her name. I must have her name." I memorized her each and every move.

"Fatima," he said without taking his eyes off her. "Fatima." He gripped his crop with both hands. As tempo increased, Fatima swayed in circles, gyrating around the stage, her waist-long black hair whipping her body into a frenzy. The orchestra rose to its feet. At the height of excitement men and women in the audience stood and danced with their own reflections in the huge stage mirror. Hermes whistled. Karla jumped to her feet, knocking over her chair, and yelling an Indian War whoop. My blood surged like Fatima's. I felt boundaries melting inside me, awakening a volcano of passion that made me squirm. Mr. Bloom offered me his flask. Shaking my head, I reached for it. I sipped a slight taste of coffee and a heavy taste of morphine, much stronger than my cordial. As I started a second sip, Karla tore the flask away from my hand but I didn't care. I found myself on my feet, swaying to the music, matching Fatima grind for grind. I closed my eyes, imagining myself bathing nude in an Egyptian pool under palm trees, my silver body melting in the moonlight.

Fevered applause brought me back to the present moment. Karla embraced me, and shouted in my ear. "We're sisters at last!" She kissed me as we laughed together. Then Karla tried to out hoochie-koochie me, but I matched her bump for bump.

When I heard Hermes snort, I ignored him as he headed for the exit. Mr. Bloom threw away the handle of the broken crop, and hugged me. "I'm famished!" he shouted. "Are you hungry, my beauty?"

Karla dived between us. "I'm always famished. Where to? "

I stepped back, dabbing my throbbing forehead with a handkerchief.

"The Hungarian Café." Mr. Bloom announced. After a final glance at Fatima, he herded us Aultman sisters outside into the moist night air.

Unbidden thoughts circled my head. Why did Fatima excite me so much? Was her dance my dance of freedom?

We reached the nearby outdoor Hungarian Café before I realized I had not even glanced at Father's old Vienna. Karla's boyfriend trotted behind us. After reaching the café, Karla motioned for me to accompany her to the comfort station. I shook my head, but as she spun on her heel, I reconsidered.

After a minute I excused myself, and sidled among the little round tables occupied by couples holding hands.

Pushing through the black door, labeled with a carved red snake coiled into a W, I entered the smoke-filled room. Perched sideways on a stool before a large heart-shaped mirror, Karla peered up at me without lifting her head, displaying the evil eye. For a long minute we stared into each other's hearts. Karla's yellow skirt was hoisted to her waist, exposing her leg with a long needle inserted into her inner thigh and pointing toward her heart.

Alone with Karla, I inhaled smoke curling from the thin Turkish cigar dangling from her purple lips. The pupils of her eyes loomed large. Unblinking, they mesmerized me with her animal magnetism. Speechless, I felt my mouth sag open, eliciting a hard cackle from Karla.

"You believe we're sisters, right?" Karla said. "Don't answer. You'll faint." Then she purred as she spoke to the needle protruding from her flesh. "Little needle should I give your twin to Stir? I've been saving it just for her. Alessandra needs her very own 'H' for heaven."

Gulping and choking on smoke, I stared down at Karla as if from a great cliff. Teetering on my toes, I felt dizziness engulf me. Tapping my forehead, I tried to awaken Mother's voice. No voice came. Shaking my head, I focused on Karla's penciled eyebrows as she awaited my response. Is this where Karla's way would lead me?

At last, the door to the comfort station swung in as a gypsy woman entered, wearing a peasant blouse like Aunt Ashford.

Before the door closed, I escaped outside into the clean night air, bumping into a succession of tables as I struggled to retain my dignity.

As I sat down, Hermes arrived, arm in arm with Karla's boyfriend, who introduced himself as Lucas. Hermes blew me a kiss. Deciding to ignore him, I watched the Gypsy violinists stroll among the tables, weaving romantic music like an invisible net over the customers. As they finished, Karla rejoined us, sitting next to Mr. Bloom who ordered food for all.

"Yogurt and chapatti. That my friends means unleavened bread, cake, flour, water, salt—and waitress—don't forget thick foamy Hungarian beer!"

In the middle of our second helping, a floor show began. Four male gypsies with bandanas of black, red, yellow, and white leaned their heads together in what appeared, to me, a mockery of a barbershop quartet. However, their voices blended so melodiously they captivated me with their strange language. I shared my admiration with Hermes, who held my hand.

While the other diners applauded polite approval, I gave a standing ovation. As I sat down I was shocked to see Sol laughing at me. Scribbling something on a paper napkin, he passed it to Karla who read it, and cackled before handing it to Lucas who shrugged. Out of turn, Hermes reached for it, spilling Lucas' beer. Without reading, Hermes handed it to me on the palm of his hand. Some of the words were fading in the foam. The first line of the gypsies' song read: "We have journeyed from far countree." By staring at the wet napkin, and moving my lips I made out the second line: "By horses, camels, and boats." I held it over the table candle for the third line: "Please invade our far countree." Taking a deep breath, and smiling for the expected humorous punch line I placed the drying napkin on the palm of my hand, and traced my thumb beneath the words: "We take—pleasure—cutting—your throats!"

Trapped on the Wheel

I pushed my chair back from the table, and dropped my hands to my side staring straight ahead at nothing. The paper napkin stuck no matter how hard I tried to shake it off. Finally, I coiled my hand into a fist, balling the lyrics into a spit ball that I tossed at Mr. Bloom. As I pushed away the chapatti dish and Hungarian beer, I sensed Hermes arising with me at the same time. We passed the tables of smiling tourists who watched us with innocent eyes.

Free of the café, Mr. Bloom bid Hermes and me adieu. He hurried to the Brazilian Music Hall with Karla clinging to him, while Lucas hesitated before tagging along.

Abandoned in front of the military encampment, Hermes and I stood, listening to a bugle playing taps. We observed soldiers stowing equipment for the night. As we wandered toward the Bedouins, their horses were startled by the swoosh of the sliding ice sled, zooming back toward us along the mile-length Midway. Grateful for the distraction of the deafening roar, I ran to the ticket office, followed by Hermes.

"Wag your tails, folks!" shouted the ticket seller, "Final ride tonight."

After Hermes bought our tickets, we squeezed into the last two seats of the long sleigh-like vehicle, runners hovering in the air over water and ice at the bottom of the wooden trough. Beneath us engines trembled water below, raising steam from the ice. In front of us, people pounded their hands on the side for the ride to start. As the engines revved, I stared along the track lit with electric bulbs, rippling like a dragon's backbones.

The brakeman shouted, "Brakes off!" Hermes pressed his blood-brother thumb against mine.

The sliding railway jolted forward, throwing back our heads, and making us scream with delight. Everything became a blur. Flashing past us like a smudged mural were Hungarian Café, St. Peter's, Ferris Wheel, Palace of Moors. Hermes hugged me. Then he turned my chin to his, and kissed me. After thirty seconds, the ice railway slid to a stop with a shudder.

The view moved too fast for me to comprehend, sucking my brain empty. Staggering from the sleigh, I almost fainted from vertigo. I laughed at my loss of control. Turning to share my feelings with Hermes, I could not find him. The sleigh was unloading from its last trip when I heard a hacking sound next to the ticket booth of the Illinois Central Railroad.

Searching, I finally found Hermes doubled over in a corner. "Time for home, Romeo," I said, helping him to straighten as I guided him to the ticket booth. "You can send for your father's car tomorrow." Purchasing our two ducats, I allowed the train conductor to secure two seats, letting him think Hermes was inebriated instead of dizzy.

Inside the train car, I felt relieved when Hermes snoozed in the seat beside me. When it seemed safe, I started to visit the train's comfort room but stopped, remembering the image of Karla with the needle inserted into her thigh, inviting me to imitate her. As I was returning to my seat, the train started to pull out of the station. Hermes was missing. Glancing out the window, I spotted him on the platform staggering in a circle. Racing to the exit door, I was restrained by the conductor.

Over his outstretched arm, I watched Hermes shrink in the distance as the train pulled away from the station.

I sat in Hermes' empty place and closed my eyes, imaging everything shrinking, the Hungarian Café, the Palace of Moors, Street of Cairo—all shrinking inside Karla's needle.

However, the Ferris Wheel in my heart did not shrink. Instead it towered and glowed, revolving like a new world churning inside me. But why?

Chapter Ten

The
BULLET
and the
PLOW

The Next Day

Hunger awakened me early in the morning, but not for food. Midway had left my body stimulated, but my heart empty. Karla's way was not mine after all. Shuddering at my encounter with her in the comfort station, I realized something else was also hungry—bed bugs biting my cheek. I must have screamed as I struggled out of bed because Odette hobbled into my bedroom.

With one glance, she took in my predicament and, turning on her heel, left the room, only to return in a few minutes lugging a kettle of steamy water. Apologizing in Creole, Odette set it down on the floor with one hand, while with the other tugged at the cap of the nearest bedpost. It proved reluctant, perhaps from rust.

Hopping onto Mother's rocker, I scratched the bites on my ankles. Why is becoming an enlightened lady such a struggle, Mother? Was it the same for you?

Odette, using both hands and planting her feet like a wrestler, gripped the cap again, wriggling it several times. Then, sucking in her breath, she yanked the cap off the bed post. Placing it like a chipped coffee mug into the large pocket of her yellow apron, Odette lifted the kettle with a grunt and, standing on her toes, poured boiling hot water down the hollow tube. She repeated this most welcome task on the other three bedposts. Bugs crawled out of the open tops and scurried down the sides.

I pulled my feet off the floor. Mother, was Ireland like this?

Odette flapped her apron at the posts, scattering bugs onto the floor, whereupon she stomped a well-aimed sole of one shoe, dispatching bugs with a series of click-click-click that delighted my ears, and almost seemed to heal my bites.

Sitting cross-legged, I rocked, feeling Mother's presence as I clasped her acorn pendant. Why did I have to make decisions on my own?

After sweeping the remnants of the crushed bugs, and depositing them into the coal scuttle next to the unlit fireplace, Odette knelt and reached under my bed to drag out the chamber pot. At arm's length, she escorted it out of the room. Maggie entered to remove the empty kettle, while Em appeared with a broom to sweep under the bed. My stomach rumbled. I slipped my bare feet into my tam o'shanter slippers that had once warmed Mother's feet, and waved away Odette as she brought me a snack of suet pudding. I asked her instead to bring my remembrance book, and canvas bag containing souvenirs from the fair.

After she left, I washed my face and hands in the lava bowl next to my dresser with a medallion of perfumed soap. Patting my face with the monogrammed pink towel that Hermes swore he had not stolen from the Woman's Building, I examined my cheek in the vanity mirror above the basin, grateful to discover no trace of bites. I needed to sort things out.

Refreshed, I wrapped Mother's comforter around my shoulders, and padded over to the window to gaze a few moments at branches of oak tree beckoning me outside.

Rejecting its invitation I clambered onto my bed, propping my back against the brass headboard, as Odette returned with my book and bag. Positioning book on lap, she then placed the bag upright between my arm and the wall.

I fingered the diamond-shaped red stitching that formed the A with its mirror image beneath it. With the stitching worn at the edges of the A, I felt that if I teased even one strand too far my initials would unravel totally.

Straightening the remembrance book on my lap, I noticed several photos had worked free when Odette transported it. With my ring finger I slid out the first one—a round sepia of Father, in his lieutenant's uniform as he stood at attention, grasping the tall spokes of his artillery cannon wheel. As I released the picture, it stuck to the dance card from my birthday ball. I did not have to look to know it was blank.

Suddenly, I realized I had no programs from performances of Karla and Aunt Ashford to make my remembrance book complete. Setting it aside, I eased out of bed and shuffled to the hallway, then down back stairs to Aunt Ashford's room on the third floor. I was glad for the distraction.

Knowing she slept so lightly relieved me of any guilt in disturbing her. One knock provoked a response of "Entre." Opening the door, I whispered, "Programs?" I observed Aunt Ashford directing Mrs. Dibbs to add the new Cleopatra cover to her scrapscreen, displaying dozens and dozens of play titles lacquered on both sides on the three panel stand. Next to her, lay a stack of theatre programs awaiting their turn. Whenever in Chicago on tour, she conducted this ritual of chronicling her career, but usually with Uncle Chilton. Standing so close to the scrapscreen, I was filled with awe.

"Close your mouth, my dear," Aunt Ashford said, her hand on the hip of a red corset that molded her figure, more than perfect. Although Karla imitated her, I would not.

I envied her beauty but I wondered if her skirt concealed needle marks. Diverting my glance to the stack of programs, I almost felt sorry for Mrs. Dibbs, who had probably been drafted because of Uncle Chilton's hangover. Mrs. Dibbs avoided my eyes. Aunt Ashford lit a black cigarillo, blowing a perfect smoke ring at the ceiling chandelier. She blew out the wooden match and said to it, "Go ask Karla. That is, if you feel free." Her voice purred like Karla's.

What I did feel was the need for fresh air.

The green cut-glass of our church filtered sunlight, dappling the minister's shoulders with the illusion of green leaves. Lately, I shared the Wetherstones' pew because Father had not attended services since the birthday ball. Karla was not with us, of course. After riding to church in the Wetherstone's carriage, Karla would smile and wander to the new ice cream parlor or to the park, until we emerged after services to join her for lunch at a local restaurant. I envied her freedom. When the services had ended, my questions about changing direction in life were still unanswered. My prayers to Mother must have been faulty. Should I be Father's Lady of the Manor? Hermes'? The fair's wet nurse? Or a student at Harper? Tell me what direction, Mother. Please.

As Hermes left church with his mother and father, I lingered because a young man had detained the reverend from his duty of pressing the flesh of departing parishioners. Obstructing the minister's exit, he said, "Answer me. What if Christ came to Chicago? What would Christ say about the rich people deaf to cries of the poor?"

I moved closer to Rev. Brackenbush while admiring the young man's boldness. I wished I could imitate him.

"Let me go, Mr. Stead. You're a demagogue!"

"Rather a demagogue than an old Brahmin."

What in the world was a Brahmin? I wondered how a word I did not know could sound like an insult.

Hermes came to usher me out like a good brother, but I insisted on watching young Mr. Stead as he flailed his arms, and whispered loudly. "Astor Street is cursed. Haunted by bones of dead Potawatimi. Astor Street is doomed!"

That was exactly how I felt. How could he know? A man with peppery muttonchops bumped into me. "Have you seen my brother?" Before I could reply, he peered over my shoulder and shouted in an English accent, "Will'm, old boy. Time to scat." He waved his arm. "Brother 'erbert 'ere for you. Off to Prairie Avenue we go!"

I was angry he had interrupted Rev. Brackenbush's answer. What if Christ did come? How would he judge Chicago? Oh my Gawd! How would he judge me?

Hermes hustled me outside church to a waiting Edith who embraced me. "What a horrid, horrid man. Accosting our poor minister!" She looked at Seth, who was opening his snuff box. "Why doesn't Mr. Stead just write a book instead? If Christ came to Chicago, indeed!"

"But what if Christ did come?" I heard myself shouting. I glanced at Hermes, who went to his father for a pinch of snuff. Why didn't Hermes feel the same way I did?

Without missing a breath, Edith replied, "Why we'd invite Christ to dinner. Of course." Edith beamed at a gathering crowd listening to her, as if she expected applause. "He certainly wouldn't be as odious as that old cowboy Seth patched up last night." She lowered her voice, and took my arm as she guided me down the church steps. "You know what that old Indian fighter does after Seth set his shoulder? He rides his big horse around our house hooting and blasting both pistols. Then to top it off, he spins his horse in a circle, and flings his white Stetson on top our roof. Who does he think he is?"

"William F. Cody," said Doc Seth.

As we rode home after lunch, I was obsessed by the image of Buffalo Bill's Stetson pitched into the air. That night I dreamed about throwing my own Stetson onto our roof, over and over.

The next day I overheard through the open register that Doc Seth brought complementary tickets to Cyrus he had received from Mr. Cody. After a few jiggers of rum, Father called in Hermes for a handshake all around. They agreed to attend Buffalo Bill's Fourth of July Extravaganza as a group. I accompanied Father, Hermes, Doc Seth and Edith to the show, located outside the gates of the fair. In the Wild West Stadium, we climbed to the upper seats at one end of the large open auditorium.

After we settled in, I took out a pair of new field glasses, Hermes' gift to make up for abandoning me on the train. At first I had refused, until I realized Hermes meant them to replace Father's opera glasses.

Cool on my eyes, they blurred, then focused onto a horseman, whose spotted pony stirred dust in afternoon sunlight. The colors adjusted to reveal a red megaphone protruding beneath a gold sombrero in the center of the parade ground. The rider's pony stopped, pawing at clay, anxious to begin. "Welcome to Buffalo Bill's Wild West Extravaganza and his Congress of Rough Riders." His high-pitched voice seemed too thin, coming from a stocky figure.

I envied the vaquero's outfit of black velvet with scarlet sash, silver buttons glittering like coins fresh from the bank. "Don't call it a show—it's an Extravaganza."

"If Buffalo Bill's show is so great," Hermes said, stuffing his mouth with Crackerjacks, "Why is it outside the fair?"

Why didn't Hermes read the rest of his guide book for the answer? I felt a restless wind on my cheeks as I noted hundreds of flags, banners, and swags celebrating our national day of birth. Dr. Wetherstone attended to a lady fainted in the heat, while Edith chatted with the woman's children to distract them. Father scanned the stadium crowd with his old opera glasses. Looking for important people from Astor Street? From time to time, he would peek at my new binoculars from Hermes, and bite his lip.

"Welcome the Honorable Colonel William F. Cody— Buffalo Bill to you folks! His bullet claimed the land, so your plow could tame it."

I was anxious to see the man who pitched his Stetson onto our roof, and thought the others in our party would be anxious too. However, I saw Father stoking his pipe, Doc Seth kissing Edith's cheek, and Hermes fumbling with his tripod in the center aisle. I seemed to be the only one in our group listening. A fist fight in the lower stands was halted when the band struck up "The Star Spangled Banner." We all stood, pretending to sing it, but the lyrics were unfamiliar. Reseated, Edith moved next to me and tugged at my sleeve.

"Pay no attention to the parade ground," she said, glancing at my new hat. "Alessandra, that sombrero your father bought you is so fetching, especially the tassel trim. Sets off your cheek bones."

"Gracious of you," I said, squirming.

Edith patted my hand, while on the field a trapper entered in beaver hat, wearing a sign around his neck: *John Jacob Astor.*

"Please look at me," Edith said. My eyes refocused. "I've always thought of you as our daughter. So has Seth. We're hoping poor Hermes' attacks of *petit mal* provoked by those rides on that awful Ferris Wheel will not—"

"Please Edith," I said, feeling uncomfortable. "Let's watch Buffalo Bill."

"How dare that man!" Father shouted. "He's riding Sitting Bull's horse. And after getting him killed."

To me, Buffalo Bill's fringed buckskins, flowing oyster hair and goatee presented the ideal image he actually lived: Indian fighter and entertainer. Using my binoculars, I followed his horse as Bill rode toward the covered box seats, and swept off his Stetson in a salute. Who could warrant such respect?

Focusing quickly, I was astounded to see that perfect face with the blond curls belonging only to Aunt Ashford. She waved her open pink fan, and curtsied to the cheering crowd. I located Uncle Chilton, sitting behind her, as he tugged at her elbow to resume sitting.

"That woman is shameless," Father shouted.

"Actress!" Edith snorted.

The booming voice of Buffalo Bill addressed the crowd from the center of the arena. "Ladies and gentlemen—meet the peerless shootist—maid of western plains—Annie Oakley!"

The crowd roared, and I noticed a table holding pistols and rifles of all sizes in the center of the field. Running as on wings, a young girl appeared, young as myself. She ran so fast her cowboy hat flew off. Held by a cord, it bobbed against her long braids as a dozen medals glittered on her chest.

"Little Sure Shot!" shouted Hermes, snapping a photograph. Focusing on her face, I discovered the brownest eyes I'd ever seen, except in a mirror. Reaching the table, she held a rifle in one hand as she threw a ball into the air. She disposed of it with one shot. Then she threw two balls, breaking both. Applause. Pieces scattered on the ground like confetti.

When I pulled my eyes from the lens, Edith was tearing apart her lace handkerchief.

Peering through binoculars again, I saw Annie Oakley grabbing a different rifle. Springing onto a pinto from the right side like an Indian, she galloped around the arena. A male assistant at the table threw six glass balls high into the air. Then Annie did a handspring on the saddle and, while standing, peppered those crystal balls at full gallop. Skidding her pinto to a stop at the table, she reached for a newly loaded repeating rifle and, of all things, a hand mirror. The band played louder as Annie rode toward our end of the field.

Beneath us, she paused and turned her pony toward the table, while she swung herself backward in the saddle. She waved, and winked right at me. Adjusting her rifle with the barrel over her shoulder, she aimed it toward the table, but did not fire. Tilting the mirror in her other hand, she kicked her spurless heels into the flanks of the pinto. Away she galloped, in a cloud of dirt toward the table, as her male assistant threw what appeared to be blue dishes high in the air. Staring into the mirror as she rode, she fired, but missed.

Twenty thousand people groaned as one. But she shifted the mirror and shoot the rifle held backwards over her shoulder, dispatching all the other dishes, while her pony raced lickety-split toward the table. Well, my lands!

Riding through the debris like a flurry of snow, Annie Oakley rode right out an open gate. She stole the show, as far as I was concerned.

However, her male assistant took all the bows. "What's he bowing for?" I shouted, leaping to my feet. "He's just her assistant."

"Alessandra," Hermes said, leaving his camera for a moment and hugging me. "It's all right. He's her husband."

At the word "husband" I looked at Hermes' face. I'd never seen him so happy. Was it the word "husband?" Was this a renewal of hope for us?

"Oh, Sander, I'm so happy."

"Don't be afraid. Share with me."

Hermes whispered in my ear. "Those photographs. Those photos I just took will make Mr. Arnold so happy."

I sat down, shaking my head, allowing Edith to hold my hand. Concerning the horse race among a cowboy, Cossack and Arab, who won? I did not know. In stunned silence among a shouting crowd, I rubbed the palm of my hand that started to ache. Letting my field glasses from Hermes dangle, I wondered if he would notice. He did not. Hermes was back working his camera on a shaky tripod. Edith moved even closer to me.

On the field, pony express riders passed pouches at top speed while flinging themselves onto fresh mounts. But to me, they just came and went. Edith opened her mouth to speak to me, but I wriggled away. "Pardon me, Mrs. Wetherstone, but I need to stretch my limbs."

Excusing myself, I left my row and maneuvered up the crowded center aisle, passing Hermes who was showing a handful of photos to a yellow-haired man. Loosening the runner cord on my sombrero, I wedged through people gawking at the show, until I reached the top of the stands.

At the last rail, I turned my side away from Buffalo Bill, and focused my binoculars on the Ferris Wheel, as it glowed in late afternoon sun. The vision I had experienced at the top of the Ferris Wheel—was it fading away? Why can't I make up my mind?

The cord scratched my throat worse than ever, so I removed the hat entirely, holding it like a purse. Cool breezes caressed my forehead. The back of my mind wondered if Karla was roaming the streets of Cairo with Sol Bloom.

Leaning over the wall, I dangled it by its golden cord until a gust of wind snatched it from my moist fingers. The sombrero tumbled over and over, rising on an updraft, sailing toward the walls of the fair. For a moment, the hat created the illusion of landing on top of the Liberal Arts Building with the big clock. After hovering a few more seconds, it spun like a roulette wheel toward the crown of a tree beneath the stadium. Instinctively, I reached out as if I could control its fate.

"Don't fall, young lady," a male voice behind me said, "I'll buy you another."

I stared at the hat, seeing it disappear as it landed in the branches. "It really wasn't mine anyway," I lied, tossing my head and flipping my braids, as I turned to face a yellow haired man who had been talking to Hermes. His bright gray eyes, pale skin and a tie depicting the American flag gave him a comic appearance. When I smiled, he took that as encouragement.

"So glad I'm pleasing you," he said blocking the sun, "permit me to identify myself. Mr. Brickton Pemberton, newsman." He bowed. "Brick to my readers."

I was glad he was attracted to me.

"Alessandra, are you all right, dear?"

For the first time today, I acted eager to see Hermes' mother. "Yes, Edith, quite so," I said, forcing my face to smile.

Taking my elbow, Edith called her husband who, breathing heavily, pursued her up the steps. "Seth, we're strolling down to the Indian concessions under the stands. Do accompany us, dear, at a distance."

I waved for Hermes to follow but he was showing photographs to little children. "Permit me to clear the path for you good folks," volunteered Mr. Pemberton, slipping his notepad into his vest pocket, as he led the way through the crowd to the exit.

While the three of us clambered down the stairs, Mr. Pemberton chatted like a magpie. "No more progressive an educator than Buffalo Bill. More reality than all this imaginary Romeo and Juliet business taught by mealy-mouthed spinsters."

Pausing at first landing, Edith faced Mr. Pemberton. Her voice carried a knife's edge. "Sir, we would not dream of keeping you from your appointed rounds."

"Ah, have no fear. Shortly I shall interview Captain Jack Crawford backstage."

We continued down the stairs, passing a series of large posters wrinkled upon the walls: Buffalo Bill rescuing a white woman tied to a stake with fire licking her feet; Sitting Bull shooting an arrow piercing the driver of Deadwood Stage; Buffalo Bill scalping Chief Red Hand in revenge for General Custer.

Reaching ground floor, we passed a bullet-scarred cabin with a sign: *Authentic site of execution of Sitting Bull.* Mr. Pemberton dropped back to whisper in my ear, "Progress—must kill—its parents." He seemed to think it was important.

Above us, the stands vibrated from stomping feet. Cheers, muffled by canvas walls, rolled like thunder. Reaching the concession tables, I was surprised to discover they were attended by women arrayed in beads and animal skins. The women possessed high cheekbones and serene black eyes.

Rows upon rows of tables were piled high with beaver hats, pottery, weapons. Edith tried on beaver hats that kept messing her hairdo. I ran to the table of Indian dolls, miniature tepees, moccasins. I tried on several moccasins, trying to walk pigeon-toe, but they were all too small. Even if I wanted, I couldn't follow Mr. Pemberton as he waved goodbye, heading to the dressing rooms, no doubt.

One table in particular captured my attention: clay pigeons. Were these the objects Annie Oakley shot when she rode backwards while looking into a mirror? Through hand gestures, I asked an Indian maiden behind a table if I could examine the clay pigeons. She nodded.

The blue saucer, four inches across, one inch deep, felt strangely thin and light in my fingers. Protruding from its side was a flat handle of iron, one inch long. Next to the stack of clay pigeons lay the traps. With gestures, I asked how the trap worked. She blushed, and stepped aside for an old squaw who had guarded the cash box. Without words, she demonstrated by touching the small arm, a string wound tight around a short upright column. At arm's end, some apparatus held the handle. The old squaw set the trap by forcing it back with gnarled fingers, securing the arm with a drop catch. She studied my eyes if she should go further.

I smiled as I looked for Edith, and saw her posing for a black silhouette cut-out. Why didn't she appreciate these women?

The old squaw pulled the line attached to the catch, releasing the arm to spring a clay pigeon into the air, if one had been attached. Her crooked finger pointed to a gear joint in the middle of the support column, enabling the trap to be set for any altitude. She explained in broken English that placing the concave side of the saucer face down, the clay pigeon would float farther and faster than crystal balls. However, the flight would be at the mercy of any chance wind. Its fate would be unpredictable even to the shootist.

My heart longed to buy clay pigeons and a trap, but my mind realized these objects belonged to the world of Annie Oakley. Instead, I purchased a color-tinted lithograph of

Annie in costume, her long hair loose this time, caressing her shoulders, her beige dress buttoned to the collar and secured with a white star broach. She wore no earrings, unnecessary really, and her eyes peered straight at me, as if giving permission for me to own it. Annie's hat sat back from her forehead, divided by a curled forelock. A clay pigeon trap lay at Annie's right side. Annie reminded me of Mother at eighteen.

Edith poked my elbow to show off an Indian shawl draped about her shoulders. She sashayed in a circle displaying both her slim waist and the black silhouette of profile she held next to her face. The two faces were both Edith. "It is I, don't you think?" She affected a mock high society Astor Street falsetto. "Alessandra, don't laugh that hard."

I laughed so much I started to cry. Edith hugged me, and I buried my face into her shoulder, imagining Mother's photograph in my room with her protective arm around me.

On a sudden a pony rode up to our table, sliding to a stiff-legged stop within inches of my shoulder. Its spotted flanks quivered as I peered up at an Indian warrior, full-bonneted, with painted face peering down at the old squaw who had shown me the clay pigeons. With fierce eyes, he stared arrows at her. Then he winked, and tossed a small leather bag that clinked when the woman caught it against her bosom. "Win!" the warrior grunted. With a curt nod, he heeled his pony backing up, turning, and loping toward the opening to arena grounds, its hooves kicking up miniature explosions of clay.

The old squaw's expression never changed. Reaching back to a buffalo hide, she removed it to reveal a shotgun on top of a treasure chest. Cradling the shotgun and lifting the lid, she laid the leather money pouch side by side with dozens of others. Then closing the lid, she replaced the shotgun with the buffalo hide covering it. I wanted to be one of these Indian women.

"Where is our warrior off to now?" I asked myself aloud.

"To procure Deadwood stage a-gain," proclaimed a Welsh lancer, walking past. Pausing, he touched his cap that made him resemble a bell boy. "With your permission, missy, that native son who almost rode you down double timed to be shot by your Billy Buffalo. All with your permission of course."

With a discreet nod, I grabbed Edith's elbow, and almost stepped into the hoop of a lasso twirled by a Mexican caballero skipping in and skipping out. Edith pointed to a husky cowboy shoeing his horse by holding the hoof between his knees, while I felt attracted to a huge framed map of the world tour of Buffalo Bill. Above the map, a banner proclaimed: *Freedom of the Trail—prairie to palace—163,000 miles.* On the protective glass, I saw my own reflection.

Edith's voice interrupted. "Are you hypnotized by that silly map?" She patted my shoulder. "What's happening to my little ballerina?"

I tried to answer, but what could I say? The aroma of lilies, from an opening in the back of the tent, captured my curiosity.

"Alessandra, we need to talk soon. For now, let's return to our seats." Edith tugged at my sleeve. "Seth must have gotten himself lost again."

My curiosity drew me to an open flap at the back of the tent. Ignoring Edith's plea to return, I approached a young lady dressed in a Parisian gown of royal blue. She wore her long auburn hair combed back, tied with blue ribbons. Turning a page in the book resting upon her lap, she glanced up revealing the brown eyes I had studied earlier in my binoculars. Her eyes said to me, "You are there and I am here, so be it." They pierced my very soul.

I felt my wrist being tugged by Edith. She guided me to a stump nearby. Placing her torn lace handkerchief upon the surface, she gestured for me to sit.

Muffled explosions from the outdoor arena celebrating the Fourth of July made my body recoil. Gasping for breath, I tilted toward the stump, sitting down with an awkward thump. I peered into my palms, and watching them tremble as if with a life of their own. I stroked both my cheeks. They felt numb. Edith placed into my hands the ivory choker she had removed from my throat to help me breathe. Studying the choker, I realized it resembled a tiny white buffalo. My fingertips squeezed the choker as my palms started aching again. Dropping the choker, my hands grasped my knees, squeezing until my fingernails bit into my kneecaps so I would not scream.

Chapter Eleven

COLD FIRE

The Next Day

*G*yrating in my nightmare, a tornado twirled my doll house beyond control, blowing out small doors and stain-glass windows, whipping flames from my candelabra to ignite draperies, furniture and little portraits of Father and Mother. Around the corner on Astor Street, the Wetherstone mansion lay sheathed in ice, its shingles glittering in a snowstorm freezing all doors and blinding all windows. I knelt betwixt and between with one side of my body scorched, the other side frozen.

I awoke. Sitting up to gather my wits, I retrieved Nellie Bly's book from beneath my haunches. Dog-eared and moist, the words were faint, but I knew them by heart, from reading myself to sleep.

Last night after Buffalo Bill's, our party had dined at Henrici's, where Hermes and I agreed to share a ride today in the Captive Balloon. Hermes had an assignment to photograph the fair from a high altitude. At first, he refused my accompanying him. He labeled me a certified coward of heights, which was true, but so what? I could wear a blindfold to prevent vertigo.

I thumbed Nellie Bly's book with my gold rope ring, just like Nellie herself, searching for my favorite parts I had already marked. "What agony of suspense and patience I suffered last night." Nellie always described my feelings perfectly. "The question is, do you want to do it?" If Nellie Bly was brave enough to go around the world, why should I be afraid to go up in a Captive Balloon? "Life is very sweet. The thought of death is the only thing that causes me unhappiness." I felt the same way as Nellie. The only quote I disagreed with was, "Wasting precious hours, I lay outside the gates of hope." I had plenty of hope! Nellie had extracted the truth that girls can do whatever boys can do. Her Maxim, as she called it, was "Energy rightly applied, and directed, will accomplish everything." I found myself humming, and then singing softly the lines to a familiar ditty. "Nellie Bly, Nellie Bly / Never, never sigh / Never bring the teardrop / To the corner of your eye."

After a hasty shower bath avoiding using yoke and tub seat, I decided to luxuriate being dried off by Odette with my favorite unbleached Turkish towels. Then, dressing in my bicycle outfit, I wolfed down a light breakfast of oatmeal, berries, and coffee.

Awaiting Hermes on the stone steps in the back area near the kitchen, I heard the real reason he allowed me to come with him today: the flipflapping of baseball cards he had attached to the wheel sprockets of his new partner cycle. It bumped across the prairie between his house and ours. As he slid to a stop at our bottom steps, I leaped to my feet, and hopped backward. Amidst clods of mud and grass, Hermes almost pitched headfirst over the handle bar of his tandem bicycle.

Ignoring my objection, we detoured to Mr. Arnold's to pick up his camera equipment before securing our destination, the gondola of the Captive Balloon.

With Hermes displaying his credentials from Mr. Arnold, we cut to the front of the line. My enjoyment was tempered by the white handkerchief Hermes placed over my eyes. However, the crosswinds of Midway were too strong, and the blindfold escaped to the freedom of the air. Rising, falling, and rising above the outstretched wings of the Chinese Theatre, the would-be blindfold undulated as smooth as Fatima's hips. It resembled a white flag of surrender. The word rolled about my tongue a hundred times so intensely I could chew upon its syllables. Sur-ren-der. I surrendered my attempts to please people.

The gondola of the balloon, tethered to a cable, was finally emptied and waiting for us. The grinding of the winch strained against the winds.

The attendant peered at my expression, and frowned. "You can't control no wind, young lady." He opened the little door in the gondola as it hovered two feet above the take-off zone.

"Sorry to be tardy," a man said, patting my back. As I turned, he passed me, and leaped into the gondola with a small basket while flashing his press pass at the attendant. The latecomer looked directly at me. "How many times do I have to introduce myself?"

"Oh, Mr. Pemberton, you do surprise me."

"From your face, I can see young Wetherstone neglected sharing some facts with you." He scowled at Hermes, and smiled at me, while reaching out his arm to escort me up. However, Hermes swung his camera case, and clambered aboard. Mr. Pemberton then assisted me.

"Let's go people, it's cast-off time!" the attendant shouted. Our big basket swayed, bounced down and up twice and came to rest. "Oh, don't forget, people, it's a twenty-minute ride. You'll be safe because we've got your tail nailed to that there cement anchor." He snapped shut the door, and triple locked it. "Be sure to wave at those observers in the nearby Ferris Wheel. They like that."

The line of people behind us rumbled and cursed.

"If youse upchuck, deposit in bucket."

Above our heads, the balloon's envelope filled with fiery gases. The attendant adjusted dials. I gripped the waist-high gondola and imagined I was sailing on the Columbus. The heavy network of ropes webbing the surface of balloon slowly slipped away, a fishing net releasing its catch. The grinding of cables reminded me of the car on the Ferris Wheel.

As we rose above the fair, I squinted between my fingers, and saw for the first time the Dahomey African Village located directly across. Hermes shouted, "Alessandra, see that war dance? Those men look dangerous, but they'll give me a great photograph."

To please him I should have looked at them, but instead, I shut my eyes. Pemberton laughed, leaning over the side of the basket. "Don't listen to him, miss. Those are Amazons. Last year, they fought to a standstill the French Foreign Legion." We rose higher.

"If I look down, I'll get sick."

"Then let me report. The women are dancing, and shooting arrows at wooden Legionnaires. My god, they haven't missed yet."

"What's the secret of their skill?"

"You don't want to know." We kept ascending.

I took a deep breath, opened my eyes, and peered up at flames inside the balloon. "I need to know."

"My headline would read: 'Amazons Amputate Left Breasts.'" He rocked the gondola. "Do you want more?"

"That will do," I said, extracting my binoculars from their case on my belt. Focusing the field glasses, I located Vienna Café, and then the fire station next to it. Peering closer, I discerned a fireman washing the side of a firetruck, one of Karla's boyfriends. What was his name? Oh yes, Kelso. I yelled, and waived at him as our balloon rose higher. I could not avoid staring at his muscular form, nude from the waist up, as he sponge-bathed the torso of the truck with surprising tenderness. I shouted at Hermes. "Take Kelso's photo!" I wondered what Kelso saw in Karla.

"Pemberton, how high will we go?" asked Hermes, changing slides in his camera.

"Hermes, why don't you try to please me for a change?"

"Two thousand feet, old sport," Mr. Pemberton replied taking notes, not looking up. "High enough to observe most of the fair as well as parts of Chicago."

As cable uncoiled, we cleared the top of the Ferris Wheel. Spread before us in the sunlight lay the White City. My binoculars located the art gallery at the North pond, the Wooded Island with those blooming roses, and the Court of Honor. The buildings didn't look so high to me. However, the South pond was hidden from view. I did not look straight down.

"After our trip!" shouted Mr. Pemberton. "You should visit Transportation—I'll drive you." He winked at me. "Holds everything on wheels—from baby carriages to locomotives." Our balloon lurched toward Chicago. "Prepare yourself for a glimpse of the Gray City."

My view was blocked by fog on the lens. Rubbing them on my sleeve, I peered through them again. I shook my head in disbelief as the lens grew foggier.

Mr. Pemberton tapped me on the shoulder. "Not your glasses, my friend," he said. "When all else fails, use your eyes."

A gray cloud hovered before, and beneath us. "We must be frightfully high to be above that cloud," I said.

"Not a cloud, Miss Aultman. That's smoke. Smoke from factories, smoke from coal furnaces, smoke from wooden houses on fire."

"Imagine living every day inside that gray curtain," I said, my eyes smarting, "and beneath that gray blanket you tuck your children goodnight." I coughed, my knees buckling, as I slid to sit on the floor of the gondola. Thoughts of poor Terese ever living in such conditions made me sick.

"Your timing, Alessandra, is perfect." Mr. Pemberton said, crouching over a small wicker basket. Undoing the straps he opened the lid, revealing a picnic lunch. Like a gourmet chef, he pointed a silver butter knife at the contents. "Eggs warm, beef cold, chicken sliced." He pulled out a small pouch and smiled. "Ice crushed." He touched another pouch. "Ice cream, strawberry only. It's my favorite."

The surprise distracted me. "Hermes, put down your camera," I said tugging at his knickers. "Partake. No! Take a photograph of Mr. Pemberton's luncheon basket."

"Too busy working," Hermes said.

I turned to Mr. Pemberton, who was concentrating on pouring green liquid into a small pewter tumbler. Finished, he handed the tumbler to me with his gray-gloved hand, although steady, the bright green liquid trembled. I held the cup but he did not release it. Instead, we both embraced it for a long moment. I glanced to see if Hermes noticed, but he was changing lenses. I felt Mr. Pemberton's eyes burning into mine. I released the tumbler and leaned back against the wall of the gondola. Smiling, he handed it to me again, and took out a box of wooden matches. As I held the tumbler with both hands, he struck a match with his thumbnail, cupping the flame in both hands to protect it from the winds, and also to hide it from the attendant who nursed a flask he tried to conceal from us.

"Now, don't panic, Miss Alessandra." Mr. Pemberton guided the yellow flame to the tumbler in my hands. "Green chartreuse," he announced as the liquid burst into flame.

Fascinated, I stared into the orange fire as parts of it turned white, then red. Mr. Pemberton leaned toward my face, his yellow hair brushing against mine. Then he blew out the flame with one breath, transforming it into a whiff of black plume. "After a moment, Miss, it will become cool enough to imbibe." As I held the cup like a chalice, the green chartreuse reflected flames from the balloon above us. I shivered with excitement at such a romantic effort to please me.

Mr. Pemberton prepared a plate of sliced chicken and cheese. Lacing the knife between the prongs of the fork on the same dish, he placed the plate onto my lap. "Try it, Alessandra, and taste the unknown." He poured a chartreuse for himself, igniting another match with his thumbnail, setting his own drink ablaze. Blowing it out quickly, he toasted me, saying, "To the future."

When I sipped, it tasted sweet as warm lime, clearing my nostrils with a pleasant rush. Blinking, I opened my mouth to speak, but no words came forth. I sipped again.

"Try some food," he said.

I placed the tumbler at the edge of the golden dish, separating the interlocked miniature knife and fork. In the center lay a shelled egg, the largest I ever saw. I sliced it, and pronged the delicacies into my mouth. I felt so secure and buoyant.

Mr. Pemberton's voice seemed farther away. "Ice cream, when you're up for it, comes courtesy of Cold Storage Building."

"Sander!" Hermes screamed. "I need you. Really need you."

Startled by Hermes' voice, I imagined him in a jealous fury, lifting me into his arms, and proclaiming undying love. Too late Hermes, I thought, as he swooped down his long arms to my neck. But then, he lifted the strap of the binoculars, taking back his gift.

"I need these to locate the area of the Chicago fire. Great view for a great picture." He flipped the strap over his neck and tugging at it, turned his back on me. I heaved a sigh of relief.

Our balloon swung northward as our attendant pocketed his flask, and consulted his pocket watch.

"I can't make heads or tails where the fire was," Hermes shouted, "Too much smoke. Could you assist me, Sander?"

Mr. Pemberton held the side of the basket to pull himself to his feet, without spilling a drop of his chartreuse. "It's three square miles, young cock," Mr. Pemberton said. "Roosevelt to North Avenue, Halsted to river." He pointed to the slums as he talked. "Perished? Three hundred people. Buildings burnt? Twenty thousand. Homeless? Ninety thousand." He swigged the last of the chartreuse. "Hot damn! That was a great story!"

Pulling a flask from his coat pocket, he unscrewed it with his teeth and refilled his tumbler. "And you know the best headlines? 'Poor Children Trapped,' 'Die in Arms of Mothers,'" he chuckled. "Hot damn! Wish I had covered it!"

I stood beside him, drawn by his energy. I would never want to change this man. "Show me those firetraps," I said, pleased to be close to him. "Who are the guilty landlords? Were they were just—boodlers?" I wanted justice for the poor.

"You should know," Mr. Pemberton said, starting to slur his words. "Aren't you Gold Coast?"

"What do you mean?"

In reply, he knelt to his picnic basket, replacing the ingredients.

"Answer me, Mr. Pemberton."

"Not the one you should ask," he replied, with a level gaze like Mother's. "Did you enjoy your ostrich egg?"

"Sir, I do not understand you." Our Captive Balloon dipped for several moments, making my stomach leap into my mouth.

"Time to anchor!" announced the attendant.

Our descent seemed much faster. Feeling woozy, I lost interest in geography. To distract my mind, I snatched the guidebook from Hermes' hip pocket to read about Transportation and Cold Storage. Glancing at the index, I unearthed so many exhibits I had missed I felt frustrated that I could never grab the whole fair into my hands at once. I threw the guidebook over the side, and watched it flutter and twirl.

Hermes was too busy taking photographs to notice. Feeling nauseous, I shut my eyes until we bumped on the ground several times. The attendant said, "Congratulations to the new auronaunts."

After Hermes and I exited the gondola and enclosures, we were guided by Mr. Pemberton toward a strange machine parked under an elm. It appeared to be a roofless carriage without a horse. "The more I'm on the move," Mr. Pemberton said, "the better I like me."

I hesitated, glancing at Hermes, who was inspecting the spokes on his tandem bicycle that always seemed to wriggle loose. Was he pouting because I was no longer trying to please him? Or was he still embarrassed from the traffic ticket for wheeling over ten miles per hour?

"Do join us, young sport," Mr. Pemberton said to Hermes, as he shooed away little boys in and around his machine.

"Oh, Hermes, yes, you must join us," I pleaded. "I've never ridden in one of these new-fangled machines. Or even seen my reflection in its fender."

"A carriage. Not a machine," Mr. Pemberton's voice was suddenly weary. "That's their slogan anyway. Get paid by Duryea Company to motor it around the fair. Hand out flyers." Hermes palmed a coin to a Columbian guard, holding up a nearby tree, to guard his camera case.

The machine resembled our family carriage, it being built so tall. But there were only three wheels. Also, the passenger seats were so high Mr. Pemberton had to assist my entrance. Sitting, I stared at a vertical contraption next to me. "That's my joy-stick," he grinned up at me, "gives one-hand control."

Hermes laid his cycle against the chassis, a pedal scratching it. "What's the moniker for this heap?"

"Remove your cycle, and maybe I'll educate you."

Hermes blinked several times, his square eyeglasses cockeyed.

"Sit across from me," I said, patting the hard leather bench backed against the dashboard. "Mr. Pemberton, I'm sure, will be kind enough to hand up your precious cycle."

"If we were motoring in England, Wetherstone, I'd have you trotting in front, waving a bloody red flag."

Hermes stomped aboard and settled himself, while facing me on the padded bench. Mr. Pemberton hoisted the cycle to Hermes who laid it across his body. Through the spokes, Hermes peered at me for sympathy. However, I remembered

Annie Oakley's eyes that told me, "You are there and I am here. So be it."

Mr. Pemberton went to the rear of the machine, where a cranking noise reminded me of the gears on the Ferris Wheel. "Mr Pemberton, where are you going?"

"Call me Brick!" The engine in the back shuddered, coughed, rattled. The racket even caused Hermes to cease tightening his spokes. Peering over my shoulder, I saw black smoke billowing. Where was Brickton? Was he injured?

The entire carriage vibrated until my body responded to its rhythm, embarrassing me, because I felt like Fatima. I avoided Hermes' eyes. How could I possibly feel safe, even with Brickton, when this contraption had no doors?

On a sudden, Brickton reappeared as if out of the ground and settled into the driver's seat beside me. Reaching for a black bulb of rubber attached to the vertical stick, he squeezed it once, twice, to elicit blasts of a trumpet. "That's my sugar pot!" he said, beaming like a new father. He frowned at Hermes. "Wetherstone, you've got to admit, this carriage beats the hot damn out of your old boneshaker." As Brickton released the hand brake, I noticed he had donned a beige hat, dust goggles, and yellow gloves that extended halfway up his arms. "Yes Miss Aultman, I drive myself to interviews."

Wonderful. Could he drive me to my freedom? I snuggled closer to the real journalist.

The engine coughed, and then jolted us forward. "Tell me, who did you interview lately?"

"No, let's discuss you instead."

"Please."

"Well, you are persuasive. My most famous interview was also my most irritating: Gentleman Jim."

"Who's he?"

Brickton swerved to avoid hitting a little boy's white balloon bobbing in our path. "Wetherstone, tell your friend about Gentleman Jim."

"I'm too busy fixing my own transportation."

"Gentleman Jim Corbett," Brickton said, swiping yellow hair from his eyes, "defeated John L. Sullivan, himself, in only twenty-two rounds. Did it scientific. Modern finesse beat old-fashioned brute force." Brickton slowed the machine to avoid a gentleman peddling a six foot front-wheeler. "Well, Jimmy spent more time in front of old Vienna swilling free beer. Shoulda sparred all comers at his own exhibit. Wouldn't talk to me, so I interviewed his agent. Warned him no one would pay after they saw Jimmy for free. Mark my words, Gentleman Jim Corbett's too undisciplined to last." He squeezed the horn, blasting a horse into rearing up, almost dumping its lady rider. "Love my sugarpot!"

"Anyone else?"

"Yes, two reporters. Young squirt from St. Louie. Called himself Teddy, Teddy Dreiser. Also one of my heroines."

"Who's that lucky person."

"Nellie Bly."

My stomach fell through slats in the floor.

"I can see you're impressed." Brickton said, "but Nellie shared a story that still puzzles me. Maybe you can solve the mystery."

I stared straight ahead.

"Nellie's riding the Ferris Wheel on a holiday when she sees a young man go crazy, pull a gun, hold a child hostage. Everybody freezes. Guess what happens?" He peered into my face. "Am I boring you?" Then Brickton laughed. "Some brazen young lady strips her blouse; she's stark naked. Then she throws it over the crazy guy's head, and wrestles him to the floor. Hot damn! That chickadee is my kind of cookie." Hermes started snoring. "But then, she gets crazy and almost pushes Nellie Bly out a window. When the Ferris Wheel lands, the chickadee walks away from a write-up." He speeds up to ten miles per hour. "It's sure a ball scratcher."

I could have written a more accurate story.

The carriage chugged to a stop in front of Transportation, with a huge golden doorway embedded with a series of receding arches, overleafed in silvery green. The reddish building looked out of place in the White City. I loved it.

When Brickton assisted me from the carriage, he bowed. "Pleasure being in your company Miss Aultman." He kept the engine running.

"You're not guiding us indoors? But wasn't it your idea?"

"Sorry missy, forgot to say. Interviews scheduled with two firebrands; young Wells, old Douglass. Way over at Haytian Pavilion."

My knees felt like buckling. Where was Hermes? Brickton touched my hand. "I'll roust your friend, Miss. That is, after I escort you to the entrance."

Hermes rolled his cycle toward me, one wheel wobbling. He flicked sweat off his brow with bruised fingers. Without looking back to the Duryea carriage, he shouted, "Pimperton, don't you have to disappear someplace?"

"Quite so, young cock. Check later on your photos and my article for the *Herald*." He waved at me, but before I could respond, he leaped into his carriage. With a shudder and a lurch, the Duryea drove away from us, belching tiny clouds of soot.

"Well, are we going to stand here all day? It's boiling," I said.

Hermes bumped his cycle up the steps past me as his pedal twisted against my skirt. When Hermes announced, "I know you Alessandra, you'll like the thousand dollar baby carriage the most." I bit my tongue. He wasn't going to get a rise out of me. He stashed the cycle behind a pillar.

Inside, the main hall felt cooler. A tour guide told his group the must-see exhibits, "Relics of all sorts—Chinese junks, Japanese rickshaws, covered wagons."

"Forget relics," I heard myself muttering. "Only new things would please me now."

"Oh, young girl," the guide said, "Your taste be more bizarre? Sled runners from jaw bones of a whale? What about the trip hammer weighing one hundred twenty-five ton that built the Ferris Wheel itself?"

"Sounds great to me," Hermes said. "What's your pleasure, Alessandra?"

Perspiration from my forehead stung my eye. "The elevator," I said. "Where does it lead to?"

Not waiting for reply, I strolled toward the bank of eight elevators. The first one of them lifted us toward the cupola located sixteen floors above. While in the crowded elevator I maneuvered as many people as possible between Hermes and me, so when the doors opened I hurried first to the window to view Wooded Island with its million trees and its pagoda with a rose garden. As I stood admiring the sight, Hermes tapped me on the shoulder, and left me to wander to the opposite side to view Cold Storage Building.

Alone in the crowd, I felt a word forming itself on the roof of my mouth, syllable by syllable. Sur-ren-der. Surrender. I gave up trying to please Hermes; I would not reform him into my ideal husband.

"Doesn't that excite you?" Hermes said, returning to my side. "Cold Storage. It makes all the ice, and all the ice cream for the whole entire total fair. Doesn't that please you all to hell?"

I stared into Hermes' face, his mouth open, but his mind closed. Did I really know this boy? I listened to the elevators heaving and falling, mechanical lungs of a dying giant. I reminded myself that I was trying not to reform Hermes, but suddenly I wondered, could I endure him? Hermes' shoulders slumped. I touched his gift locket at my breast. "Another time for Cold Storage, Hermes," I said, holding his hand. "Maybe with all that ice, we could even skate together there. Remember skating on the pond between our houses when we were children?"

"Lollapalooza!" Hermes shouted spinning on one foot. "Let's do it now!"

❉   ❉   ❉

After Hermes and I took a brief tour of the ice-making facilities on the ground floor of Cold Storage, we hurried up several flights of stairs to the ice rink on the top floor. While I rented skating shoes, and buttoned them, Hermes went to the near-to locker he rented to store his antique speed skates. To passersby, he pointed out the nickel plate and buffing, but he hid the ankle brace in his pocket. Just before we glided onto the ice, Hermes took out the ankle brace, and strapped its steel rib at the rear of each skate, connecting the russet leather straps around each ankle. His old weakness reawakened my feelings for him in our growing years. By not viewing him as a future husband I felt more comfortable.

On the ice rink other skaters slid past us as Hermes ridiculed the wobbly ankles of a lady skater in front of us. As we tilted around the border of the circle of ice, I slipped, losing balance. Hermes interlocked his right arm to save me from falling. We whooshed past the slower skaters, as people sipped drinks on the raised platform surrounding the ice rink.

With gathering speed, we leaned forward, my left hand and Hermes' right hand grasping each other. Once again I noticed our hands had corresponding brown moles, so that together they appeared to belong to one person's body. Such a sight used to comfort me with reassurance I would never be alone in this world.

"Hey look, no windows!" Hermes yelled. Indeed, the only light was unnatural but I had been too absorbed with my thoughts to have noticed.

The people at tables were focused on our feet; were they noticing Hermes' ankle brace? In front of us, a woman with the wobbly ankles lost balance and fell. Around her body, gray fog swirled as we skated past her, our hands separating. Her male partner pointed toward the door with the stain glass porthole. "It's coming from there!" he shouted.

A blur of smoke oozed under the door, and rolled toward the rink. "Fire!"

Trapped on the Wheel

A woman screamed, tables overturned, electric lights flickered. Darkness.

❂   ❂   ❂

I opened my eyes. An Indian squaw's blanket, smelling of smoke, enwrapped me. The squaw, breathing whisky, was not looking at me. Instead, her black eyes were rolling in their sockets as she stared upward at black waves of smoke avalanching downward from the roof, lava from a boiling volcano. A man nearby shinnied up a lamppost for a better view of the fire on the roof. A minute later he slid down, tears creasing his St. Peter's cheeks. Young lovers shouted to locate each other; parents tugged at children to leave the scene. On the rooftop, flames like tongues of devils licked at tall towers. I stood as a horse-drawn fire truck skidded to a halt at the entrance to Cold Storage. Jumping off the truck in a swirl of gray smoke, men in big boots and drawn pole axes stomped a pathway through the throng of laughing sightseers and skaters. The fire brigade, lugging ladders and water hoses, charged like Hermes' football team returning a kickoff toward the burning building. A pumper truck, with six plow horses, pulled up amidst scattered applause.

As the good squaw reclaimed her blanket from me, I realized suddenly that Hermes was nowhere to be seen. My God, was he still in there? Perhaps reading my emotions on my face, the good squaw patted my hand, shook her head, and pointed her arm, a dozen bracelets jingling. In the distance at the other end of the building, I saw Hermes pedaling away on his tandem through a crowd rushing pell-mell. Avoiding a collision, he tumbled off his cycle. When he stood, he saw me, on my toes, waving as I screamed his name.

I thought I saw Hermes mouth the word "camera."

"Children!" a woman screamed, exiting, "Children trapped inside!" Hermes was lost to my sight. I sank down and squatted next to two little girls bawling. Mechanically, I reached to untie my ice shoes, and noticed they were neatly stacked against an oak tree.

"My baby is dying in there." A tearful mother tugged at the fireman pumping water at the rear of the truck, who ignored her.

One of the little girls crying next to me snuggled under my arm. "Baby Brother—trapped in comfort station," she whispered. "Crawled away—not my fault." The younger child said, "She ran. It's her fault. Mom will kill her when she comes out."

"Do you mean a baby's still in there?"

Without wasting another breath, I tiptoed in my stocking feet across the cement sidewalk, dodging firemen coming out coughing smoke. Before entering Cold Storage I paused, regretting that Hermes had ridden away. For a camera? Which one of us was on a fool's errand? I followed several women into the entrance. Inside, the cold smoke engulfed my body.

"Where are the babies?" I shouted.

"Trapped in public comfort upstairs," The woman behind me said. "Now move it."

Seeking a corner on the jammed landing, I wrapped my shoulder scarf around my face, leaving space for my eyes, as another mob rushed downstairs to exit. When an opening occurred, I flung myself upward along the wall.

At first floor, a tall fireman outspread his arms, pole axe horizontal in his hands, "Stop people! Back you go!"

The incoming mob, mostly women, knocked him backwards. When I reached the firemen, he was doubled over, braced against a wall, and holding his private parts, the pole laying on the floor across his boots. Resisting the urge to aid him, I ran down the hall, searching for the comfort station.

Screams of children led me to the far end, a half dozen women at my side. Several of us hurried in. Huddled next to the water closets were several little children. Some hugged; some fought each other. Others splashed water from the toilets onto their faces. I scooped up a little boy because he possessed almond eyes like Terese. Smoke made him cough. A fireman appeared with his rubber coat open, a little girl's blonde hair bobbing under his arm. Behind them, flames flickered down the wall. "Everybody out! Fire in roof towers. Ready to collapse."

The little boy, clinging to my neck, kicked me in the ribs as I staggered to the hallway again. A beam, caving onto the floor, sounded like thunder. I took the scarf off, and wrapped it around the boy's face. By now, we had reached the head of stairs. The fireman who had been against the wall was gone, replaced by a buxom woman of color in coveralls. When I approached her, she stared at me wide-eyed. "Good! You all's got one. Down you go, honey." The stairs were only partially crowded. "Stay close to the wall!" she shouted. I jammed my shoulder, hugging the boy who clung to my neck. He reminded me of Cerby, the time I found him lost in the woods. Smoke burned my throat.

Reaching the exit, I found a fat fireman pointing a turned-off water hose at us. Spreading his feet, he swung a hip, and popped open one of the double doors. As we wedged through the opening, I planted a kiss on his stubbled cheek. Outside, I stumbled over to the tree, handing the little boy to the Indian squaw. She enfolded him into her blanket as she had accepted me earlier.

I paused, wiping my face on my sleeves, soiled from smoke. Were those geysers of flames engulfing the towers on the roof? As small as midgets, firemen waved their arms begging to be rescued. Instinctively, I waved back.

A woman appeared at the entrance, her dress on fire. The fireman at the door rotated the nozzle, and sprayed her so forcefully she was knocked to the cement. When he turned off the spray, she shook herself and shouted, "Babies! My baby's still in there, for God's sake!"

Fighting through the gauntlet of women grabbing at my arms, I reached the entrance. Desperate, I elbowed the fireman at the door to one side, and climbed the stairs. I started coughing as I inhaled the oily smoke. Why was I being so foolish? I realized my scarf still protected the little boy's face. Covering my mouth with a handkerchief, I searched second floor, but found no one. When I reached third floor, I heard voices from the roof shouting orders I could not understand.

On fourth, I reached the room containing the skating rink. Pushing open the porthole door, I waded into water, ankle deep. Burning timbers from the ceiling hissed as they fell. No one was in sight. Failure drove me to desperation.

Resuming my ascent, I waded toward the final flight of stairs to the roof. Each thrust of my limbs murmured for me to stop.

Feeling shame in finding no baby and guilt in breaking taboo, I was desperate to recover something. I needed to rescue some one. Anyone.

I found a narrow wooden ladder leading to the roof and ascended it toward the hatch. Grabbing the middle rung, I reached up to touch the flat roof door. Hot. Scorching my fingers, I pushed anyway. Heavier than I needed. Turning my body around on a rung, I positioned my back against the hatch, and stepped up. It rose slightly, then dropped. Stepping up another rung, I pushed harder. The hatch felt like a yoke across my shoulders. I pushed again as I heard a man's voice shouting, "Watch falling slabs!" What was I doing? Why was I here?

By now, the smoke was so thick I could barely see. Gathering what strength I had, I pushed again. At last, it raised just high enough for a hot blast of air to sting the back of my neck. I realized the hatch was a double door, which proved a blessing. I peeked out at a scene of chaos: fire hoses bursting, water spewing in all directions, ladders flaming, men running.

As I tried to absorb the scene, something heavy fell onto the half-open hatch, setting it on fire. My hand got caught between the doors. I hung there as the hatch burned. As the ladder broke in flames, my wedged hand still clutched the edge. Then the rung collapsed beneath my foot, and I fell, pulling the half burnt door down upon me. My body smacked against the floor at the bottom of the ladder. Fire, smoke and voices filled my ears as I lay beneath the burning door, my fingers searching for Mother's pendant.

"My Gawd, I had no idea somebody was under the hatch."

"I'm jumping down," shouted a second voice. When he pulled the burning wood off me, he shouted, "Christ, her hair's on fire!" As the fireman covered my head with his jacket, a third voice shouted from the hatch. "Out of the way Mike." Dropping to the floor beside me, the third voice said, "I'll take her down, your bad back."

As we descended, I thought in my groggy state that I heard a baby crying. I summoned the last of my strength to punch my fists into the small of his back.

"Ba—baby. Go save baby."

The fireman hesitated, then stopped to listen as I passed in and out of consciousness. Flames cackled all around us like a hundred Karlas. He shifted my weight, but continued down the stairs. Then he handed me over to the fat fireman at the exit.

"I believe I know this lady. I'm going back for the baby."

I heard myself moaning. Exhaustion overwhelmed me as my dead weight fell into the arms of the fireman with the hose. He dropped it, hissing water and whipping around like a snake. As I sank into a black hole, my last thought was of the baby.

Chapter Twelve

Journey to Jubilee

Tuesday, July 11

Pain awakened senses: smell of burnt flesh, as if flat-irons singed a wedding dress; tastes of sulphur on lips, mingling with blood so thin so cold; touch of cloth layered and bound too tight, suffocating pores; the whole body a mummy awaiting burial. Last sense to awaken was sight. A faint light seeped through a single strand of bandage stretching across closed lids.

❋   ❋   ❋

"Doctor, Doctor, no sign of life?" The words, once so far off, drifted on dark waves like wreckage from a sunken ship. "No sign of life!" the voice continued. "None. And how many days? Perhaps, perhaps we should—that is, you should—well, you know!"

What poor soul was she talking about?

Then a second voice spoke. "Stop that! Complain again and you won't be allowed—" Words drifted closer, carried like white caps on waves, words and waves slapping against the shore, before whispering past to disappear in silence.

❋   ❋   ❋

Cool air irritated the hands, hot and stiff. Fingers struggled to move, struggled to twitch.

"Oh, awake are we? Must ask you one question before I re-apply my axel grease. Nod your head."

Darkness engulfed my eyes.

"Oh, that's all right. Here's my question—anyway. Are you still a true believer? You must trust my medicine to heal your burns." The voice was fading. "Can't you nudge one nod for old Doc Seth?"

❖ ❖ ❖

"Yesterday your eyes popped open, finally. Your old Creole told me. You don't remember the fire at all? Lucky for you."

My eyes tried to focus on the young lady. Amber hair. Ivory fingers caressed a book with double A on cover.

"Mean anything Stir?" A smirk twisted purple lips. "You're really faking it, aren't you?" She sucked her teeth. "That's what I'd do."

Bandages around my chest choked off breathing. Struggled to sit up.

"Gawd, you can move! Doc lied to me."

Coughing.

"I'll just leave it on your lap." She opened the large book and straddled it across my bandaged legs. "Off to rehearsal. Besides, I found out what I came for!"

❖ ❖ ❖

Eyes opened, surveying a mantle crowded with junk—flattened opera hat; old ballet slippers bronzed and useless; photograph in gold frame of two young peasant girls. Above mantle, a bell-shaped light green area outlined a missing mirror. Why no mirror on wall?

Out of sight, a door creaked open. Odor of burning cigar. A shuffle of boots. A hacking cough. Was it Father? Door creaked a second time, and clicked shut, like a thief. Was it Hermes? Left eye felt a tear. Deep breath from chest stuck in throat. Eyes closed. Was this a hospital?

◦ ◦ ◦

"Wake up, handless maiden! Good doctor is here!" Placing a black bag on an old rocker, he pushed it once. Squeaked. "Memory?"

My eyelids closed again.

"Come out of hiding. Unwrapping day, for that beautiful head." Cold scissors at base of bandage, enwrapping head. "Ready?" Snip, nibble, snip, nibble, around jaw bone, left cheek to temple. "Don't squirm." Good doctor cradled bandaged head and said, "Odette, come in now. Need you." Heels on wooden floor. "Hold up her head from behind. Time to remove bandages for good. Your father wants you to be perfect before he sees you."

The brain pretended it was someplace else.

"Your good fortune. The starving poor you're not," the doctor said. "You'd be neglected in a filthy infirmary. Now you're cared for in your own bedroom." Stale air leaked onto left cheek. Gentle hands caressed head while doctor lifted cocoon of bandages like a beehive. Assaults of air. "Don't touch your cheek. Itching is good sign. Needs more black grease. Later, mirrors come. Not now."

My head leaned back on towel, eyes staring at ceiling. A fly struggled in a cobweb. More it wriggled, more enwrapped. Looked away. My forehead oozed sweat, a trickle rolling down bridge of nose, paused, slid to edge of eye, stinging. Eyelid twitched, but no fluttering of eyelash. Why no fluttering of eyelash?

"That's right, you sleep. Odette, rub her feet and hands like she's a little tyke again. Ointment needs soaking time."

❦ ❦ ❦

Door slammed against wall. High heels stabbed across the floor. "Errand of mercy, this!" A rocker creaked. "Oh, Mother wouldn't mind."

My eyes peeked at amber-haired young lady in rocker squinting at room. "Not a single one to see yourself by. Now, set yourself for surprise of your life." With that, she slipped out from behind her a large heart-shaped hand mirror, and held it up. "Behold the woman!"

In the glass, blood-shot brown eyes blinked without lashes, without eyebrows, forehead extending to top without a single strand of hair. Was this really my head?

"Stir, your skull's pitch black as a witch's heart."

The blonde lady dropped the mirror onto bed, and stood cackling. "At last! You look like me the night Cyrus finished with me." She sat on edge of bed. "But now, you do look worse." She reached out, smearing black grease from my cheek. "Cyrus will be finished with you too," she whispered in the ear. "Tell me, how does it feel? You used to call me the white crow. Consult the mirror I brought you, and tell me what to call you now."

She picked up the mirror, but the grease on her fingers slid the mirror behind the headboard, crashing on the floor. She kicked the rocker. Heels stomped toward the door that slammed, rattling objects on the mantle, the flat opera hat bouncing off and falling on its rim, popping open and rolling in a circle.

❦ ❦ ❦

"Today we walk! Don't you want to walk for my son Hermes? He'll be seeing you soon. You must move your bones."

With that, my knees felt themselves being bent, lifted and swung free over side of bed onto chilly floor. Odette knelt, encasing my feet in eiderdown slippers. The rest of body hoisted upward, swaying and buckling until good doctor said, "First step most important. No first step, nothing." Odette draped something around my shoulders. "Your mother's comforter."

One step, shaking. Then pause to gather breath. The other leg, shaking. Third step firmer. No pause necessary.

Fourth step bold, but too long, lurching all three bodies toward the fireplace, until good doctor pulled away toward the model of a small house in a corner of the room. The body staggered ahead, but legs folded, and sank down to sit Indian style.

"Rest here a moment," the good doctor said. "Do you recall your dollhouse?" But as he touched the forehead for fever, his hand trembled.

The stomach climbed the lungs, gathering strength until a growl erupted from the mouth and spewed forth a stream of hot vomit, bursting into air, and descending like poisonous rain upon the roof of the doll house.

✺ ✺ ✺

Awakened by cawing of crows outside the open window, my body refused to lie abed any longer. Reaching for the cane left by good doctor over the headboard, the fingers stroked the handle, a silver headed fox. Filling the hand with cane, and rising from bed like a marionette with tangled strings, my body wobbled toward the writing desk near the window.

Opening the center drawer, the hands somehow knew a yellow notepad would be there. It was. My body sat on edge of a straight-backed chair, not knowing what to write. I said a quiet prayer to Nellie Bly. Give me the courage that you possessed as a reporter.

Dipping the point of quill pen into an opened inkwell, the hand then hovered over the yellow sheets, black India ink dripping.

One word surged in my heart like a hot coal. Fingers gripped the pen, and scratched that word in middle of the paper. Then it scribbled the same word into a circle, moving paper with the other hand around and around, until the entire page was filled with that same one word.

My teeth started to grind. Ripping off the top page with one hand, the other dipped the pen into inkwell, and stabbed the same word in the center of the second sheet. Over and over, the pen point scarred the paper, until the movements released the fox-head handle hanging on the back of the chair to clatter upon the floor.

"Allow me," said the good doctor, retrieving the cane and placing it across the desk. He picked up the loose page, and chuckled. "One word you write, again and again?" He tossed the page back on the desk, "Goot!"

My hand gripped the sheet and fisted it into a wad the size of a baseball.

The good doctor sighed, and picked up the notepad filled with that one word—OUT.

"I'll send Alsace to carry you upstairs to your old nursery. Fresh start and all. No, a moment wait. He's garnering week's groceries in Lincoln Park for Mrs. Dibbs."

My fist squeezed the paper baseball.

"I know. Curlin's returned, he is, from driving Cyrus to La Salle Street."

The body pushed itself back from the desk, as one hand reached for the cane.

"You won't need my cane upstairs, my girl. Sit on floor all you want. Play with your old toys." The doctor headed toward the door. "Send Curlin, I will, for your journey upstairs."

※ ※ ※

Rousing from a catnap at the desk, my eyes slowly focused. A man, crouched near the writing desk, said, "Don't be afraid, Missy. Doc Wetherstone gave me orders." His black eyes bulged. "First time ah done seen you in a month since yuh—" He held up a heart-shaped mirror, cracked. "Found this here under bedpost." He wriggled the stem, glinting a ray of sunlight onto the broken glass. "Beg pardon, Miss, but I ain't never seen you like this. Breaks the human heart." Then he chuckled. "Lookie, here." He angled the mirror to include both faces, separated by a vertical break, snaking down the center of the mirror. One face with gold front tooth, one with vacant eyes. Curlin whispered hoarsely, "Halleluijah," pointing at our two faces in the mirror, both black as pitch.

"For the first time Ah feel a member of this here family!" He sat the mirror down, lifted the chair containing my body, and lumbered toward the door as Odette appeared with clothes across her arm. He hugged the chair as he threw his head back and, roaring with deep emotion, sang, "After the ball is over / If you could read them all / Many the hopes have vanished / After the ball—"

※ ※ ※

As the last lyrics echoed off attic beams of the nursery, Curlin angled the chair through the open doorway. The eyes perceived the good doctor, arms folded, standing with legs spread. He blocked the window covered by a black horse blanket, sunlight framing it. "Place the chair here, next to the mat." He pointed to the center of the barren room. "Gentle, boy, gentle."

Curlin frowned, and set the chair onto the bare floor, a father caring for a sick child. My eyes peered at his strong face, and blinked. Curlin winked back. Then his index finger touched his lips to seal our little secret.

The doctor cleared his throat, "Dismissed, boy, after you put her on the mat."

Curlin nodded, kneeling at the chair to position my body. Before rising, he squeezed my hand. As Curlin headed to the door, my body on the mat felt an electric shock bolting through it, strong enough to roll it off, and toward the door pursuing Curlin. Both my fists reached out on the floorboards, shoulders hunching forward, knees swinging against fists; the fists then stepping forward, like feet, to repeat the crawl.

After half dozen hops, the knees felt splinters. Odette entered, breathing heavy. My fists beat against Odette's shoes as my knees swung forward. Odette knelt and opened her arms. My body rose to its knees, fists flailing against Odette's bosom, striking again and again. Odette flung her arms around my body, and I began to weep. A flood of memories—keys for Father's favorite servant, Karla's evil eye, Hermes blood brother thumb pressing mine, Nellie Bly spinning a globe, Brickton lifting me into his Duryea.

"Crawl this way, Alessandra," the good doctor shouted, flopping to his knees onto the floor. "Cross pattern. Not like a frog. A lioness. Cross pattern." His right arm and left leg reached out, followed by his left arm and right leg in unison. Odette stopped crying, muffling laughter with her apron, as the doctor wriggled away from her across the floor. "Follow me, Alessandra, crawl this way. Repeat and repeat."

As my eyes watched his derrière see-sawing toward the opposite wall, they also noticed, for the first time, the wainscoting lined with children's toys: slate blackboards, a dozen majestic dolls, an Egyptian Ouija board, a prismatic top, a shoo-fly rocking house, a balky metal mule with a frustrated driver. What child lived here?

"Fallen asleep, my dear?" The good doctor's voice was edgy. "Imitate me."

He dropped to his knees, and started cross-crawling to the opposite wall, joined by Odette.

But my eyes were hypnotized by a Minerva indestructible metal doll. Its curly hair crowned a beautiful throat encircled by a necklace with an acorn pendant. My mind thought of the word "Mother."

The door opened, and suddenly the doctor stopped in mid-motion with right arm and left leg raised high off the floor. Turning, his face showed shock, then embarrassment.

Following doctor's gaze, my body turned to door, and saw a man, big as a bear, smoking the stub of a cigar. He snorted, and threw the stub to the floor. He ground it under the heel of his boot without taking his gaze off the doctor. Stepping back, he slammed the door, upsetting the Minerva doll onto her side and rattling a China tea set. He looked so familiar.

"Just remembered. Other patients await." The doctor stood, brushing his knees and his spats. "You've earned a full meal today, my girl." He glanced at Odette who rose to her feet in stages. "Bring her favorites." He walked toward me. "What would your favorites be, Alessandra?"

Odette flapped her apron at a horse fly. "Coffee, of course, sir." She rocked on her toes. "Then oatmeal with brown sugar, whole wheat toast with orange marmalade. And then—"

"I'm asking Alessandra."

"And then either mutton chops or broiled sheep kidneys," Odette said, finishing.

"Well, keep her cross-crawling. Borrow knee pads from maids and gloves from Curlin." He left the room, motioning for Odette to follow him into the hallway. She closed the door behind them.

My ears listened to tumblers sliding against metal and thudding into place. The eyes darted about the room, pausing at the window where edges of blanket partially covered it, revealing tips of iron bars.

My body sank into its haunches, and my eyes stared at a future of solitary confinement.

✦ ✦ ✦

When my eyes finally closed that night, a nightmare came to visit me. Fog filled a toy workshop. My eyes peered at Nellie

Bly lying on her back upon a mat in the center of the room. A bear smoking a cigar straddled her chest, reciting in a pleasant sing-song voice the tale of little Karla who burned to death playing with wooden matches. The bear drilled a twisted spindle into the young girl's heart. Leaving the prismatic top embedded, the bear then recited the tale of little Hermes who was a naughty boy sucking his thumbs, and refusing to stop. The boy's Mother, sharpening scissors, smiled and proceeded to clip off, clip off, the boy's thumbs.

When the metal doll cried, the bear's huge head revolved, searching for the noise in the toy room. My eyes shrank farther down behind the doll. The bear roared, reaching down a huge paw toward my eyes, pulsating like a red burning cigar. More fog poured into the room. Eyes went blind.

❊ ❊ ❊

"*Mon dieu!*" Odette screamed as she entered the nursery. "Toys! All your little babies!" Chewing edges of her apron she hopped in front of the cold fireplace as she pointed toward the pile of furry animals and metal toys overflowing the base of the flue. She swept her arm around the walls that were emptied of the little army of toys that had lined them. How did they all wander into the fireplace?

❊ ❊ ❊

When the doctor visited next, he carried a cat. Placing it gently on the floor next to my body on the mat, he said, "You watch Cerberus. Study how he strides, cross-pattern." He glanced at the fireplace, now without toys as he lit his pipe, placing the box on the mantle. "Das gut! Toys, you are beyond. Also beyond black axel grease. Now Odette applies aloe."

My arms reached out, and grasped the cat who purred when hugged to the breasts, but the smell of aloe made the cat sniff and leap to the floor, scampering. Was the cat seeking a mouse or a hole for escape?

My ears listened to the heavy trod of Curlin coming in, carrying an army cot like a log for the fireplace. "Here, where the floor has dried." The thud of the wooden limbs upon the floor. "Now, carry her to the cot, and remove the mat."

Eyes shut, I waited for strong arms to lift my body. Curlin strode to the mat and swung me to the cot. "Gentle, don't waken mistress. Now bring up her Mother's rocker."

When my torso sagged onto the cot, my nose sniffed the musty stench of canvas cloistered too long, cheeks feeling fresh oil of maple as the cot gently rocked like a cradle. My body drew up knees, and hugged them to my breasts as Cerby perched on a shoulder, licking my ear.

After arising early and rolling off the cot to use the oval rubber-lined bed pan, my body crawled cross-pattern to the rocking chair facing the wall. A box waited upon a seat upholstered with a green and gold coat of arms. As my body crouched beside the rocker, fingers lingered, tracing the seat's pattern. Other fingers tipped the solid birch runners to set the rocker squeaking.

Like a disobedient child, my body reluctantly followed directions and sat. A wooden box greeted the derrière. My body rose just enough to retrieve the box and place it on the lap as Cerby leaped onto it to pry up a corner. Whiffs of charcoal sent the cat onto my shoulder. The movement wriggled the rocker until my knees bumped against the wall. My little finger lifted the corner. Might it explode? Was it a box of fancy Opera Mix? Removing tissue covering the charcoal sticks, my fingertips fondled the pieces. Which one to use?

With a screech, the cat landed smack-dab in the center of the opened box, flipping the charcoal pieces in all directions. The cat sprang to the floor, racing to hide under the cot. Only one piece of charcoal remained in the box. The choice having been made, the next thing was to order fingers to seize the stick, then brace knees against the wall, and stretch as far as possible. My arm swiped an arc with charcoal upon the wall.

That done, my body collapsed into the rocker, exhausted. Eyes traced a half-circle, an eyebrow for a giant. Then my fingers swept a semicircle under the arc with such a flourish the stick broke. With a stub of charcoal, my fingers drew small circles within the large globe, over and over. Lurching the rocker sideways to an untouched space, my arm performed the same actions until most of the wall was covered with circles of all sizes. Fingers ached, but lips smiled.

A gentle knock on the door was followed by Odette bursting into the room. With her foot, she slammed it behind her as she carried in a lady's bathrobe. "Mam'selle, put on!" With both hands, Odette pulled my body to its feet as she flung on a blue and white striped terry cloth, flipping up the hood, and drawing the sash too tightly at my waist. Staring into my face, Odette moaned, stepped back, and spat on the edge of her apron. With both thumbs, she rubbed the cloth on my face, removing smudges of charcoal until a knock on the door forced her to stop.

Odette sat my body onto the rocker, positioning it like a throne. She hobbled over to open the door, its frame revealing a lanky young man adorned in a gray checked cashmere suit with high starched collar and black cravat. Holding his hands behind his back, he rocked on his toes. Tip-toeing into the room, hands still out of sight, he stared at the charcoal circles covering the wall, until he stumbled over the cot, sending a red velvet heart-shaped box out of his hands to spray brown missives and white wrappers all over the floor. The cover skidded across the floor banging against the baseboard, while the bottom tumbled into the unlit fireplace. The young man sprawled on all fours.

Locking eyes with him, my body left the rocker to crawl a cross-pattern around the cot, while the young man sat on the floor with a confused expression. Halfway around, he imitated my crawl, trailing my body the rest of the way. When cherry pieces stuck to his knees, he stopped. With that, the young man stood, a bit unsteadily, one hand attached to his trouser by melted chocolate. As he crouched, he stared at the wall half-filled with circles. Then he snapped the fingers of his other hand.

"Wheels!" he gasped, "bicycle wheels." He stepped to my body, raised me to my feet and gave me a hug. "Sander, how clever of you!"

My body felt his hug awaken memories only half-remembered: a waltz under chandeliers that shivered in a breeze, an embrace in a gondola that bobbed on the waves. But, then the hood fell from my bald head.

The young man stepped backward, his mouth dropping open. "Alessandra, I had no idea—Dad doesn't talk about his pa—"

My body sank into the rocker, hands restoring the hood.

"I know the answer!" the young man shouted, "You need light." He strode toward the window, showing new confidence. As he tugged at the horse blanket, he said, "In case you may have forgotten, I used to be Hermes." Half the blanket fell free. "Don't answer me. You can't talk yet. Remember?" One corner of blanket proved stubborn. "Dad tells me to recall last time everything seemed normal." He hop-scotched back to the rocker, missing most of the chocolate pieces. "Let old Hermes turn your beautiful face toward the light." He pivoted the rocker like a sled, and skidded the runners closer to the window. With a kiss atop the hood, he reached the corner of the window still covered, and announced with a flourish: "Worship the sun!" As he yanked the blanket fully away, he dropped it onto the floor. Sunlight pierced the room like a police spotlight.

My hands hid my eyes as my throat tightened. With an animal grunt, my body pulled the hood down to cover the face. Both hands kept waving the young man out of the room until he closed the door behind him, the knob twisting. My body bent in the rocker, sobbing.

❂   ❂   ❂

"Young parishioner," a new voice bounced off the walls, "missed the pleasure of your lovely face in the Wetherstone pew."

My ears did not know which was more irritating, the booming voice of the stranger or the cawing of the crows pecking the window pane.

"Doctor Wetherstone instructed us to re-introduce ourselves: Reverend Milton X. Brakenbush, God's humble servant."

Odette brought a chair for the visitor. He shook his head when he saw the small seat, whereupon she left the chair, and reappeared with a wider, armless one, that he also rejected. Odette placed that chair next to the first one, and stood in a corner. In a moment, Curlin carried in a wide corner chair with three limbs. He slid the chair too strongly against the back of the visitor's knees, collapsing him with a thud onto the seat, his Bible dropping to the floor. From his sitting position, the minister bent over to retrieve it, but was prevented by his mid-section.

Odette picked up the Bible, dusted it on her sleeve and handed it to the Reverend. Then with a curtsy and a grimace, she and Curlin departed.

Rev. Brackenbush inserted fingers into his vest pocket, extracting a timepiece while he blew dust off his Bible, "Won't waste your precious time, young lady." He peeked over thick glasses but his eyes, buried in puffy cheeks and hidden beneath hanging brows, made the detection of color impossible. His throat rumbled. "Your *pater*, the good Mr. Aultman requests your unworthy servant to counsel you as to your neglected duty as a daughter." He paused. "Well, what say you, girl?"

My fingers touched the bandage at the throat.

"Oh yes, of course. Your voice."

My eyes started to moisten.

"By Jove, but that's the very point you see. You must want to know: why you? Everyone needs answers." He rippled the edges of his Bible like a deck of cards. "By Jove, we specialize in answers."

My body sagged in the rocker, temples throbbing.

The Reverend's voice took on a darker tone. "Miss Alessandra, seize the moment. Examine conscience." He started to wheeze. "Have you honored your pater? Obeyed his will? Your pater represents Gawd Almighty. Disobey him, you disobey Gawd!" He stamped his boot on the floor. "Listen! Ga—your Father is punishing you by his absence. The moment of repentance is at hand." He glanced at the circles on the wall, licking his dry lips. "I see you have drawn the symbol Omega many times. Good. Omega, the end. The Lord indeed is the end of all things. Perhaps, there is yet hope for you." Then he belched, "By the by, could we have a glass of water? Parched lips."

My throat choked with questions. Did Father love me anymore? Was obedience the only reason he loved me at all?

At the threshold of the open door, Odette appeared, frowned, and disappeared.

"Any questions of clarification?" He produced a red checkered bandana from his sleeve, like a magician. Mopping his forehead, he tossed shocks of white hair out of his eyes.

Odette returned with a sky-blue glass and offered it to the preacher. With trembling hand she poured ice water from a dark blue pitcher. With uninterrupted gulps he devoured the water, spilling drops on the front of his black suit coat. He held out the glass for a refill. Once done, he shooed Odette as if she were carrying a bee hive.

My stomach rumbled, feeling empty.

"We can tell from your eyes you require proof of your sins of disobedience." The Reverend straightened in the chair. "We submit as proof your very own pitiful condition. Item, you cannot remember that dreadful fire. Item, you lost your hair. Item, you lost your voice too. Item, your hands are singed. Item, you caused the death of that young fireman, oh what's his name?"

Odette interrupted by offering to refill his glass. He shook his head, handing the empty glass to her. She stood in a corner.

My chest felt squeezed by a vice.

The Reverend patted a generous stomach, revealing two loose brass buttons on his white vest. "We must be cruel to be kind, as that Protestant poet wrote so long ago." He started to move toward the rocker, but my hand waved him away. "We take no pleasure in your pain, despite what unbelievers like Dr. Wetherstone may claim."

Words to defend the good doctor sprang from the heart but choked in the throat.

Reverend reached to take out his pocket watch again, but this time a folded piece of green paper drifted to the floor. With an agility that startled, he knelt to recover the paper. Standing, he blew on it as if it were the spark of life. Unfolding the check, he smoothed it across his belly, smiled, and pocketed it. "Due to Mr. Aultman's generosity, my church may now purchase that ultra expensive Hammond Queen organ precious Lord so much deserves. Blessings upon you, dear child."

How could Father afford it? Did he borrow from Mr. Palmer again?

As the minister ambled toward the door Odette trailed him, performing a little Creole dance, while silently applauding his exit. When she returned from the hallway, she brought a second box of charcoal sticks. After picking up the debris, she left.

Alone, my eyes studied the circles, the wheels, the omega on the wall. Something was still missing. Would rolling a stick of charcoal between my palms tell me? I remembered a man rubbing a pocket watch in his hands, like Aladdin's lamp. Freeing one hand to grip the cane and squeezing a charcoal stick in the other, my body shuffled toward the wall. Swaying, I placed the point of the charcoal at the exact center of a circle. The stick broke, dropping at my feet. With the remaining half, my fist drew a dark line straight down, then it drew a straight line like an axle across the center. Stretching upward to the top of the arc, and re-gripping the stub, my hand pulled a line down to the center, as if releasing darkness from the green wall.

After a minute, my hand gripped a new stick from the box and in a fury proceeded to fill in all circles with X's, then all circles with T's, until the entire bottom of the wall seemed to roll with charcoal wheels.

Throwing away the stub of charcoal onto the horse blanket at the base of the window, my hands grasped the grid. I leaned elbows against the iron, not minding the sharp discomfort that pinched my skin, my chin resting against a horizontal bar.

My eyes gazed through the dirty glass at birch trees bowing to the wind. Small American flags snapped in the breeze on top a gazebo. My eyes perceived a garden overgrown with weeds. My heart ached to pull the weeds and dig into the black soil to plant seeds. Who was the neglectful gardener?

✸ ✸ ✸

"Stir, you're improving!" a young lady's voice screeched off the walls of the nursery. Turning from the window my feet lost balance, entangled in folds of blanket. "No more ballerina for you," said the young lady posing upon the cot, kicking off one white sandal, while wriggling the other. "Impressed with the purple bow over my instep?" She stretched her short body encased in a navy blue reefer jacket with shoulder cape and collar, trimmed with white braid. Despite the heat and the droning flies that had followed her perfume into the room, she appeared unnaturally cool with her transparent skin and purple lipstick. "That dreadful Reverend X. Rumplestilskin. He just waddled past me." She sat up on one elbow. "What did he want with you? Exorcism? Or do only Catholics do that?" She suspended one leg over the edge of the cot, and toyed with a fallen shoe with her bare toenails, painted purple. "Maybe if I ever attended church, I would know. But Alessandra knows Karla's real church is the stage." Her green eyes widened. "Enjoy those iron bars? My idea, you know, for your safety."

Suddenly, she sat up and reached for her shoe. "Your stone face is making me nervous. But then, it always did." After slipping on one shoe she said, "Thought I would find you perched on your high and mighty throne." She twirled the loose shoe in one hand. "Is Alessandra still searching? Take it from little Karla: life's a crap shoot, a Ferris Wheel of misfortune." She wedged on her second shoe and stared at the floor. "Even when you win, you lose."

She jumped to her feet, stomping like an Indian. "Sundays! I love Sundays, especially now they allow the fair to stay open on Sundays, despite blue noses like Reverend X. Birdinbush. Thank Gawd I talked Cyrus into backing the fair on Sundays. Told him it added money to his pocket as an original board member of the fair."

Karla spun on her heels and strode to the door, as my body shuffled to the rocker. At the open door, without looking back, Karla said, "Can't remember your own sister, Alessandra? Can't remember your own name?" She peered down at her shoes.

"Nobody likes their own name." Then she turned around. "Choose any name you want! Here's a once-in-a-lifetime chance. Re-christian yourself."

As my body sagged in the rocker, Karla trotted back into the room. She squeezed my shoulders, and kissed the top of the hood. A swirl of perfume brought images of a girl dancing alone on a stage in front of admiring men. Peering deeply into my face, Karla shouted, "Sister just remembered something, didn't you!" She rotated the rocker in circles until my knees banged against the wall. When the rocker stopped spinning, my head tilted backwards on the headrest. My eyes saw Karla's head upside down, decapitated. For the first time a belly laugh stirred deep inside me, and rumbled upward to my throat, bursting into a gurgle.

Karla stepped away. "Don't laugh at Karla. I swear she wi—" Running to the door, she stopped, "Oh the perfume! Well, Stir, it's called 'Fatima.'" She posed with one hand on hip, while her other hand gestured toward the wall filled with charcoal bicycle wheels. "Karla will have all those zeros scrubbed away by tomorrow morning!"

Opening the door, Karla screamed, "Sister, are you deaf as well as mute?"

My body thrust itself upon its feet, as both hands ripped at the bandage at my throat. My whisper became a cry, then a scream, as my body rose on its toes and my ears heard one word pour forth from my mouth, "Nooooooo!"

Karla cackled like a small fire just beginning to burn. "See, Alessandra? Karla knew you were a fake!" She slammed the door as my body swayed, roiling like a burning bush.

❂ ❂ ❂

"What does Alessandra need?" Doc Seth said, finishing his examination. He smiled, "No need to talk. Already, I know. Your own bedroom." He patted my wrist. "Your father would be here for you, but it's hard for him to see you as anything but perfect."

I sat up, excited by the thoughtfulness of a man called my father but furious at a sister called Karla. I needed to see both Hermes and Father, but small steps first.

"Your hands need to work. Knead bread. Dig garden." He examined my knees and soles. "Calluses you got? Das gut!" He applied salve to my throat. "A few words you can say now. But don't overdo." He frowned. "Remember doctor's orders. In a fortnight, we celebrate Jubilee at the fair."

"What?" He was distracting me. I wanted to bury Karla in the garden.

"Day dedicated to coloreds, honoring old friend Douglass. Invited we are to hear his speech." My cheek felt flushed. "So I invite you too, along with your father."

"Tomorrow?" I had to get out of this room.

The good doctor laughed, the gap in his teeth showing. "No, no. Fourteen tomorrows, my girl. First, work hands outside in garden. Later, break bread with Cyrus, so he can see what a good doctor I am." He took out a tongue depressor. "Your father looked in on you from time to time, was afraid you would notice him."

I closed my eyes. I didn't understand such a father. How could he have a daughter like Karla? And also a daughter like me? Too much time has been lost.

"Now your tongue, it can stick out."

※ ※ ※

After a sleepless night, I followed doctor's orders and prepared to garden. Odette assisted me into a blue gored skirt with a yellow cotton scrim blouse. My aching sinuses were soothed by squeezes of the silk-netted rubber ball atomizer. With the aroma of jasmine lingering in my bedroom, Odette informed me of my favorite quick breakfast: hot oatmeal topped with clumps of brown sugar, raisins and honey-buttered toast of cracked wheat. Several times I dunked the ball of black coffee into a big mug, resting upon a glazed porcelain tray. Finished with breakfast, I smiled at Odette, who helped me descend the back stairs to the outdoors.

In the garden, I rejected gloves to sink my hands into overturned earth. I crumbled clumps of hard soil in my fingers, as if kneading dough into loaves of bread. Squatting in my leather apron, I studied the tall weeds that had first drawn my eyes to the garden, through the bars of the nursery window. I stared up at the fourth floor to the window, almost buried behind branches.

"Dreaming of me again, Alessandra?" said a young man's voice, standing over me. I squinted up at him. "You look at everybody as if for the first time." He adjusted his square glasses. "It scares me."

Not knowing what to say, I heard myself snapping my fingers, "Tools."

"You didn't use to give orders."

I stood, knees trembling like a foal, and gazed around at small railroad cars chugging on the track circling the lower lawn. "Just who are you, young man?"

He bowed, clicking heels. "Used to be known as Mr. Wetherstone. To my intimates, Hermes. Remember? You wore my locket everyday. 'Til the fire tore it off and melted it."

Before I could reply, a male servant lugged a dirty carpet bag that rattled. "Pardon miss," he said, placing the bag at my feet, "Tools, including your favorite one for weeds."

Dust stirred from the carpet bag. "My, my favorite?" Would I know that?

"Do you want me?" said the young man who called himself Hermes. Then his face flushed pink. "I mean, do you want me to pick it out for you?"

I squatted next to the carpet bag with its dark-blue faded tapestry. Unclipping the latch, I spread open the wooden handles on the top like jaws of a beached giant turtle. Taking a deep breath, I closed my eyes, and reached both hands into its pried mouth.

"Your body's trembling, Sander. Let me do it."

Ignoring him, I closed and opened my hands. Kneeling, I plunged my arms deeper. My eyes still shut, my hands roamed around the little cave for tools, bumping knuckles against what seemed small bricks of iron, long wooden handles, claws that trapped my fingers. I wriggled them loose, scraping skin. At the bottom of the carpetbag, I touched a small spade, shaped like half an ice-cone with a long round handle that felt hollow. My hand clasped it like an old friend from long ago.

Rocking back on my heels, I clanked the tool up through layers of metal and wood, like Lazarus arising from the dead. "Here it is!" I shouted raising my favorite clawed weed puller above my head, as my eyes opened in triumph.

I stood and spun like a dancer. Losing balance, I started to fall into a rosebush when young Hermes caught me in his arms. Then he swung me like a carousel, my feet off the ground, one arm around his neck. It felt familiar. As the garden spun, the toes of my sandals scraped the gravel path, slowing us like a bicycle brake. In the rising dust we hugged, staring into each other's eyes. His blue pupils were pools for plunging, but dust invaded my nostrils, and forced me to sneeze. As we released each other, I stomped my foot in frustration.

"Don't! My glasses!"

Then Odette's voice called from the shadow of the gazebo. "Mister Hermes, midday recess."

While grasping my hand, Hermes scooped up his glasses, and pocketed them. We strolled toward the gazebo, inhaling the aroma of onions, cabbage, boiled potatoes and lamb. Odette handed each of us a frosted cut-glass of lemonade with sprigs of mint. As we stepped up into the gazebo, we beheld dappled squares of sunlight on a small folding table, two amber dishes displaying offerings. Sitting side by side with a young man, I should have felt comforted. Instead, I could not take my glance from the red sticky flypapers suspended from rafters. Twitching in the wind, they revolved to reveal black blotches all along their spines like bullet holes. A baby fly was flirting with following its parents, still flapping their wings, their little bodies captured on the flypaper. The baby hovered above them, circling. I could look no longer.

    Clamping my eyes shut, I squeezed one hand around the lemonade glass, and the other on the handle of my clawed tool. Although surrounded by summer heat, I shivered in the shadows.

❋   ❋   ❋

Finally, the time arrived for Jubilee Day at Haytian Pavilion, bringing me the anxiety of first breaking bread with the man the good doctor called my father. Why wasn't Father constantly at my side? Why was he hiding behind the scene pulling strings, and treating me like a marionette? Giving orders to dress me in clothes he alone selected?

    After being dressed for the occasion in a room Odette insisted was my old bedroom, I stood before a full-length oval mirror in clothes ordered by him: a lady's tailor-made suit consisting of jacket and long skirt of wool serge. The fly-front, with cuffed sleeves, topped the skirt with inverted pleat in the back, and a graduated flounce on the bottom. A silk ribbon band circled the waist.

    Everything was funeral black.

    Odette combed back the forelock of my wig that had been blocking my vision. The large mushroom-brimmed hat, trimmed with a large Alsatian bow of black liberty satin, hid a silk cable wire fronted by a brass buckle. Atop the hat, a large cluster of pink artificial roses huddled on one side. Chantilly lace draped over, forming a veil. The hat was all black.

I felt tears in my eyes. Then I realized the tears were prompted by braces, shoulder and back with steel stays to anchor my bones into an unnatural perfection, aborting my breath. I felt impaled.

Odette must have read my face. "Accustomed, you will grow." She stood between me and the mirror, studying my face. "You must be on time for the first breakfast with your father. You must go down now."

I took two steps toward the door. The gong of grandfather's clock vibrated from the dining room through my steel stays like a tuning fork. It shook my very soul. I stopped. Then one word burst from my mouth. "Nooooooo!"

With both hands, I lifted the mushroom hat from my head like a crown I voluntarily renounced. I threw the hat against the mirror; it bounced, and hit Cerby on his tail, sending him screeching for the exit. However, the closed door caused him to skid against it. I ripped at my throat, snapping buttons to free my spirit.

Odette screamed. Flinging open the door, she escaped, followed by Cerby at her heels.

Fighting free from the buttonless tailor-made jacket, I pulled it over my head, and flung it at the wall. I ripped the buttons of the black blouse of mercerized sateen with its fake pearls, and I sent it scattering across the wooden floor. Throwing the blouse on the bed, I jammed my thumbs into the cast-off snaps, springing shoulder and back braces loose. I shed its snake skin, dropping it at my feet.

Unfurling the long skirt, I twirled it twice before letting it fly. Standing in my underdrawers, I remembered I'd forgotten one more thing—the wig. I pitched it into the flames of the burning fireplace, setting it ablaze. I stared as the straight brown hair blackened into curls. The wig, resembling a tiny fallen tower, hypnotized me until its smoke made me cough. Opening the partially stuck window, I let out gray smoke. Still coughing, I searched for a hat. Finally I decided on a baseball cap of the

Chicago White Stockings. I jammed it down on my bald scalp. Since the world is run by males, why not dress as one? From the costume closet, I chose leather pants, red shirt, and leather vest. When I stood before the mirror fully dressed, I saw a need for boots. Tucked in a dark corner were a pair of brown cowhides; they fit snug and secure on my feet. After adding an orange kerchief around my throat, I marched out of the bedroom, and down to breakfast with the man who claimed to be my father.

When I arrived, only Mrs. Dibbs was in the dining room, her arms folded and a smirk upon her face. She informed me I was too late; Mr. Aultman had already left for the Jubilee. I was ordered to follow with Doctor Wetherstone's family.

Personally, I felt relieved.

* * *

My bald scalp itched as if crawling with fire ants, but I refused to scratch. Had the fire ants escaped from the garden with me?

I squirmed at the end of the pew seated next to the good doctor, our party awaiting among a small audience for the featured speaker, somebody named Douglass.

When Doc Seth noticed my squirming, he touched my hand and glanced at my head. "Gut!" he said patting my knuckles. "She's healing goot! The more itch, the more heal."

If I could have moved away from him, I would have done so, except I was wedged into the corner of the shoulder of the pew. What could I do? It would be ungrateful to hurt his feelings.

"Alessandra, those clothes are not what I ordered!" Father shouted at me from the end of our pew."

"Since I am ordered to please you," I whispered back, "shouldn't I dress as a boy? Now you can finally have your son. You could even name him Alexander!"

Father's eyes bulged. I felt secure next to the good doctor. Nowhere to be seen were Sister Karla and her new boyfriend from Fort Sheridan. As I looked for them, I was surprised to observe that half the congregation was white. Seated behind me, Brickton anticipated my question. "No mystery, young lady. They know Frederick Douglass is half-white himself."

I pointed to the stage where notables were seated. "Is one of them Douglass?"

"No, he's just a poet named Dunbar. Really a clerk Douglass hired. Lady to his left is Harriet Beecher—" A loud rumbling outside interrupted him. "Trucks," he said, "the trucks have arrived."

"Hush!" said a voice on the other side of Doc Seth. Hermes leaned across his father's lap and slapped my wrist, "and stop picking at your fingernails."

I hadn't realized that to distract my mind from the itching, I'd pestered my nails. The ends were worked off, mixed with dried blood where black axel grease still lingered.

"Watermelons!" Hermes yelled, half standing, "I smell watermelons."

"Quiet, son," Edith said, seated next to him. "This is like a church."

"And by the truckload!"

"Knew there'd be trouble today," Brickton said, "Told the *Herald* to send me." He unbuttoned his hunting jacket, revealing the butt of a derringer in a shoulder holster. "When I saw you come in, I just had to change my seat."

"A gun? Just for a speech?" I managed to say, admiring his power.

"Gillmore's band was scheduled to play here."

"Where are they?" Hermes said.

"Cancelled. Cancelled last minute. All white."

Part of the congregation applauded as a colored woman left her chair next to the young poet. She cleared her throat and began to sing "Never My God To Thee."

In the vestibule, dozens of coloreds in rags elbowed their way into the pavilion, carrying gunny sacks that bulged.

"They're just waiting for a signal," Brickton said. "Why don't you tip your baseball cap, Miss Aultman, and see what happens?"

Applause for the singer's rendition rippled throughout the audience. The stench of gasoline, exhaust fumes from trucks, and broken watermelons invaded my nostrils. My eyes could barely focus on the poet-clerk, about twenty, taking center stage. Speaking with a voice like vinegar, he recited a poem he composed, "The Colored American," but the newcomers chatted so loudly I could hardly hear the poet.

Doc Seth muttered, "Where are those Columbian guards?"

After Dunbar finished his poem to a scattering of applause, the gunny sacks in the back snapped open at the same time. At that moment, from the wings of the stage ambled a huge colored man with a massive head of salty hair. He resembled a regal lion. As he paused at the podium, I noticed that those colored newcomers were edging along the walls toward the stage. The speaker placed a sheaf of papers before himself on the stand.

A tap on my shoulder. "Two lynchings of negras this summer so far. Maybe Douglass will be the third." Brickton bit his pencil. "Hot damn!"

The featured speaker, head down and hands shaking, rippled the pages. Skins of watermelon rinds popped within the pavilion. Were they being stabbed with knives? Sounds of munching on melons and twanging of pulp seeds filled the air. Then slices of watermelon and blackseeds ricocheted against the speaker's stand. Douglass did not look up. Brickton broke his pencil point. Cursing, he bit into the wooden tip.

What would I do if I were Douglass?

The speaker's chin jutted up, his nostrils flaring like a thoroughbred at the starting gate. He eyed the crowd, then took the stack of papers in both hands and, stretching his arms, dropped his prepared speech straight down to the floor of the stage.

"Damn him," cursed Brickton. "Now I've got to take notes!"

Douglass' deep voice thundered from the stage. "Men talk of the Negro Problem—" A few people applauded. "There is no Negro Problem." Colored people with gunny sacks booed. "Problem is whether the American people have—" He paused, examining the unruly crowd with calm eyes. "Whether the American people have honor enough."

Mr. Aultman stood up. Was he going to defend the speaker?

Chunks of melon flew past. The speaker did not flinch. Other pieces flew between two white dignitaries while others struck the American flag, smack dab on the stars. "Whether the American people have patriotism enough."

Mr. Aultman stalked out of the other end of our pew, with Aunt Ashford scurrying after him, but Uncle Chilton sidled closer to us. I felt the anticipation that something new was being born inside me.

Dozens of melon chunks filled the air, shattering against the seal of the Haytian government. Other slabs spattered people onstage. In the audience negra and white men stood shouting. Women screamed for police. "For the American people to live up to their constitution." A wedge of melon smacked Douglass's shoulder. His expression did not change. Bravo, I shouted to encourage the speaker. Bravo! "We Negroes love our country." The sound of rumbling trucks surrounded the pavilion, engines roaring. "We Negroes fought for this country." A white woman fainted, and was carried by a Haytian guard to a side exit. "We ask only that we be treated as well as those southern soldiers in the Civil War who fought against our union."

Doc Seth and half the audience including me stood, and applauded. Hermes slid next to me, taking his father's place. He reached for my hands, but I put them into my leather pockets.

The good doctor sat down and leaned over Hermes. "I'll wager your itchy scalp that you've forgotten."

What did he mean? Then I laughed at myself, and rubbed the button on the crown of my cap. Suddenly I realized the need for a public comfort station.

"The *Herald* desires your opinion of the fair, sir," said Brickton.

"Here it is—a cultural Frankenstein! That's what the fair has become."

"May I quote you, Dr. Wetherstone?"

"A racial nightmare!" the doctor added, "Ida B. Wells is right refusing to attend. Where in the fair are the colored exhibits? The colored workers? The colored fairgoers?"

"Shut your big mouth!" hollered a white man sitting in front of him.

Doc Seth stood up. "Well then, at least where are the colored Columbian guards?" As the two men shouted nose to nose, hecklers in the pews took sides as pieces of watermelon started to pelt them while Mr. Douglass continued his speech.

Another man in front of Doc Seth stood tall, raising his voice. "What about the White City?"

"Whited sepulchers."

Catcalls from the audience greeted me as I stood on the seat in support of the Negroes. I felt closer to them than my own family.

A guard ordered us to leave. Disturbing the peace. Of course we refused, but when he was joined by two Haytian ushers we were escorted to a side exit with the good doctor shouting to the audience, "Read the pamphlet 'The Reason why Colored America is not represented in the Exposition by—'" A guard tried to silence him, "Ida B. Wells."

Once outside, I realized in our haste I had not thought about my difficulty in walking. We were greeted with the sight of a hundred trucks, bumper to bumper, engines vibrating, horns blowing. Blue clouds of gasoline burnt my throat. Where's that public comfort?

Freeing my hand from Hermes, I excused myself and wedged my body between two trucks. I stumbled on uneven ground, falling to my knees. Bits of watermelon flew past my ears as truck drivers pelted a crowd of coloreds at the open windows, listening to Douglass' words. Hunching my shoulders to gather strength, I stood and stepped over slabs of melons littering the grounds. At the rear of the building, I saw a public comfort station. Hoping that no one was from Astor Street, I hurried through the angry throng. They threatened by snapping emptied gunny sacks. After a quick glance at my boy's outfit, however, they cleared a path for me.

Remembering to swing my shoulders and not my hips, I yanked the peak of my baseball cap down over my forehead.

Approaching the station, I saw expressions of frustration on women returning from public comfort. Lurching toward the clutch of women crowding the door, I heard a series of groans from other women just arriving. When I reached the entrance, I was stopped in my tracks by a large sign screaming—*FOR MEN ONLY.*

Men, colored and white, lounged to both sides, chuckling as they observed the scene.

Taking a quick breath, I hitched my leather pants and, throwing out my elbows, marched up the ramp past the women to open the door. I was disappointed to discover the comfort station empty. After relieving myself and washing my hands, I exited, bumping into a huge truck driver who gave me a double look as he scratched his privates.

Pausing on the platform of the ramp, I studied the crowd. Shirtless men with tattoos spat tobacco at each other's boots, while women in babushkas bit their lips, staring at me with watery eyes.

As other young girls approached the comfort station hopefully, I turned on my heel and grabbed the sign *FOR MEN*

ONLY, slipping it under an arm like a baton of a major demo leading a parade. I marched down the ramp and through the stunned crowd, as women cheered, and men shouted, "Traitor!"

Stomping on every piece of watermelon I could find, I swung my shoulders and glared at men who were blinking and shaking their heads. As I rejoined our party waiting beyond the ring of trucks, I saw Curlin perched in the driver seat, shotgun across his lap, a worldwide grin across his mouth. As I stepped up into the open carriage accepting Brickton's hand, I laughed: at Mr. Aultman losing his cigar from his gaping mouth, the good doctor beaming like a new father, Edith hiding her face in shame, and Hermes looking for a comfort station of his own.

As I settled into the carriage and laid the sign across my trousers, I felt the mixed emotions of completing a long journey to Jubilee while at the same time anticipating a direction yet to come.

Chapter Thirteen

mirror image

Friday, August 25

Rocking on my feet in front of the full-length mirror in my old bedroom, I would have sworn a bald young man stared out at me, with penciled eyebrows and artificial eyelashes from Karla.

On a top corner of the oval mirror dangled the sign *FOR MEN ONLY* that I had removed last night from the public comfort station behind the Haytian Pavilion, a souvenir from what Karla had rechristened the Columbian Masculine Exposition.

Although I had ordered Odette to assist me in my deception, she fled the room, bumping into Karla who cursed at her. Slapping me on the back, Karla began to attach her own anchor brace on me to square my shoulders, providing me the illusion of a barrel chest. Despite my previous reservations, I acquiesced, and allowed Karla to harness me. "We do seem to be trading places, Stir. Am I now closer to Cyrus than you are?"

The steel springs and overshot of elastic webbing forced me to feel like a mouse caught in a trap. The crush on my chest nearly made my heart stop. "What do you mean, Karla? Are you closer to Father now?"

"Spread your arms, Stir, while I put my boyfriend's shirt on you." Before I could object, I felt the cool blue silk envelop my bare arms, and embrace the nape of my neck. When Karla faced me, she drew the shirt front together, tugging downward and fastening the bottom button first, then upwards, all the way to my throat. Lifting the collar, Karla stared into my face, as if to hypnotize me with her evil eye, turning her good intentions bad. When I crossed my eyes, she burst into laughter. "Then, Stir, I'll hang you instead," she said, as she looped the string tie over my head like a noose. Clutching the two silver tips, she slid the guide up the red string to secure the silver dollar under my chin, after which Karla folded the collar over the string and patted my barrel chest.

From the costume rack, I selected beige corduroy knee britches. Stepping into them and hitching them up, I realized my hands were sweating. I rubbed them against the corrugated texture of the trousers. To tighten the cowhide belt, I took a deep breath, and hooked the round silver buckle of a buffalo into the tightest hole.

Sitting on my bed, I drew on long brown stockings. Karla knelt before me, lifting one of my feet while holding a high-low shoe. With her other hand, she slipped the leather shoe on me and said, "Your Herkimer would love doing this." It felt snug above my ankle.

When I stood before the mirror, Karla cackled because one stocking sagged into a clump at my ankle. She tugged the errant sock, removing its wrinkles by tucking the elastic top under the knee of my britches, making it as smooth as the other one. Standing to one side, Karla studied my reflection. She frowned. "Your scalp?" She glanced about for a hat, while I put on my red and white striped tennis cap. Grabbing the white Stetson, Karla knocked the tennis cap off, planting the Stetson firm on my bare scalp, and securing it with a drawstring so firmly it bumped her knuckles against my jaw.

Recoiling from the blow, I examined my chin in the mirror above the basin and detected no visible damage. Feeling invincible, I posed in front of the dressing mirror, adopting what I thought was a cowboy's male stance with toes out, shoulders square, thumbs in belt.

"You can't pose like that," Karla said, "You look like you're Mr.—ah—Pimperton."

"What?"

"Think Buffalo Bill."

"How?"

"Don't wriggle your hips. Roll your shoulders, like you're elbowing through water."

"I know. I know."

Practicing the stiff-legged male stride before the mirror, I tilted the Stetson over one eye. The telephone downstairs rang once and ceased: Hermes' signal he was ready to accompany me to the fair. Scooping the contents of my purse into my deep pockets, I hastened out the door forgetting to thank Karla, who said, "Hips, Sister, too much hips."

❋ ❋ ❋

The Illinois Central Railroad car was so jammed by the Saturday crowd that Hermes, pouting, and I, grinning, stood holding onto ceiling straps. An older gentleman with white sideburns offered me his seat. Without thinking, I accepted, but the very instant I sat down, it dawned on me what I had done. As I met the old man's eyes, he winked. I did not look at Hermes. Instead, I noticed a lady who bulged in the middle.

Tipping my Stetson, I rose and presented her my place. As she sat down, she smiled and said, "Thank you, young man."

Disembarking at the station near Buffalo Bill's Wild West, I watched the eager faces of people arriving for the Extravaganza, and almost envied their past memories. I would not have traded places with them however, because I had the rare opportunity to recreate myself. He thought more people would recreate themselves if they only could.

When I told Hermes he said, "I don't need to recreate myself. It makes me nervous when you appear masculine."

"You could too, if you tried."

Our destination was Mr. Arnold's Photography Studio. Once inside the tent, we mingled with recruits hoping, as I did, to be hired as commercial photographers. Kissing me on the cheek, Hermes left me to race to an attached smaller tent to receive his individual assignments for the day. With mixed feelings about being kissed because of my male clothing, I peered around, and saw that a woolly-haired man had observed the kiss. With a nod and a wink, he shuffled toward me.

Instinctively, I withdrew to the other side of the tent, scuffing up sawdust covering dried mud. To prevent the cold chill of feeling an orphan, I touched Mother's pendant beneath the blue silk shirt.

The clang of a cowbell announced a small man atop a wooden crate. His pencil-thin mustache quivered like a rat's tail beneath a long chiseled nose he used to peer down upon all assembled. He handed the bell to an overweight Columbian guard. "Good morn, one and all. You see before you Harlow H. Huggins, administrator of the fair. This morning I shall indoctrinate you, me, myself this morning because Mr. Arnold, himself, is…well, indisposed."

The man next to me whispered with whisky breath, "This guy's old man's president of the fair. Or can't youse tell?"

Mr. Huggins continued, "Before one goes further, please remove all your hats as a sign of courtesy and respect to yours truly."

I started to take off my Stetson when I realized that my nude scalp would be exposed, and might draw attention. What to do?

I edged toward the exit flap. Another Columbian guard, with squinty eyes, stood, arms akimbo, blocking my escape. I faked a sneeze, and said to him, "Handkerchief, buddy."

With reluctance, he pulled one from his pocket. It depicted the Ferris Wheel in vivid colors. Snatching it out of his hand, I tied a knot at its four corners. Then I took off my hat, and plopped the knotted kerchief on my head to cover my bald pate.

Returning with hat in hand, I sidled into the crowd. By now, Huggins had put on a pair of kid gloves. "Later, my assistants shall demonstrate the usage for the eight-inch by ten-inch camera with tripod." He smirked at an even smaller man in the corner playing with a camel-hair tassel on a swagger stick. "Some of us call it a reproductive camera."

Someone muttered, "Catch the bloody duke at the wall, will yuh?"

"Remember, boys, photograph only buildings, not people." The Columbian guard distributed circular photographs to us as examples of the types of pictures to take. "If you are hired, and only a few will be chosen, it will be as professionals, not amateurs. Amateurs are licensed at the fair for a fee, but not encouraged. We provide no darkrooms for amateurs."

He pronounced the word "amateurs" with the same tone I would use for "rodents." Mr. Huggins stretched his arms out, gloved hands entwined. "Mr. Arnold retains all rights, repeat all rights, to all photographs you take. Plus take no ugly pictures. Therefore, no stock yards, no homes of working men, no South Pond. Especially no Midway photos. The Midway is scandalous!"

Mentally, I thanked him for providing a list of places I intended to visit and photograph.

"We have these Columbian guards to enforce rules. Everyone at the fair taking a photograph must be licensed. All, with one exception, of course." Mr. Huggins nodded toward the gentleman with swagger stick, jodhpurs and ascot tie. "Our most welcome visitor from England, late of Indya, the Duke of Newcastle."

Somebody whistled. The Columbian guard at the flap reached a long arm into the crowd, and collared the offender, escorting him to the exit. "Order in the ranks," Mr. Huggins said. "To continue, keep onlookers out of your picture frames. It is best to use a timer, so that people moving will just disappear from the photo as if they never existed."

A nudge to my shoulder sent a shiver down my spine. Detected? Arrested?

"Young man," a familiar face whispered. "Come with me." He wriggled his middle finger at me, and pointed toward the exit. To keep from being exposed, I followed. At the exit, he said to the guard, "My friend here is sick from a hangover. The lad needs fresh air."

The guard shook his head.

"Or else he will vomit all over those bright shingles on your shoulders."

The guard let us out.

When the flap dropped behind us, I said to Brickton, "Is my disguise that bad?"

"Not actually, only half-bad. I knew you'd be here this morning." He smiled at my expression. "Hermes told me."

"He shouldn't have revealed my plan," I said, whipping the handkerchief off my head and slapping on my Stetson. I shook the flap as hard as I could, until the guard stuck out his bare head to see the trouble. Unable to resist temptation, I smacked his own handkerchief flat on his head, flipped the canvas closed, and tied its straps around the guard's head, tight as I could.

Then, Brick and I ran. Away from the photography tent we ran beneath the elevated railroad tracks hand in hand, past the outside exhibit of Transportation, until we collapsed out of breath on a bench. Between our gasps, we laughed. Brickton said, "What am I running for? My Duryea is parked back at the tent!" He laughed louder, and gave me a squeeze.

"This time," I panted, "This time, I deserted Hermes."

Over his shoulder, I saw the Cold Storage Building, with its blackened shell, torn towers, and windowless scorched walls like a cremated gigantic elephant. Did memories begin to smolder in my mind? None that I could tell.

Brickton's eyes, however, were focused on something else. "Look past Cold Storage. Near the rail terminal."

I didn't respond. In the back of my head, I heard a faint noise: Why was it the screams of men? I felt a dull ache.

Brickton stood, and hitched his belt. "Tucked in the corner of the fair lives the Kodak fiend! Some people call him Mr. Eastman." He blinked his eyes in mock fright.

"Will he see through my disguise?"

Our elbows hooked together, we ran until we stopped outside a building with a modest sign: *Smith, Crimp, and Eastman.*

Inside, I damped down my forehead and upper lip with my sleeve. Excessive perspiration always embarrassed me. As I did so, masked workmen wearing rubber aprons, and rolled-up shirt sleeves faced walls lined with metal counters, trays, tubes, bottles. Assisting them were women in calico dresses, hustling back and forth with supplies, aiming to please. I felt relieved that I was not one of those women, thanks to Nellie Bly. She was successful in a man's world by dressing like one of them.

As Brickton tried to snuggle close to me, I heard a worker near us mutter, "Better do it over. Mr. Eastman don't accept sloppy."

I was liking Mr. Eastman already.

My attention was drawn to the center of the laboratory, where a small meeting was being conducted by a slim young man in a gray suit with vest and cravat. Was he the son of the owner? Talking to six men and one young lady, he held a large glass of milk in fingers stained green. Possessing a banker's air, his thin voice carried above the hubbub of workers at their posts. "Photography is no more a fad than bicycling. Believe that. Take pictures of people, not things. People are most important. Fix their images. Fix images of people doing ordinary actions. Follow famous people, and fix memories of their human moments."

My heart went out to him.

"Mr. Eastman, what famous person would you suggest?" asked the young lady in her red bonnet, "And do you think they would regard me with enough respect to submit to a photograph?"

She made me happy not to be wearing a red bonnet.

Mr. Eastman took a sip of milk and patted his van dyke. "Do not be afraid. Being a photographer is a most suitable occupation for a young lady."

Brickton poked me with his elbow. I poked him back.

"Our staff has already photoed Gentleman Jim Corbett, Susan B. Anthony, Jane Addams, and, let's see who else, oh yes, Dwight Moody, and last week the entire White Stockings baseball team." The men in the group applauded. "So, if a famous person balks at a photograph from you, just rattle off this little list."

"But Mr. Eastman, I possess such a poor memory."

"Then my secretary, Miss Whitney, shall write it down for you, and you can photograph it."

The men laughed. I felt my cheeks blush in embarrassment for her.

"However," Mr. Eastman said, "There is one exception to the rule about famous people. Mayor Harrison must not be disturbed when escorting his young fiancé. Photograph Mayor only alone."

What did he mean?

The workmen along the wall snickered.

What was so funny?

"You volunteers represent Kodak. Whenever tourists see your Kodak, please explain how it works. Three easy steps—point, click, crank. Not ten steps like those bulky wet cell cameras. Tell tourists about dry cell being superior to Arnold's wet plates. Also mention Kodak's one hundred images before reloading." He pointed to a map of the fair on the wall. "Those stars are Kodak Kiosks. There, a tourist can exchange his spent Kodak for a new camera, containing one hundred new exposures. Each shot is easy as snapping off a shotgun blast. That's why we call it a snapshot."

I could learn from this man.

By this time, we had joined the little group.

"And now let us introduce this month's Kodak Girl!"

Whistles greeted a young lady, who cavorted into the lab, wearing a lengthy blue and white striped swim suit, sleeves the size of legs of mutton. She twirled an open parasol over her shoulder, while beaming a practiced smile. Mr. Eastman toasted her with his glass of milk nearly empty. She struck a pose leaning on the parasol, now closed, and proclaimed with a charming lisp, "We member," she purred, "If it's not Eastman, it's not Kodak!"

Workers chanted a slogan as if one word: "Take-a-Kodak-with-you," as they waved at the Kodak Girl who exited, twirling her parasol.

I felt sorry for her.

"And now let me introduce my secretary, Miss Alice K. Whitney." She appeared wearing a lace blouse, high collar, and a man's long black tie. I wouldn't be caught dead in her garb. She grimaced at the new interns, all of whom were taller than she. "Miss Whitney, here, will conduct you into the next room for further indoctrination. Then in the shipping room, you will be issued your own cameras." The group applauded.

"Thank you for your kind attention. You have made my mother very happy."

After the crowd left, Brickton advanced on Mr. Eastman, "Time for our interview?" He introduced me as "Al Aultman," and explained my interest in photography.

"No more suitable work," Mr. Eastman said, staring into his empty milk glass. "Excuse us for a moment, Mister Aleman. You already heard orientation so you may join the other gentlemen in the shipping room. Fill necessary forms." Then Brickton waved me away from his interview, adding, "And we do the rest!"

I strode into the next room for further indoctrination as an official Kodak photographer with all the other men.

❋   ❋   ❋

That night I couldn't sleep, and I couldn't tell anybody about my feelings. At first, I regretted having no one to confide in, not Odette, not Hermes, not Father. Only Mother could I tell, and she told me to keep it to myself. I followed her advice, and over the course of the next few weeks, I discovered something. Keeping my own counsel provided a source of energy. I realized, that if I stopped asking the question of who I was, I could pour the energy into who I wanted to become.

I was exuberant passing my acid test with Mr. Eastman, and accepted the position of a male photographer. For my first assignment I interviewed widows of the thirty workers who died constructing the fair. Some of them allowed me to take photographs of their children, but only if they received free copies. I gave my interviews and photos to Brickton for possible publication in the *Herald*. On another day, I interviewed street sweepers who labored all day for bowls of soup. I felt moved by their wives with their sunken eyes, so I gave hard candy to their children.

One of my best interviews was with the Esquimaux from the Yukon, who told me about broken promises. Instead of good pay, they received only poor food and no fresh water. Every day in the summer heat, they were forced to wear fur coats to please tourists, or else no rations for themselves and their children. If the Esquimaux complained, their white manager cursed them as "chattels." I wondered, were these the same bears who walked as men that I saw from the Illinois central? They had appeared so romantic. All these facts I wrote up, adding photographs, and handed them to Brickton He was always impressed, but disappointed that his editor rejected my submissions. Odette told me to read the *Herald* each day to check on Brickton, but wouldn't that be showing a lack of trust?

After some experience, I was anxious to interview doctors. Since the fair was constructed on a swamp, why didn't the doctors object? I discovered that even though they feared a smallpox epidemic, as Doc Seth wrote the *Tribune* every other week, they had not planned a program for smallpox vaccination. They claimed Mr. Ellis on the board would just kill it.

For my next assignment, I asked Mr. Eastman if I could document cruelty to Indians, but he advised me not to do it, saying, "The whites don't want to hear about it." Despite his opinion, I skipped his morning meeting and, clipping the ankles of my trousers, bicycled directly to the military encampment in Midway. As rumor had it, today was a special day. An overflow crowd inside the west gate made me glad I had brought my full one hundred exposures. My article about cruelty to Indians must become the first one Brickton's editor would purchase. How could he resist? It might even make page one of the *Herald*.

After paying admission, I slipped a coin to a Columbian Guard, who escorted me to the foot of the outdoor gallows, roped-off for dignitaries. The Master of Ceremonies, a white man with a megaphone, proclaimed that this event was the official one-time-only performance costing ten times the regular admission, conducted inside the military encampment for security purposes. I noticed soldiers cradling Springfield rifles as they guarded the perimeter of the enclosure. It made me feel less safe.

Two large Indians in white men's work clothes stood on the gallows. One rocked on his toes, making the platform creak. The impatient crowd had been drinking and eating for hours.

I felt a cold chill cross my heart.

"Folks, have you all paid your way in?" Laughter and curses. "Then meet Chief Two Bites and Joe Strong Back." I fingered my starch collar as I gulped. "They're each ticketed to make a whole month's pay, in less than ten minutes." Boos from the crowd. I thought what could they possibly do for so much money. "Let's get started," someone shouted. With a gesture from the Master of Ceremonies, the two Indians removed their shirts ever so slowly, until several pistol shots from the back of the mob speeded them up. Then the master displayed a Bowie knife, glittering in the sunlight. The crowd roared its approval. A wave of excitement swept through me. I readied my Kodak and jotted a few notes for Brickton. He would love this.

The master ordered the two Indians to turn their naked backs to the crowd. Like General Sheridan inspecting the troops, he strutted past one Indian to approach the other. Then he raised his Bowie knife into the air. The front row gasped. I stared; is he going to stab him? Stepping aside, he laid the point of the blade on the chief's back, large muscles twitching. Was it cold? Then the Master of Ceremonies stepped sideways, and placed the blade vertically on the chief's back, slowly slicing a deep gash downward, then a second gash, then a third, a fourth all parallel to each other. As the master moved away, his female assistant, an Indian maiden, sponged their blood as the mob whistled and hollered for more. I could not believe my eyes. Why didn't the soldiers stop this atrocity?

After wiping the bloody blade against his buckskin trousers, the master approached Joe Strong Back, and laid the point of the blade against his bare back. I almost fainted in anticipation, dropping my Kodak to my feet. With deliberate ease, the master repeated the slicing ritual on Joe Strong Back as his female assistant sponged and sponged. Somebody must stop this. I bit my fist to keep from screaming.

When the master strode to a table, he sheathed the knife and held up a long piece of rawhide cord. Lifting it over his head, he snapped it three times like a whip, driving the crowd crazy with lust. Retracing steps, he reapproached Chief Two Bites. The master handed one end of the cord to his assistant. Then, with the delicacy worthy of Doc Seth, he inserted one end of the thin cord into one of the vertical slits, wove it through, and out the second slit to guide it into the next, and out the last. He was as skillful as the devil himself. As he threaded the cord through the openings of flesh, people pushed closer, silent as a morgue. Someone in the crowd flashed a wet-cell photograph. Was it Hermes? My hands felt paralyzed, my body rigid. I was hemmed in. I could not pick up my Kodak from my feet to take a single picture to save my soul. I clamped my eyes closed.

The roar of the crowd forced my lids to part revealing the master bowing to the mob as he pulled the end of the rope until it snaked out of Chief Two Bites' back. Then the master measured it with his outstretched arms, like a tailor for a suit.

He inserted the end of the rawhide into the first slit of flesh, in-and-out and in-and-out, weaving the slits together. Then he ordered both men to stand back to back, joined by the same rawhide cord that he knotted as tightly as Siamese twins.

After an eternity of the mob celebrating with cat-calls, rifle shots, and the pitching of Stetsons into the air, the master picked up a pistol from a table. Slowly, he stretched out his arm, and aimed the pistol at the two Indians. The crowd gasped, and drew silent. Was he going to murder them and pay off their families? I jumped with fright as he shot into the air: once, twice, three times. Did it signal the end of this one-time-only atrocity?

The people continued cheering and whistling. Some cowboys leaped onto the gallows platform to mop up spilt blood for souvenirs with their bandanas. The two Indians were shuffled toward backstage by armed guards. Then five white lassos from the crowd encircled the bodies of the two Indians, spinning them around and around, until the white ropes made their bleeding red flesh seem almost white.

Why had I disobeyed Mr. Eastman? Refusing to cry, I retrieved my Kodak, shaking off blood and tobacco juice as I stumbled through the mob to a tree at the perimeter of the compound.

Soldiers were hugging each other. "All bound up like they done to us!" An officer riding up on a white horse shouted, "I missed it! Round up two more Potawatomie!"

How could I ever forget what I just saw? I threw my Kodak into a trash barrel. Elbowing my way to my bicycle my heart was filled with questions. Why couldn't I stop this evil? Why couldn't I photograph it? Was photographing evil without stopping it suitable for a young lady? Or for that matter a young man?

❀ ❀ ❀

When I shared my revulsion at the mutilation of the Indians with Brickton, he reacted strangely. "Hot damn!" he shouted as he parked his Duryea in front of the Aultman manor. I had enjoyed our Sunday picnic on the lake shore much more than attending church. But why didn't he comprehend the evil?

"Wish I had been there. Why didn't yuh tell me? So where are the photographs for my article?" He switched off the ignition, which surprised me because he always kept the engine vibrating, even during our picnic.

"Well, I don't like reporting evil. Nellie Bly exposed evil; she didn't profit from it." I started to jump down from the machine, but my Gibson skirt caught where the door should have been and stopped me.

"Hey, I'm talking," Brickton said, lowering his voice, "but you're not listening."

Taking a breath deeper than usual, I did not know how to say the unpleasant truth.

"I'm not a patient man, Alessandra. Where's the bloody photos?"

"The camera was lost."

"Lost! Where?"

"After it was over. As I was leaving, a Columbian guard confiscated it."

"Well, Ally, which is it? Lost or confiscated?"

I really wished I had gone to church. I should have listened to Mother, but I hadn't heard her voice in a long time. And Nellie Bly was becoming a memory.

Brickton took off his right glove with his teeth, and stroked my hand. "You've changed, Alessandra. At Buffalo Bill's you were so beautiful. On the Captive Balloon, you were so romantic."

He let go my hand, took out his flask, and jiggled it. Nearly empty. He replaced it in an inner coat pocket. "But you never once lied to me."

"I'm not—"

"I could have got those photos on page one of the *Herald*. Christ, the boss would have loved me. Maybe even a bonus. Maybe an assignment to Atlanta."

A lace curtain in our front window had been pulled aside. I said, "Page one? Published? But they never published any one of my photographs before, Brick."

Brickton shifted uneasily behind the joy stick. "Let's talk about something else."

"No we won't talk about something else. Tell me about my photographs!"

"Ally, since you look so lovely in your Gibson, why on earth do you ever dress as a boy?"

I jumped out of his Duryea, but into a puddle.

"Don't go, dear Ally, I'm dying to ask you another question."

"No, if you don't want to answer me—"

"Tell me, when you wear men's clothes, what's your favorite item? The buttons?" He leered at me. I hated him when he leered.

"If you don't answer my question, why should I answer yours?" I sauntered away while Brickton. shouted behind me.

"Oh, by the by, say hello to your father, he's peeking at us from behind those lace curtains."

※ ※ ※

That night I could not sleep, brooding on the question Brickton had asked me. I'll never understand men. Take Hermes. He knows I'm working with Brickton—so he doesn't phone me anymore. Why? Tossing in bed, I dismissed Odette who was pestering me with opium cordials. I listened to oak branches whispering outside my open window. In the darkness, I prayed. As I descended into sleep, I thought I heard a whisper, sounding like Mother's voice, repeating one word that made me laugh, "Pockets."

Yes, my favorite part of men's clothes were pockets: first Father's pockets, then Hermes', then Brickton's and now my own pockets. I realized that pockets meant control, unlike purses, which were burdens. As I giggled at myself I resolved not to share my secret with anyone. I needed to carry the power of control into my life as an enlightened lady journalist. But what were my chances of success?

※ ※ ※

As September waned, I felt the need for inspiration since assuming the role of a male photographer had become routine. Perusing my McNally's guidebook, I realized I had yet to visit art galleries in the Fine Arts Building. Wanting companionship, I took the initiative and phoned Hermes.

When he learned I would be dressing as a boy he claimed a previous commitment. Was it with Karla? I really didn't need his companionship after all.

Taking my cycle, I determined to visit the gallery on my own. Inside, I stared at dozens of oil paintings, letting images wash over me like fall breezes. The best ones made me wish I had brought my replacement Kodak. In particular I loved Winslow Homer's *March Wind*. It shows a woman atop a knoll, her back to me, holding her bonnet on her head against a rising wind of a March day, darkening, her full skirts billowing like a sail. She didn't need to disguise her strength. Even in the stuffy gallery, I felt a wind from the painting on my cheek. In the next room, I found Homer's *In Fog Warning*. A dory heaves up one side of a huge wave, revealing the contents of his rowboat, two large halibut flapping at the feet of a fisherman. He hunkers down, alone in the boat. In the storm, fog threatens to hide his mother schooner before he can return safely with his catch.

That picture so unnerved me, although I did not know why, that I begged Hermes to accompany me the next day. I promised him not to dress as a boy. Maybe Hermes was right, after all, to be scandalized by my male attire. Was it true that I had sold out being a female for a dishonest advantage? Why couldn't men be less fearful and more accepting? These questions always brought me a migraine.

When Hermes saw me in my Gibson he took charge of our agenda, making me hate myself for being powerless. First, he insisted on seeing the most popular picture at the fair. "Sander, how could you have missed it?" he said, grabbing my wrist, and marching me up the stairs to a gallery jammed with people crowding in front of a large, five foot high, six foot wide golden frame.

Wedging into the room, I heard an unseen woman sobbing in a corner. A barrel-chested man with a diamond stick-pin in his cravat muttered to himself as he sidled past me to the exit. "By Gawd's wounds, I'd rather possess that one picture on that there wall than this whole bloody gallery."

As the man moved beyond us, I saw a tour guide speaking to a gaggle of elderly ladies. "Old Chicago cannot have gone entirely to the proverbial dogs. Not when Chicagoans become enthralled by this simple homey scene we see before us." He pointed a yard stick toward a picture I could not see, it being hidden by ostrich feathers adorning a tall bonnet directly in front of me. Was this the most popular picture at the fair?

After the guide and his little group trekked to the next gallery, we progressed closer to the wall. Encamping near its golden frame, I studied the oil that displayed a sparse room inhabited by rustic people. Hermes intertwined his fingers with mine as I smiled. Studying the center of the painting, I saw a middle-aged woman, hair pulled back tightly like mine used to be. In the bright window light, she places both her hands firmly upon the shoulders of a young man facing her, but looking beyond. He holds his hat firmly in one hand, while the woman peers into his face, as if to memorize each line of his flesh, as if to transfer her strength to him, like mother to me. The young man, her son? He seems to peer into a middle distance, like Hermes accuses me of doing. The lad is not focusing on a young lady. His girlfriend? No, probably his sister. She pets a large hound, crouched beside her, the dog's head cocked like Edith. In the background, sits an old man sharing their same expression: acceptance of the unknown. Next to him in a doorway, slumps a little girl. She sags against the door frame as she stares at me with the look of loss that makes my eyes moisten. In the open doorway, stands a stranger wearing his hat indoors. Carriage driver? At the edge of the picture frame, another man with his back to me, holds a carpet bag. The boy's father? In the foreground, waits a vacant wooden chair. Does it belong to the young man who is leaving home?

Dropping Hermes' hand, I touched the title mounted on the wall beside the painting. The brass felt warm. I found my palm emigrating across the etched letters of the title like a sentence in Braille. Stepping back, I reached for my Kodak to photograph such painful beauty, but realized I was without it. Instead, I fixed the image of the painting in my heart until it filled to overflowing. Why did I identify with the young boy leaving his nest?

As if from a cave, I heard Hermes' distant voice echo the title of the most popular painting at the fair, "Breaking Home Ties!"

Chapter Fourteen

All That Glistens

Monday, October 9

The crisp wind off the lake cooled my cheek. Our party stood high on the roof of the observation deck atop the Liberal Arts Building, looking down on the Court of Honor. The railing trembled in my gloved hands with each gust of October wind. My body, although hemmed in by Mr. Aultman on one side and Hermes on the other, felt strangely relaxed and self-contained, clothed in a sky-blue touring outfit. As Mr. Aultman sucked on his empty pipe, Hermes pointed his arm at the floats parading around the Grand Basin and encircling the Administration Building, commemorating Chicago Day.

The bands, a dozen bodies wide in a mile long parade, weaved like a huge anaconda in the afternoon sun. From this altitude, it was impossible to discern the carpenter's guild from the plumber's. I leaned over the railing for a closer peek.

"Alessandra," Hermes shouted, "Remember your fear of heights!"

"What?" From my photographer's jacket I extracted the pocket spyglass I'd purchased for myself using the fee the *Tribune* paid me when I sold my own photos and articles of last summer's tour of Harper College. Extending the draw lens, I focused on the Columbian fountain located at the west end of the basin beneath us.

"What are you smiling at?" Hermes said to me. "You must be dizzy by now." His new eyeglasses glinted with sunlight, hiding his pupils from me. How little he understood. To cheer him, I swung my spyglass, and pretended to study his face. "What are you worried about?" I said. "Your mother is with us." Collapsing the lens, I returned the spyglass to my coat pocket.

Hermes sighed, and blew a kiss, leaving my side to stand beside his mother.

A walking stick tapped behind me. I ignored it. A moment passed, and then another tap. As Mr. Aultman turned, Dr. Wetherstone said to him, "Cyrus, old boy, does it really seem twenty years?"

A burst of wind rattled the power cords of the large unlit searchlight nearby in the corner.

I pretended not to eavesdrop.

"We think we're so much better off now, don't we Cyrus?"

Mr. Aultman turned his back to Doc Seth. He hunched his shoulders.

"That was one wild night," the good doctor persisted. What did he mean?

Mr. Aultman spun around. "I hate that expression." He glanced my way, as he whispered, "Herself used to say that."

"I mean the fire."

Mr. Aultman moved to the side of the searchlight. Once out of crosswinds, he slumped against the turnbuckle, and took out his tobacco pouch to fill his pipe.

Edith edged into the place Mr. Aultman had occupied. She studied my face with her maternal stare. Did I detect a tear in her eye? "Poor Alessandra," she said, patting my hand. "Sometime photographer by day, sometime college freshman by night." She clucked her tongue. "But little memory of her past."

I searched for Hermes to protect me, but he was feeding the pigeons at his feet.

Mr. Aultman growled, "No Lady of the Manor would ever go to college!"

"On that we can agree, sir," said Hermes.

"Leave the poor girl alone." Doc Seth put his arm around me. "She may favor Cyrus in appearance, but she has her mother's trusting heart."

Edith opened her mouth to respond, but instead glanced away to peer down on thousands of people following the parade along the canals. "They're so tiny you could almost step on them." Shivering, she tightened the shawl around her shoulders. "I wonder if any of those young ladies in the parade have ever dressed as boys." Then she yawned. "Thank Gawd, we're above all of them."

"I see your eyebrows are grown back." Doc Seth said to me. Over his shoulder, I watched the smoke from Mr. Aultman's pipe swirling a halo around his head. Beneath the halo, he tilted a flask to his lips. "Alessandra," Doc Seth whispered, "Look at me."

"Ask her about her newspaper class," Hermes said, placing his chin on his father's shoulder. "That's what she really cares about." Then, he peered over the railing. "Joined the school paper. Think she's William Randolph Bloody Hearst." His shoulders slumped.

"According to your father I'm only trying to recreate myself." I said, putting my arm around his waist. I placed my cheek next to his, and whispered the first lyrics of the student song I heard at a night football game against Northwestern. "There's more Profs than students / But Harper doesn't care." Together we chanted, "Profs spend days in research / Their evenings at the fair."

A dozen gulls from Lake Michigan swooped above our heads and veered toward the Grand Basin, then over the bandstand along the canal. As I lost sight of the gulls, Hermes voice chanted softly: "T'was life upon our campus." He tilted his forehead to touch mine as we sang together. "Profs on continuous fling / Lil Egypt goes round and round." I welcomed the feeling of companionship with my blood brother.

Hermes brightened and began to wriggle his body in a Saint Vitus dance. But then his mother cleared her throat, freezing Hermes in mid-sway, leaving me to finish the last lines of the song alone.

"Not doing a goddam thing! / Not doing a goddam thing!"

Mrs. Wetherstone gasped, clutching her breast. "Too chilling for me on this deck." She stomped her foot. "Seth, dear."

The good doctor winked at me. "I'm comfortable, Edith."

Without taking her eyes off mine, Edith reached out her hand to Hermes.

While the pennants lining the roof snapped in one direction, and then the other, Hermes' head pivoted between his mother and me. Then he took off his glasses, and rubbed his eyes with his knuckles as if trying to awaken from a bad dream.

Unexpectedly, it was Mr. Aultman who marched toward the elevator. Edith tiptoed after him and latched onto his arm. "Good ol' Cyrus! Instead of Seth, you may escort me down to the chocolate kiosk in the lobby."

"Then to the bar."

I reached out for support from Hermes, but already he had skipped to his mother's side to take her other arm, his eyeglasses rattling near my feet.

Doc Seth moved closer to me, his face reddening with embarrassment. "Young lady, you are still under my care." He touched my forehead. "I won't abandon you."

I stepped backwards. "No, you go with them. I need a few minutes by myself."

Edith whined near the elevator. "Dr. Wetherstone, we can't hold the elevator just for her."

With a pained expression, the good doctor shrugged, and ambled away. I sighed as the four of them crowded into the elevator. As the door started to close, Hermes shouted, "Sander!"

Instinctively, I stepped toward him.

"Eyeglasses! Don't step on them." When the doors closed, Hermes' voice became muffled. "Bring them when you come."

Shaking my head, I retrieved his glasses, one lens chipped in the corner. I secured them like eggs in my coat pocket. To cheer myself, I extracted my spyglass from my inner pocket, and extended the draw tube. The Moroccan leather felt soft even through my gloves. Leaning on the railing I steadied my elbows. From my high vantage point, I was able to detect the barest outline of the tallest blade of the highest windmill. What lay in the background out of my sight? The wind shifted. I shivered like Mrs. Wetherstone and turned up my collar. I pocketed the spyglass, being careful not to use the same patch pocket as Hermes' eyeglasses. After a final glance down at the tourists, I hurried toward the elevator. In a minute it opened, allowing a young couple to emerge. As they strolled past me, I studied the young couple. He was a short sailor, leaning his head onto the corsage attached to a tall girl who smiled, despite a missing tooth.

From inside the open elevator, I was jealous of their little world. Would I ever create my own? Near the searchlight they kissed while I stared at them, until the sliding doors became a wall between them and me.

※ ※ ※

Our party of five boarded the Electric Launch carrying a hundred tourists to the Wooded Island. The launch was festooned with banners, flags, and well-placed beds of mignonette flowers. Their delicious perfume seduced my memory into recalling my first class at Harper College. The same flower filled the window boxes next to me in the class room. Shafts of sunlight illuminated the large room originally meant to be a chapel, but alternating as a science laboratory, a glee club recital room, and a lecture auditorium.

The thirty of us students gathered in one small front corner on straight back chairs forming a type of defensive British square. As an unclassified student I awaited the teacher. To give my nervous hands something to do I made a notation to purchase an orange sweater worn by a beautiful girl in the first row, emblazoned with the school slogan "I will." Atop her upright hair she proudly wore a shell pin, making my own locks feel stringy. Her complexion, the color of pink carnations, made my face feel scarred.

A male student made a late entrance, sporting a footballer's haircut as he wore maroon knickers and a letter sweater with "UC" on his chest. How lovely he limped.

Plopping down in the first row next to the beautiful girl, he threw his arm around her waist, making me regret my lonely lamblike mien.

Inhaling another breath, a mignonette filled my sinuses causing me to sneeze into my lavender handkerchief. At that moment, a side door creaked open and in strode an imposing man attired in black cap and gown.

He fingered a black walrus mustache and adjusted round eyeglasses. Instantly we all stood at attention out of respect while his deep-set eyes inventoried all of us with a single sweeping glance. Removing his mortarboard and placing it on his table, the teacher introduced himself as Professor John Dewey. We sat muttering excitingly, our shoes shuffling like a herd of cattle.

"Ladies and gentlemen, behave. The classroom is not a dormitory. Behave as you really are—children of the Enlightenment. Yes, the eighteenth century, a mere hundred years ago, proved once and for all the supremacy of reason through science and education."

After we settled on our chairs, I noticed the footballer had removed his arm from the girl's shoulder. She slid her chair away from him as Professor Dewey continued, "You students are all equal as human beings, a self-evident truth."

Far above the professor's head among the rafters a dozen pigeons cooed, flapping their wings. I noticed droppings on a wall of cubby holes, bulging with hundreds of objects labeled, and thick with dust. Noticing us staring, Professor Dewey chuckled. "You see before you shelves of student inventions rejected by the patent office. Were they failures? No, experiments. We always learn from experiments. Education should be an experiment. Too often, it isn't. Education at Harper College is an experiment; that is why we are different from Harvard, Yale, Princeton. Here we believe in service to students and society."

What was he talking about? I heard the footballer tap his shoes, and cough too loudly as if in mockery.

Stopping his lecture the professor said, "Are you nervous, lad? If so, good." Professor Dewey's Roman nose snorted and his long neck seemed to extend even farther. "Learn to stick your neck out. Take risks. Don't harbor fears of embarrassment, boredom, cowardice, or too much reverence for the past."

I harbored them all. How could Professor Dewey know me so well?

"Your pathway, lad, is called doubt. You must endure not knowing, must suspend judgment, must search for truth. Focus on results, not your bloody intentions."

I found myself staring at the window boxes of mignonette flowers and pretending I was living here, instead of Mr. Aultman's rowhouse.

❁   ❁   ❁

Toward dusk, our party stepped from the electric launch onto the southern tip of Wooded Island, with the aroma of pepper lingering to mix with roses. I wanted to share with Hermes what my botany professor at Harper had informed my class: that roses released their most beautiful aromas as they were dying. Walking ashore from the dock, we headed to the outdoor tent of Germania Club. As we trudged inland, the odors of rhododendrons and lilies grew stronger. The winding pathways, fringed by shrubbery and wildflowers, were bordered by willow trees bowing to autumn wind.

As we merged with strolling sightseers already on the island, Mr. Aultman set his own pace far ahead. In front of me, Hermes, sandwiched between his parents, occasionally peered over his shoulder. After he stumbled, his mother motioned for him to keep his head straight forward.

I extracted my Kodak, its cord already around my neck, to photograph beauty only. Crimson butterflies circled bull thistles. In the midst of danger, safety. I crouched for a closer shot.

My thoughts were interrupted by the voice of Dr. Wetherstone. "Well, young lady, are we feeling faint?"

I let the Kodak swing, relaxed, on my bosom.

"Recall anything of your first week at college?"

"When I try to remember anything, I get confused," I said, shooing a honeybee hovering above my forearm. "I had my first Latin seminar last Tuesday. Professor Hall was tardy." I stood to shake the bee. "Extremely tall, like Alsace, but with gray hair and beard." I snapped a photograph of a little boy with mouth brimming with popcorn. "The prof wore his black gown and mortar board, but his tassel made his eyes cross, reminding me of Karla."

"Your voice. Sounding stronger." Honey bees encircled the good doctor's head. "Recall anything else?"

"Professor Hall rambled on about the difference between free will and determinism. I didn't know what he was talking about, but I loved it."

"Then why are you frowning?"

Forgetting the camera, I peered into his eyes, "I overheard a boy in Cobb Hall. At the next table. He said to his classmate, 'She won't remember anything we do to her.' And then they both laughed like hyenas."

Doc Seth put his hand on my shoulder. "Alessandra, see those columbines heavy with bees? These flowers nod their heads. Memory, they don't need."

I heard Hermes announce that he saw the rose garden first.

"Doc Seth, on the observation deck this morning you said 'one wild night.' What did you mean?" People bumped against my shoulder as they ran past us to see the rose garden.

"My dear," the good doctor said, seeming to choose words carefully, "That night, Old Chicago died, and so did Cyrus's parents. They were lost in the great fire." He stopped, and touched my hand. "Didn't the old bear ever tell you the details? Cyrus and his parents were collecting rents from their real estate in the poor—"

A fly bit the nape of my neck. Was Brickton right about slum landlords?

"Ach, Cyrus arrived too late to save them." He hurried ahead of me. "My Edith is waving at us. Catch up, Alessandra."

When the two of us rejoined the others, I was dismayed to see a chain metal fence surrounding the rose garden. I had hoped the roses would be wild and free. Close to the entrance, we discovered a Japanese tea house. The four of us sat at table, while Mr. Aultman trudged onward by himself, ahead of a group of strangers. Sipping lukewarm darjeeling tea, we were served wafers and sweet meats.

Hermes waved his new guidebook. "Don't know the fate of my last one." He glanced my way. "Last time I had it in the Captive Balloon." I sipped my tea, admiring the delicate Japanese waitresses in their colorful kimonos, as they bobbed among the tables, smiling and bowing.

Leaving the tea house behind, we hiked onto the trail again. After several turns in the path, we came upon a muscular man, shirtless, talking to a dapper little man. "There's Ziegfeld's son, Florenz," said Doc Seth, "That short squirt who scheduled those awful military bands from Europe. Famous even though a kid. Next to him, his latest discovery, the Great Sandow in exercise clothes."

Hermes said, "Wow, strongest man in the world. My hero."

"There's Brickton," I said, "trying to interview Great Sandow." Suddenly the strong man bent, clipping a bloom from a stock of snapdragon.

Edith pointed her finger at him. "Naughty man! That's against rules. Read the sign."

"Hush, wife," whispered the good doctor, "he might hear you."

"That's the point."

A crowd gathered around the Great Sandow while he held the tiny cutting between his thumb and index finger with surprising tenderness. We stood close, but as outsiders. Great Sandow spoke English with a German accent. "Now, friend Brickton, ven ve vere children in beloved Bavaria ve took blossoms und pressed them thus." He raised the bud to his eyes. "Und if mouth of bud opens vide it prove a sign calling us home from fields." Great Sandow kissed the tinted bud. On tiptoe. I could swear I saw its rosy lips part in a perfumed smile. The crowd aahed its approval, including me.

"That brute must be stopped," Edith muttered.

As if reacting to an alarm bell, Hermes rushed toward Great Sandow, "You there. You're breaking the rules!" He seized Great Sandow by the elbow while throwing a side block into him, only to richochet against a tree trunk. The Great Sandow glared at Hermes, half-wrapped around the tree. I moved closer. Great Sandow peered into his hand and, seeing the blossom gone, stalked toward Hermes with the pace of a mortician. Reaching down and placing his hamhock hands under Hermes' armpits, Great Sandow lifted him straight up off the ground, at arms length holding Hermes, wriggling his toes. Great Sandow studied him with the objective curiosity of a scientist eyeing a new specimen.

Brickton took notes, I snapped a shot, Mr. Ziegfeld chortled.

As I snapped more shots, Doc Seth pleaded with Mr. Ziegfeld to persuade Great Sandow to release Hermes unharmed.

Finally, Ziegfeld shouted a plea in German, and after a third try, Great Sandow responded with an outburst of his own that did not resemble a prayer. He dropped Hermes into a thornbush like a sack of rotten potatoes. Great Sandow brushed his hands, and the men in the crowd patted him on the back. I moved even closer for another shot. He beamed at me and posed, flexing his biceps, "For guard, Great Sandow loves Cherman Chepards."

He glanced at Hermes, alone on the grass, pulling thorns out of his clothing. "Dogs vell-bred animals." I had to agree with the Great Sandow.

A Columbian guard pulled up on a safety bike, and started to disperse the crowd.

"Why don't you arrest that man!" Edith shouted from the bench, her head in hands.

"No need, Edith," Doc Seth said, sitting next to her. "Case terminated, let's move on. Cyrus must be in the Germania tent by now."

※　　　※　　　※

As our party approached the large red and blue striped tent, the singing from inside grew louder and my anxiety facing the man called Father grew stronger. *"Ist das nicht ein Schnitzelbank? Ja, das ist ein Schnitzelbank."* Doc Seth started to sing along. *"Ist das nicht ein Schnickelfritz? Ja, das ist ein Schnickelfritz."* As our party left the main trail, I saw a large placard in front of the tent: *Germania Club Celebrates Chicago Day (Members Only).*

Entering the open-ended tent, we heard the final lyrics, "Ist das nicht ein Haugenmist? Ja, das ist ein Haugenmist!" As hundreds of people in the tent applauded themselves, I saw the Aultman table in the form of a huge horseshoe covered with a red tablecloth, ends pointing to the entrance. At the head of the table, Mr. Aultman sat between a gray haired corpulent man on his right and a beautiful lady on his left. Above their heads, Chinese lanterns swung with incoming gusts of wind, as if enduring a tossing sea.

Mr. Aultman's false collar was missing, revealing his large Adam's apple, but his forehead was smooth as a child's. A half-empty bottle of Schnapps shook in his grip, while his other hand raised a glass for a toast. He had stood before we had a chance to be seated.

The lady of beauty spotted us, smiling like a perfect hostess. Who was she? Doc Seth strode ahead to embrace her and plant a kiss, while Mr. Aultman froze in mid-toast with arm in air. Doc Seth then sat next to the lady who received a pressing of flesh from Edith followed by Hermes, myself and Brick who I was glad to see had joined our party after his interview with the Great Sandow.

As we settled into our chairs, I looked to my left at Uncle Chilton, Aunt Ashford, Karla, and her new West Point boyfriend. None showed any welcome.

Instead of finishing his toast, Mr. Aultman sang, *"Ist das nicht eine Gefahrlichesding?"* Then he glanced about the table. Total silence. He sang the line again, and waited for response. Finally, Doc Seth stood up and sang, *"Ja das ist eine Gefahrlichesding!"*

The tension broke, and everyone laughed, except Karla. Doc Seth leaned across the table, and clinked Mr. Aultman's half-filled glass with his own unfilled one, while motioning to sit.

Waiters, with their white gloves holding tapers, lit the candelabras on our tables. A barbershop quartet at the far end of the tent sounded a pitch pipe, and began to sing, "Daisy, Daisy, Give me your answer do / I'm half crazy…"

From the corner of my eye, I saw lady beautiful tilt forward in her chair. "Alessandra, honey, what was your favorite ceremony today?"

She knew my name?

Before I could answer, Mr. Aultman blurted out, "My favorite part was when they presented one million, five hundred sixty-five thousand, three hundred dollars on a six-foot long check!"

"And seventy-six cents," said the lady's companion. "That final check covers the total cost of the fair. The rest of October is pure profit."

"Potter, I feel like I'd written the bloody check myself."

Potter frowned. "And I assume my check will follow, Cyrus?"

"Starting tomorrow, Tuesday, October tenth," Mr. Aultman said, "A new day. My rebirth into the gray."

"At—least—out—of—the—red," Potter said.

I was disappointed in his not confiding in me. More proof he was not really my father.

"At the risk of repeating myself, what was your most memorable moment? I'm really asking because of my desire to hear that honey voice of yours again."

My cheeks flushed; I wished she had not noticed me at all. I stared at the flames of the candelabra directly in front of me, until the fire seemed to consume me. I fought against the return of a fear of flames.

"She is still under my care, Bertha," Doc Seth said, "and ordered to save her voice."

"Alessandra's come so far," Edith said smiling, "and done so well. Haven't we, my dear?" Her smile did not include her eyes.

The waiters placed crimped cod, and oyster sauce before us as Mr. Aultman stood up. "We Aultmans have the great honor of hosting the Palmers today, Potter and Bertha, to thank them for their support both financial and emotional. Here's to working closer in the future!" He sat as everyone applauded.

Mr. Palmer stood and raised his glass. With white hair thinning and silver muttonchops billowing, it was hard to believe he was the beautiful lady's husband, and not her father. "Most gracious of you Cyrus, old sport. To return the courtesy to you all, as my Kentucky princess would say, so let me toast the entire Aultman family, especially Oscar's son and my current real estate partner, Cyrus." The clinking of wine glasses. "A most devoted son who transported, in his own hands, two precious urns across the ocean to Ireland. These urns contained ashes of his departed parents Oscar and Cathleen, both of whom I also dearly loved. Thereby Cyrus fulfilled their written wishes."

"Here, here Cyrus!" shouted the good doctor. Edith shushed him. Why didn't Mr. Aultman share these things with me?

"By the by," Mr. Palmer said sitting down, "What year was that? Seventy-two?"

"No, four, seventy-four."

"That's when you and Cora met, wasn't it?" Bertha asked.

"More Schnapps."

Edith muttered, "Time for the entrée."

"Mrs. Palmer," said Karla, disentangling both her hands from her new boyfriend's. "Why don't you ask Cyrus if he met someone else in Ireland before meeting Cora?"

Aunt Ashford put her hand on top of Karla's. "The entrée is making its entrance."

Indeed, silver trays of curried rabbits and roast suckling pigs descended upon our tables.

"Mrs. Stark sends her sympathies," Bertha said to me. "She misses your assistance at the Children's Building. Terese asks about you."

"Who?"

"Terese, the little gymnast, don't you remember?"

Scampering around our horseshoe table, a girl of five pulled an orange balloon above her head; she seemed to be taunting a two year old boy who pursued her. The balloon hovered above a candelabra, and then popped. The boy started to cry, while the girl strolled away to the far side of the tent, dragging the shreds of his burst balloon across the canvas carpet.

"Ah declare," Bertha said, fanning her face. "This here is the most entertainment little ole me has had since Opening Day.

I'm never allowed out of office, you know." She looked at her husband. "Am I, Potter dear? Except to chair a meeting or attend one of Potter's speeches." She lifted her glass. "So kudos to you all. You have rescued a neighbor's little ole soul."

Later, with the table cleared and dessert ordered, firework explosions outside the tent startled everyone. I needed fresh air. At my side, Hermes was gulping down my leftovers. Brickton pulled a chair next to Mr. Palmer for an interview. Edith had taken Doc Seth to a corner of the tent behind our table, and seemed to be furious with him.

When Karla left for public comfort, Uncle Chilton moved to sit next to her boyfriend, and touched his hand. Aunt Ashford smoked a cigarillo in her silver holder as she stared daggers at Edith. Mr. Aultman had spilt his Schnapps on Mr. Palmer's lap, and he was apologizing to both Potter and Bertha as he refilled their glasses.

My temples throbbed, too many pieces missing from my past. I could not wait for dessert to come. Pushing myself back from the table, my hands clenched and unclenched. At the table there seemed so much hate beneath the surface, like a beautiful garden covering quicksand. Standing, my legs shook until my knees locked.

I shuffled away from the table. Perhaps if I joined Karla in public comfort, I could ask her what she meant about his meeting someone else before Mother.

"Alessandra, you are not excused from leaving the table!" Mr. Aultman's voice cut into me like a pair of scissors. People at adjoining tables stared at me. Instinctively, I adjusted my brown wig. I felt at a crossroad, glancing first at the path to public comfort, then at the white runner leading to the opening where we had entered. Rocking on my feet, I felt the palm of my left hand start to throb.

"Alessandra Aultman, are you deaf as well as mute?"

With his tirade burning my ears, I pivoted on the balls of my feet in a movement strangely familiar. As I strode through the opening, a cool breeze refreshed my face. Nighttime had fallen. The darkened sky formed a perfect background for yellow streaks exploding into gray clouds. Walking farther, I watched rockets flash over my head, criss-crossing before erupting. As my eyes grew accustomed to the dark, I detected a bench with its back to the tent. Approaching it, I passed a series of tiny yellow and green luminaries lining both sides of walkway. As I passed them, the wicks in the pod burned molten wax, like tiny volcanoes.

Settling on the bench, I inhaled the crisp night air before I heard footfalls on the gravel behind me. "Your father sent me to retrieve you." Hermes said, standing at my side.

"Is that what you want?"

"I, I don't believe it's my place."

Taking a deep breath, I inhaled the aroma of melting wax. "Hermes," I said without looking at him, "your mother needs you." Overhead, the sky blazed with rockets exploding into brilliant fragments. Hermes' footsteps headed back to the tent.

Fireworks blossomed instant gardens of transparent giant roses, lilies and orchids of unexpected hues of olive, ochre, and mauve expanding and evaporating into gray black vines. As they faded, rockets soared, fragmenting into large gauzy sponges of gold leaf, egg white, and indigo that slid across the night sky before fading into webs of red and violet smoke. Flowers of the gods.

As I chided myself for such lofty thoughts, I heard footfalls again. Hermes, I thought, you don't know how I really feel anymore. I peered at the sky. Someone stood behind the bench without speaking, and for a long time I seemed to be communicating with that other person without a word. After a dozen more bursts of flowers in the sky, I arose from the bench. We sauntered, side by side, the two of us, back to the tent, without touching hands.

Returning to the table with Brick, I saw a blue flame leap from a tray on a cart between the two limbs of the horseshoe table. "Baked Alaskan dessert," Brick said, chuckling at my expression. "Remember our chartreuse?"

I barely heard him; more concerned was I with the empty chair where Mr. Aultman had sat. Doc Seth came up to me and clasped my hands. "Not to fear. Where he's wandered off to, I can guess."

The Palmers were bidding adieu before the good doctor asked them to pause. "As Cyrus' best man years ago, I feel licensed to state his appreciation honoring us with your presence tonight. So fond farewell." Then he spoke to his son, "Hermes, my boy, play the man. Escort your mother and Alessandra home on the I.C." He nodded to the Palmers, who then quickly departed. "So, Ashford, what are you up to?"

"Well, Chil and I are headed for Midway." She glanced at Karla who nodded. "With Karla and her West Pointer. Unless something better—"

"This is the beginning of another wild night," the good doctor sighed, staring at the Baked Alaskan burning itself out. "Don't disturb your mind, Alessandra. Mr. Pemberton and I will bring the big bear home to you tonight."

We never reached the train terminal. Edith telephoned her house, and ordered her driver to meet us at the fair's coach park. Edith hated trains; they reminded her of traveling in Ireland years ago, and she'd never gotten over it.

When her driver arrived, she instructed him to proceed to the Aultman residence. During the ride, the only noise was Hermes singing, "Daisy, Daisy, give me your answer do," as he peered at me, expectantly.

Edith insisted that she and Hermes escort me into my house. Once inside, we had our capes, hats and camera collected by Hustings. We sat in the dining room in front of a dying fire, while a servant brought more wood. Odette insisted on serving me opium cordial. I told her once again I hated it.

Instead, I ordered Napoleon brandy. Edith asked for ice water for herself and her son. Sitting in silence, we listened to the crackle of the flames. I sat by the fireplace, with Edith keeping the dining room table between us. Hermes remained standing. Edith seemed to be trying awful hard not to say something.

The servant entered with libations. Edith sipped ice water, "Son, you look flushed," she said. Hermes opened his mouth to speak, but instead gulped his water down without taking a breath. He avoided my eyes.

Edith clicked the tips of her long fingernails on the wooden table top. The moment Hermes finished his ice water, his mother dismissed him. "Hermes, my dumpling, your mother is concerned about your health. Do take our carriage, and go home. Before you go to bed, have Mildred make you a hot toddy, and have her rub camphor on your chest. But first, inform Chas to transport me later. Alessandra needs company until her father arrives." She leaned her cheek into her hand. "Don't you my child?"

Hermes stared into the empty glass in his hand, as if willing it to fill again. Finally, he set it down on the sideboard, and sidled over to plant a kiss on his mother's cheek. She accepted it, and waved him away. Avoiding my expression, he shuffled past me, and out the door.

After the latch clicked behind him, Edith smoothed her lap. "Now that we are alone. Alessandra, are you listening?"

I looked around for my brandy.

"Remember, I have always loved you. Always felt toward you as a mother toward her daughter. Especially, dear, during your recent illness. You have always returned affection not only to me, but also to my husband and son." Edith patted the seat of the chair next to her.

"Are you trying to help me remember?" I asked, "Or to feel guilty?"

"No, young lady, guilt should be a natural feeling just like, just like, memory. But you are recovering now, according to Seth." She cocked her head, as if peering around a corner. "All those social conventions you have broken during the last month and a half. Do you even remember? Should I elucidate?"

"Have I asked you to?"

Edith stood, and moved around the table to occupy the chair next to me.

The servant presented a tray with Napoleon brandy. I grasped it with both hands.

"My dear, don't misunderstand. I take no delight. But I do have my duty. Remember, I was your mother's maid of honor." Edith stiffened her back with a smug expression. "I must speak the words poor Cora would have said, if she had not sacrificed her life giving you birth."

"Mrs. Wetherstone, you are so knowledgeable, so I know you can clear up one fact for me. Would you?"

She reached over, and touched my knee. "Of course, little one."

I took a breath, and sipped brandy from the snifter. "Why didn't Mother have her sister Ashford as maid of honor?"

Edith took her hand back, as if shocked by electricity. "See what I mean? You are not yourself. The Alessandra, I knew, would never have the cheek to ask that question."

"While I'm at it," I said, "remembering, that is, why did Aunt Ashford stop Karla from pursuing her question tonight? Did Mr. Aultman meet someone else in Sligo before he met our mother?"

Edith stood. "If this topic continues, I shall leave this house and walk home."

"It's not far, you know. Just around the corner."

"Yes, on Astor Street, where Cyrus would give his life to live. He's such a social climber on the backs of—"

I swirled the brandy in my snifter.

Mrs. Wetherstone pulled her chair and sat facing me, our knees touching. "Alessandra, what's happened to you? I prayed with Reverend Brackenbush many hours for you to come to your senses. Marry my Hermes. He loves you so much he's tongue-tied whenever around you. Especially when you sometimes dress, unconventionally."

I finished the brandy in a gulp.

"See what I mean, dear, you didn't use to drink at all, at least as far as I knew. Besides, drinking's not healthy. Your body used to be a ballerina's. Remember our dream we planned? Your own ballet studio one day." Edith leaped to her feet. "What's happened to the dream?"

At that moment, I overheard muffled voices singing outside the front door. Some words wriggled through. "Ist das nicht—"

Suddenly, Edith crouched in front of me, clasping both my hands. "Alessandra, quickly. This may be our last talk together. I've been trying to help you. That conduct of yours this morning on the roof was so unlike the old Alessandra. It was so, dare I say, modern?" Edith took a deep breath, and waited for me to speak. "Say something, please!"

I put down the empty brandy glass. "Edith, I do love you. You're the wife of the good doctor who saved my life. But I am eighteen years old. I do not need to justify myself to you, to anyone. Only to my own heart. Which rests in Mother's hands, and God's." I stood up. "I don't think you understand," I said, peering down at her as she rocked on her heels to sit on the floor. "In fact, don't try to understand." I reached down, taking her hands, and helping her to her feet. "Just accept me as I am now. Accept the fact I will never be your daughter-in-law." I hugged her. Her body sagged in my arms, as if without bones.

The snapping of a key in the lock, followed by curses loud enough to summon Hustings, hurried Edith and me to free ourselves. The open door revealed Mr. Aultman, arms hooking around the necks of Doc Seth and Brick, all three singing "Schnitzelbanks."

Rushing toward them, Edith's voice rose an octave higher. "Mr. Seth Wetherstone, I demand you escort me home this instant!"

Ignoring her, the three men staggered to the chairs in the dining room. Edith grabbed at the good doctor's arm. He pulled away. "On my oath, woman. Can't you see I'm doctor here?" They settled Mr. Aultman into his wing chair at the head of table. Releasing him, Brick grinned at me. "The old coot was dancing hoochie-kootchie!"

"Where did you find him?"

"Right where I knew he would be." Doc Seth said, puffing out his cheeks. "German Village, Midway."

"Two buxom Fraulein waitresses," Brick added. "Hot damn!"

"Quiet, Mr. Pemberton," Doc Seth said, "decorum, remember, decorum."

A shoe tapping on marble told me Edith was waiting in the hallway. "Mr. Wetherstone, I'm ready to walk home."

"My dear, I'm doctor. That should explain it all."

"So Cyrus is more important than your own wife?"

"Please accept my being a doctor, dear. But, then, you never really have, have you?" I wanted to kiss Doc Seth.

"The neighbors. What will they think of you if I walk home at this time of night?"

"I concur, Edie, that's why I prescribe exercise for you."

The slamming of the front door must have been heard as far away as Germania Club.

"I've injected Cyrus to settle his nerves," Doc Seth said, rolling his own shoulders to take the kinks out. "Last time I saw Cyrus this bad was—but it might be that damn mercury hat he always wears." He squinted at me. "Mercury seeps into the brain. Drives a soul crazy."

In the meantime, Brick had spotted my empty brandy

snifter, and had tracked down the maid for a Napoleon for himself. Mr. Aultman had fallen asleep in his chair. I straightened his twisted suspenders.

"Come to think of it, I'll need my bag from the house, after all." He chuckled, revealing the gap in his front teeth. "Should have asked Edith." He gave me a penetrating look, which lost some of its power because of his missing pince nez. "Mind if I shortcut across your lawn?"

"Your father's no longer a strong man." He glanced at Mr. Aultman. "Keep him quiet. Whiskey him, if necessary. Be back shortly."

"Must you leave him?" I felt sorry for him all of a sudden.

"What about hospital?" Brick said.

With a pat on my hand, Doc Seth said, "Have to re-supply my bag." With that, the good doctor left the house. Brick and I stared at each other for a long time. "Should we take your father to his room?"

"No, he couldn't stand it."

Mr. Aultman awoke, gripping the arms of the chair, and tried to rise. "Stand? Bloody well yes, I can stand!" He fell back into the seat.

"He's half daft," said Brick.

"Wild night," He muttered into his chest. "One wild night."

I felt my breath choke in my throat. "What had happened?"

"One wild night ruined it all."

What was ruined? A knock on the front door brought Hustings, grumbling, to open it. When he did so, the stink of whiskey flooded into the house. As she entered, Karla exclaimed, "Some half-wit broke their key in our lock."

Following her, Aunt Ashford and Uncle Chilton stumbled, arm in arm. "Surprised?" Ashford asked, standing in the vestibule. "Our cab drove behind your carriage. Tonight, we hoped the Aultman house would erupt like a volcano."

Karla twirled with arms outstretched. "I brought Midway madness into Aultman house!"

Hustings took their wraps.

Karla collapsed onto a chair by the fireplace. "Come clean," she said to me, as I glanced at Brick finishing his brandy.

"What are you talking about, Stir?" I asked.

"That's my line." Karla snapped her fingers and ordered a mint julep. "You've been talking like me for a month. What's happening?"

Ignoring Karla, I watched Aunt Ashford wipe Mr. Aultman's forehead. She poured a glass of ice water from a pitcher, spilling some onto her pink handkerchief, and placed it on the nape of his neck with a thoughtfulness that surprised me.

"Leave alone." He swung away, and hid his face in the crook of his arm on the table. "Tortured me long enough."

Aunt Ashford stepped away and appeared to think a moment. About what? She drew her arm stiffly to one side, grabbing the water pitcher, and raising his head up, flung the ice water into his face. "You wicked old bear! You started all this." She threw the empty pitcher into the fireplace, and watched it shatter.

I jumped to one side. Karla stayed put, and smiled. Brick took out his notepad; Hustings slid the dining room doors closed.

"Across a bloody ocean you came, Cyrus. Across Ireland to Sligo. You came to bury your parents, but you stayed to sleep with me. First! Before Cora!"

He shook his head again and again. Ashford moved to his side, embracing his head against her bosom. "And you loved me first. You know you did, Cyrus Karl Aultman. You know you did." Then she lowered her head to touch his, and started to moan. "But why in God's name did you rape my sister?"

"The old bear is down," Karla cackled.

I collapsed into a chair.

Karla glided to Ashford's side. They embraced and kissed.

Suddenly energized, he sat up straight and shouted hoarsely, "One wild night ain't no bloody love."

Ashford cackled like Karla. "One wild night."

"Cora," he groaned, "Where's darlin' Cora?"

"In Ireland!" Uncle Chilton shouted. I had almost forgotten he was in the room. "Died giving birth. You killed her, Cyrus. My own brother's a killer."

"No!" I screamed, "Father, tell him he's a liar!"

He peered down at his hands.

"Chilton!" Ashford said, "You've waited twenty bloody years. Waited for the right moment. Now speak up. Seize the moment, or forever crawl." She gave Chilton her evil eye.

Uncle Chilton centered the widow's peak of his toupee. "Well?" Ashford said. "Now's the time." He stood, and wiped the palms of his hands on his striped trousers.

"Do it!" hollered Karla.

"Stop this!" I shouted.

"Brother of mine," Chilton said, voice thicker and lower-pitched than I ever heard it. I expected him to wink at me, but he did not even look. "My belly's full of Cyrus' high and mighty airs. The last twenty years? Hell! Try fifty. Try all my life." He shuffled toward him, "Never good enough. Not for you. Not for your god damn parents."

I dropped my brandy glass.

"Oscar and Cathleen adopted me—they chose me!" he screamed into his brother's face. "You were just their natural mistake."

"Remember they cut you out of their will," Ashford hissed, "Don't forget that part."

"Oh yes," Chilton said, as if under her spell. "They cut me out, so I've had to crawl to you, Cyrus, for pennies ever since." He pulled his brother's hair, lifting his face, slack-jawed and drooling. "You shoved it in my face every day."

"And in a way you can never forgive," Ashford prompted.

"And how did you do it? By never mentioning it!" He slammed his brother's head down on the table top. "My name's not even Aultman," he said, as if to himself. "Don't even know what the hell it is."

"Hot damn!" Brick muttered, writing on the backside of the pages. "My headline—Midway Madness."

I wanted to cry, but I could not.

"Don't forget little Karla!" Ashford shouted.

Karla grabbed a poker from the rack, and shoved it into the collapsing wood in the burning fireplace. "Don't you remember, Cyrus? When I was twelve? One night you came home too late for my birthday party—dead drunk, falling upstairs, smashing open your forehead." Karla glared at me. "Stir was paralyzed with fright—just like she is now." Then Karla shook the handle of the poker, stirring sparks. "My heart ran to help you," Karla said to the flames. "But you thought I was mocking your public embarrassment."

"Karla, stop," I shouted, as Uncle Chilton, back to the wall, slumped to the floor, sobbing. Aunt Ashford stepped to comfort Karla, who waved her away.

"And when I reached you—terrified you were dead, guilty that somehow it was my fault—what did you do?" Karla extracted the poker, white hot and smoking, and advanced toward Father, whose head and shoulders sprawled on the table. With a flick of her wrist, Karla signaled Aunt Ashford to pull his shoulders back and straighten him in the chair. The smoke from the poker made him cough and squint. "Cyrus, why don't I burn off your eyebrows and eyelashes like that night when you pulled out all of mine? Why don't I set fire to your hair like you shaved off all of mine?"

Aunt Ashford stepped toward Karla. "Don't forget, don't forget it was me who gave you wigs, who gave you a mask to wear in a man's world."

"Yes, and I hate you for it. Every time Cyrus looked at me he saw you, Aunt Ashford, but instead of hating you he hated me." Karla raised the smoldering poker above her head with both hands, smoke coiling upwards like a soiled snake.

I screamed. Was Karla going to strike her father?

With a primitive yawp, Karla drove the poker straight down into the table, burying it between his hands. It penetrated the wood and stood upright, tiny flames rising at its base. She wriggled the poker out of the tabletop, and hurled it into the fireplace. "Cyrus, now you're the child!"

I covered my ears, not believing a word.

The clatter of the poker aroused him to his feet, looming like an old bear. "Cora's alive. I know it. Where's my hat? No, get my opera hat. Cora and I are late. Didn't know they had bloody operettas in Ireland." Then he started to sing off key. "Things are seldom what they seem / Skimmed milk masquerades as cream."

Aunt Ashford took a handkerchief, and dabbed the blood from his forehead. Then, she sang softly, "So they do / So they do."

His eyes opened wide. "Ashford, is that you? My little Ash?" His face beamed and he shut his eyes. "Last night we loved each other, didn't we? Don't deny it! But Ash, now I can't remember lyrics to the rest of our precious song." His forehead seemed split in half, his vertical vein pulsating. The left side of his face twisted into a sneer. "Ach, yes, I remember now. After you, I had your sister. Did I pretend your sister was you?" He scratched his temple. "Or pretend you were your sister?" He opened his eyes as he sank into the chair. "I remember now, Ash. My first night in Sligo we sang in your dressing room, after I sneaked backstage and exchanged a few drinks. Just bumming around, trying to forget two urns in the hotel safe."

Ashford sang to him. "Black sheep dwell in every fold /All that glistens, all that glistens—"

Cyrus roared in triumph, "'Is not gold' that's right ain't it, Ash?" he peered around for approval.

Aunt Ashford turned away from him, tears streaming down her cheeks, like St. Peter's tears. She buried her face into Chilton's shoulder. Karla eyed Brick who eyed her back. I grabbed my mouth with both hands.

Mr. Aultman's left side of his face twisted again, closing his eye totally shut. A stranger to me. His head snapped against his left shoulder as he half stood, reaching across the table. Toward me? He folded into his chair, just like his old opera hat.

Karla lit a cigarette, Aunt Ashford and Uncle Chilton embraced, and Brick beamed, snapping his notepad shut.

I approached Mr. Aultman, feeling somehow it must have been my fault for being born, just like Karla always told me, but as I bent to kiss his lips and beg forgiveness, he muttered over and over a single word, "Onewildnight."

Then the door burst open, and the good doctor entered and stopped. Gasping, he dropped his medicine bag of cures. With a hollow thud, it landed on all the broken hearts in that room, including mine.

Chapter Fifteen

The Truth

shall set you free

The Next Morning

*I*n a recurrent nightmare Father and I live in a Palace. Mr. Potter Palmer comes to collect his fee, reversing the sign hanging about Father's neck from *Real Estate Broker* to *Slum Landlord.* Father orders me to hold Mother's pendant, and to please him I do. As he says, "Alessandra you are loved," the pendant dissolves in my palm.

Mr. Palmer calmly twists off my hands, depositing them into my little dollhouse. "Without hands," I cry, "what could I do?" In response Father employs additional servants to wait upon me. He orders Karla to become my scapegoat, punished for all my wrongdoings. Although I possess no hands for a wedding ring, Hermes begs me to marry him. Mr. Palmer attaches a pair of silver hands that fit perfectly. To please Hermes, we are married in a large golden cage. My salty tears rust the silver hands, and my handicap returns with a vengeance. "What could I do now?" I sobbed, unable to stop crying. Seeking solace in my gazebo, I find it had been replaced by a huge fountain, flowing with bubbly black water. Easing my body into the fountain, I lean my head back until my neck rests on the edge. I feel a new complacency seeping into every pore of my body. So what if I can't do anything for myself? A tightrope sways above my head. In the middle, Little Terese is poised between steps. I start to applaud, but my silver hands hook each other. Terese screams and loses her balance, descending like a broken kite into the fountain's deep waters. Without thinking, I dive beneath the foamy waves to rescue her. Fighting against the force from the large water pipe, I feel my lungs bursting.

Finally, I encircle Terese with my arms. Springing upward, I emerge with Terese, both of us entangled in seaweed. At the surface, I am amazed to discover she had become a little baby. Reaching over the side of the fountain, I lay her gently down onto the marble. Staring at my wrinkled palms, I realize that the silver hands transformed themselves into my own flesh and bone. My fingers flex with the power of newly restored life. At last, I feel able to do everything myself.

A bloodsucker bites into my cheek.

Awakened, I sat bolt upright in bed.

Did my nightmare reveal the truth about *The Handless Maiden*? All my life Father used that folktale to describe me to Doc Seth. However, they would never explain it to me. I knew when I understood that I would be free of the nightmare.

I found my hands clasping my throat. Was the bite real? Only one way to find out. Freeing my hands, I saw one bed bug squashed against my palms.

Jumping out of bed, I ripped off the ivory sheets and red blanket, shaking them at arm's length. Discovering no more bugs, I took a deep breath, rubbing my hands on my chemise nightgown. Although I was alone, I still chastised Odette for not pouring hot water down the brass bedsteads each day. Common sense. Must I remind her?

Then I detected an oder like turds. I sniffed at my hands, but realized it was not, as I had hoped, the remains of the bug. The fumes seemed to come from beneath the bed. Odette, couldn't you empty the chamber pot? Why should I reach under the bed and pull out the pan for inspection?

Glancing about the room, I noticed the wall clock in the corner. My Gawd. Two minutes to noon. I must have been exhausted from Chicago Day.

And the basket with freshly ironed undergarments? Where was it? Was laundress ill?

A bad start for today. but at least I could read my article about the fair in the *Tribune*. I always enjoyed finding my newspaper freshly ironed, and waiting outside my door. Looking in the hallway, though, I found no newspaper. Instead, I stepped onto a maid's box and overturned it, sprawling brushes, cloths, and damp tea leaves used for carpet brushing.

Stepping over the inexcusable mess, I hastened to the comfort station down the hall. I really needed my customary dose of laudanum. The good doctor prescribed it when I was ill, and it worked so well, why not continue it?

Hurrying past the staircase, I ignored loud voices from downstairs in the vestibule. Once inside, I flung open the wooden door of the medicine cabinet, and reached for the bottle, but my hand froze in midair. Empty! Slamming the cabinet, I shouted in my head: who do I bloody blame for this!

After I washed my hands, I postponed my sponge bath to exit to the hallway, where I heard a babble of voices coming from downstairs. A gaslight was still burning. I turned it off. Then a second, and a third. Why did I have to do this? The pounding of a heavy object made the racket suddenly cease.

After extinguishing the other jet, I leaned over the banister.

Far beneath me, I saw the front of a long table perpendicular to the hallway. Uncle Chilton was holding the barrel of a pistol in his fist. He banged the butt on the table again.

"Quiet! Remember, we will employ only servants of houses on Prairie Avenue, past or present." I heard snickering from people in a line that stretched to the front entrance. "Our coachman will carriage you back to Prairie. Right now, Curlin is rounding up more applicants on the south side." Murmurs of disapproval. "Come to the front of the queue if you have credentials from the following six families—Marshall Field, Philip Armour, John Glessner, Frank Lowden,

William Kimball, George Pullman. Everybody else to the rear. Hustings, close the damn door, there's a draft."

Reality was worse than my nightmare. What was happening? Wait until Mr. Aultman returns from LaSalle Street. Or maybe he's still abed after such a painful night. I laid on the floor in the hallway, and peeked between the railings, feeling like a disobedient child. Chilton sat down, but then shot up again. "Let me add that Miss Ashford, and I, prefer German and French servants. Irish need not apply. Today we are replacing all positions in the Aultman household except coachman, butler, and, of course, chef." A dog barked in line. "If you own a dog or cat drop out. No animals are allowed in this house."

Why was Uncle Chilton in charge? I stood, bumping my head on the banister as I returned to my bedroom. What did all this mean? As I rubbed the bump on my head, I decided to delay going to Harper today.

To visit Doc Seth for some answers, I slipped into my favorite Gibson Girl outfit. While doing so, I studied the scrapscreen. On one side, Odette had created for me a montage of pictures to jog my old memories, while the other was to establish new memories for myself. I stared at this collection of overlapping newspaper clippings, photographs and tinted postcards of the fair. She preserved them with a coating of lacquer on three panels, head high.

While reluctantly attiring myself in female clothing, I had to slow down to relearn buttoning the shirt. Squinting into the oval mirror, I searched for Mr. Aultman's face, as it must have been when he was eighteen. But all traces, young or otherwise, had disappeared.

With my Gibson properly in place, I picked up my Kodak with fifty exposures still remaining. Slipping the camera into its case, I was careful not to disturb my personal valuables I had stored there, instead of a purse.

I hastened to the door, but paused for a last glance in the mirror. Did I swing my shoulders too much? Stopping at the threshold, I surveyed the bedroom and shrugged. I felt like an outsider.

Descending the several staircases, I recoiled from the stink of whiskey. Rings from shot glasses surrounded Chilton on the table as he sat in Mr. Aultman's wing chair, interviewing applicants. Straightening my spine, I readjusted my grip on the handle of the camera case.

Sidling down the stairs, I sank into a pit of people pushing each other in line. People jostled others into dropping credentials on the floor; some spat tobacco juice, cursing all the rich bitches on Astor Street.

"If approved by yours truly, your next step is to wait in line at the dining room door opposite the guard at the parlor. Final approval is done by Miss Ashford Larken in the dining room only."

Reaching the parlor, I was stopped. A West Pointer in uniform held his arm, decorated with sergeant stripes, across the door to block it. "No, Miss, it's the dining room to apply for a position."

Recognizing him from the Germania tent last night, I smiled at his formality, but felt grateful for his seriousness in fulfilling his duty. "I'm Alessandra Aultman, young man." He did not even blink. "I'm Karla's sister?" He frowned. "Have you forgotten dinner at the Aultman table? In Germania Club tent? On Wooded Island? Last evening?" He wet his lips, bent toward me, peering into my face, his arm still barring the door. "Well," I giggled, "I'm glad someone else forgets."

He snapped to attention. "Begging pardon, miss. Mixing me drinks no excuse. Went to Midway after Karla went home." He smiled a killer smile. "How forget a beauty like yourself?"

"Where's Mr. Aultman?"

"Pardon miss? Oh, he's interviewing hired help."

"No, not that one."

"Above pay grade, miss." He smiled. "Want me to ask around?"

"No, no!" I shouted, being manhandled by the applicants in the crowded hall. I must breathe.

Squeezing out the front door, I walked around to the stables where my cycles were stored. Choosing the Rover with its drop-curved frame to accommodate my Gibson skirt, I placed my camera case in its basket. In less than a minute, I pedaled around the corner to the Wetherstone's.

After dropping the kickstand to balance the cycle, I tripped over the first step at the door. I knocked, and took a deep breath.

A dozen carriages clattered past on the cobblestones of Astor Street before the door opened. Their butler, Abram, scowled when he saw me, his bald head shiny with sweat. "Not Miss Aultman?" the butler said. "What are you doing here?" The door was pulled ajar.

"Hello, Abram. Is Edith at home?"

"Regret Miss, but I have standing orders from Lady of the Manor that you are, what she terms, persona non grata."

The words were no more out of his mouth than I overheard Doc Seth's voice in the background. "From here, I'll take it, Abram. Edith does not understand the modern journalists' need for education. She is incommunicado."

Abram's face disappeared from the half-opened door, replaced by the good doctor who swung it fully open. "Come in, my dear." Inside, the quiet of the house was so loud it enabled me to hear a door handle on the second floor click, and then click again.

Hugging me with one arm, Doc Seth led me to the parlor off the vestibule. He motioned for me to sit on the divan with the high back. "Judging from your face, Alessandra, a glass of claret you could use."

I sat on the divan; it did not yield. "No thank you." I looked into his face. "Doc Seth, I need to know, what is happening?"

"I do not know."

"But you must. How is his health?"

The doctor shrugged.

"You're his doctor."

"And best friend, yes." He sat in a chair near me. "Let me tell you. Bright and early I arrive with bag in hand at your house to examine my patient." He wrinkled his brow as if it were painful to remember.

"Yes?"

"Met at the door I am by servants leaving the house. Trampled over."

"Odette. Did you see Odette?"

"Who? Oh, no Odette. But Chilton I see. He announces in no uncertain terms that no longer my services are required. All the while, your Aunt Ashford folds her arms, and taps her foot, standing behind him." Then he chuckled. "Like a witch cackling at sparks from a Halloween bonfire." He glanced at my face. "Sorry, funny to you none of this is." He adjusted his pince nez. "What plans now?"

I squirmed against the high-backed divan for support. The horsehair beneath the tapestry felt as hard as a wall. "Don't know." Its wooden railing pressed against the nape of my neck, dull blade of a guillotine. I squeezed my hands. "What's happening to us?"

The doctor brushed lint off his white trousers. "My dear girl, do you want facts? Or do you want truth?"

I gulped. "Some of each."

Doc Seth pursed his lips. He spoke as if thinking aloud. "Daughters require fathers to share these things." "But then, Cyrus seems unable to provide that service at present."

I sat straighter. "Yes, you're right. I regret not seeing him before I came here."

"How to begin?" He stood and paced the room. "Maybe the great fire of seventy-one? Well, your father risked his life to rescue his parents, Oscar and Cathleen, who had risked their lives trying to save their tenants on the south side. To spare you painful details, your father failed, failed to save the two people closest to his heart." He sat down, and stared at his spats. "Just like that fireman friend of Karla's, what's his name, at Cold Storage? You must remember, it was in all papers. The young man who lost his life returning to rescue a baby who was not there."

I rubbed my throat. It felt smoky and dry. "May I have a glass of water, please?"

"Forgive me." He motioned to Abram at the door to fetch water.

Doc Seth then sat halfway on the divan, and held my hand.

"Remember, your father loves you as much as he loved his parents, but it's hard for him to show it. Cyrus braved an ocean voyage to Ireland carrying the urns with their remains. He arrived in depths of despair. There, he found Cora Larken, the woman he loved. And she loved him. They married in county Sligo. I was best man, and my Edith maid of honor. They settled down. Nine months later, Edith and I returned to Ireland for delivery. You and Karla were born as fraternal twins in Ireland." He squeezed my hand. "Regret I do. Your mother I lost." Abram entered the room. "So you see? Oh, here's your water."

Quickly he stood, too quickly, and turned his back on me, as a cold chill possessed my spine.

"No thank you," I said, "I don't need water now." My heart was chewing on the half truth Doc Seth was telling me.

He marched to the window. "So you see, the truth, the truth I have just told you, shall set you free."

I stared at his back. "But not happy."

"And sometimes, my innocent," he said to the window, "sometimes the truth can bring you joy."

I did not understand a word. Why was he treating me like a child?

"Would you want Chas to drive—"

"No, thank you. I need to do things myself." I stood. "I have my cycle."

"As you wish." The good doctor faced me with his handkerchief covering his mouth. "Harper College. Are you scheduled today?"

"Yes, I'm a little delayed, but in time for the Convocation tonight, thanks to you."

Doc Seth stood with hands clasped behind his back. "Remember, Alessandra, you can always rely on old Doc Seth."

I tried to peer into his gray eyes, but sunlight had transformed his eyeglasses into tiny mirrors. "If I had any doubts of your love, you proved to me today how much you want to protect me, in your own way."

"Dasisgut! Leave your worries with me, my dear."

"Give my regards to Mrs. Wetherstone."

✵ ✵ ✵

As I rode my cycle, each pump on the pedals relived the moment when the good doctor stood too fast after telling me his version of the truth. I recalled the little sigh that escaped his body, telling me he felt relieved it was over. But what was over? The story? The secrets?

Such important items would have to wait for an urgent one, the railroad train. I stored my bike in the baggage car before I boarded.

As I rode on the Illinois Central in an aisle seat, I closed my eyes, wondering if I had ridden it before. Why couldn't I remember? I could recall some events but not others. Why couldn't I remember the fire? Was I really the one who sent that poor firefighter back to rescue—

When the train chugged to a stop at Midway I retrieved my cycle. Feeling lighter, I pedaled to the Harper campus north of Midway's wall.

❋ ❋ ❋

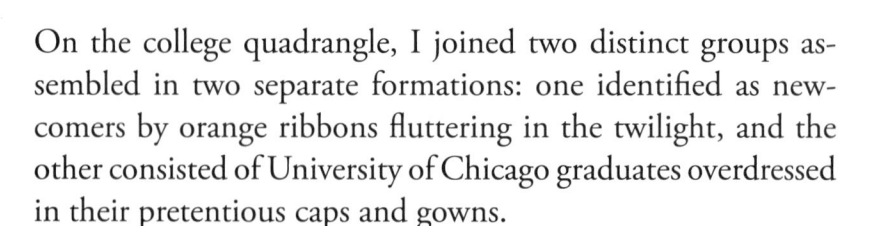

On the college quadrangle, I joined two distinct groups assembled in two separate formations: one identified as newcomers by orange ribbons fluttering in the twilight, and the other consisted of University of Chicago graduates overdressed in their pretentious caps and gowns.

My amusement at the contrast was tempered by regret that Doc Seth could not attend the Convocation because it might reveal to Edith that he was secretly financing all my expenses at college without her knowledge.

Sensing my mixed emotions, my new classmate rolled her large black eyes, grinned and said, "Sweet bitter?" Rachel waved her flowing sleeve of red, black, yellow hues. Adjusting her tribal headgear, stacked high above the large gold earrings dangling to her bare shoulders, Rachel appeared every royal inch the young African princess from Liberia. Pointing to my sky-blue Gibson, she rocked her head in approval, with such a regal bearing. It seemed hard to realize that the white girls at Foster House refused to room with her. I knew that if I were not stuck living at Mr. Aultman's rowhouse then—

At the blast of a trumpet, we began to march while a drum kept cadence. Our formation approached a huge English gothic building of solid red brick with blue Bedford stone trimmings. Along its granite walls were running vines, perhaps hoping to develop mature and dignified. "My Gawd!" I whispered to Rachel, "Looks like a museum." The student in line behind us snorted and said, "That's what it is, the Walker Museum of Science."

We entered to the soothing notes of the Glee Club rendering the university's song. The melody poured much needed unction upon my heart.

"The City White hath fled the earth,
But where the azure waters lie,
A nobler city hath its birth.
The City Gray that shall never die.
For decades and for centuries,
Its battlemented tow'rs shall rise,
Beneath the hope-filled western skies,
'Tis our dere Alma-Mater."

Although the fair was lost, I gained the gift of college, thanks to Doc Seth. He told me I had exchanged an illusion for a vision. As the last extended note echoed off the beams of the museum, we were seated on our folding chairs in the front rows.

As the scraping of chairs subsided, President Harper assumed the podium. After greeting every administrator and honored guest in attendance, and every group present, he proclaimed in a mellow voice, "The first year's work of building the campus is finished, the foundations, at least in part, have been laid." Some graduates in their caps and gowns snickered behind their programs. Was it due to the fact that the president himself lacked a house on campus?

"We are congregated this evening to honor our graduates of the University of Chicago and to welcome our incoming neophytes to Harper College, as signified by their orange ribbons. Welcome one and all." The large throng of parents, relatives, friends, and other students, including Hermes, all rose as one and applauded so loudly the glass containers of scientific specimens from Geology and Mineralogy Studies rattled in their cabinets lining the walls, making Rachel giggle. "Students, boys and girls, faculty, and administrators are all of one body, united and equal in all ways under God's light."

Somehow Professor Harper's cherub face and his hair parted in the middle lent an air of innocent faith that disarmed me.

and caused Rachel to move closer to touch my hand. I dabbed the corner of my eye.

As I perspired in the crowded museum, I yearned for a mouthful of sherbet. I licked my lips. To distract my thoughts, I endeavored to listen to President Harper saying, "To plan is poetry. To build is prose." He added sentences that lodged between my ears. "You must invite doubt and fear. Doubt about your abilities, and fear of failure. These traits are prerequisites to learning. To succeed add two more: trust and curiosity. Trust in people for stability and curiosity with your whole heart to risk change."

I counted all the obstacles that had blocked my journey to Harper.

"If you students wait until all difficulties have disappeared, you will wait until the end of your life. Remember, patience is not always virtue."

As I pondered his words, the rest of the Convocation ceremony came and went. What remained for me were the words "doubt, fear, trust, curiosity." To me it sounded much like Nellie Bly, but enlightened.

With the university song flowing over the congregation, we exited the Walker Museum into the muggy autumn night. As we wended our way to Foster House, Rachel led the way by raising her long rainbow sleeve and chanting, "Fol-low me," making me laugh with delight at her boldness.

※ ※ ※

The crickets, pulsating in the surrounding darkness, echoed the rhythm of my heart. Deep inside me throbbed the conviction that I was in the perfect place at the perfect time with the perfect people. Nevermind that some students mocked the gerry-rigged buildings by calling them, "Harper's bazaar." Nevermind the interiors were labeled, "Empty monstrosities." To me, the buildings reminded me of people in my life.

After traversing the campus, now turned into a morass by recent rains, I perceived the porch lanterns of Foster House, swinging in the breeze, and flickering behind the cottonwood branches. I glimpsed the tall figure of Rachel waving for me to catch up. In the background, over the wall, towered the top half of the Ferris Wheel, its lights blazing. I vowed to experience one last ride.

Nearing the front porch I smelled the aromas of popcorn and Japanese incense, enwrapping Rachel and me while we embraced. The wind caught my skirt, and twisted it tightly about my legs, making me almost lose balance. Rachel, howling at my awkwardness, hid her mouth behind her hands, the double rings on each of her ten fingers glittering like fireflies.

The twang of a mandolin strumming "After the Ball is Over" created an invisible web, luring us off the wooden planks and toward the tea-rose vestibule of Foster House. At the open door we were met by Doctor Alice Foster, herself, in her gingham apron. As she hugged us, she said, "Welcome ladies, all you girls are beautiful gifts. You must enjoy my homemade white fudge." Then she whispered in my ear, "Well I must confess, I somehow singed it."

"That's perfect," I said, grinning like a fool, "That's exactly how we both love it."

"Stay," said Rachel, reaching out to me.

"No I can't, they need me at—well, maybe overnight only." My long orange ribbon, blown about by a breeze, was tamed by Dr. Foster who patted me on the shoulder. Arm in arm in the vestibule between Dr. Foster and Rachel, I felt I had arrived at a new home.

※ ※ ※

After classes, Brick had promised to meet me at Foster House. Responding to the honking of sugarpot on Brick's Duryea, I found myself grabbing Rachel's wrist, heavy with large bracelets, to insist on her sharing the ride. Dragging her onto the veranda, I spotted Brick's machine sliding to a muddy stop. Without a word, I released Rachel, hopped down the steps, and jumped through the car's doorless side.

"Love to see that!" shouted Brick, lifting up his yellow goggles. "Not one hot second lost. Our own private drive together."

"Rachel, come join us!"

Brickton revolved the engine.

"She's my new best friend," I said, my voice drowning in the noise. "We take classes toget—"

"Ally, we're gone!" he said, "Wastin' petrol."

While I motioned to Rachel I heard Brick whisper hoarsely, "No nigras allowed." He spun the car wheels in place.

"What?"

Then he shouted, "No nigras allowed!"

"Brickton, I thought you were sophisticated." I started to wave for Rachel to hurry when I stopped at the sight of her.

Rachel, instead of cowering in the face of racism or furious at the indignity, presented the picture of serenity. With arms akimbo, and a smile upon her lips, Rachel apparently did not need a manor to be a lady, nor even a country. I was certain she spoke better English than I, Afric. Oh, how I envied her self-composure, her freedom to be herself.

Then Rachel pointed to the side porch containing a cycle rack. "My Gawd!" I shouted, "I had forgotten it."

With a shake of his cap, Brickton clambered out muttering, "Only for you Ally." He trudged through a rain puddle to retrieve my cycle, without a glance at Rachel. Returning, he deposited it gently on the bench opposite us.

"But why—"

Brick jolted his machine forward, as we headed for the new Lake Shore Drive.

Why did I betray Rachel to be loyal to Brick? Is that what adults did? Brick complained, "No reporter needs no books at no Harper. Gets in way of raw experience, it do. Ally, you're wasting your bloody time."

When I tried to explain my need for education to become an enlightened Nellie Bly, he would honk his sugarpot and laugh.

We followed the scenic route up to Fort Sheridan. There we parked and watched the soldiers parade. When Brick tried to put his arm around me I would have none of it. I insisted he drive me back to the rowhouse. On the way he asked questions about my classes, but I did not reply, knowing he really did not care. Instead, I pondered the image of the young princess of Liberia, my new best friend, and wondered how she had changed me.

After awkward silences, we finally parked in front of the house, the machine vibrating beneath my body as I awaited his apology.

"Behind schedule," Brick said. "Interview with Sol Bloom; what a firebrand he is." He removed my cycle from the bench and bounced the tires upon the grass.

Biting my lip, I exited the Duryea and pushed my cycle to the footscraper at the front stoop where I pretended to remove gum from my sole, stalling so he would have time to reconsider. A raindrop spattered the back of my hand.

The roar of his engine told me that Brick left in a cloud of soot, dodging a dump truck filled with broken lumber chugging from the back of our house.

Before I reached the front door, it opened with Hustings peering out at me, his stony face unchanged, but his eyes clouded with tears.

"Mr. Aultman?" I asked.

Hustings nodded to the parlor as he allowed my entrance. Pausing to touch Mother's pendant with trembling fingertips, I recited in my mind a brief prayer. Hustings pushed aside the parlor door.

Standing with my back against the closed door, I set the camera case upon the floor. With my fingers twitching, I noticed the harp-piano had its bench inverted to perch atop a canvas covering. Why was it moved toward the exit? The open roll-top desk had surrendered its contents in stacks of drawers spilled upside down on the floor. In the center of the room, Mr. Aultman slumped in a tall cobra-backed wheelchair, his shirt off, bare chested, suspenders fallen to his side. His left arm hung straight down, useless, his bare feet immersed in a basin of water. Kneeling at his left side was Karla, sponging her father's feet as if washing a baby's. Tilted forward, he reached across with his good right arm to pet Karla's head as he muttered, "Cora, Cora, you've come back to me."

Neither person sensed my presence. I moved closer, until I could almost touch the smooth side of his face. When I touched him, he slanted his head away from me for a better look as he grasped my Gibson skirt. "Cora, Cora. You've come back to me." I pulled my skirt free, and stepped aside as Karla hummed, "Nearer My God to Thee." I waited for Karla to acknowledge me, but she continued to sponge his feet without looking up.

I realized, in that moment, that Karla was the new Lady of the Manor. She had taken Mother's place in Father's heart. I inhaled deeply. I realized that now I was free. I touched Mother's pendant.

Without taking my eyes off them, I backed toward the door. I was shocked to see that Mr. Aultman's portrait had been moved into the parlor. Who had moved it? With a final glance at the lion-headed cane depicting him as he used to be, I retrieved my camera case, and left the two of them together in silence, surrounded by the healing sound of water.

In the vestibule, I needed consolation. I headed upstairs towards my bedroom to lie down, temples throbbing.

There, I found no Odette to hover over me. Glancing toward the window, I saw a gentle mist slanting down the dirty glass, like veins upon the palm of my hand. I imagined I saw the image of Father with his new Lady of the Manor he called Cora, washing his feet. The mist brought me the realization of neglecting October chores in my garden. Damaged pockets of grass needed reseeding. Leaves must be raked just enough to prevent smothering. Perhaps I should also split geraniums to store safely indoors before winter.

I sighed, imagining my own favorites withering—herbs, chive, rosemary. In a recent letter from Hermes, he had chided me for not pruning my Christmas cactus. For myself, the roses with faded blooms needed deadheading by shearing them midway down the stems, leaving half the leaves on the plants before covering them.

Feeling reenergized and headache gone, I decided to work in the garden despite the thin drizzle. Dressing in old clothing, I made plans to plant a remembrance tree of the fair near the gazebo, perhaps a sugar maple. I rolled a souvenir scarf, picturing the Ferris Wheel, and tied it over the crown of my Stetson, fastening it under my chin. After I buttoned my yellow slicker, I tugged on my woolen gloves and lugged my carpet bag with tools as I sauntered down the rear stairway.

Once outside, I inhaled the brisk fragrance of my own garden. For the first time since I could remember, I felt welcome. Now where should be the site of the new maple tree, which side of the gazebo?

In the gazebo's place was—nothing. Without my gazebo rising above my garden, it appeared decapitated. I gripped the handle of my carpet bag tighter. The wind behind my back blew a familiar voice from the house.

"It's true then. Ashford told me you were spying on me, and Father. And now you're sneaking around."

I turned, and faced Karla at the half-open door I had just come through. The mist grew thicker. "What happened to my gazebo?"

"Oh, Mother and I decided. That old thing—Uncle Chil didn't care," Karla said, "The gazebo just had to go. Too quaint. We wanted what our neighbors already had. A badminton court. It's all the rage on Astor Street."

I dropped the carpet bag. "What? Did you say you and Mother decided?"

"Naturally, so to speak."

"Are you insane? Mother died, giving birth to—"

"No, I did not!" Aunt Ashford's face bobbed upon Karla's shoulder. In the mist, it gave the illusion of two heads on one woman's body. "That was *your* mother who died," Aunt Ashford said, "not Karla's."

Karla cackled. "Stir, you killed your mother because you just had to be born!"

I laughed at them. "Go tell that to Cora!" I wiped the mist from my mouth; it felt like a spider web. "Karla, are you telling me, that you're not—that we're not—" I felt invisible manacles melting from my wrists.

"Not is the proper word," Karla said. "We're not knotted as sisters."

"Who told you?"

"Me!" Aunt Ashford elbowed Karla aside. "I told my daughter. My pact with Cyrus was for me to remain silent for eighteen years in exchange for his raising Karla as his own daughter—which she was. We vowed that neither one of us would tell. That pact terminated after the ball is over."

A storm was brewing overhead. "You both played me for a fool."

"Type casting." Karla said.

I peered down at my feet. An angleworm, half emerged, was being devoured by a blackbird. "That explains the gap," I said to the ground, "whenever we got too close. How the word 'Stir' from your mouth seemed an insult." The blackbird flapped its wings.

"So now, you're just a half-stir."

Closing the screen door, Aunt Ashford said, "There's nothing left for you here, Alessandra my dear."

A moan from the front of the house sounded like an old bear dying.

"Are you going to stand in the rain all day, half-stir?"

I heard myself chuckling. I threw my head back and untied my scarf. Shaking off the Stetson, I twirled it around my wrist like a wheel, as the wind freed the scarf from my throat. A high-pitched war whoop burst forth from me. Squeezing the brim of my Stetson, soggy from mist, I spun my body around and around. Stopping on *relevé*, I pitched the hat with all my strength, aiming for the roof. Letting it go, I watched the Stetson soar into the sky, headed for the weathervane, but it fell short, hitting a chimney and tumbling down the shingles on its brim, until it tottered halfway over the side of the roof.

The sky, the color of buttermilk, rained on my face, bathing it clean of any invisible webs. I howled like a bear cub at the October sky, letting its waters baptize my eyes.

I might have stood in my garden forever, if not for the slamming of the inside door behind the screen. The noise awakened me to attend to my garden while time remained.

Bending to the fresh-smelling earth, I opened my tool bag.

✦ ✦ ✦

In high spirits the next day, I phoned Hermes to ask him to escort me around the fair on the elevated. After I finished talking about Harper, which seemed to annoy him, I changed the subject. What was his favorite painting at the fair? Hermes' choice was a scene from the Middle Ages in Florence, during the time of Savonarola. He said it shows a procession of nude men and women lashing themselves with barbed whips to purify their souls, while a dying man is borne on a litter by the others. The painting was called *The Flagellants*.

I hung up the phone.

I telephoned Brick. We met at four o'clock downtown at Chicago Harbor and sailed again on the whaleback steamer

Columbus. I wanted to stay on deck for the view, but Brick insisted on huddling together in the barroom, located in the hull of the boat, away from the wind. We snuggled onto stools at the end of the bar. "I don't want opium cordials," I said to the barkeep, a young man with a handle bar. "Hate them."

"Got us a little stash of them there laudanum," he said, "Calculated to ease you off the opium, with a dash of alcohol. State of well-being. Says so on the label."

Brick produced a leather flask. "Fill up my little buddy here," he said, handing it to the barkeep. "And pour me a side of absinthe."

"And what will your beautiful wife have to wash down the pills?" He looked at Brick, who looked at me, while I shook my head, wanting Brick to order for me.

Brick rubbed his new mustache. "Do you happen to carry on board the current craze, Mariani wine?"

"Bullseye, it's all the style."

"What is Mariana wine?" I asked.

Brick received back his flask. "That's one tasty tonic, laced with coca direct from France."

"Too exotic," I said.

"No fear, lassie," the barkeep said. "Didn't you see our sign?" He stepped aside to reveal a large poster taped to the corner of the huge mirror behind him. It competed for attention with the bottles on the shelf. The poster displayed an image of the Pope. "See that small print at the bottom?" The barkeep stared at the ceiling and recited, in sing-song fashion, the words on the poster with his hand over his heart. "His holiness Pope Leo Thirteenth writes he has fully appreciated the beneficent effects of this tonic wine. The Pope has forwarded to Mr. Mariani a token of his gratitude—a gold medal bearing the Pope's august effigy." Then he beamed at us. "Good enough?"

Nodding, I swallowed the pills with a sip of Mariani wine as Brick pocketed his flask. He withdrew his hand from his jacket, and took my hand. His skin felt warm and yielding. He stroked the cord holding my Kodak around my neck, pulling me slowly toward him. As the barkeep served the other end of the bar, we kept our eyes fused into each other.

The tilting of our stools told us the steamer was swinging into the dock of the White City. Brick paid our tab, and we joined the other passengers hurrying on deck to disembark. He held my hand, towing me in his wake until I broke away and trotted ahead.

After stepping onto the pier, we strolled arm in arm, alongside the movable sidewalk, ignoring the hollow train entirely. We sauntered past series of benches with lovers entwined, with children restless, with old people peaceful. I took snapshots as we walked along. Reaching the end of the movable sidewalk, we entered the fair itself and beheld the Casino directly in front of us, connected with the peristyle to the Music Hall on its right.

After I snapped a few photos, I also snapped the red garter Brick wore around his muscle. "Let's go left," I said, "where Santa Maria's docked. Great photo."

"But Casino's right here." Loose change rattled in his pocket. "Might be my last chance to gamble," he teased.

"Brickton," I said, taking my hand back. "First, the elevated train."

"When you refer to me as Brickton," he said, "I know I'd better obey."

As Brick and I ascended the steps to await the el, I glanced toward the lake shore and saw the huge building containing the Krupp Gun Exhibit. The lettered sign "Deutschland" on its façade was being dismantled by a crane.

On the platform bench, Brick and I held hands. The elevated arrived too soon, squeaking to a stop. We boarded. As it chugged ahead encircling the south pond, I took a photograph. The train swung past the stockyards. I took three shots. At my side, Brick drank from his flask. When he saw me noticing, he said, "I need to tell you something important today. Need to swallow some courage!" He took another swig.

"Yes?"

"Oh, see the Cold Storage Building by the wall? At least what's left of it?"

I did not look.

The elevated pivoted, and I saw over the wall the top of the stands of Buffalo Bill's Wild West outside the gates. I regretted missing it.

The train stopped at the photography tent of Mr. Arnold to let passengers off and on. Was Hermes there? There was a time I had hoped so.

We saw the Ferris Wheel revolving. I snapped a shot even though I knew we were too far away. "Can't kill that wheel!" Brickt said, "Made Ferris a fortune. No wonder the bosses want it shut down by suing him in court. But he'll keep that wheel rolling, even after the fair is over!"

Finally, we passed the Haytian Pavilion, where Frederick Douglass stood his ground amidst broken flying watermelons. I shared some of Douglass' courage by asking Brick, "Wasn't there something important you needed to tell me?" He frowned and peered out the window. I prayed he would ask, but also prayed he would not.

At the terminal of its north loop, the elevated stopped. Brick got off first. Had he changed his mind? On the ground, with my back to the canal, I squeezed my hands into fists as I held my arms straight down at my sides.

Brick took the flask out, and seeing it empty, placed it in his hip pocket. He held my left hand with both of his. "Alessandra, we have known each other only a short time. However, the feelings we have for each other—we communicate without talking. We can share everything." He paused as the elevated train rattled on its return trip.

Taking my other hand, he melted them together. "Dear Ally, thanks to you, my boss is impressed with my reporting."

Sedan chairs, hurrying past us, nearly knocked me over. Brick did not notice. "My reward is to cover the next fair from ground up in Atlanta. Construction's underway." He grabbed my arm like a vice. "Ally, come with me. We work so well together. I write the stories. You take the snapshots."

Instinctively, I pulled back and covered my mouth.

"How do you feel about it, honeylamb?"

I almost lost my balance.

"Don't mean to frighten you, Ally, but don't Pemberton and Aultman make a great byline?" He looked at his watch. "Oops, sundown, must get to my interview with the Board of Directors." He signaled for a sedan chair. "Get in," he ordered, as he gave the two bearers instructions. I did not move. "Aren't we headed in the same direction?" He got in and stretched out his arms to me. Lifting the sedan poles, the bearers started trotting in place, shaking the sedan chair.

I noticed that Brick's hands trembled. On a sudden, he seemed vulnerable. Instinctively, my hand moved toward his. Would he be my path to freedom? I observed the fingers of my left hand, palm up, unfurl as if from a cramp. My blood surged through my veins to my fingertips. With my heart straining toward his heart, I searched his eyes.

Brick smiled, pursing his lips. "Hot damn," he said, "now you can be my Nellie Bly!"

The speaking of that name awoke me. I stepped sideways. "No!" I shouted, "That's not my name." Passersby turned to stare. "I'm not Nellie Bly. I'm not Lady of the Manor. I'm not a ballet teacher. And I am certainly not the bottom half of no byline. I know who I am now. I'm me—Alessandra Cora Aultman. Me, myself, and I."

Brick glanced at his watch. "And in due time, you shall add my name." He shook his head. "But now I'm late; this is taking too much of my time."

The bearers had stopped trotting in place. "Deliver Mr. Pemberton wherever he bloody needs to go!" I shouted.

Brickton's mouth dropped open.

"Administration Building, isn't it?" I said to him. He nodded, leaning back into the shadows of the sedan.

The porters trotted away to cross the bridge to the south, and I watched them disappear.

❂   ❂   ❂

I resolved not to hand control over to Brickton, or Hermes, or Mr. Aultman, or the fair, or anyone else. I decided to spend time with an equal. I asked Rachel to be my guest on Woman's Day. I felt the need to share with her the workings of our republic by demonstrating women in control. The two of us cycled on that cold morning, pausing from time to time to take Kodaks of oak trees letting go their last leaves.

Arriving cold in the assembly hall, I noticed some ladies huddled by the two roaring fire places. To warm our riding skirts we cozied up to one group, and listened to their chatter as firelogs crackled and smoked. "Two laws are pending," said one lady waving a longnette. "Who remembers?" A little cross-eyed redhead answered, "Equal pay for equal work, nationwide. But I don't recall." A lanky lady whispered, "I do: un-uniform mar-marriage and di-divorce laws, nationwide." "Good for you Gladys," said the first lady twirling her glasses by their stem. The other ladies murmured, "Certain to pass." "Twentieth century, you know, only seven years away."

Yes, yes I thought, especially since the twentieth century already began with the World's Fair. On a sudden, an organ thundered a prelude, signaling the start of the meeting. All the ladies snapped to attention and filed to the rows of folding chairs. Rachel and I hustled to front row seats.

After an opening prayer, a beautiful lady entered. I remembered having seen that noble bearing in the tent of the Germania Club. What was it she told me? There was a little gymnast who had missed me.

The beautiful lady was introduced as Bertha Palmer, president of the board. As she welcomed the women's organizations, I snapped her photograph. Rachel jumped in her seat with the click of the Kodak, losing her composure for a second.

"Now to represent Women's National Suffrage Association is our beloved Susan B. Anthony." Miss Anthony declared her organization to be the cornerstone of the women's movement. Despite her boast, I was impressed with her as she related in a matter-of-fact tone the travails endured by women fighting for equal rights for forty years. "The World's Fair," she proclaimed, "provided us women a public forum to display the contributions of independent women to the arts, the sciences, and society at large." After her, group after group spoke praising themselves. I shared with Rachel the three simple steps of the Kodak: point, click, crank.

Of all the words, only two sentences by Bertha Palmer were worth my remembering. "Man by leaving to woman the control of the heart left to her the destiny of the nation. As long as woman rules the home she rules the world." I heard myself shouting, "Here! Here!" I leaped up. "As long as she is free to choose." Rachel pounded me on the back.

The ladies discussed the fate of any unmarried woman. What could she do with her life? I tried to recall what Nellie Bly believed. I retrieved Mother's pendant from beneath my green peasant blouse and kissed it. Rachel nodded approval. As I squeezed the pendant between my palms, its warmth comforted my cold hands. With my thumbs, I rubbed the pendant's acorn, while inhaling a deep breath. But still I could not remember.

Releasing air slowly through my nostrils, I tried to recall Nellie Bly's face, but I could not even picture her features. What had happened to me? Rachel placed her arm around my shoulder.

I sensed my shoulders beginning to relax, and melt into my body. Tears of relief moistened my eyes, transforming shafts of sun from the skylight into a half rainbow. Breathing deeply, I allowed a welling inside me surge upward like a fountain, a fountain of joy, joy in not needing to remember Nellie Bly's motto because I was already living it, joy at being my own person, joy in being finally free. Rachel's dark eyes, warm and unblinking, told me she understood.

I started to kiss Mother's pendant, but stopped. When I returned the pendant beneath my blouse, it felt cold. Realizing that loss can lead to freedom, I savored the taste of joy in my mouth as around me the meeting adjourned.

❋   ❋   ❋

Afterwards, I felt drawn to the Children's Building next door and I pleaded with Rachel to stay with me. In the fading twilight I pointed out the motto above the door. "The Hope of the World is in the Children." Tears welled in Rachel's eyes. Why did I feel I had been here before?

Peering out the window, a woman with steel gray hair shook her head at us. Then her face disappeared. A minute later, she reappeared with her double. Both women laughed. Then the first woman vanished to open the front door and exclaim, "Miss Aultman, Lord bless you!" She shouted over her shoulder, "Jenny, go fetch little Terese. Her American aunt has finally appeared."

Rachel put her hand in front of her mouth.

The gray haired woman advanced toward us, her arms outspread, face beaming. Before I could react, she enveloped me in her arms, overwhelming in a kiss of garlic. "Where you been, girl? Terese misses you so much. She keeps Mrs. Bates awake all night. Now the fair's ending, so Terese doesn't know what's next."

My cycle collapsed sideways. Rachel stepped backwards.

"Oh, just leave it. My sister will care for it."

"Don't think—I, I've had the pleasure?"

"Oh, I forgot. Your memory. Got burned up in Cold Storage fire, didn't it?"

"Only partly," I said, "Some things I—" I reached out for Rachel who took my hand.

"Hey, Jenny, front and center!"

With that, her twin emerged from the Children's Building with a small Oriental girl about eight years old. As the girl approached me, her almond eyes, unblinking, searched mine as if digging for my heart. A few steps away, she hesitated, pursing her mouth, her eyes now blinking in disbelief. She heaved a deep sigh, and struggled to form a single word. "Ah-Tee-A?"

"Me and Mary, we taught her a few words. You know, to distract her from being an orphan, and all."

"What?" I looked at Rachel and shook my head in denial.

"Her guardians were journalists. As soon as they had their articles finished, they left her."

That's the worst thing, I thought, being abandoned. I put my arm around Rachel's waist.

"We was just gonna take her for a final fling on the Ferry Wheel," Mary said, rocking on her toes.

"To stop Terese from nagging us—" Jenny started to say.

"—with her eyes," Mary said, finishing Jenny's sentence.

"But now her aunt Alessandra has returned, just—"

"—just like Lazarus," Mary finished, clapping her hands.

"Soyoumisscansaveusthetrouble!" Jenny shouted as one word, glaring at Mary.

"No no," I said, "You see, I, I don't seem to recall—" I avoided the little girl's eyes, focusing on Rachel.

"But Terese recalls everything," Mary said, tongue in cheek, "even the secret portal to Midway."

"That's the place with the huge spinning wheel," Jenny added, folding her arms.

Something tugged at my Gibson skirt. Looking down, I saw bright eyes smiling up at me. I held out my hand. After a puzzled frown, Terese placed her small palm within mine, more moist than my own. Were we both orphans? I peered into her almond eyes, and remembered a rooftop playground for children. I remembered a little eight year old girl with deep set eyes I could sink into like a fountain of black water. Reaching down I lifted her little body into my arms, and hugged her, a long lost part of me, restored.

* * *

At Midway, bonfire barrels glowed like nightlights for an arsonist. To one side, old Vienna's blackened timbers resembled charcoal sticks, the Palace of Moors' roof had collapsed, and the bazaars of Cairo Street were half-buried in drifts of sand.

My common-sense shoes, and Rachel's sandals, squeaked on the wooden boardwalk. The vibrations made Terese giggle. "Mice?" she said, behind her fingers. Dozens of people wandered among the ruins. I heard a megaphone shout, "Admissions still only fifty cents. Ride the great wheel. One revolution only, but uninterrupted." Staring up at the Ferris Wheel twenty five stories high, Rachel staggered, and searched for a bench.

As I tried to locate the ticket booth, Terese whistled, fingers in her mouth, and started to skip ahead. Gripping my camera case tighter, I ran to catch up. The case banged against my shin all the way to the booth. When I looked back Rachel was pointing to the height of the wheel with one hand, and holding her head with the other. How anyone could be afraid of heights was beyond me.

After paying admissions for us both, I limped into an open Pullman car on ground level. I watched parents race their children up the stairs to other carriages.

Our car was empty. No fresh paint assailed my nostrils. No music assaulted my ears.

Upon our entrance, I saw several stools with bent necks. Shattered window glass littered the floor. Terese skipped back to my side, and tugged at my hand to hurry. Against an inner wall, I set the camera case. With a grunt of triumph, Terese grabbed the case, and dragged it to the farthest corner.

Before I could stop her, Terese unlatched my case while the door behind me slammed shut. The thrust of engines starting threw me to the floor. The opened camera case slid on patches of glass, as if on ice. When the carriage lurched off the ground, photographs flew all over me.

Terese, after brushing off the photos and patting my back, helped me sit up. With blood on my hands and glass embedded in my cheek, I must have presented a sorry sight. I braced myself for Terese's taunts, but she did not laugh at me. Instead, her eyes misted as her little fingertips tweezered glass needles from my forehead and palms.

Assisting me to my feet, Terese guided me to a stool, where I discovered my knees were scratched. I should have dressed with long trousers. As I rested, head in hands, the electric lights flickered. I stared at images gazing up at me from round photographs strewn helter-skelter upon the carriage floor: Buffalo Bill spurring his white stallion onto its hind limbs; the Big Clock shading lovers beneath the largest building in the world; Mayor Harrison waving his arm to crowds as his fiancé recedes in the background; Frederick Douglass and Ida B. Wells handing out pamphlets; Columbian guards lounging against the Casino's huge double doors.

While I pondered, the carriage rose higher, allowing me to see the lights of Harper campus on the other side of Midway. Their buildings in the gathering dark were half familiar.

The ripping of thick paper brought me back to Terese sitting Indian style on a stool, lap overflowing with photographs. Her face beamed with happiness as she tore my pictures into little pieces.

"No, no, Terese," I shouted, "those are my memories!"

Reaching her side, I uprighted the camera case to extract my Kodak. I waved it to get attention. "Capture today's memories for yourself!" Replacing photos in her lap with my camera, I leaned into her face and mouthed the words, "Kodak easy. Three steps. Point, click, crank."

As we reached the top of the ride, Terese shook her head in disbelief.

"Yes, it's true," I said.

Terese clapped her hands, yanked my camera from me, and threw it across the carriage to clang against a hollow fire extinguisher.

"No, no Terese!" I shouted, "Not my camera. It's my future."

Terese shook her head until her long braids whipped around her throat.

"Yes, it's true," I said, "And the truth shall set you free."

She stood and high-stepped across the carriage with arms folded in defiance. When she sauntered back, she had the camera strap around her neck as she grunted the words, "Fee? No want fee! Want cam'ra!"

"No, Terese," I said, "Not my camera." I removed the strap and put my camera on a stool. I touched Mother's pendant at my bosom. "Here, this is my past." I unclasped the silver chain and kissed it.

The cap of the acorn had lost its corrugated ridges and grooves, having been caressed by my thumbs over the years. It had gained the unity of smoothness with the shell. With a sigh, I realized that if stored too long the acorn would turn rancid.

Embracing Terese, I secured the pendant around her neck. "You need this now," I said, "I pray, Terese, let yourself be guided."

The Ferris Wheel descended in a rush toward the earth. Terese's almond eyes widened with fear. "You are loved," I said, "We are all loved." I squeezed her little body. "The truth shall set you free, free not happy. But better than happy." I needed to say it, even if Terese couldn't hear it. "The truth, Terese, shall bring you tears of joy!" I blew into her ear to make her giggle.

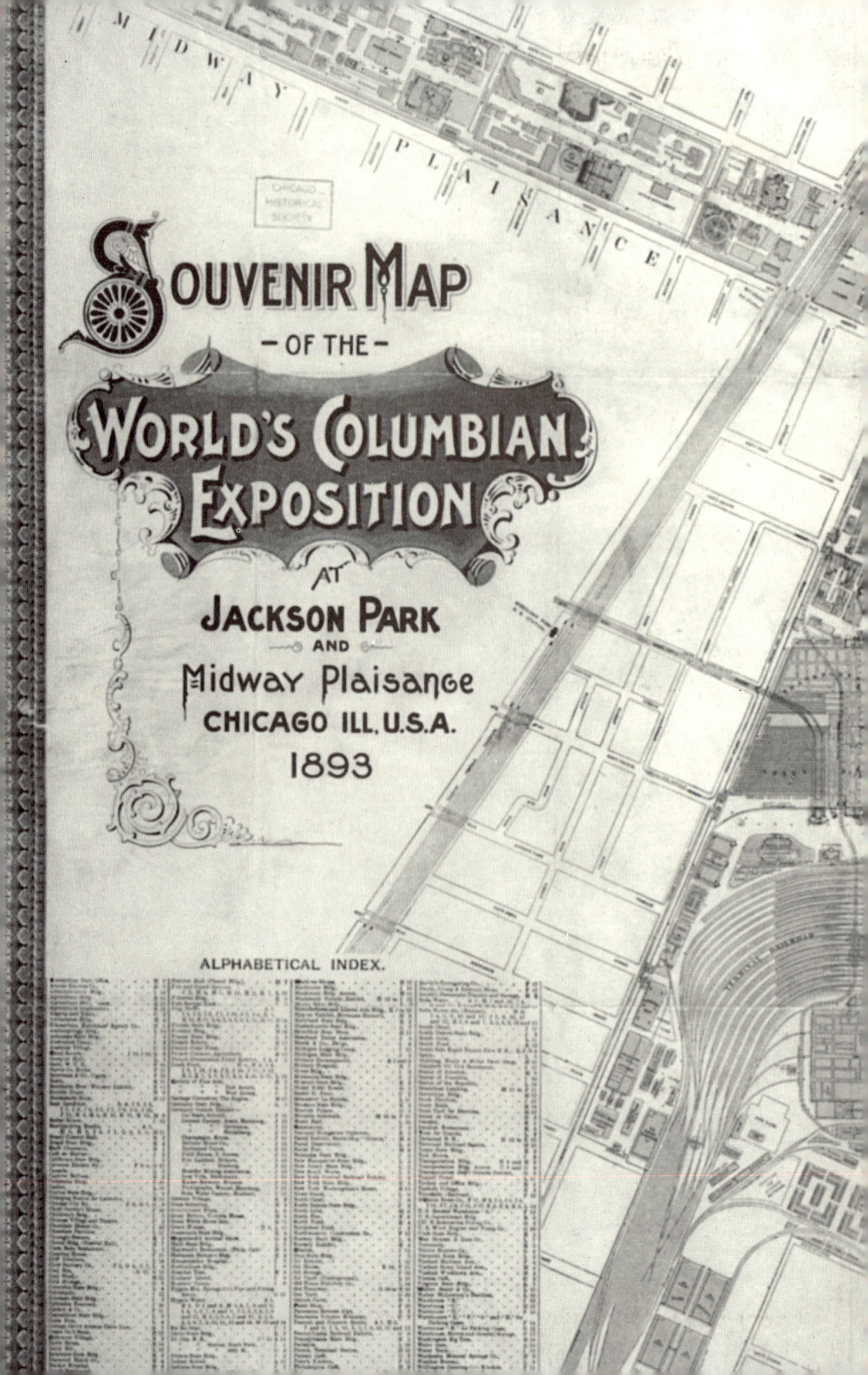

Souvenir Map
— OF THE —
World's Columbian Exposition

AT

Jackson Park

AND

Midway Plaisance
Chicago Ill. U.S.A.
1893

ALPHABETICAL INDEX.